Hold High the Flame

For Myrna
With Best Wishes
Frances Burke
Christmas '97

First published in 1997 by
Saga Publishing, an imprint of
Gary Allen Pty Ltd
9, Cooper St
Smithfield
NSW 2164

National Library of Australia
Cataloguing-in-publication data

Frances Burke
    Hold High the Flame
    ISBN 1 875169 69 5

    I. Title

    A823.3

Printed in Australia by
Robertson Printing
352 Ferntree Gully Rd
Notting Hill
3149

Cover design by
David and Traci Harding

Typeset and produced in Australia for
Gary Allen Pty Ltd by
Allan Cornwell Pty Ltd,
25, Churchill Rd,
Mt Martha,
VIC 3934.

Hold High the Flame

Frances Burke

SAGA

Frances Burke is intensely interested in history and has written several period novels set in both England and Australia. Happily married to a Sydney businessman and with three sons, she is a keen traveller whose interests include music and antiques. Her work has been widely published in Australasia and the U.K., and one of her novels, *Endless Time,* was a winner in the Random House Novel Competition of 1991.

I acknowledge with grateful thanks the support and editorial help of my good friend Trisha Sunholm, my editor Julia Stiles and my agent Selwa Anthony, all of whom have helped to shape the final effort.

This book is dedicated to the memory of Australia's first Nightingale Nurse, Lucy Osburn, who was Lady Superintendent of the Sydney Infirmary from 1868 to 1884, and whose experiences there were similar to those of Elly Ballard in this novel.

PART ONE

Chapter One

Heat swathed the cabins and outbuildings in suffocating layers. It pressed down upon the animals, restless in their stalls; on the mongrel panting under the wooden boardwalk just outside the bar-room doors; in huts and lean-tos folk tossed and sweated on their blankets, wondering who would be next, hoping it would be another, and trying to pray through lips already dry and cracked.

Up in the hills the heat writhed beneath canvas shelters to twine itself about the sleepers, who moaned and cursed from the depths of their fatigue. Nearby, axe heads lay buried in the hearts of their bloodless victims, the great Australian cedars. Gums drooped, trailing exhausted leaves in the dust, and grasses crackled under the feet of men dragging their cartloads of corpses uphill, the rumble of iron on stone covering the sound of laboured breathing. Few words would be said over these poor remains. The town had no clergyman, and the doctor could spare no time from the living.

The hotel, the one properly constructed building in this small village called the Settlement, was a cavern from Hades lit by wavering lanterns and smelling of beer and spirits. There were other smells, too, biting and pungent—frighteningly medicinal: the acrid stink of sweat and terror, of foul bodily fluids: the indescribable odours of humanity in extremis, without hope.

'Pass me the scalpel.' The voice, harsh with strain, came from a figure stooped over a trestle, his arms bloodied to the elbows.

A young woman silently handed him the instrument, then steadied the patient, a bearded, barrel-chested man lying quiescent, ready for the blade which would sever his forearm. Did he know it, the woman wondered? Did he understand that this meant farewell to his livelihood, to his high standing amongst his fellows as the fastest feller of trees in the colony?

Eleanor Ballard shook away her thoughts. Lips compressed, she helped her father clamp the bleeding vessels as he worked to save what he could of the mangled limb.

The man could count himself lucky to be in the hands of Robert Ballard, Eleanor thought. The sweetish smell of ether hung about the table, and the patient's eyeballs had rolled back. He was quite out of the world. With her foot, Elly shifted the bucket into place beneath the trestle. Savage shadows danced on the wall beside her; voices beckoned, moaned, whimpered. She closed her eyes to rest them for an instant, feeling the sweat sting beneath her lids.

It was monstrous, she thought, that two such disasters should strike within so short a time. The Settlement, reeling under the sudden blow of fever, had scarcely realised the danger before an eruption of tempers in the cutters' camp had brought more trouble and death. Back in the hills, where the tall lovely cedars brushed the sky, in a dirt clearing dotted with the detritus of camp life, the interminable, unbearable, heat had done its work. Beneath its goad, knives, fists and ugly emotions had gone into frenzy; and when it had ended, some lives had ebbed away into the stony dirt, while for others life balanced on the edge, as did this man's. His arm was now a stump, useless for swinging an axe. Useless for most things.

'Eleanor, I need your help.' The surgeon turned, his face lardy in the lamplight, the skin slick yet endlessly furrowed, the face of a Methuselah. He was forty-nine years old.

'I'm here, Father.' Elly straightened her tired back. There were only the two of them. At the onset of the epidemic a few women had offered to help, those without young children, mainly, but now even they'd fallen away. There were too many sick. And the rest huddled in the fetid huts, most likely brewing the fever in their own veins, awaiting their turn.

Elly helped to move the patient onto the floor—there were no mattresses—then hurried back to a corner where her two youngest charges lay in an uncomplaining stupor. The little boys huddled together, their sweat-soaked blond hair mingling, their arms wrapped about each other, trying to provide the comfort their dead mother might have given. Elly's heart lurched painfully as she knelt beside them. They looked ... empty, past hoping for someone to take away the pain, the heat, to tell them it was all a bad dream.

'It is a nightmare,' Elly murmured to herself, as she wrung out yet another cloth to lay on a man's brow heated like a stove lid. She helped an emaciated figure, a woman this time, upright to cough and sip water. When the lad beside her failed to respond, she searched for his pulse then, after a few moments, sighed and pulled a ragged shirt over the gaunt, untenanted face, mentally adding one more to the next load of bodies to be moved.

'Come quickly, Eleanor!'

Alerted by his tone, she hurried to where her father bent over yet another tormented body.

'This man's choking to death. Help me get him on the table.'

Together they struggled and heaved, hampered by the man's whooping efforts to breathe. Then, abruptly, he fell limp. Dr. Ballard gave him one last thump to the back.

'It's no good. I can't find any obstruction in the throat. We must cut him.'

Together they began their well-rehearsed routine. Tracheotomy. Elly had assisted only twice before but she knew the procedure by heart, had studied the journals, listened to her father's advice. As she poured chloride of lime over her hands and soaked the knives, needles and thread she went over each step.

Her father moved jerkily back from the trestle. His hands dropped. 'You do it Eleanor. You're perfectly capable. I ... I will attend to the next case.'

Elly looked up sharply. 'What is it? What's wrong?'

With an obvious effort, Dr. Ballard straightened and walked away, saying over his shoulder, 'There's nothing wrong. Attend to your patient at once while I attend mine.'

Obediently Elly forced aside her concern and gave her attention to the man whose life depended upon her. Neck stretched hard back. No time for ether. Pull the skin tight below the hollow of the throat, draw the blade downwards through the skin, keep to the exact midline. Now divide the muscles. Wipe up the blood. Insert the knife tip into the windpipe, twist delicately. Ah! Air was sucked into the opening and expelled with blood and mucous. The man's breathing gurgled and bubbled hideously, but it was the sound of life.

Elly's tightened shoulders relaxed as she wiped away more blood, watching the man's cheeks change from grey-blue to pink. She delicately inserted forceps into the upper part of the wound and closed them around the obstruction, withdrawing a lump of wadded material.

Her father appeared beside her and took the forceps. He peered at them, snorted, then dropped the wad on the floor. 'Tobacco plug. What next! Sew him up smartly and don't forget the piece of cotton for drainage. I hope to heaven the fellow hasn't developed the fever already. He's got enough of a battle against sepsis under these conditions.'

Dr. Ballard looked around him with bloodshot eyes and his laugh was a bark. 'What a scene! Straight out of Dante. This goes further than tragedy: it's an absurdity.' He nodded approvingly as Elly cut the final thread then stood back, her hand on the patient's pulse, her gaze checking her work for leakage.

'I think the worst may be over, Father. There were fewer cases brought in today.' Elly washed carefully in an inch of water in a basin, then wiped clammy hands down her apron and tried to tuck back wisps of fine blonde hair that had escaped from her plaited crown. She longed desperately for a bath, to strip off heavy petticoats and tight-sleeved bodice, to peel away stockings and toss her boots into the corner. To feel clean water lap over her body. What utter bliss. What idiocy, to dream of water where there was none. With the creek bed dry and barrels lined in slime, and not a drop of rain in four months.

It's Christmas in two weeks, Elly thought suddenly. How terrible—a festive season lined with fresh graves, and only the half living to toll the bells. I must be light-headed. She turned to her father and saw him stagger.

'Father! You're not well. You've been doing far too much.'

'It's nothing, girl. I'm weary, of course. Who would not be?' He shook his head angrily, a gesture at his own weakness rather than at her. 'I'll have a drink and sit for a minute.'

Slumping onto a bench, he drained a long draught from a mug standing on the bar counter. Beer, the only fluid left in the Settlement. Even the children drank it. Elly shrugged and took a gulp from her own mug. Just about any liquid would do to wet her throat. But her father worried her. He was killing himself over this epidemic. Always generous with his time and skill, he'd come close to also giving away his health to this motley crowd of creek dwellers and brawling timber men.

She'd never understood why he'd chosen to bury them both here in the Settlement. There were so many other places they could have gone to in the Colony. If he'd wanted to leave Sydney Town, there was always Parramatta or Liverpool, or even Bathurst over the mountain range. There were townships with amenities such as decent houses, shops, parks, perhaps even the luxury of a running river. Why did they have to come north to these cedar hills, to frontier country? They were not pioneers. They wanted nothing from the land. Her father's superlative skills were wasted here on so few, when he could have headed a great hospital, healing and teaching on a much grander scale.

Surreptitiously, Elly studied her father. He was still, for his career, a relatively young man, a graduate of Edinburgh University Medical School, a postgraduate student at the Charite in Paris, and the colleague of such men as Professor Rokitansky in Vienna, who still corresponded and kept her father abreast of the latest developments in the medical world. Why had he chosen to bury himself in this desolation? Why? The years had been so long. Twelve years since Mother had passed away, leaving them to work out a relationship that sometimes seemed to Elly more student and professor than daughter and father.

She sighed and sipped her warm beer, reminding herself of her good fortune to have Robert Ballard as her mentor. It was Elly's great grief that she had been born female. She knew women did not study medicine, especially not women without means, buried twelve thousand miles from the great teaching centres. But she'd worked alongside her father, been allowed to experiment, to gain experience from him as a son might have done.

'I've no time for namby-pamby females,' her father had growled, levelling his pipe at her. 'For a woman, you, Eleanor, are exceptional. You have a brain and, by Jehoshaphat, I'll see you use it!'

Elly's breast had swelled with pride. For she had done it. She'd slaved to prove herself as good as any son, fit to stand beside a great surgeon and assist him in every possible way. The college training could never be hers. The letters MD would not be attached to her name. Yet there were compensations. After a decade of the kind of intensive training few women could hope for, she'd become an experienced nurse who could think for herself. It was hard to understand just why nursing should be regarded as so lowly by society, and relegated to the unskilled and unfit. There had to be a place for nursing as a profession. How many women fretted their lives away uselessly as dutiful daughters or idle wives, when the right training could turn them into productive members of society? There must be hundreds in every city who would welcome the chance—compassionate, capable women perfectly suited to caring for the sick.

Elly pulled herself out of her daydream. She put down her mug and smiled at her father. Later, when there was time, she'd broach the topic with him, see what he thought. Light flickered on her father's nearly bald scalp as he bent slowly towards her, a surprised expression on his face. Elly's smile stiffened. She rose and took two steps forward. For an endless moment her father hung there, as though caught by some invisible hand. Then he slipped from the bench and fell on his face only inches from her boots.

Elly dropped down in a pool of grubby skirts. With shaking hands she raised his head as he vomited over her and onto the floor. His congested eyes seemed to plead with her.

'Father! What's wrong?'

His eyelids flickered and closed. His body convulsed, then stilled. Elly continued to grip his head between her hands, crazily convinced that while she held him he could not die.

'Father. Wait! Don't leave me. Father!'

But she knew he had.

The heat hung over the Settlement for another week, and so did the fever. Then, as suddenly as the cloudburst that came and turned the one crooked street into a quagmire, slowing wagon wheels and engulfing boots in glutinous sludge, the fever went. People opened their doors and closed the gaps in their decimated ranks. They got on with their lives. Widows with children still left alive hid their resentment at God's will and started the baking. Those left childless took their desolation to the unmarked humps of yellow clay in a hastily widened clearing on the hill, there praying for acceptance, or went off to drink themselves into oblivion. At least one ended her pain with a rope over a sturdy branch.

Elly did none of these things. She went on as her father would have wished—serving the sick and convalescent, making up nostrums as she'd been taught, alleviating pain where she could, delving into her tight-packed store of experience to help her fellows. She grew thinner. She mourned privately. She worked harder than the logging bullocks.

A few weeks later a stranger came into town, riding on a high perch wagon which proclaimed in large painted red and black letters, *Doctor Harwood's Remedies, Famous Throughout Europe, Greater Britain and the Americas, Relief for Sufferers of Divers Ills.* For the benefit of those unable to read, there were also representations of bottles, pill boxes and an enormous wooden stethoscope, eye-catching and with a certain lurid attraction. Like the forerunner of a circus train, the wagon lumbered down the crooked street, demanding attention as it threw up sun-caked clods in the faces of the urchins who followed.

Elly stepped hastily aside, half inclined to laugh at the procession, now enhanced by two brown dogs, a flock of hens and Mrs O'Bannion's pig. It lacked only a trumpet and kettledrum, she thought. And was that Dr. Harwood himself? The angular driver wore a battered topper and a coat of dust so thick that nothing else could be learnt of him. Elly put the strange entourage out of her mind, hurrying on to Bessie Flaxman's cabin. Bessie, a shrivelled, prematurely aged woman of thirty, had scalded her foot badly, yet still dragged herself around caring for seven children and a feckless husband who couldn't even arrange to have himself carried off in the epidemic, much less feed his household.

14

I'm becoming an acidulous spinster, Elly thought. Either that or I'm more like Father than I know. He'd have put the fear of God into Tom Flaxman by now. He's done it before. But I can't. I'm a woman, and I'm learning what it means now I have to stand alone. Oh, Father, I miss you. I still feel so guilty. If only I'd known more, if only I'd tried harder to prevent you working yourself to death. You must be so disappointed in me.

She stopped at the cabin door to gather herself, drawing about her the professionalism her father always insisted upon, then knocked and stepped inside. The dirt-floored room was dim after the sunlight. She had to push past the hovering man with his foolish grin like a slice of melon in a week's growth of stubble to bend over the woman who lay on a cot in the corner, weeping in pain.

'Don't worry Bessie, I'm here to help you.'

A week later Elly stood in the same doorway wondering why she had bothered to come. Bessie lay with her leg elevated, simpering at the man anointing her foot with lotion and talking with the speed and assurance of a fairground spruiker. Tom lay on the floor, either drunk or asleep, while the children ran wild.

Elly felt like a jealous discard. Yet, she wondered whether she merely envied the stranger who had walked straight past her into the confidence of her father's patients, the people she'd nursed and helped back to health, or whether she was more worried about his expertise. She knew his treatments were not what her father would have given. And Harwood charged outrageous sums for his pills and tonics, while making even more flagrant claims for their efficacy. It couldn't be right to cover Bessie's healing skin with layers of heavy bandage then tell her on no account to put foot to floor for another four weeks.

With a nod at her own thoughts, Elly stepped inside the cabin. 'Good day, Bessie. I hope your leg has improved. Good day to you, Dr Harwood. I notice you favour excluding air from the healing flesh, with no exercise for atrophying muscles.'

The man appeared to unfold himself, like an angular measure hinged in several places. When erect he looked down on Elly's five feet four inches by a good foot. His manner, too, was lofty, suited to the importance of his calling, although he couldn't have been much more than thirty. His oddly piping voice seemed incongruous, even adolescent.

'My treatments vary with each patient, Miss Ballard. I would not normally trouble the lay mind with explanations but you, with your smattering of medical knowledge, might appreciate the information that a swaddled bandage has lately been found to counteract the injurious humours prevalent in the atmosphere of the countryside hereabouts. The resinous gums exude a most unsavoury noxious odour which must be kept from the healing flesh—protected, also, of course, by my own special remedy against such fumes.'

Elly's indignation swelled, but she concealed it. 'Dr Harwood, I know it's not my place to question your treatment. I'd simply like to draw your attention to my father's experience in similar cases to Bessie's. I have his case notes if you'd care to see them and verify that the treatment of choice, once the new skin has formed over the wound, is clean air plus gentle exercise. My father—'

'Clean air. Precisely, Miss Ballard. Not an atmosphere laden with the fumes of resinous gum trees.'

'I believe you are mistaken, sir.' Elly's temper increased a notch. 'The air in the countryside is a thousand times cleaner than in a city. As for the gumtrees, their eucalyptus oil has only the most efficacious effect in many, many illnesses. I've *seen* this for myself.'

Harwood managed to look both aloof and amused, staring down his long nose and piping: 'Young lady, permit me to point out who is the qualified medical practitioner here. Whatever your limited experiences, they are not to be compared with my own. I must ask you to leave me with my patient.'

Elly tilted her head back to meet his gaze and tried to sound more pleasantly amenable than she felt. 'Of course I'll go, if you want me to. Yet I could be of assistance to you. I know the townsfolk and the background to their troubles. I can assist you in operations, care for your patients in convalescence. I can even make all my father's notes available to—' His look of dismay stopped her dead. What had she said? More urgently now, seeing denial in his face, she added, 'Dr Ballard's large experience in care of burns would be valuable—particularly in the matter of muscle atrophy caused by immobilising the limb ...' Again she stopped, warned by something in the atmosphere.

For some seconds Harwood stared down at her, his cold eyes locked with hers, which were as vividly blue as the southern summer skies and, at present, just as hot. 'I'm not answerable to you or any person other than my confreres,' Harwood spat, 'and I certainly do not require your assistance. Kindly leave, Miss Ballard.'

Angry tears stung beneath Elly's lids as she swept out, aware of Bessie's hostility and Dr Harwood's barely repressed contempt. She hurried off down the dusty street towards her own small cabin, set at a distance from the others in the shade of several eucalypts, the trees so despised by Dr Harwood. She breathed in their aromatic scent as she sped inside to throw down the medical bag which accompanied her on her visits to patients. Ex-patients, more like. Dr Harwood had made it clear he didn't want her anywhere near them.

Having placed the kettle on the fire, she sat down in her father's chair, a solid Windsor wheel-back that had come from his home in Scotland and stayed with him throughout his travels. That chair, more than anything else, reminded Elly of her father. He'd occupied it when seeing patients, exuding the confidence that helped start the healing process; and again, each evening after dinner, he'd been there, book in hand, pipe drooping, for an hour of quiet companionship. While she had this chair, her father's presence remained with her.

Her half-tame currawong swept down from the trees to land on the windowsill, cocking a golden eye. Sunlight burnished his elegant black back and a stream of liquid notes poured from his throat.

Elly glared at him. 'That man is a charlatan,' she told the bird. 'He can't possibly have earned a medical degree. Father would have stripped away his pretence within a day. "Injurious humors" indeed!'

The currawong carolled, and Elly dragged herself out of the chair to make a pot of tea. She took a knife and tin from the dresser, carrying them to the well-scrubbed kitchen table. Only the heel of a loaf remained, dried hard in the heat, but she could soften it in the tea. Cutting an extra slice she absent-mindedly fed pieces to the bird while she turned over her problem.

This new man had swallowed the loyalties of the Settlement as easily as a snake taking eggs in an untended nest, and he clearly planned to be rid of her. That alone increased Elly's suspicion that he wasn't the qualified medical man he pretended to be. Might he be afraid of revealing himself in front of someone with even a small amount of medical knowledge? If he was acting a part while intending to take over her father's practice in the Settlement, he couldn't risk having Elly around to question his credibility.

A shadow passed across the window and Elly looked up to see Old Susan peering in. She beckoned and the old woman's sun-furrowed cheeks screwed themselves into ingratiating lines as she hastened through the door and dropped onto a bench, sighing, her body sagging like the week's wet wash.

'Can you spare a drop o'tea, Elly? I got something to tell you.'

Elly reached for a second teacup, recalling that Old Susan took almost as much pleasure in the fine china as she did in swilling the brew around her toothless gums while dreaming up new, interesting symptoms to confound the doctor. It was easy to give her pleasure. 'What did you want to tell me?' Elly asked.

The faded eyes followed her movements as the pot was heated and tea carefully measured then ladled in. 'Some'un should warn you. There's talk in the town.'

Elly replaced the kettle and straightened up. 'What kind of talk?'

'Bad talk. That new doctor's been saying things ... like you don't know what you're doing.'

'I know he wants to prove himself superior.' Elly hid her worry under a smile.

Still Old Susan looked worried. 'I don't know about that, but I do know he's blaming you for Juniper Jones's bad back and Millie Cross's baby's croup and—'

'All right, Susan, I understand. It's no good me pointing out that Juniper disobeyed my instructions to stay in bed and instead went out and chopped wood until he collapsed, or that the Cross baby lies in a damp cot and never sees the sunlight, or any number of other cases where people refuse to help themselves. No doctor on earth can cure human willfulness, but Harwood has to see someone take the blame.'

Old Susan nodded, although it was doubtful whether she appreciated, as Elly did, the crux of the situation. The townspeople needed to believe in Harwood's skill. They were delighted at their luck in obtaining a new doctor so suddenly after the death of the old one, and of course they believed he would naturally be superior to any unqualified female, however useful she'd been in the interim. As well, Elly knew that her passionate dedication to her patients, her fear that he would harm them, had delivered her into his hands. He was using her own outspokenness against her, deriding her methods from the pinnacle of his own unassailable professional heights. Well, if she wasn't wanted here, if the loyalty of her neighbours had shifted, she supposed she would have to leave. There were other towns where she could put her skills to good use amongst strangers.

Depressed at the thought, she finished her tea and sent Old Susan off with a piece of loaf for her supper.

Two days later, on her way to the store for supplies, Elly heard a terrible cry behind her, and turned to see Molly O'Bannion rush from her cabin screaming that her Maureen was dying. Elly dropped her basket and ran, half the loiterers following. Inside the cabin she almost fell over the pig; then, righting herself, she discovered that Dr Harwood had managed to get there ahead of her. His lean shape bent over a child who writhed on her cot, her lungs straining for air. The doctor had taken his tin of medical instruments from his pocket, laying out the contents on a box beside the cot. He fumbled amongst them, dislodging flakes of rust and nameless other encrusted materials.

Elly pushed up the canvas over the window to let in more light. 'What is it? An obstruction?' she asked.

Harwood turned a sweating face to her. 'God knows. A nut or fruit stone perhaps.'

'Have you put her over your knee and thumped her back?'

His nod was unconvincing and, seizing the small body, Elly tried the remedy several times but without success.

The little girl now lay limp in her arms, all her failing energies concentrated on drawing the next breath.

'I can't shift it. What about forceps?'

He said sharply, 'I've tried, dammit. They will not reach.'

'Cut her throat.' It was the mother, Molly O'Bannion, panting from her hysterical outburst. Her fat face had turned the colour of dough and she clutched at her breast as if something pained her there. They barely had time to register shock at her words when she continued: 'The old doctor did it. He cut into Jim Ridley's throat to save him. Ask her. Ask his daughter.'

She pointed at Elly, who shook her head. 'Too dangerous. Let me try the forceps.'

Dr Harwood rounded on her. 'Kindly put my patient down again and move back. I am about to make an incision.' Sweat oozed from the pores of his face to trickle down his chin. His pale eyes shifted away from Elly's as she laid the child back on her cot.

'Wait. Do you … Are you familiar … ?' She stuttered to a stop. Drawing a deep breath, she said firmly, 'Those instruments have not been cleaned since their last use.' She swept around to face the small crowd that had pushed into the cabin. 'Someone fetch my medical case for Doctor Harwood. Dorothy O'Bannion, bring me your father's whiskey—at once.'

She turned back to see Harwood hovering over the small patient, his dirty scalpel poised in uncertainty.

Elly couldn't help herself. 'Stop!' she cried. 'Wait! The child can still breathe a little …'

With an arm like a whip Harwood swept her aside, sending her staggering back into the arms of the onlookers. 'Stay out of my way. Keep her off,' he ordered.

Hands clamped down on Elly's shoulders. She stopped struggling and willed her tone to be reasonable. 'At least clean the blade first with the whiskey, and swab the child's throat with it before you cut.'

Harwood turned his back and proceeded with the operation.

There was a sudden mewling sound, like a kitten whose tail has been trodden on. The doctor gasped then straightened up. Elly tore herself free and sprang forward.

'What is it? My dear Lord, you've nicked the jugular vein!' Her face as pale and sweaty as his, she plunged her finger into the wound to apply pressure. With the other hand she scrabbled at the coverlet to blot up the blood. 'Quickly, what are you …?' She stared at him. He had frozen, his expression glazed, the dripping scalpel arrested in mid air.

Elly let go the coverlet and shook him.

With a jerk he dropped the scalpel and reached for the forceps, rammed them into the wound and rummaged as if clearing a blocked drain. Before Elly could react, the forceps had pushed her finger aside, widening the nick into a hole. Blood poured over her hand, warm and viscous.

'Look what you've done.' Harwood's voice was shrill. 'I told you to keep away, you stupid woman. Now it's too late.' He thrust her aside with bloody hands. Molly O'Bannion screamed and once again Elly found herself restrained by others. She watched helplessly as Dr Harwood made futile attempts to stop the flow of life from little Maureen O'Bannion's body. The child grew steadily paler. The blood streaming onto the floor slowed to a steady drip, then stopped. With a last flutter of the lips the child stopped breathing.

Silence filled the cabin, except for the moaning mother kneeling by the cot. Sick with anger and frustration, Elly locked gaze with the spurious doctor. There was now no doubt left in her. No true medical man would have made such a dreadful error. But while she sought for words to express her feelings, he began to defend himself by attack.

'This woman is a danger to your community,' he piped. 'I hold her directly responsible for the child's death. Due to her interference at a crucial point in the operation my blade was forced against the main vein in the neck and irreparable damage occurred.'

Elly saw the ring of darkening faces harden against her, sensed the growing anger. She could practically smell it, the age-old urge to find a scapegoat.

'That is a lie,' she said calmly. 'It was *your* hand that made the slip. When I tried to help you stop the bleeding, you pushed me aside and compounded the damage with your forceps. You have the hands of a bullock driver, and with them you have killed a child.'

Uproar broke out behind her. As helpless as a doll, she was pulled about by the men and women holding her and others who tried to join them. Molly O'Bannion turned a tear-ravaged face to her, screeched 'Murderess!', then collapsed.

Elly had to shout to be heard. 'Listen to me. You don't know anything about this man, this so-called doctor. Have you questioned his credentials or heard any good report from someone who has had dealings with him? How do you know he's qualified to touch your children? Ask him for proof.'

Several heads nodded. The room quietened, while the imprisoning hands relaxed enough for Elly to stand alone and rub her bruised shoulders.

'Bluff, pure bluff.' Harwood's voice had reached it's highest pitch, emerging as a squeak. 'I resent your attempt to impugn my character. I will have you know the crowned heads of Europe—'

'Will you stop pontificating and attend to the poor woman at your feet?' Elly indicated the prostrate Molly O'Bannion. 'And someone might take care of the child's body. Then I suggest everybody else go outside. This is no place to conduct your kangaroo court.'

Her tartness had an affect. People began to move out, until only Elly, Harwood, Molly and the women about to lay out the child were left. Molly had recovered her senses, without any assistance. She sat staring hopelessly at the wall, her grief etched into her puffy face. Elly prepared for battle. Her deep anger at the unnecessary death overlaid her personal response to the accusations. For the sake of the township she had to prove this man a dangerous idiot.

Harwood gave her no chance. Grasping her arm he thrust her out the door to face the encircling men and women.

'This woman,' Harwood began in the high voice that no longer seemed comical but instead carried the conviction of a powerful orator, 'this woman has killed one of your children. Because she has formerly been useful when supervised by her father, you've been led to believe that her skills are equal to those of a proper practitioner. But she is not a doctor. She has not been properly trained or accredited. She's merely an assistant. Yet she holds a high opinion of herself, even deeming it proper to interfere with a surgeon at work. Therefore she is dangerous. Shall you harbour a ticking bomb in your midst? Shall you go about your daily lives never knowing when she may explode into a furore of false medical activity and kill someone else? Shall we live with that?'

'No!' It was a united roar from twenty throats. Old Cyrus Bennetts, the hotel rouseabout whose smell kept others at a comfortable distance, and whose ulcerated leg Elly had treated over long weeks of battle with infection, shook his fist at her. His stubbled face was twisted with hate. Women who had cried over Elly in gratitude when their children recovered from the fever, and others she had trudged miles to help, leant towards her to hiss, even to spit. The tremor in her legs moved up through her spine until her whole body shook.

She could hardly believe what was happening. They couldn't turn on her, even if they did prefer Harwood and his remedies. She'd done nothing to deserve such hatred. Surely they knew she'd never harm their children in any way. But she read only animosity in the ugly faces, almost unrecognisable as belonging to friends and neighbours. This unthinking mob frightened her. It was as though the crowd had one face, one accusing gaze, one menacing voice.

Harwood tightened his grip until it was painful.

'Let me go at once,' she whispered, 'or I'll kick you.'

He released her, perhaps in surprise, and Elly confronted the crowd. Choosing one person, Old Susan, who had as much cause as anyone to be grateful to the Ballards, Elly addressed her directly.

'Susan, you know me better than that. Will you listen to a stranger who knows nothing about me?' Her gaze swept their avid faces, noting each one. 'All you good people, my friends of years, I ask you to remember who I am, and for how long my father served you all. He was a brilliant doctor who chose to make his skills available to you when he might have been acclaimed in the world. He never refused a call for help. He cared desperately that none of you should suffer.'

Harwood raised his voice above hers. 'We all know and appreciate the work of Doctor Ballard. But he's gone, and his daughter brazenly tries to assume his mantle.'

Elly spread her hands. 'That's not so. Few trained *men* could emulate Robert Ballard. I don't aspire to do so. But he taught me well. I'm experienced enough to help you in many ways. What happened here today—'

Harwood shouted her down again. 'She's only a woman. Listen to her. Her humility is false. The truth is, she believes herself to have equal standing with a professional man. Does not her arrogance demonstrate the danger? How often has she failed you— you, Juniper Jones, still as crippled as the day you fell down, despite this woman's efforts? And you, Colgrave. Did she give you back the power in your legs? Will you ever swing hammer to anvil again before you die? No, you will not, because *she* failed in her treatment, overreached herself, in fact, and condemned a good man to a life of misery.' He pointed dramatically to the brawny fellow balanced on rough crutches, his limbs hanging uselessly between them.

The crowd roared ominously, but Harwood raised a hand. 'This woman should be got rid of before someone else dies. I urge you, friends, to wrench out this canker in your midst, to dismiss it from your lives.'

'Yes, yes. She should be punished. Let's hang the bitch.'

In vain Elly shouted that no-one could have helped the two men named, that she was not responsible for Maureen O'Bannion's death. Her words were buried beneath the united voices hurling abuse. This wasn't happening. It was a nightmare, like the fever 'ward' in the hotel that night—the worst of dreams that had turned to harsh reality when she gazed down at her father's corpse.

The mob began to move in on her. She backed away, coming up against Harwood, who grasped her arm once more.

Again he held up his hand. 'Wait, friends. We're all reasonable folk. We do not return blow for blow, harm for harm. A life has been taken. Very well. But we are not monsters to demand a life in revenge. Let us simply remove the killer from our society. Let us—'

'Run her out of town,' someone shouted.

'Yes. Yes. Run her out of town.'

The mob halted, then took up the refrain. 'Out of town. Out of town.' They surged forward.

The women got to her first. 'We'll fix her before she goes. Child killer!'

Old Susan, protesting, was hustled to the rear, while Molly O'Bannion ran forward and spat in Elly's face. Others held Elly down as several more brandished shears with which they attacked her braids. Elly screamed and struggled madly but couldn't break free. The shears clashed, one blade carelessly gashing her forehead as it tore at the silken strands now falling about her neck. She ceased to scream, her horror too great for expression. She felt blood drip down over her ear, heard the hissing breath of her tormentors, smelt their rank sweat. She closed her eyes against the faces, the awful faces.

At last they finished and the women fell back. Elly was dragged to her feet, then shoved and jostled along the crooked street, Harwood at her side, guard and guardian, protecting her from physical attack. How kind. She swallowed hysterical laughter. Accuser, judge and jury—but he didn't want to be branded executioner. She stumbled along in a daze. They passed the hotel, where less than a month ago she had slaved to save these people and their dear ones. Past Bessie Flaxman's cabin, where Bessie lay obediently resting a leg that she would never use fully again. Past the pathway to her own cabin. Here Elly halted but was roughly forced on again. Then the realisation came to her. They truly meant to run her out of town, without preparation, without food or water, or even a hat to keep off the fierce sun. But they couldn't. They wouldn't do it to an animal.

Looking ahead she saw the street straggle to an end, vanishing into the encroaching bush. It was so vast, so impenetrable, unbroken miles of trees and undergrowth, nothing save a stony track winding away towards a limitless horizon. Heat, dust and incredible loneliness. That's what lay ahead of her. A desolate road to oblivion. Elly stopped suddenly so that Harwood cannoned into her. 'Listen to me,' she began.

In answer, he gave her a push, strong enough to make her trip. She fell hard, grazing her hands on the stones, twisting her ankle under her. As she picked herself up she heard her skirt tear at the waist. Slowly she brushed away the clinging dirt, tested her weight on her ankle. It hurt, but it was bearable. Then she raised her chin and faced her tormentor.

'Keep moving. And don't think you can sneak back after dark,' Harwood warned. 'There'll be nothing left of your home by then. We'll burn it down.' He forced her on.

About half a mile down the track he called a halt. By now the crowd had dwindled to ten men plus a couple of the more energetic women, still buoyed by mob excitement and a hope of more drama to come.

Harwood pulled Elly around to face him. 'This is far enough.'

She returned his look calmly, forcing down her despair. 'You're sending me to my death. I can't survive without provisions or a horse. You know how far it is to the nearest township.'

For a moment the pale eyes lit, and she saw in them real hatred—for the things she'd said about him, for seeing through him. Then Harwood smiled, saying softly, 'We are always in God's hands. Let it be your comfort—while you live.'

Chapter Two

The Christian mission squatted on a hillside a mile from the village, its bareness contrasting with the stepped green paddy fields and farmlets of a lush Chinese river valley noted for its abundant harvests. The mud-brick walls of the mission dispensary, chapel and living quarters, set in lopsided fashion around an unpaved courtyard, appeared to be slowly crumbling into the earth. Shutters hung awry, letting in the winter winds and the monsoonal rains. Roof tiles were chipped or lost altogether. Any attempt to grow trees in the hard-packed earth had failed, while a row of empty flowerpots only added to the starkness. The one concession nature had allowed within the walls was a persimmon tree, sheltered by the eastern gate. It had survived against all odds and in summer became a miracle of glossy green leaves and golden globes of fruit. The rest of the mission remained, botanically speaking, a desert in a sea of plenty.

With its air of brave isolation, the mission was shunned by most villagers until someone needed the Red-Hair doctor; and the few converts wisely kept a low profile. Imperial edicts forbidding Christian worship remained in force and all rights of foreign trade and residence were confined to the seaport of Shanghai, many miles down the Yangtse River.

Pearl knew this as well as her foster parents, Ada and Morris Carter, representatives of the London Missionary Society, stalwart medical pioneers in the Land of Sinim for five years. The clinic and dispensary, plus the evangelical work, left little time for gardening or repairs, at which the doctor and his wife were particularly inept anyway. And somehow the place failed to prosper under the hands of hired workers. Yet the Carters maintained their cheerful determination and persevered with God's work.

Like her foster parents, Pearl accepted the inherent risks of running a Christian mission. However, unlike the Carters, Pearl was a fatalist. She didn't expect the current peace to last. Sold into slavery by her natural mother at the age of five, used as everything from pot-scourer to bed-warmer, then bought and fostered by a largely incomprehensible white couple who introduced her to the first comfort and consideration she'd ever known, Pearl kept her own counsel. Made pragmatic by circumstances, she had accepted their kindness, their God and their training in nursing skills, while squirrelling away small valuables and practising self-defense techniques against the day when the axe would inevitably fall.

That day came one cold January while Pearl worked in the dispensary making up a wound poultice for a patient in the hospital room next door. Her glossy black braid hung down over the collar of her warm padded jacket, thumping lightly against her back as she pounded her pestle and, for perhaps the thousandth time, called down a blessing on the foreigners who cared for her. She had rice in her belly, a sleeping mattress of her own, and no expectation of blows or curses if she failed to please. In return, she worked carefully and meticulously, and held in her heart an inarticulate love for the white woman who tried so hard to mother her. Pearl's own family had been lost to her so long ago she never thought about them, except for Li Po, her older brother. Him she remembered—a boy carelessly affectionate towards an unwanted girl child, saving her tidbits from his meals, helping her small stumbling feet across ditches in the paddy fields, until the day he left for the great distant city of Nanking, never to return.

Pearl stopped work to inspect the mash of yarrow leaves in the mortar, then spun around as, without warning, the window shutters banged back and a man sprang into the room, shouting and brandishing a sword. His coarse short hair was held by a bandanna and his loose jerkin and breeches were belted with a sash.

Pearl froze, her usual technique when under attack.

'Death to all Manchu pigs.' The assailant rolled his eyes and swung the sword high.

'I'm not Manchu.' All the same, Pearl dropped the pestle and scuttled under the workbench. Her accent was quite different from his. Maybe he had not understood.

The sword stayed high while the man hesitated.

Pearl peeped out at him. 'Look, my feet are not bound. I am a servant.' She thrust out a small, sturdy foot in its leather slipper.

'Come out,' the man ordered.

Pearl sidled out from under the workbench, keeping her distance. Not liking the man's expression, she put a convincing whine in her voice then dragged her jacket away from her neck to expose the brand on her upper arm. 'See? I bear the slave mark. I am but a lowly cockroach in the house of the *yi*.'

The man nodded and, lowering the sword, looked around. His fierce expression changed to one of disgust. Clearly there were no valuables here to be scavenged.

'Where is the gold? Show me it.'

'What gold? We have nothing of value, except salves and potions for the sick.' Pearl spread her arms wide, wondering whether she could keep the man here while she alerted the mission. Was he alone, or were there other raiders with him?

Then, from the yard outside, she heard screams, shouts and the clash of weapons. It rose to a clamour that seemed to rock the walls; voices chanted above the hubbub, broken now and then by a horrible wailing. 'What's happening? Who are you?', Pearl cried in terror, lunging for the door; but the man caught her by her braid and dragged her back.

'I am a Triad brother of the Taiping, the Great Peace,' he said. 'We bring death to the Manchu usurpers and peace to our land under the new Heavenly Emperor.' He spoke as if by rote; not with conviction.

'Peace? That doesn't sound like peace. Why are you attacking the mission?'

'We sweep the land clear before us. We make way for the true

Emperor.'

Pearl wasn't listening. In a sudden brief lull in the uproar she heard a familiar woman's voice. She tore at his fingers. 'Let me go.' Twisting unexpectedly, she freed herself and sprang towards the door, then stood transfixed. In the courtyard bodies lay in pools of blood on the hard-packed earth. More bodies were crammed in the gateway, slain as they fled, one figure even hanging over the high wall, legs dangling. Two or three attackers were busily looting their victims, while the rest chased after the mission workers fleeing downhill towards the village.

'My mother!' Pearl put a hand to her mouth to stifle a scream. She'd seen the pile of petticoats flung in a heap across the hospital step a few feet away, the arms outthrown as if in supplication. But where the head had been, only a bleeding stump remained. Ada Carter had died trying to protect her patient. Straddling her was a giant of a man, his boots carelessly planted on his victim's skirt to reveal an immodest amount of stockinged leg. He had dropped his bloodied blade to tear the small gold hoop earrings from the severed head.

Pearl's mind went blank. All her senses failed her. The courtyard disappeared, the distant screams faded, the smell of blood and fear no longer existed. For one blinding instant she was pure pain. A great crimson sea rolled in, swamping her; on a tide of insane rage she surged forward, stooped to grasp the fallen sword with both hands, then swung it high to arc down onto the arm holding that grotesque trophy. The giant spun to face her, his expression one of total astonishment. Blood pumped from the hole in his shoulder, hosing the soil and the corpse of his victim. Then something hit Pearl on the side of the head and thrust her into oblivion.

She woke to darkness, pain down the left side of her face and neck, and the smell of cooking fires. Frosted stars hung overhead and a cold wind stirred her hair. Voices came from shadows clumped around the fires. Many men and many fires. This was a camp. She was surrounded by the rebel army, a prisoner. Why had they taken her but slain the others ... her mother ... her mother ... Acid tears burned Pearl's eyes. She brushed them aside fiercely, discovering in the process that her wrists were bound together with a thong.

A voice, not familiar, but not wholly strange either, said, 'Rise up, woman, and come to the fire.'

Stiff and bruised, Pearl got slowly to her feet. The movement caused the wound on the side of her head to start seeping and she felt warmth trickle down her neck as she walked into the firelight. A tripod sat over the flames where a man squatted, stirring a bubbling pot. Pearl recognised her attacker, the Triad who had wanted to cut her down. When he rose he seemed even taller than she remembered. She had to tip back her head to meet his eyes.

'You, servant woman, are now my slave. I am a leader of fifty men. You will give me honour.'

Pearl said nothing. It had always been safer to maintain silence and be watchful.

Perhaps the man took this for defiance for he stepped forward and slapped her face. Head ringing like a temple gong, Pearl fell to her knees, her hands rising to her wound as she felt the trickle of blood increase to a flow.

'Get up, slave. Serve the meal.' The Triad plucked a knife from his sash; Pearl flinched, but met his gaze. He laughed as he cut the thong around her wrists. 'Disobey and I will slit your nostrils.' He turned aside, ignoring her.

Dragging herself upright, Pearl crossed to the fire. A wooden bowl and spoon lay there, and she served the savoury stew of what smelt like chicken and root vegetables, taking it to where her captor lolled on a pile of bedding, and presenting it subserviently.

'Your meal, honoured master.' Her tone was conciliatory. Her eyes were not visible beneath her lowered lids.

He grunted, dismissing her. Others came to the pot to help themselves, some glancing at their leader's new acquisition, most simply interested in the food. Pearl crouched in the darkness beyond the circle of firelight, but her thoughts were not on food. The picture of her mother's dead face, hanging by the hair from that animal's fingers, would not leave her. The pain in her heart was so great, far worse than her torn scalp; it was living agony.

In the darkest hour of that windy night Pearl drew within herself, into that stillness of the spirit that no-one else can touch, and there she swore a great oath.

'By the spirits of my ancestors whom I have not known, by all the Gods of heaven and earth, and by Jesus Christ, Son of the most high God, I swear I will escape this slavery and avenge my parents' deaths. I swear this by ... by my mother's book of holy writings, and may I die in torment if I do not fulfill this oath.' She touched a finger to the bloody ooze at her temple, then drew it across her lips. A life for a life, if necessary.

The pain in her heart eased a little after this, allowing her to think. The man who had cut down her mother could not have lived long, with his lifeblood pumping from him like a river in spate. But he was only one. These others, these Taipings or Triads, this army of butchers, were just as responsible. She knew her foster father must be dead, along with the mission workers. Why leave any witnesses to the slaughter? And she guessed the village would by now be a funeral pyre, with the animals and grain taken to feed the murderous hordes rolling across the countryside. Where were they headed? They must have a destination in mind if they really planned to replace the Son of Heaven who ruled China. Peking itself? Was it not many hundreds of miles to the north? Her foster father had said so. Although whether his words could be replied upon, Pearl was unsure, since he had not succeeded in explaining to her satisfaction how there could be two Sons of Heaven, one seated at the right hand of God the Father and the other upon the silken cushions of the Imperial throne.

Her new master summoned her and she obeyed silently. Her moment would come.

Pearl slipped easily back into the attitudes and responses of a slave. As long as she swiftly obeyed orders and hid her true feelings, she was treated well enough, although kept busy foraging for twigs and dung for the fires and for edibles for the pot. After she'd laid out her master's bedding at night and prepared his opium pipe, she was free to creep away to attend to her own toilette, before being either tied to the ox cart or first used to assuage any bodily urges her master might still have after a long day's march or an even more tiring day of killing. Several more villages had fallen victim since the mission had been overrun. The other members of the Triad company clearly feared their leader too much to interfere with his spoil, but they watched her jealously; and since

Pearl had discovered the enormous size of the army, of which her master's group was a tiny part, she'd given up any immediate plans for escape. Surrounded by some eighty thousand men, women and children, smothered in dust as she plodded along tied to the ox cart, Pearl was lucky if she saw the sun and made a rough guess at her direction.

From the first day she had been made to wear her braid tied up under a beaded cap, while her slight seventeen-year-old figure remained hidden under padded jacket and pants, so that everyone except the Triad's men knew her as a young boy. When she dared to query the cap she was told: 'These Taiping have strange ways. They are of the Hakka tribe in Kwangtung who wear their hair long and bound in a turban. Any man found with queue and shaven forehead is taken for a Manchu and sent to his ancestors.'

'Why must I be a man?' At the time Pearl was combing her master's short locks and massaging his neck. He humoured her.

'Because the leader, Hong Xiu-juan, has a new religion which permits him to smash the old gods yet forbids rape of females. The women and children of the camp live separately and march with us under guard. To stay with me, you must act as a man slave.' He shrugged. 'We are Triad. We march with the Taiping to overthrow the Manchu, but we do not follow their ways.'

Pearl said softly, 'Does Hong Xiu-juan say there shall be no violence practised against the Red-Hair *yi* or innocent villagers?'

Her captor twisted about and caught her arm, bending it back painfully. Her face was inches from his, her gaze steady.

'You grow bold, slave. I do as I will. And when the Imperial troops attack once more you will be glad these weaklings have the Triad beside them to make real war. The Emperor's men take delight in delivering prisoners to the death of a thousand slices.' Then he forced her down on the mattress and took her, careless of his watching men.

Tethered at night like one of the oxen that pulled the carts, Pearl lay on the cold earth and thought about the future. She had heard some say they were headed for Nanking to the east, the intended new capital where, with the help of this army of thousands, Hong Xiu-juan would make himself Heavenly Emperor. Pearl knew they would succeed. Evidence of their cruel ruthlessness abounded, although she doubted that the Imperial troops were worse. The forthcoming battle would be a bloody event, but it could present an opportunity for escape.

Some days later, scouts warned of the enemy's approach and the rebel army grouped, ready for attack. Watching her captor sharpen his blade and organise his followers, Pearl understood how much these men enjoyed the prospect of a fight. She heard them rally one another, wagering on the number of heads they would cause to roll, the promise of spoil. There was no mention of their own deaths or mutilations, no sign of fear. Nor did they discuss the cause they supposedly fought for. The Triads did battle for themselves, for excitement and freedom from the humdrum life of a peasant. They were animals, and she despised them.

Sent with her master's cart to the rear with the women, children and baggage, Pearl made her preparations. First she retrieved the small, sharp blade she had long ago concealed in the lining of her padded jacket for such a moment. Her jacket was a treasure house, a survival kit, with a pocket even holding needle and thread to restitch the lining. With the blade she slit her bonds then climbed up into the oxcart, crouching down out of sight of the milling women and children aroused to a ferment over the imminent attack. Pearl went first to the opium chest, taking from it a sticky pellet of raw drug. From her secret cache in the jacket she took a silk bag, emptying into her hand a pinch of herb-like powder which she rolled into the opium. She did this with several more balls before, satisfied at last, she replaced them and closed the chest. Then she searched for her mother's earrings, finding them tied in a bag with other valuables stolen from bodies still warm and dripping their lifeblood. There was dried blood on the golden hoops. Pearl held them in her shaking hand, taking a moment to regain control. She also picked out the biggest, blackest pearl she had ever seen, threaded on a piece of silk.

'What are you doing there, boy?'

Pearl jumped as if scalded. Still crouched amongst the boxes she turned to see a woman silhouetted against the glaring sky. In the distance she heard the roar of the sea—only the sea lay many miles to the east, and what she could heard was the voice of war.

The woman leaned forward, peering in. 'Thief!' she screeched.

'You rob your lord. Thief! Thief!'

Pearl sprang, her outstretched leg hitting the woman under the chin, knocking her backwards in a heap. Jumping down from the cart, Pearl ran, dodging and weaving amongst the startled crowd. Some tried to stop her only to find she was not where she'd been a split second before. A boy, older than the rest, grabbed at her arm. She sliced his knuckles with her knife and he let her go with a howl. She raced on.

Now there was a baying mob on her trail, infected by the battle excitement, hardly knowing whom they chased or why, driven only by bloodlust. Pearl slipped under a cart and crouched there, panting, easing the fire in her lungs. Dozens of blue-trousered legs ran past. She waited for a long time, then slipped out the other side to mingle with a quieter group of people who stood peering northwards to where smoke and dust rose in a huge pall, darkening the sky, and from where rose a roar like that of a beast from Hell itself.

Quietly, ghostlike, Pearl threaded through the crowd and began to creep away to the south. She picked up a pot and pretended to be fetching water, moving slowly backwards until finally she reached the lip of the vast plateau where the army had camped. Throwing aside the pot then, she ran down the slope, tripping and rolling and scrambling to her feet again, braking with her heels where the angle grew steep, cannoning off rocks, until at last she reached shelter in a clump of trees. There she flung herself down, her chest labouring like a blacksmith's bellows. Looking up into the trimmed bare branches she saw they were mulberry trees, planted in rows leading down to an expanse of water where sampans were towed by water buffalo, men fished and children played. It was a painted scene, peaceful, in total contrast to the fighting and bloodshed she'd left behind.

She thought of her captor, taking his ease after the battle, if he survived. He would be weary and furious that there was no slave to prepare his pipe. He'd take one of the pills and swallow it. Eating opium was an easy way to satisfy the drug craving. And with it he would swallow the deadly powdered mushroom.

Filled with fierce satisfaction, she forced herself to her feet and hurried down to the river.

Chapter Three

T he sun was at its zenith, bearing relentlessly down upon the earth. Elly felt it as an actual pressure that flattened her hair against her skull in a sweaty mat. All that was left of her thick gold braids was a rat's nest of chopped ends which she couldn't bear to touch.

Still stunned by the violence of events that had overtaken her so suddenly, she plodded along the middle of the track, stirring up dust that clung to her damp skin and masked her face. Stinging flies and midges clustered there, seeking moisture from her eyes, lips, skin. Listlessly she brushed at them with a swatch of gumleaves. She'd been walking a long time since being herded out of the Settlement like an animal, followed by catcalls and the ugly epithets heard in rough timber camps. Her throat was parched, her unprotected skin on fire. Numbed by shock, she hadn't even flinched when a stone was thrown at her, narrowly missing her head. Eventually they'd stopped following her, headed back, no doubt, for a refreshing drink at the hotel, the dead child and her grieving family already out of mind, and Elly herself ancient history.

Which was just what she was likely to become if she didn't find help in a day or so.

Elly stopped to tear off a long strip from one petticoat and wound it around her head against the scorching sun, then set off once more. It was no use turning back to further abuse. She'd been warned. The thought that by now her home, all her possessions, her father's precious chair, would be ash and rubble, brought her close to despair.

She walked for hours until the sun was replaced by stars shimmering overhead in the heated air, until the moon disappeared, leaving her to feel her way through confusing shadows, sometimes running into an outstretched branch or tripping over a stone. The rough track had been carved by the bullocks pulling cedar logs to the river, where they were floated down to a mill. However, due to the drought this summer, the water level had dropped and it was unlikely a team would pass by in time to help her.

When the light failed completely Elly found shelter under a fallen tree; then, digging a hole for her hip in the sandy soil, she tried to sleep. By this time her empty stomach had contracted into a tight, painful knot and her body ached mercilessly. Utterly drained, she lay shivering despite the lingering heat. Since her father's death she'd managed to keep going, but now the last of her courage was seeping away. She longed for him as a child would, although he'd not been a demonstrative parent and had seldom touched her in affection. What would their life together have been had her mother lived? she wondered. The rosy memories were no doubt overcoloured, yet she recalled her mother as a warmth that had gone from her life, a loving protectiveness which had abandoned her. Had Mama lived, would they have stayed in Sydney? Would there have been young brothers and sisters? Perhaps. Yet despite her husband's skill, Mary Ballard had died giving birth, her tiny son following not long after. God, according to the minister who had buried them both, had needed them in heaven; His will must be suffered and accepted.

Elly wished she had a strong religious faith to sustain her. Her father's logical mind and the clarity of vision which made him see his fellow men and women for what they truly were, had long ago destroyed his belief in a heavenly father.

'God is called upon by those in need and neglected until need arises,' Robert Ballard had said. 'He's blamed for disasters, condemned for not answering prayers in the required manner, claimed as defender of both sides in battle and used in blasphemy as an outlet for inarticulate rage. God is a convenient construct, an answer to the eternal cry of "Why?", not a reality.'

His young daughter, who'd watched the suffering of humanity but could find no reason for it, agreed with him.

Which means I'm on my own, she thought, listening to the night sounds of the bush and reasoning that she had nothing to fear. There were no nocturnal predators in the Australian bush—well, none larger than a rat. Not even the dingoes prowled after dark, did they? No, she was sure they didn't. Which left only one kind of hunter, man himself. The blacks. But they were afraid of the night spirits. She'd heard that, she was sure.

At last she slept, fitfully, wakening to a blazing dawn and the chorus of birds high in the gum trees—and a terrible hollowness within. She struggled to her feet, then sat down on a log to tighten the bootlaces she'd loosened the night before. Light-headed from lack of food and water, she licked the dew from gumleaves. It wasn't sufficient to quench her thirst, but it was something, and she winced as she ran her tongue over cracked lips. A search of the scrubby growth beneath the trees disclosed a few flowering plants but no fruits or berries. She tightened her belt and, because there was nothing else to do, set off down the rutted track, hoping it would soon begin to slope downhill towards the river. Would it be salt, so far up from the mouth? More likely brackish. Whatever. If she could find water, she'd drink it.

But as the hours passed, the track remained level. She didn't dare leave it, despite the fierce heat, for fear of being lost in the forest, which was closing in on both sides, thick with undergrowth. The gumleaves drooped dispiritedly, each tree the same as the next, a mind-numbing sameness that could quickly disorient any traveller. A thousand bush cicadas shrilled in Elly's ears, drilling through her brain. Her eyes ached. Her tongue had become a wad of dry felt, so swollen it impeded her breathing. The flies were maddening, and her arm itched and stung where an ant had bitten her. She staggered along, scuffing in the sandy soil, only half conscious. Her feet were two lumps of pain which extended up her legs; each step jarred her knees, while her face and hands were on fire.

Knowing she couldn't go much further, she considered crawling off into the bush, into the blessed shade, to wait for death. It
would be so much easier. Yet she couldn't do it. Something goaded
her on, a stubborn determination that ignored her many pains
and forced one foot ahead of the other, forced her to stay aware
and upright for one more minute, then one more minute after
that.

As the afternoon shadows drew in, Elly sensed another presence. She stopped and, shading her aching eyes with her hands,
stared into the bush, her heart thudding against her ribs. No-one
there. She tried to call out but her voice died in her parched throat.
Was that darkness beside a paler tree? A figure? No. Her eyes had
tricked her. She saw a branch wriggling across her path. Another
hallucination, she thought. Next I'll see a mirage of Sydney Town
itself. The branch curved and reared a smooth flat head. Eyes like
boot buttons stared at her. Snake! With an inward scream Elly
threw herself backwards, overbalanced and fell. The strike was a
knife-blade in her arm. As the snake slithered off into the bush,
Elly glimpsed the red underbelly. A black snake—highly venom-
ous.

God have mercy on me, she thought, her senses slipping away.

Chapter Four

The city had fallen. All twenty-two miles of Nanking's great walls were breached. All but two of the thirteen original Ming gates had been destroyed, the gate-keepers and beggars who clustered there left to lie in their own blood. Shops, temples, houses, all had tumbled into smoking ruins, while twenty thousand people lay hacked or burnt to death among them.

Pearl, crouched in a barrel amongst the rubble of the Protestant mission where she had taken refuge, listened to the sporadic crackle of musketry and decided it sounded far enough away for her to creep out down to the river. For that was the only way of escape: a highway to the sea and a ship to take her in search of her brother. She would hide on the wharves, scavenge for food, await her chance. She thought, with a mixture of compassion and derision, of her missionary hosts, buried beneath their own fallen roof. How could they have been so stupid as to believe the Taiping promises of brotherhood in Jesus? This was an army of beggars, pirates, deserters, the country's scourings whose only aim was ravishment and plunder. The high visionary outlook of Hong Xiu-juan, their leader, had degenerated into fanaticism, allowing the extreme brutality that would forever discredit the movement. Pearl had tried to disillusion the missionaries, describing the sacking of her home and her foster mother's murder. However, these had been seen as isolated incidents carried out by disaffected troops. Everyone knew the Triads were thugs, but they formed only a part of Hong's great army. Doubtless, when Hong himself arrived, the Church Missionary Society would make fruitful contact, which would lead to the Christian word being spread throughout China. With their eyes fixed firmly on the Holy Grail of conversion, the missionaries had ignored the almost overwhelming obstacles to China's Christianisation, putting their trust in the Divine Will instead. And thus they had died, in the fires set by invaders too filled with bloodlust to differentiate between friend and foe.

Pearl had arrived in Nanking a few days earlier, having worked her passage on a fishing boat. She'd headed immediately for the House of Five Lanterns, where western friends of her foster family lived and evangelised discreetly, regarded by the locals more as an entertainment than a source of trouble. Here she obtained news of the brother she had not seen since her babyhood. Mrs Edna Horbury, tall, angular, self-satisfied as a wading bird in a fish-filled pond, had broken the news in a tediously roundabout way.

'I'm sorry if you hoped to find Edgar here. When your family … er … dissipated, as you know, Edgar sold himself as a labourer. Later he was able to come to us but he was never … well, he was never a success, you know. Too independent, by far.'

'Edgar?'

'We gave him a proper Christian name, you know, one we could pronounce.'

'His name is Li Po,' Pearl said firmly, irritated by the arrogance.

'Yes, well, as I said, he was with us for a year, then he ran away. It was most inconvenient, you know. We had to train another boy in his duties and it's difficult to find a family that will sell a male child, as you know.'

Pearl tightened her lips. 'Li Po is not a boy, he is a man.' Her heart had become a weight in her chest. Her brother, her last remaining relative, had left before she could reach him.

Edna Horbury bridled. 'You are just a little impertinent. I'm sure my husband and I did our best for the b … for Edgar. We were quite hurt when he left us without a word, you know.'

'Do you know where he went? Is he still in Nanking?'

'I really couldn't say.'

Pearl saw that she'd given offence, and hastened to alter her tone. 'Mrs Horbury, I apologise. I was too abrupt. My excuse is my anxiety to find my brother. He's all I have left in the world.'

'You have the Lord Jesus, my child, and are therefore never alone.'

'Of course.' Pearl's voice was smooth. 'And if my prayers are answered I will find my brother. Could you be instrumental in answering those prayers, Mrs Horbury?'

Edna Horbury succumbed. 'Well, do you know, I just might be. Thomas, our gardener, was Edgar's friend. They may have kept in touch.'

When consulted, Thomas, a gnarled tree stump of a man at home in his setting, was able to provide an answer which only added a load to Pearl's weighted heart. Her brother had heard about the great gold strikes in a land of the Red Hairs far to the south and had gone to make his fortune.

'Left China!' Pearl sank down on her haunches and laid her forehead on her knees.

Thomas tittered. 'He heard that gold hung from the trees in this land, this Ostrahleeah. He told me he'd come home with a sackful to buy the house of a mandarin and live in it and forget that he ever bore the mark of slavery.'

Gold that hung from trees? Pearl shook her head. Li Po would be disappointed. But at least she now knew where to find him. She rose and thanked Thomas for his help, then turned to his mistress.

'I will follow my brother to this Ostrahleeah. How do I get there?'

Edna Horbury allowed herself a superior smile. 'My dear, the place is practically off the map, thousands of miles away. You could never travel such a distance.'

'I must. Where can I find a ship to take me?'

When the woman hesitated, Pearl said impatiently, 'I will find out for myself.' She paused, choosing her words carefully. 'Mrs Horbury, ma'am, my foster mother always told me that if ever I needed it, I could rely on your kindness. Could I please stay with you for a few days until I make my arrangements? I want to leave Nanking before the Taiping arrive.'

Hospitality being offered and accepted, Edna Horbury had set herself to explain to this half-pagan child just how she had mis-judged the God-worshipping Taiping leader. Pearl had listened, argued, then given up in the face of such monumental assurance. However, she had not been alone in appreciating that the river made a swift highway. The rebels also had taken to the water, and within three days had arrived at the city walls. Pearl had left it too late to leave.

By dusk the rampage had ended. Certain by then that whatever was left of the city had quietened, Pearl climbed stiffly out of the barrel and picked her way cautiously through the narrow streets blocked with clay bricks, shattered tiles and shards of timber, the remains of narrow houses butted hard against one another yet not strong enough to withstand deliberate attack. The air was thick with smoke and the nauseatingly sweet smell of roasted flesh, over-laid with charred wood. Even the inevitable miasma that cloaked China in a stinking pall—decayed garbage, over-flowing sewers, faeces spread in the paddy fields, putrefied remains floating in the canals—even this had been temporarily overcome. Accustomed as she was to unpleasant smells, Pearl wrinkled her nose and covered it with her sleeve.

She remembered these streets as busy arteries leading to the markets where all the world gathered to gossip and haggle over the produce brought in from the countryside; where rickshaws jostled chairmen transporting high-nosed mandarins to the pal-aces for audience with equally high-nosed officials; and street ur-chins and beggars blocked passage to the many temples, whining, importuning.

Pearl's eyes filled with tears, the first she had allowed herself to shed since war swept away her world. The tears became a torrent and, shaking too much to continue, she crept into shelter under some fallen pillars to give way to her grief. She didn't weep for the destruction, or for the mass death surrounding her, but for her-self and the loss of two good people, who had cared enough about their fellow men to leave home, comfort and loved ones to bring a gift of knowledge to a country lacking that knowledge. It didn't matter that they were unwelcome, that their message had little relevance for the people they tried to help, physically and spiritually. They had ignored the very real risks they ran and in the end had given their lives for their beliefs. All that Pearl knew of goodness and self sacrifice came from them, and she wept bitterly for her loss.

Two weeks later HMS *Hermes*, carrying the Governor of Hong Kong, Sir George Bonham, docked at Nanking. While the representative of Her Britannic Majesty endeavoured to see Hong in person, and the self-styled new Emperor of China frustrated these endeavours, Pearl, now ragged and half starved, slipped aboard the vessel, along with a group of eager sightseers. Avoiding the crew members trying to contain the unexpected crowd, she found a hiding place below deck where she stayed until the ship weighed anchor for the coastal city of Shanghai, far away to the south east.

Discovery was inevitable. When a shout of surprise was accompanied by a fierce jerk on her plait, Pearl rose uncomplainingly from behind the crate and allowed herself to be dragged on deck to the accompaniment of a few kicks. She only began to struggle when her captor thrust her head and shoulders over the side rail and seemed about to throw her into the river, until a peremptory voice stopped his game.

'Seaman, put that child down and explain his presence aboard one of Her Majesty's vessels.'

The sailor knuckled his forehead, while firmly twisting his other hand in Pearl's plait. 'Stowaway, sir. Just giving him a bit of a fright, like, before taking him before the mate.'

'A stowaway, eh? Hardly any wonder, really.' The speaker, young and elegantly, although plainly, dressed, was clearly accustomed to command. He rubbed his chin and looked amused, then beckoned to Pearl. 'Come here, boy.'

Feeling her queue released, no doubt reluctantly, Pearl approached the speaker. Here was authority, and she peeped warily from beneath lowered lids, seeking evidence of his character and temperament.

His smile grew as she went down on her knees in obeisance, hands clasped before her.

'Rascal,' he said in fluent Chinese. 'There's no humility in you.

I saw your face when you were being manhandled. My name is Meadows, and I'm the Governor's official representative. So, who are you?'

His brows rose as Pearl replied in perfect English: 'I am a fugitive from the Taiping, honoured sir. I came aboard your vessel to escape the city before I could be recaptured and executed. If, from the kindness of your heart, you will give me passage to the coast I shall remember your honourable name in my prayers.'

'Well, I'll be blowed. What cheek.' The bosun, drawn by the crowd around Pearl, stood hands on hips, glaring. 'Give 'im to me, sir. I'll deal with the mudlark.'

Meadows shook his head. 'You still have not told me your name, boy.'

Pearl drew herself up. 'I am Li Po, honoured sir, foster son of Dr & Mrs Morris Carter, lately of the Protestant mission near Pai Hu.'

'I see.' Meadows fingered his chin once more. 'I've heard what has been happening to the missions when the rebels pass through. You are a fugitive indeed. Were your foster parents killed?'

Pearl's lids hooded her dark eyes. She nodded.

'Poor child. How old are you … eleven, twelve?'

Again Pearl nodded, as if choked beyond speech.

'Too young to fend for yourself. What would you do if I did permit you to stay with us as far as Shanghai?'

'My brother lives there, honoured sir. He will give me shelter.'

'Hmn. Well, I expect you eat little enough and you certainly don't take up much space. You can stay aboard and make yourself useful to the cook. Bosun, the lad is not to be interfered with. He'll sleep on deck, not in the foc'sle, and if any harm comes to him I'll hold you responsible.'

The bosun all but snarled, 'Yessir', then turned to vent his aggravation on the crew, roaring orders as they scurried to their stations.

Pearl bowed her forehead to the deck but Meadows pulled her up. 'Don't kowtow to me, lad. A western man stands on his two feet, wherever he is, or with whom, and you should do the same. Now, go to the galley. Say I sent you.'

Pearl bowed. 'Permit me to thank you, honoured sir. I shall

make a special prayer to the Almighty for your protection.'
  'Eh? Oh, thank you.'

Once assured of safety, Pearl enjoyed the two hundred mile trip through the fertile valley of the Yangtse. It was a broad river, often divided by thickly wooded islands, and during this season the days were cool and dry. She spent her free time up in the bows watching the paddies and tiny farm fields glide by; the peasants gathering the winter harvests of wheat, beans and barley; the water buffalo working or drinking at the river's edge where long coarse grasses grew. There were fields of tobacco plants, orchards of lichees and mulberries, and acres and acres of rice. A bountiful land where none could starve, unless ravaged by invaders.

There was always something new to see—the hills above, looking down on every shade of green; the banks dotted with fortresses and pagodas; fishermen out in their sampans, two or three men to each boat, with cormorants fastened by one foot to a long string secured to a man's wrist, a ring around each bird's throat, tight enough to prevent it swallowing any catch. The men sat the birds on the edge of the sampan where they peered intently into the water, plunged suddenly, then came up almost instantly with a fish. They never seemed to miss, and they fought fiercely to retain the prey they could not eat. Pearl was rather sorry for them and thought the men deserved the fierce pecks they received.

Her protector ignored her most of the time, keeping to the quarter deck area reserved for the Governor and his entourage. Occasionally, however, he would spend a few minutes conversing with this oddity he had rescued. He was with her when they passed a tributary river crossed by a bridge hung with the bodies of several dead cats.

Meadows was shocked out of his usual urbanity. 'What in God's name are they doing there?'

Pearl hid a smile. 'They are there to prevent the ghosts that walk by night from attacking travellers.'

'Do you believe that?'

Pearl shrugged. Her blood told her such things were true, while her training denied it. Sometimes she believed, sometimes not.

She changed the subject. 'I heard the men say we do not go as far as the river mouth; that Shanghai stands on a smaller river.'

'That is so. Ships can't pass the shallow sandbars in the Yangtze delta, but the Huangpu has a good channel to the sea. Shanghai is about thirteen miles upriver from the mouth. It's an extraordinarily busy port, has been since the British forced it open.'

Pearl had been taught that the trade treaties forced on the Chinese by western countries were a good thing, since they had allowed the entry of missionaries. The consequent flooding of opium throughout the country was accounted a necessary sacrifice. She had her own thoughts on the matter but kept them to herself as Meadows went on happily expounding the value of trade through the open ports.

He turned to say something, then suddenly fell quiet. Then he exclaimed and turned Pearl towards him, peering intently into her face.

'Why didn't I see it before? The skin is drawn tight over such exquisitely regular bones, the eyes, so beautifully shaped, and the lashes long, the mouth ... You're not a boy named Li Po. Who are you?'

Pearl tried to pull back, shaking her head so that her braid danced.

'No. Answer me,' Meadows insisted.

Pearl stopped resisting him and he let his hands drop. 'My name is Pearl, but the rest of my story is true. I am travelling to Shanghai to seek my brother, whose name is Li Po.'

'And the fugitive story—the mission, the dead parents?'

'All true.' Pearl's lips tightened. 'It's not safe to be female in this land. Twice I have been a slave. It will not happen again.' Her hand darted inside her jacket, and the small, wicked blade flashed in the sunlight.

Meadows gave a soundless whistle. 'I believe you. You fooled me finely, Pearl, but I can't do much about it now. We will soon come up to Baoshan where we turn into the Huangpu River, and then it's only about another forty-five miles to Shanghai. You may as well stay aboard.' He laughed suddenly. 'I don't know why I should worry about a little firecracker like you. You'll succeed in whatever you try. But I'd keep a surly face if I were you. In repose your features show your sex.' He went away, chuckling.

The following night *Hermes* anchored to the north of the walled city called On the Sea, and Pearl slipped ashore. Having a good understanding of the Triads, she knew they would not be long content to rest in Nanking. Shanghai would be their next conquest, and she had to stay ahead of them.

Chapter Five

Elly woke in darkness to what seemed like another nightmare. She was lying flat on the ground, aching all over, her arm a fiery agony that burnt through to the bone. Moaning, she looked up into the face of a stranger, his face planed and shadowed by firelight, his eyes curiously intent as he stared into hers.

'Who … ? What are you doing?' Elly shrank back as the man's fingers closed on her arm like hot pincers.

'This will hurt you. I'm sorry.' His voice held a rough sympathy. A hot ember of wood appeared in the man's free hand and dipped towards her.

'Don't! Don't do it!' Elly's protest ended in a scream as awful, searing pain burst in her flesh and she fainted.

Her mind seemed to float for a time, turning in lazy spirals that gradually ascended until she was aware of daylight and the drift of wood smoke and, overhead, the warbling notes of the magpies' morning song. She lay still, savouring the comfort of warmth, peace, freedom from pain. Memories flitted across her mind, of the harsh sunlight on the track, of thirst and exhaustion—of the snake! She jerked involuntarily and a sharp twinge in her upper arm brought the memory vividly to life. She'd been bitten by a black snake. What had happened afterwards? There had been darkness and a man who frightened her, hurt her.

Footsteps crackled on broken twigs and she looked up fearfully to see the stranger standing over her.

'Awake at last. How do you feel this morning?' His voice was reassuringly normal, of a pleasant deep timbre, without emotional inflection. It might have belonged to any educated Englishman. Nor did his tanned and shaven face reflect the passion of a madman who attacked people with burning coals.

Elly's momentary panic was dispelled by anger. Heaving herself up onto her elbows, she bit her lip against a stab of pain, saying sharply: 'Who are you? Why did you attack me?'

'Attack … ! My dear young woman, you're delirious. I'll fetch you some water.'

'Never mind the water. Answer me, if you please. I distinctly recall you brandishing an ember in my face before … before …'

'Before cauterising your snake-bite and thereby saving your life. Look at your arm if you don't believe me.'

Elly glanced down at the neat bandage on her right upper arm and realised that, apart from that first jab, it barely hurt at all. 'The treatment for snakebite is scarifying, then suction of the poison from the point of entry and washing with whatever clean liquid is available.'

'Which is exactly what I did, with the addition of a native remedy—cautery, followed by application of a herb and clay covering. I've known it to be very effective.' The stranger squatted down beside her and she smelled the familiar mixed odours of wool, leather and pipe tobacco that so reminded her of her father.

Soothed by the association, her interest caught by this new bit of medical lore, Elly felt her anger dissipate. 'Is it so? I wish I could have told my father. He always said he'd have liked to know more about native medicine, if he could have communicated with the people. How did you discover the treatment?'

'Oh, in my travels I've learned a thing or two.' The man turned his head to whistle two notes, and the bushes beside Elly parted as a small brown body barrelled through in a flurry of barks and whipping tail, to stop short, eyeing Elly enquiringly. 'This is Pepper, famed as a snake catcher, and may I introduce myself also, Paul Gascoigne at your service.'

'How do you do, Mr Gascoigne. Pepper. My name is Eleanor Ballard and I've remembered my manners at last. Thank you for saving my life. I couldn't have survived another day on the track, even without the snake bite.' She studied him—a tall man of about thirty, broad, loose limbed, dressed sensibly for the bush in boots, moleskins and a many-pocketed jacket. His lean face was intelligent and strong-jawed, and his eyes were a clear green verging on grey, with sun creases at the corners. A mass of dark unruly waves needed cutting, unlike her own, thought Elly with a sigh. As for the man's manner, he projected an air of confidence that was comforting to her. She felt none of the customary wariness of a woman alone with a strange male in isolated surroundings.

Paul held out his hand. 'Come, Miss Ballard, and join me for breakfast. You may perform your ablutions down at the water hole beyond that stump.' He handed her a cloth wrapped around a sliver of soap. 'And then you can explain to me why you were alone on the bush track close to death.'

Elly accepted his help to extricate herself from what must be his own bedroll, waiting until the world had steadied around her before taking the washcloth and making her way barefoot through the scrub to the waterhole. This lay well back off the track, screened by mimosa bushes. Alone, she'd have passed it by, never knowing it was there. The pool, dark, cool and deep in the shadow of the gums, was so inviting that, with a glance around, she removed her bodice and knelt to plunge head and shoulders into the water, scrubbing the worst of the dust and sweat from her hair and leaving it standing in short damp spikes all over her skull. Wriggling her top back over her wet chemise, she brushed down her gown while deciding how much of her story she would tell her autocratic saviour. Still raw from her recent ill-treatment by the people she had once called friends, she hesitated to expose her humiliation to a mere acquaintance. Then she shrugged at her reflection. There was precious little dignity left for her to clutch.

Pushing aside a mimosa bush in full golden bloom, she re-entered the small glade where a camp fire burned with a tripod and a billy on the boil. A saddle sat on a stump beside a couple of packs, and a sheet of canvas hung across a branch, shielding the bedroll. As she watched, Paul Gascoigne took down the canvas and rolled it tightly, securing it with a leather strap. Elly heard horses grazing nearby and smelt the gum bubbling in the eucalypt branches on the fire. She stepped forward as Paul raised the pot lid.

'Would tea suit you, Miss Ballard?'

She thought this question the sweetest music she'd ever heard. 'Tea! I could die for a cup of tea. You can't know how I've longed for one.'

His face lightened in a half smile which hovered, then disappeared. 'Well, hold onto life a little longer,' he said. 'The water has boiled already.'

Elly sat on the bedroll sipping from a steaming mug, watching the light change the trees from shadowed sepia to all shades of green against the dawn sky. She felt oddly content. Pepper lay in similar repose across her feet, his acceptance complete, while Paul moved about the camp, tidying and packing, soon to move on. Elly felt a flutter of panic at the thought. What about her? Would he take her with him? Where was he headed? To the Settlement? She couldn't go back there. That life was finished. She had to start a new one, somehow, somewhere far away.

When Paul brought his mug of tea and took a seat on a log, with one eye on the bubbling porridge pot, Elly collected herself, ready for an accounting. But he forestalled her.

'Miss Ballard, are there any others of your party lost and wandering in the bush? Should I try to arrange a search?'

Elly cleared her throat. 'No. I had no party. I was alone.'

His brows rose and he waited.

'My story sounds strange, I know,' Elly began, 'but I beg you to believe it is true. I come from a small village called the Settlement, back in the hills above the Myall River. It services a cedar cutters' camp and, as far as I can see, that's its only reason for being. My ... my father was the doctor there. He trained me as his assistant, and when he died recently I took over his practice as well as I could.'

Paul raised his mug and blew gently at the rising steam. Elly noticed his hands, long and muscular, burnt brown by the sun. He said, 'This Settlement place was singularly fortunate in having two medical people in residence.'

Elly's mouth twisted sadly. 'One would have thought so. However, a newcomer, a so-called doctor by the name of Harwood, arrived and set about undermining people's faith in my skills. At first I felt there could be room for both of us, but he obviously did not. When I offered to act as his assistant he rebuffed me. I now realise he was waiting for the opportunity to discredit me publicly.' She paused. 'He did so at the cost of a child's life. Blaming me for his own incompetence, he swayed the people against me. They attacked me and drove me out, knowing that without help I would die on the track.'

Paul dropped his mug. He bent to recover it, saying in an even tone, 'I find it almost incredible. To do that to a woman.'

'To anyone,' Elly said fiercely. 'The one thing about this harsh country is the way it breeds bonds between folk for protection. We must stand back to back and face its hardships together. The people of the Settlement broke that bond.'

Paul's head came up. 'Well said. It's imperative that we support one another if we are to survive and turn this land into a thriving, self-determining community. The inhabitants of your Settlement sound to me like the worst kind of low-minded idiots … Did they do that to your hair?'

Flushing, Elly raised her hands to her spiky head, then let them drop. 'Yes.'

'An unnecessary refinement of cruelty. I shall not bother to visit the Settlement. It's crossed off my list.' He got up and ladled porridge into a bowl, adding brown sugar, and handed it with a spoon to Elly. His own share went into his empty mug.

Seeking to change the subject, Elly asked: 'What list is that? Do you travel to all the settlements north of Sydney Town?'

'As many as I can reach in a given time, when I can be spared.' He concentrated on his porridge, seemingly at the end of his explanation.

But Elly was intrigued. 'I should like to hear more about your travels, if you please. Do you ride out for pleasure? What do you hope to achieve?'

Evidently willing enough to oblige, Paul began to outline his purpose. It seemed he was politically ambitious, hopeful of eventually gaining a seat on the colony's Legislative Council, despite the firm hold of the wealthy property owners. But to do this he needed the support of the less important members of society, for them to push for their right to a vote and to representation by men who had their interests at heart.

'Our time will come,' Paul promised. 'The small people are gaining strength and they want a voice in their governance. We'll not end up with a class-ridden society like the one back home. Here we all start equal. Self government will bring with it the chance for men of intelligence and integrity to govern—men with the good of this young country at heart.' He stopped abruptly. 'You must pardon me for haranguing you like this, Miss Ballard. I'll descend from my podium immediately.'

'No, no. Go on. I need to talk, to listen to new ideas. It's been so long … And I like to hear someone express such commitment. My father believed this colony would one day head a nation of strong, fearless men and women. He wanted to live to see that day.' She faltered.

'You're grieving for him still. I'm sorry for your loss, amongst all your other tribulations.' Paul got up to fetch a meaty bone for Pepper.

The little brown dog gazed up at him with adoration, then fell to his breakfast. Paul pulled the floppy brown ears gently, spoke a few words in an undervoice, then sat down with his back against a handy sapling, crossing his long legs in comfort, relaxing as fully as a man at home in his own favourite chair.

The niceties of social behaviour had little place in the bush, reflected Elly, settling herself on the bedroll. She wriggled her bare toes and grinned privately. Time enough to resume boots and propriety when she arrived back in civilisation. She looked up to meet Paul's speculative gaze.

'Miss Ballard, circumstances have caused me to limit my circuit of the townships on this trip. May I offer you my escort to Sydney Town?'

Elly flushed. 'Has my plight influenced your decision, Mr Gascoigne? I shouldn't like to think you had abandoned your journey for such a reason. I could quite easily find employment in the next settlement you visit.'

'No doubt your skills would be welcome there. Yet, would you not prefer to begin a new life in completely different surroundings, away from unhappy memories? I assure you, I had already turned back towards town.' His half smile said that he understood her dilemma, knew how relief warred with chagrin at her vulnerable position, underlined by her anxiety not to burden a stranger.

He understood entirely too much, thought Elly. It irked her to be so beholden, but what choice was there? She'd best be gracious and find some way to even the balance later. 'I accept your offer with gratitude. However, you must let me earn my way. Show me how you break camp.' She reached for her boots.

They made an early start before the heat struck and, despite her sore arm, Elly worked diligently, approving Paul's careful loading of the packhorse, his checks to see nothing galled the animal. Finally he mounted Elly behind him on a saddle blanket and led the packhorse jingling in the rear. Pepper ran ahead like a scout, flushing out birds and lizards and, once, a giant goanna which sent him into prudent retreat. The great striped lizard eyed him, tongue darting furiously, then sped up a tall tree, its claws gouging the trunk as easily as knife blades.

At Paul's insistence, Elly wore his hat while he tied a handkerchief about his head over a bunch of damp leaves; his absurd appearance helped her put aside her shyness at his proximity. She'd never before sat pressed against a strange man's back and buttocks. The sensation caused her decidedly mixed reactions. A ladylike withdrawal was hardly possible, nor even appropriate. Despite her efforts to tidy herself, she felt that nothing could turn her from this shabby vagabond into the gentlewoman she'd once been. Strangely, the idea didn't bother her.

I've changed in other ways, she thought. I'm tougher. People will never have the chance to ride roughshod over me again, and whatever the future holds, I'll deal with it. There's work for me to do. I'd like to show the world what a woman is capable of in medicine. I'd like to see women trained to nurse professionally, competently and with the informed compassion so often lacking in the care of the sick. I could do it. I know I could. And I believe I will.

Trotting along in the cool early morning, with a breeze whispering through the leaves overhead, the horse's gait smooth beneath her,

Elly had an urge to talk. She missed her conversations with her erudite father, and she was naturally curious about people. She also found Paul Gascoigne to be polite but irritatingly silent and self-contained. He had proved quite adroit at avoiding her questions so she found herself doing the talking, describing her years at the Settlement, her father's work and the disasters that had struck the whole village recently.

When she finally stopped, her feelings and her story spent, Paul said over his shoulder: 'You'll feel better for having relived it all. Emotions put into words have a way of shrivelling, their power to hurt dissipated.' He added quietly, 'Would that I could follow my own advice.'

But Elly thought she must have misheard him, for he then went on to describe some of the sights of Sydney and its lovely harbour setting. Elly's early memories of the town had been wiped out by grief at the loss of her mother and the passing of nearly twelve years, and her interest was aroused. However, their conversation became desultory as the temperature rose, and soon after midday they stopped to eat and rest the horses. Elly drifted off to sleep in the shade of a banksia tree, waking surprised to find the shadows long, with the sun a melting bubble on the western horizon.

'Do you want to go on for another hour or so?' Paul asked. 'We can camp here for the night. There's no urgency to reach the river.' He had made a brush from twigs to curry the horses' manes, which were badly tangled with dust and burrs. Elly watched the long brown hands stroking smoothly and wondered why she shivered in the warm air. She tried to read his expression but it was neutral. Obviously he believed that, as a frail woman, she needed to pace the journey.

She said, abruptly, 'Let's go on.'

'As you wish. I'll saddle up.'

Elly bit her lip and rushed to help clear camp.

The track had changed to an intricate web of light and shadow through which the horses' hooves pranced, kicking up puffs of dust. The daytime bush sounds had ceased, while a breeze carried the shrill calls of birds disputing their chosen branches for the night. In places the track sloped quite severely, and sometimes hooves slipped, the horses held up by the rider's firm hands. Despite her resolution Elly was tiring, so, to distract herself she began questioning Paul.

'Why do you travel so much? You said you preached self-government to people. Do they listen? Are they genuinely interested?'

He said over his shoulder: 'Indeed they are, from the squatter hoarding his acres of pasture land and greedy to add to them, to the man who grows vegetables in his home garden. Land is the wealth here, and I believe it should be equitably divided, not kept in the hands of the few, as it is at present. We need true representation of all the people. That's why I'm interested in politics, spending my life talking to any who will listen. Other, more influential men think the same way, so we are working together to bring about change.'

'You say people when you mean men. What about the contribution of women? They work as hard; they have intelligence. Why not harness their power to your political wagon?' She felt him stiffen.

He half turned to look at her. 'Women are not interested in politics. Their expertise lies in other fields.'

'Only because they've never been tried. Or are you one of those men who see a woman as an adjunct, a background figure against which a man struts and orders the lives of others?' Elly's tone was too tart, she knew, but she never could be ingratiating where her beliefs were at stake, and she truly believed that her sex was underrated. She also admitted to herself that something in her needed to prick this man's self-assurance.

Paul spurred the horse into a fast trot, before replying coolly, 'I don't agree that is the common view of women. They have a necessary part to play in family life, wielding power in the home, which is their natural place. But women in public life would be a scandal and a mockery to their femininity.'

Bumping uncomfortably on her steed's rump, Elly replied, 'Aha. So you are one of those men, afraid of challenge. Afraid to think of women as intellectual equals.'

'Not at all. I prefer to think of them as nature's counterpart to men, a restraining influence, less driven by the need to achieve, to conquer. Female softness is a necessary balance, to be preserved and protected at all times.'

Elly snorted, seeing that further argument would not only be futile but could lead to an uncomfortable clash with her rescuer. 'Very well, Mr Gascoigne, we shall talk of other matters.'

Paul slowed as they reached the top of a steep incline and retorted: 'We'd best not talk at all while on this slope. I think we should find a reasonably level place to camp. The sun's almost gone, but the river is still a mile on, if my reckoning is correct.'

Elly fell silent, contemplating her reticent companion, wondering what lay behind his wariness.

Once at the river they progressed more easily, spending the night on a grassy bank with the sluggish murmur of the water in their ears. They broke camp early, and a few hours later came to a large lagoon known as the Broadwater. On its banks they found a mill where they bargained for passage on a log raft being drifted across to the next section of river. This shallow stream, unnavigable by anything but a flat-bottomed barge, passed through thick rainforest and followed the coastline down to Port Stephens.

Sore from the unaccustomed hours on horseback, and disgruntled with her silent companion, Elly appreciated the change of scenery. They were now travelling through swamp forest and sand flats dotted with tea-trees and cabbage palms. At times the gums and banksia closed in, at others they gave way to open heath, which followed the gentle slopes of old dunes where wallabies and dingoes came down to the river to drink. Birds called, swooping down from the forest, so many and in such variety that Elly could name only a few. At night, when they pulled in to the bank, above the hum of mosquitoes she could hear the sea.

Ten miles from the Broadwater the river debouched into Port Stephens, where Elly and Paul bought passage on a paddle-wheeler carrying milled timber down the coast to Sydney. By this time the two had taken up diametrically opposed positions on just about all subjects. Forced into each other's unrelieved company day and night, they seemed to disagree every time they spoke, finding their only refuge in silence. While Paul appeared unruffled, Elly had begun to find the bush oppressive and she needed human noise to keep it at bay. Sometimes she began a deliberately provocative conversation just to goad Paul into a response—any kind of response, as long as he talked to her. When he opposed her, she would purposely adopt an unreasonable stance, driven by some demon of contrariness to pursue a route that could only lead to discord and further restrained silence on Paul's part. When they finally boarded the coaster, she welcomed the chance to escape his company. Conscious once more of her appearance in society, she sacrificed a petticoat to fashion a scarf, hiding her ragged hair, and carrying off her odd appearance with a composure worthy of Paul Gascoigne's.

After an uneventful trip, the coaster hove-to overnight, well outside Sydney Heads, then, in the pearly dawn light it took a pilot onboard and slipped into the harbour. Elly stood at the prow, absorbed by the beauty surrounding her, green hills, golden sandstone cliffs, white sandy beaches. 'How lovely. I'd forgotten how lovely this place is.'

She spoke to herself but Paul, coming up behind her, said in a softer tone than she'd heard for some days, 'It must surely be the most beautiful deep-water harbour in the world, and the safest.'

She turned around. 'Mr Gascoigne ...'

'Miss Ballard?'

'I'd like to apologise for my behaviour. You've been more than kind, while I repaid your generosity with carping and argumentativeness—'

He smiled down at her. 'Say no more. The shoe fits us both, I believe. I've been every bit as difficult to live with. Shall we agree to part friends?'

'I'd like that.' Elly held out her hand, which he grasped firmly.

'Miss Ballard, what will you do? Have you somewhere to go when we dock at the Quay?'

She turned back to watch the rapidly approaching roofs and spires of Sydney Town. 'Thank you for your concern. I shall do very well.' Her tone was sufficiently discouraging, she thought, but Paul Gascoigne was not easily put off.

'Miss Independence came a fall, if I remember my nursery tale correctly. Come, will you not oblige me? I'd like to call one day and pay my respects, once you're settled.'

Elly straightened her shoulders as if going on parade, aware of mixed feelings—not quite defiance, not quite amusement. 'Then, sir, you had best apply to the Sydney Infirmary.'

Chapter Six

The clipper *East Wind* rode at her anchor off the British settlement in Shanghai, graceful as a seabird even without her great sails set, her raked prow dipping in the wake of passing junks as if in the majestic courtesy of an empress to underlings. Men swarmed about her thousands of yards of rigging and scurried across her decks, lowering into her holds the precious tea and silks she'd crossed the world to carry to home markets.

Twenty-four hours later she weighed anchor, slipping down river to clear the mouth and enter the muddied waters of the China Sea.

Jo-Beth Loring had been glad to see the coastline disappear into the horizon. She stood at the stern, a statuesque figure with the wind playing in her bright coppery hair while she farewelled yet another foreign land. All the while she was aware of the activity of the ship, the crack of sails, the rigging creaking, the men scurrying to orders given in a clear deep voice that was echoed by the bellowing bosun. That clear voice had attracted her from the moment she came aboard to meet its owner, Captain Petherbridge, a golden-bearded Atlas who overtopped her not insignificant height by at least ten inches, a strong man who clearly controlled his ship and crew without resort to the usual bullying and threats. Mentally she contrasted him with the spoilt young males back home, more interested in the polish on their dancing pumps than the set of a sail in the wind above a canting deck, or a prow shearing through a silken sea. It was men like Captain Petherbridge who braved the elements, circumnavigated the globe, who really lived, while the owners in the counting houses kept their white hands clean and worried how to invest their profits. At the thought of the long weeks ahead at sea, Jo-Beth smiled. Then, taking one last look at China, she went to inspect her well-appointed cabin.

Lying on the bunk, her arm flung across her face, she felt weariness seeping through to her bones. How tired she was of travel, tired of new sights, sounds, smells—honest to goodness, the smells in the Far East were beyond description—tired of being dragged from ship to ship by her globe-trotting Papa, of trekking miles to admire a temple, shrine or pagoda. She'd seen too many ancient crumbling cities; explored their noisome alleys; bounced along like a parcel in carts drawn by skeletal runners; been outstared by a populace who thought her a giant with hair of flames; and chased by beggars whose miseries turned her stomach. Today they'd visited the markets to see carcasses of cats, dogs and rats, among the more recognisable animals, hung on long stretched strings. She'd given grave offence, she feared, by not eating the dinner provided by a local Chinese dignitary who conducted business with Papa. Well, she couldn't help it. Her mother could scarcely devise a greater punishment than the present situation; besides, she was beyond caring.

A strangled cough emerged from behind the curtain pegged across one corner of the cabin. Jo-Beth sat up, narrowly missing the timbers overhead. Nothing happened for several minutes. About to lie down again, she saw the curtain bulge and she bounded to her feet.

'Who's there? Come out at once.' Without waiting for a response she strode forward and pulled the curtain aside to reveal a ragged Chinese boy curled tightly against the bulkhead, thin hands clasped around baggy-trousered knees.

'Good gracious! What on earth are you doing there?' She peered into the grubby, emaciated face, her manner softening. 'Don't be frightened. I won't hurt you. Come into the light where I may see you.' She stood back and beckoned.

The boy rose gracefully and walked into the pool of light shed by a ship's lantern. It swung in an arc that followed the vessel's motion, creating jigging shadows around the cabin walls. Glancing at the lantern, the intruder allowed satisfaction to chase the apprehension from his face. Jo-Beth wondered whether it was because they were at sea and could not put back against the wind. She studied the face. It was guarded, the strong brows adding character, the mouth sweet and pink ... Without warning she twitched the cap off and a thick braid knotted with red thread tumbled down.

'Well, well. I think I've caught a stowaway, and I think she's a girl. Now, how do I discover your name, stowaway? And what do I do with you then?'

The girl raised dark almond eyes. 'I can answer both questions. My name is Pearl, and you should take me to the captain of this vessel, who will most probably throw me in irons.'

Jo-Beth sat down suddenly on her bunk and stared, then laughed. 'I must look like a startled haddock. But then, who would expect to find a Chinese girl aboard, and one who speaks such good English?' She paused and the twinkle left her eyes. 'As to the irons, that's nonsense. I'll see to it. However, I'm afraid you're right about the captain. He's in a terrible mood. You seem quite unconcerned at your possible fate, I must say.'

Pearl's thin shoulders shrugged. 'I was warned, but I could not come aboard in any other way.'

'Why did you risk it? Where are you going?'

'To Australia.'

'But why?'

Pearl shook her head and closed her lips. She eyed Jo-Beth measuringly.

'How did you know we were headed there? My father only two days ago insisted this ship be diverted to take us to Australia, and mighty angry the captain is, too, I may tell you. He's a Boston man, a clipper man, not used to being thwarted. However, since Papa owns the line ...' Again Jo-Beth paused. 'How I do run on. I guess I must be lonelier than I thought.'

Pearl bowed, sagged, then dropped to her knees.

Jo-Beth stooped to catch her, feeling like a Gulliver against the smaller woman's frailty. 'Oh, you're just about worn to a thread. How long is it since you ate? Oh, dear. Don't swoon on me. Here, sit on this chest. Have a sweetmeat.'

She fetched a cup of water and watched Pearl devour a handful of dried plums, waiting until she had recovered. When the younger woman put down the cup and met her gaze, Jo-Beth said: 'It's no good, you know. You'll have to tell me about yourself if you want my support. Stowaways are always put ashore at the first opportunity.'

Pearl blinked, reminding Jo-Beth of an exotic cat, one with a typical feline desire to reveal little while still having its own way. If Pearl had had a tail, its tip would have been quivering while she considered. Then she let out a sigh, as if releasing all the tensions that had brought her this far. 'You are kind. I will tell you my story.' This she proceeded to do, as prosaically as if she were listing laundry.

Watching the expressionless face, Jo-Beth recognised the truth. No wonder Pearl was so guarded. Her bald recital was all the more telling for its lack of emotion, and it touched Jo-Beth deeply. She sat back on her bunk and surveyed Pearl, trying to match her control.

'I'll help you. It's infamous that you should suffer so much only to be defeated at the end. We'll go to Captain Petherbridge and explain ...' Her voice trailed off as she frowned, eyeing Pearl's filthy jacket and trousers, her gaze dropping to the ragged slippers, now bound in strips of cloth. 'But those clothes will never do. First impressions are all important. Of course, my gowns will be too large, yet ... yes, I think I have just the thing.'

Pearl stood up, swaying a little. 'I must keep my jacket.'

Jo-Beth shook her head and the burnished curls flew. 'It's beyond cleaning, I'm afraid. I'll get you another—'

'No!' Pearl's expression was fierce.

'But ... Oh, very well. We'll manage somehow. No jacket tonight, though. Not for your interview with Captain Petherbridge.'

Their gazes clashed, grey eyes meeting black in equal determination; yet a smile quivered at the corners of Jo-Beth's mouth.

Pearl suddenly relaxed, then straightened up and removed her filthy jacket deliberately and slowly, folding it away behind the curtain where she'd hidden. She smiled, holding out her grubby hands. 'Where shall I wash?'

An hour later they faced Captain Ethan Petherbridge, who, having overseen the clearing of the river mouth, now stood at his ease, surveying the great sails stained by the sunset to crimson and gold and strung to a mast reaching over eighty feet above the deck.

Jo-Beth studied his grim face and decided he must be entertaining thoughts of shipowners being boiled in oil or strung up to their own yard-arms. She favoured him with her best smile, then indicated Pearl's diminutive figure, now garbed in a peach satin quilted jacket with one of Jo-Beth's skirts hastily gathered up and pinned from top to bottom. Her braid had been secured in a neat knot, her feet shod in a pair of slippers meant as a gift for a younger Loring cousin. Silhouetted against the last brilliant rays of light, her race was not immediately apparent.

'Good evening, Captain.' Jo-Beth's voice was cream, with the practised assurance of a debutante three years 'out' in society.

He raised his cap, and sunset light set his blond hair and beard aflame. 'Miss Loring, Miss …' He frowned. 'And who is this? I had no …' He peered. 'Damnation!'

Pearl bowed. 'Honoured sir, I freely admit to having stowed away on your ship and ask your pardon. I am, of course, prepared to pay my passage, if you will permit me.'

Something like a growl issued from the captain's throat as Jo-Beth said hurriedly: 'Please, Captain, be generous. This lady, Pearl, is the orphaned foster daughter of missionaries, an educated Christian woman. Why, she's practically an Englishwoman. She cannot be left to the mercies of the cutthroat rebels who have killed her family and forced her into brutal slavery.'

Captain Petherbridge found his voice. 'I see no evidence of slavery …'

Pearl slipped her jacket from her shoulder, displaying her brand. Then, adjusting her clothing, she said serenely, 'I escaped to Shanghai where I overheard a clerk in the shipping office speak of your changed orders to sail for Australia. He would not allow me to buy my passage, so I came aboard and hid. It was necessary. I must find my last living relative in the land of the south where men seek gold.'

The captain had regained balance. 'Not on my ship.'

'But Captain—' Jo-Beth began.

Another voice cut across hers. 'What's this? What's this?' A short, rotund man strolled towards them, cigar at an angle, his fat little hands grasping his coat edges and resting comfortably on the swell of his stomach. 'I thought I heard an argument.' He stopped to stare at Pearl.

Captain Petherbridge stiffened. 'Good evening, Mr Loring. I've been explaining to Miss Loring how it is we are unable to accommodate her ... friend ... on the voyage to Sydney. She will be put ashore at first landfall, wind permitting.'

'My daughter's friend, you say?' Josiah Loring peered short-sightedly at Pearl. 'My gracious. My goodness me. But she's—' His voice failed.

Jo-Beth glared at her father. 'Pearl is Chinese, yes. Not a cannibal islander. She needs our help, Papa, without any unthinking prejudice.'

'Unthinking ... !'

'What have we here, might I ask?' Amelia Loring's voice boomed across the deck, clearing the way for her massive presence. No concessions had been made to a constricted life aboard ship, and her crinoline, as stiff and round as an upturned tub, threatened to sweep the deck free of all obstruction, including other people.

'My love ...' Josiah Loring did a little backwards dance step, as if trying to disassociate himself from the scene to come.

Jo-Beth, quailing inwardly, moved a protective step closer to Pearl and prepared herself for yet another battle with her mother.

Mrs Loring repeated herself more loudly. 'I said ... what ... have ... we ... here?' Her bosom, perched aggressively above her corset, heaved with the force of her words, and beads of jet swung and clashed.

How harsh Mama's voice is, to match her temperament, Jo-Beth thought. Well, I've faced up to her often enough, I know the price; I'll do it again for this poor waif.

Afterwards she realised the issue had never been in doubt. Josiah Loring might have the power to alter the destination of a vessel in port; his wife might have the power to alter his decisions; but no-one on earth or ocean could supersede the power of a ship's master at sea, which Ethan Petherbridge made quite clear, without regard to anyone's feelings, adding: 'I never make judgements without having heard the full story. This young woman will give me her reasons for her action, which I shall weigh before coming to a decision.'

Pearl bowed. 'Your mother bore a wise son. May I say that I am prepared to pay my passage.' She calmly unpinned her braid, producing from its depths the great black pearl filched from the Triad's hoard. Even Amelia Loring ceased her storming to gasp and stare. Her hand, outstretched, clutched at thin air as the captain took it from Pearl's palm, slipping it in his pocket.

'That will be ample reimbursement. If you remain aboard, I shall have the pearl valued when we reach Singapore and refund the difference.'

Jo-Beth, momentarily stunned by her parents' routing, had stood like a stock, for which she berated herself afterwards. It was Pearl who had been gracious, almost regal in her thanks as the Lorings left in dudgeon, dragging Jo-Beth with them. Jo-Beth was disgusted with herself. Prepared to be the heroine of the piece, she'd instead found herself relegated to the background. The handsome captain had barely noticed her, Miss Josephine Elizabeth Loring, belle of Boston, accustomed to male admiration, to the gnashing of female teeth as she swept by. It was more than perplexing. It was unheard of.

But the thought of her parents' reaction to their defeat brought a smile to her face; and back in her cabin, which Pearl could now enter only in the role of servant, she hugged the girl delightedly.

'Wasn't it just the greatest thing? He was like a Greek deity on Olympus calmly making his decrees. And Papa's expression! And Mama's! Oh, there was never anything like it.'

Pearl tittered delicately in her sleeve.

Jo-Beth's voice softened. 'He's a fine leader, clearly respected by his crew. I've travelled with several ships since leaving Boston and I can tell you the men are usually either cowed or slovenly and defiant. But this is a happy ship, because of Captain Ethan Petherbridge.' Disregarding her listener's amused expression, she went on. 'He's not precisely handsome, of course—too rugged and unpolished. Yet there's definitely something lion-like about him, with his curly blond mane and beard, and his eyes so golden brown and narrowed, seeking the horizon.'

Pearl was dismissive. 'God or lion, he is certainly massive, as well as badly scarred from temple to lips. Yet he can be kind. I will allow him to be a strong man, in mind and body.'

'He must be, to vanquish my parents.'

Pearl's brows rose. 'Do you dislike your family so much?'

'About as much as they dislike me. I'm a terrible disappointment to them, you know. They wanted a submissive, featherbrained doll, accomplished only in the "ladylike" arts, one who would ornament the family name and marry to please them. Instead, they have me, over-endowed with an independent mind, not to mention a love of shocking folk.' Jo-Beth let her grin fade. Sighing, she pulled back the bedcovers. 'I'm sorry you have to act as my maid, but it's the only way my mother can accept your presence. Captain Petherbridge doesn't want to antagonise my parents further.'

Pearl's cat smile expressed understanding. 'I am not troubled by this. I believe your captain is wise to maintain the peace aboard his ship whenever possible.'

'You're so forgiving, Pearl.' But she saw Pearl stiffen.

'Not forgiving. I yield a skirmish to win the battle.' She bowed and left for her bed in the narrow cuddy next door.

Jo-Beth lay in the darkness listening to the sounds of the ship, which always seemed magnified by night. There was no silence out on the ocean but a rhythmic pulsation—a creaking and tapping and flapping and the thud of waves against the hull. The ship's bell sounded the new watch and feet padded by the door. The cabin rocked gently. Jo-Beth fell asleep, curled tightly in upon herself, like a child.

As the great clipper followed its course south, the long days stretched ahead with little to fill time for the passengers. For Jo-Beth, lonely for companionship, it was an opportunity to build a rapport with the most interesting woman she'd ever met. Pearl, mysteriously oriental, seventeen going on fifty, challenged the traditional western view of womanhood. She fitted no pattern, refused to be restricted to one; and Jo-Beth, wildly rebellious against the physical and intellectual constraints of her life, found her fascinating.

Pearl was equally as curious about Jo-Beth. 'Have you truly been almost around the world? Tell me again about riding the camels.'

Jo-Beth laughed. 'Malodorous, cranky, rough-haired ships of the desert, but still infinitely preferable to being shut up all day in a horse-drawn omnibus to bump across the sandy wastes. We were glad enough to reach Suez, I tell you, and board our Pacific and Orient Steamship vessel. That part of the journey through the Red Sea then down the western coast of India was truly beautiful. At night one could smell the land, the odour of spices and tropical growth borne to us on a humid breeze. Magical.'

'I have never before been beyond the Great River.' Pearl sounded almost wistful.

'Ha. Well, you may have my travels, willingly. We fled Boston in a snowstorm, like criminals absconding. You see, I had disgraced myself, caused a scandal, thus ruining my chances of an advantageous match. Mother couldn't face her friends' false sympathy. She also thought we would have a better chance of husband-catching in London, if we could get there ahead of my reputation. This failed, of course, and Mother rightly blamed me; so, after eight wasted months we abandoned hope and took to travelling instead. Papa adores it, even, for once, standing firm and refusing to return to Boston until he's ready.'

'What did you do that was so scandalous?' Pearl sat like a tailor on the cushions of the saloon, her legs crossed under her, her borrowed skirt a bunched and crushed impediment.

'I fell in love with a married man and tried to seduce him.'

'Seduce? I thought the word applied only to men, those who bother to bedeck their intentions, that is.' Pearl curled her lip.

'Not always. In this case, the desire was mutual. Unfortunately, or perhaps not, my plan was discovered and I was bundled back home, my virginity intact. I could hardly say the same of my back and legs after Mother had finished the whipping.'

Pearl nodded. 'But that is not what troubles you, is it? Did your lover fail you?'

In the ensuing pause, Jo-Beth struggled to hold her voice steady. 'He didn't want me. It was all a game to him, so when he tired of it … He made a fool of me, played with me like a toy to be handled and fondled intimately, then threw me aside. He also acquired a fine story to regale his friends with over port and cigars.'

'Ah. Humiliation. That stings.'

'Betrayal, which is worse. I've learned my lesson. I'll be the one piping the tune in future.'

Pearl looked sceptical, but held her peace.

The weather grew humid as they entered the tropics—a blessing, to Pearl's mind, since it drained Mrs Loring of sufficient energy to drive and insult her daughter's new servant. Making no secret of her contempt for Asians in general and 'the Chinese trollop' in particular, she had kept Pearl busy cleaning and mending, away from Jo-Beth; the result being that Jo-Beth turned for distraction to a far more dangerous pastime—the ensnaring of Captain Ethan Petherbridge.

Pearl, viewing the relationship between the two, was entertained, although mystified. To her, love meant the bond she had shared with her foster parents. It had nothing to do with the often brutal attacks on women by the male half of the human race. Having had her maidenhead wrenched from her in lust and pain before she left childhood, she regarded the physical act of love a mere mechanical chore, while the emotional bond between man and woman remained an enigma. Her companion's continual preoccupation with the opposite sex made little sense to Pearl.

However, Jo-Beth's unsubtle approach, the pouting, the seductive smiles suddenly switched to pettishness, the parading and the coquetting, which had originally earned Pearl's scorn, became amusing when it was clear that the gallant captain remained unimpressed. Confronted by these womanly wiles, he merely raised a satirical eyebrow then withdrew. His imperviousness drove Jo-Beth into a frenzy, and she spent hours plotting new ways to entangle him. Yet the more she strove to impress, the less success she had.

'He looks at me as if I'm a child misbehaving,' she wailed to Pearl in the privacy of the cabin. 'It's an affront, and I won't accept it. I had half of Boston at my feet, let me tell you, but this uncouth giant, this bumpkin, simply curls his lip when I encourage him a little. His brown eyes glint with secret laughter. Oh, I could just slap him!'

Pearl, having already suffered an hour of this, was snappish. 'According to you, the men of Boston are pallid worms, and a week ago you were comparing the captain with a Greek god. Hardly surprising he might treat you like a child.'

'Well, I'll make him regret his attitude. You just see if I don't.' The injured beauty flounced away, leaving Pearl to her work.

However, the idea that her behaviour had indeed seemed childish must have taken hold on Jo-Beth. Pearl noticed a definite change in her manner towards the captain who, in turn, began almost imperceptibly to alter his attitude, seeking the women's company a little more frequently, joining in their conversations and showing an appreciation of the more sophisticated weapons in Jo-Beth's social armoury.

There was no doubt she could be a delightful, witty companion when she chose, well read and, for a young female, well versed in world affairs. She even played a good game of chess. As for her appearance, a face so vividly expressive had no need of classical features. Pearl doubted whether Jo-Beth had grasped the truth, that her allure lay in her vivacity, in the wit and intelligence that fought her parents' stultifying control, in a spirit that refused to give up. Little wonder that Ethan Petherbridge had finally succumbed.

Yet, as Pearl soon realised, the captain was that rarity amongst the males of her acquaintance: a moral man who was not a prig. He might be entertained, even strongly attracted by Jo-Beth, but he would not take advantage of her. Jo-Beth herself seemed unsure of her effect on the captain, and Pearl grew weary of the nightly session before she could go to her bed.

Jo-Beth paced the short length of the cabin, skirts swinging, her hands locked together. 'Sometimes I fear he has a heart chipped from some Arctic glacier; yet his smile can melt my bones. Pearl, tell me, is he merely humouring me? I couldn't bear to think so.'

Pearl tried to answer. 'I don't believe—'

'Do you know, today he held my hand to assist me onto the

upper deck but did not release it for fully ten seconds, all the while gazing as if seeing me for the first time? I swear his touch caused a frisson from my toes to my head.' She halted to face Pearl. 'Tell me, who is the magnet and who the needle? Could I be the victim of my own plotting?' She laughed, but her unhappy face told the true story.

'Captain Petherbridge is scarcely likely—' Pearl began.

'Oh, no doubt it was just a breeze brushing my skin that made me shiver. Yet I wish … No, never mind.'

Pearl held her peace, but followed the growing attraction between the captain and her friend with increased interest.

The still shadows lay deep around the lifeboat, but within those shadows there was movement, as two figures clutched and strained together, mouth upon mouth, breast to breast, thighs pressed so hard against one another that the pulsations throughout Ethan Petherbridge's body shook Jo-Beth as if with fever. She *was* on fire. Her corset and petticoats stifled her. She longed to be free of them, to know this man's flesh against her own.

Ethan's hands were at the neck of her gown and her own hands went up to tear at the collar, pulling it aside to allow Ethan's questing fingers to enter. In her wildest moments she'd never known such sensation, such a slipping of the boundaries as her body's demands overtook her will. Her numbed mind allowed one brief clear thought to form—I've won, but this is folly—then sank back into chaos as a hand closed on her breast, sending a current of exquisite lightning through her. Nothing existed beyond his arms and the taste of his mouth on hers.

'My own beauty,' Ethan murmured against her lips, then stepped back from her, withdrawing his hand and closing the neck of her gown with precision.

Jo-Beth clutched at the chain on the lifeboat while the world still reeled around her. When it steadied, she opened her eyes, struggling against her confusion. A stray beam from a lamp on the masthead revealed Ethan's expression, amused and uncompromising. His voice, so thrillingly deep, so expressive, now had the edge he reserved for ordering his men.

'That's what you wanted, isn't it? Are you now satisfied?'

The moment stretched while Jo-Beth absorbed the shock. Ears ringing, her breath trapped in her throat, she was immobilised. Then she felt a blush rising to flame in her cheeks. Her hand raised to slap him but was caught and trapped between his. Her swift indrawn breath tangled in a web of angry tears and she choked, furious with herself, with him, with the whole situation.

'You can't go on behaving this way, you know.' He sounded maddeningly reasonable. 'You'll end by ruining yourself. You must know it. I respect your intelligence. I admire your wit. But at present you're behaving like a fool.'

'How dare you! Let me loose!' Still incoherent, she tried to tear her hand free, without success. With her other hand she raked the skin of his fingers, then heard him laugh as he drew her closer, forcing her to look up into his bearded face.

'Little cat. Be still and listen for once to someone who has your welfare at heart. Oh, yes. All appearances to the contrary, I am not entirely unwounded by your arrows. You might even say I've reached the point of surrender, but only on my own terms.'

Jo-Beth had recovered her voice, which she made as glacial as possible. 'I'm not interested in your feelings or your terms. Release me at once.'

Surprisingly, he did, so suddenly that she rocked back against the lifeboat, almost losing her footing. Steadying herself, she rebuttoned her collar with shaking fingers, then clutched at her hair slipping down, knowing she resembled the slut he had all but named her.

Ethan watched her, his voice warming as he said, 'You're still young and inexperienced, despite your efforts to convince me otherwise. I understand your need to rebel against the confines of your life, but this is not the way, my dear. Believe me.'

'Why should I? You know nothing about me, except—'

'Except that through habit, wishing to annoy your parents, you determined to enslave the nearest eligible male. It's a dangerous game if you meet the wrong opponent. Fortunately, I've fallen in love with you and will protect you from yourself.'

'You ... I ... Protect ... Ohh!' Jo-Beth was dumbfounded by the arrogance of the man so sure in his judgement of her, yet blind to the fact she had tumbled into the very pit she'd dug for him. The truth had hit her with the hurricane of passion only minutes before: she'd fallen in love with her intended victim. It was fully thirty seconds before the rest of the captain's statement penetrated.

'Did you say you loved me?' Her incredulity wrung another laugh from him.

'I did say that. Do you dislike it?'

She thought about the past few days and how her casual desire to capture this man had escalated into a driving need. Could he possibly feel the same—that the game they played had become a hunt in earnest?

She recalled the heat between them, her desire to bury her whole body in his, to know his flesh on hers … and shivered. 'How can I believe you?'

'A man who didn't love you might not have stopped when I did.' He stepped forward, raising her hand to his mouth. The brush of his lips reawakened a quiver of excitement. 'I do love you, Jo-Beth. I love your untamed spirit, your perfect body, your eyes so full of truth and courage. I want you by my side as I sail the oceans. Will you come with me, my heart?'

Jo-Beth felt herself respond immediately. What a life that would be. Change, adventure, untrammelled save for the loving restraints of a husband who had earned her respect. Searching his face in the dimness, seeing only the gleaming eyes holding hers, she knew she wanted him, whatever the cost. And there would be a price. This man, straightforward, toughened by his lifestyle, would not compromise. He would never give way to her unless convinced she was right. She'd have to fight him at times, but she knew he would never use his great strength against her. Yet could he grant her the freedom without which she would shrivel into bitterness and defeat?

'Would you really keep me at your side always, wherever you go, as much a companion and friend as wife?'

'Always. You need never fear chains again, my lovely rebel.'

'Then I will love you and marry you, Ethan Petherbridge, and we'll sail the world together.'

Chapter Seven

Elly stood inside the door in the stone wall and gazed across a stone-paved court to the building facade. It was the centre one of three—long, double storeyed, the pillared verandahs giving a chilly shade on this crisp March morning. A sharp wind blew uphill from the harbour, rattling the square-paned windows and pressing Elly's skirts against her legs. Gum trees and young Moreton Bay figs clashed their leaves around the old Convict Barracks on the corner, and dust flew up, discouraging the usual Hyde Park saunterers. It was no day for lingering to admire the view, magnificent as it might be. Bracing herself, Elly grasped her meagre bag of necessities, supplied against her conscience by Paul Gascoigne, and walked up the front steps.

Peering into the porter's empty office, she crossed an unswept lobby, feeling grit crunch under her boots. At the foot of a staircase she turned left down a hallway but had only gone a few yards when a door sprang open and a man darted out, almost knocking her over. Elly reeled back, dropping her bag.

'Who the hell are you?' The man paused, eyeing her closely. 'I beg your pardon, madam, but I'm in the devil of a hurry.' He grabbed the bag, thrusting it into her hands and closing the door behind him at the same time. Narrow as a churchyard rail, he emitted a medicinal odour that reminded Elly of her father, while the stains and smears on his coat proclaimed his calling all too well.

Elly said quickly, 'Sir, can you direct me to the matron's room?'

Already on his way down the corridor, he called back over his shoulder. 'Upstairs to the right.' Then he disappeared through another doorway.

Elly retraced her steps to the lobby and climbed the stairs, which creaked under her feet, as did the bare boards on the top floor. White-washed corridors ran to left and right, the walls cracked and dingy and broken intermittently by scarred doors, one of the nearest bearing a sign with *Lady Superintendent* printed on it. She knocked loudly, since the building resounded with voices calling, moaning, some even shrieking, all muffled by the closed doors, but still distressing to hear. Elly was startled when, her hand raised to knock once more, the matron's door opened and a starched cap shot out almost in her face.

'Come in. Come in. Sit, do. I'm that distracted today I don't know whether I'm on my head or heels.' The owner of the cap, a dumpling of a woman in a tight black bombazine dress and the tiniest boots Elly had seen on an adult, fluttered back to a table squeezed in under the window and sat down.

Wondering whether everyone in the building made a habit of going through doors like charging bulls, Elly followed her into a room lined by wall cabinets which reduced the available space to a slit little wider than the window. She took the only other chair, opposite the table, and found herself face to face with the woman. Sunlight pouring through the uncurtained glass, cruelly revealed lines of worry in a skin like pitted tallow. But the woman smiled hopefully as she held out a hand to Elly.

'I'm Mrs Box, the matron, only the Board prefers the title Lady Superintendent. My dear, welcome to the Sydney Dispensary and Infirmary. We take in the poorer citizens on recommendation, you know. Now that transportation has ceased, the old idea of a convict establishment has gone forever.' She took a breath. 'You have come in answer to the advertisement, of course. Now, tell me all about yourself.'

Through the thin wall Elly could hear quarrelling voices and the clang of metal being dropped. She raised her voice to speak. 'I'm afraid I know nothing about an advertisement, Matron. I landed at the Sydney Quay only twenty minutes ago and came straight here in the hope of obtaining a nursing position with you.'

The plump shoulders sank. The starch seemed to go out of the matron's bonnet. 'Oh, dear, how vexatious. I did so hope ... You seemed like someone ... A definite improvement on the usual style of applicant ...'

Elly studied the woebegone face. 'What is the difficulty, Matron? Perhaps I can help.'

The woman shook her head. 'I don't know ... The Board said it must be someone well qualified. I can't go on without a trained assistant. But it's almost impossible to find ...' Her hands picked agitatedly at her collar.

Elly's heartbeat quickened. 'You're seeking an experienced nurse? What qualifications must be met?'

The woman peered at her more closely, her interest sharpened. 'Why, well, experience in nursing, of course, plus the control of staff and patients. It would be such a help if you could make out reports for the board of directors. Mr Deas Thomson—he's an Honourable, you must know—is most particular in the matter of reports. But there are so few women able to ...' Again she drew in her breath. 'Could you do it?'

Elly thought rapidly. Dared she try for it? 'I believe I could satisfy the Board as to my suitability, Mrs Box. How many wards are there?'

The matron began to tick them off on her fingers. 'There are seven in all: two female, both on this floor, with twenty beds to the ward, although we fit more than one person to each bed. There are two honorary physicians plus two honorary surgeons on staff, augmented by the divisional surgeons, with Mr Hugh Houston as our resident in charge.'

'How many nursing staff?'

'We have three female nurses with twelve wardsmen for the male patients.' Mrs Box paused, perhaps in response to Elly's changed expression. 'We are sadly understaffed, but the Board has promised this will change. I could perhaps arrange a slightly higher salary—should you prove satisfactory.'

The hastily tacked-on phrase amused Elly, now well aware of Matron's desperate need. Well, she'd give good value and earn the extra money. 'How much are you offering, Mrs Box?'

'Twenty pounds per annum, all found.'

Elly grimaced. Well, it would keep her alive. 'Matron, I'd like to apply for the position. I could start immediately.'

Mrs Box glanced at Elly's meagre luggage and rose, clearly re-assured by Elly's own need for somewhere to stay and earn her keep. 'Come and I'll show you the wards. Oh, dearie me. I quite forgot to ask your name.'

'It's Eleanor Ballard, Miss Eleanor Ballard.'

'Then, Ballard, you may begin your duties on a probationary basis tomorrow at six a.m. Do you have any baggage to be collected from the Quay?'

Elly, flushed, shook her head, and found herself bustled out into the corridor.

Matron Box indicated a nearby door. 'These are the nurses' quarters, which I'll show you later. Now, here we have Ward Five, a men's ward. I should warn you that we are fearfully overcrowded, due to the recent influenza epidemic, although, thankfully, this has begun to wane.' She flung open the door.

Elly looked over the smaller woman's shoulder, and was stunned. The room was chaotic. Ambulant patients ran up and down in their nightshirts, some clearly feverish or semi-demented. Those confined to bed lay like waxworks, either comatose or physically unable to move, with at least two and often three men to a bed. Clearly a meal had recently been served. A wheeled wagon stood inside the door with metal dishes piled high. Several more dishes lay on the floor, their contents discharged over the boards and trodden in. Nearby, two men struggled with a third, who was na-ked and yelling as they tried to force a nightshirt over his head. A bowl of water had been spilt over the bed. An elderly man held his head, shrieking piercingly, on and on, while two others clutched a torn blanket at each end in a grim tug-of-war. A young fellow whose hair sprung up like a fox's brush danced a hornpipe on the wide windowsill, while two others chanted and beat with spoons on the bed ends. It was an uproar.

Mrs Box, looking annoyed, trotted up to the dancing sailor and dragged him down from the sill. Her voice somehow rose above the cacophony. 'Get back to bed, Billy Wales, at once. If you're well enough to dance, then you're well enough to be discharged.'

Billy obeyed sheepishly, but immediately joined his friends in beating time to the sea shanty. The shrieking man had his hands pulled away from his ears as Matron called for the wardsmen to leave their naked patient and come tie Mr Abrams's arms to his bed. The screams died to a keening wail. Matron turned to Elly.

'It's not always so noisy,' she bellowed above the uproar. 'Come outside where we can be heard.' She closed the door on the ward. 'I'll send someone to take away the wagon and clear up the floor. Oh, dear, we could use twenty more staff, I'm sure. They do their best but ...' She sighed.

Elly said: 'That man who was shrieking, surely he's deranged. Shouldn't he be kept apart from the other patients?'

'He should, of course. But that's a luxury we are denied. Now I'll show you the lower floor, with the operating theatres, as well as the board room and ...'

'Could we see the women's wards first?' Elly's thoughts were grim. It would be better to know all she had to face.

Mrs Box frowned. 'I don't see why. They're just the same.' But flicking a glance at Elly's determined expression she weakened. 'Oh, very well.'

Elly followed her down the corridor until they stopped outside a room where a minor battle seemed to be raging, then entered.

'I won't. I won't,' screeched a young woman with ragged shift and unkempt hair streaming as she ran down the ward pursued by another woman in cap and apron brandishing a ladle.

'Yes, you will, Annie Moon,' the presumed nurse said, cornering her prey and advancing on her with ladle poised.

Fascinated, Elly watched her throw her considerable weight against the recalcitrant Annie Moon, then literally pour the contents of the ladle down her throat. Annie spluttered, cried and sank down in a heap in the corner.

The nurse poked at a childish figure in the next bed. 'You're next, Charlotte Perkins. Open wide.' She went to a stone jar standing on the sill and refilled the ladle. When she turned around, Charlotte had disappeared under the bed. Dragged out, she was pinned uncompromisingly to the mattress, her nose held and the dose administered. Charlotte choked, spat and bit her tormentor's arm. A vicious slap knocked her flat on the bed where she began to sob, her thin frame shaking as if with an ague.

Elly's eyes questioned the matron, who shrugged. 'Nurse Jenkins administers the black cordial because she has better control. They don't like it.'

'The black cordial?'

'To open the bowels. It's a rule of mine that each patient has a dose each day to cleanse the system.'

'Surely an aperient may not suit all circumstances; recovering surgical cases, for instance?'

'No exceptions,' said Matron, firmly. 'Rules are made to be followed.'

Elly swallowed a retort, saying instead: 'Your Nurse Jenkins is severe. What does the girl Charlotte suffer from?'

'She's subject to epileptic fits. Someone brought her in off the street last night, unconscious.'

'Has a doctor examined her?'

'Not yet. There's been no time. Mr Wykeham will see her this afternoon.'

Meanwhile, thought Elly, the poor child is subjected to the black cordial while being bullied into another fit. She held her tongue, however, and followed Matron down the ward as she greeted each patient, enquiring kindly about their comfort. Some ignored her, going on with their moaning and mumbling as if too preoccupied to attend to anything else. Others answered according to their natures—sprightly, grumpy or with a flow of invective drawn from the slums. Matron answered all with a smile, then passed on to the end of the room where a card game was in progress. Ignoring the players she pounced on a bottle half hidden under a cot.

'Jenkins, get rid of this.'

'I'll do it for ye.' A woman of middle years, with a grossly swollen belly, picked up the bottle and with one heave raised the window. A wave of noxious fumes poured in, making Elly gag.

'Shut it at once.' Matron sprang forward to slam the window down. Jenkins grabbed the bottle and gave the fat woman a push, knocking her over.

'What on earth is that?' asked Elly. 'A tannery?'

'The drains,' snarled the woman on the floor.

'The privies,' said another.

'Doctor Houston just farted.' Annie Moon poked out her tongue at Nurse Jenkins then hid behind the matron.

Matron sighed. 'I'm afraid that since our move to the central building we've suffered terribly from proximity to both the privies and the mortuary. Also the drains need repair. The cesspool is right under our windows.'

Elly didn't hide her shock. 'But that's appalling. It's so insanitary.'

Matron shrugged. 'We keep the windows and doors closed while we continue to petition the clerk of works. Nothing happens quickly here, as you will discover, my dear.' She closed her lips, as if regretting her confidences to a mere underling.

I wonder whether I want to make any more discoveries, thought Elly. Am I making a decision I'll soon regret?

Nurse Jenkins's sharp nose twitched and, elbowing aside two patients, she marched up to Matron. Her carrot coloured hair peeked out from under a grubby cap, vying for notice with a face pin-pointed with freckles. Her pale eyes drilled into Elly. 'Is she coming on the staff?'

'Perhaps,' answered Matron. 'I'm showing her around the hospital.'

Jenkins's gaze would have penetrated a brick wall. 'You never did it for the others, or for me. Is she going for your place, then?'

'Manners, Jenkins. Manners, if you please.' Mrs Box seemed more amused than affronted. She moved towards the door, trailed by the nurse still firing questions at her.

Elly followed slowly, taking in details: the crowding, two or three to a bed, the noise, the lack of privacy, all of which she'd expect to find in Bedlam, not in a general hospital. There were mentally disturbed patients mixed in with the seriously ill and helpless, children and frail aged; and it seemed the preferred form of treatment was coercion. While the ward appeared superficially clean, the boards remained unhealthily damp from scrubbing, and in places the ceiling hung down, swollen from rain seeping through an unpatched roof.

Elly was hit with a sudden urge to take over, to change matters. It would not be easy, but in time, with patience and hard work and the right staff, it could be done. Wasn't this what she'd longed for—a challenge to show the world what nursing could be? If she could ingratiate herself with Matron, make herself indispensable, then suggest small improvements …

In that moment she made her decision. She would join the nursing staff and let them discover, too late, what a whirlwind they had acquired.

Two months later Elly sat in the narrow room that was Matron's power centre, pondering her immediate future. Copies of old reports lay before her on the table, demonstrating what would be expected from her at the next inspection by the weekly committee, plus the more detailed report required for the monthly meeting of the board of directors. Since Mrs Box's recent collapse from liver disease and her subsequent departure into her sister's care, Elly had found herself Acting Matron by default. None of the other nurses was remotely capable of administration, and at the hastily convened special meeting of the Board, Elly had been all but begged to take on the temporary position.

The only protests, predictably from the unamiable Jenkins, had been swept aside, and Elly had proceeded to clear out the rubbish of ages from Mrs Box's wall cabinets—bundles of yellowed papers including old laundry lists, details of patients long dead or departed, notes on ward requirements from the dispensary and stores.

Amongst the mildewed sheets, rusted canisters, whose purpose she could only guess, and jars with their mysterious contents hardened and caked at the bottom, Elly had found only a few useful utensils and some linen that could still be salvaged. Judging by the vermin trails in the dust, no-one had bothered to look inside for months, and her opinion of Matron Box sunk. The woman had clearly been unwell, but this was the accumulation of years. Elated at her sudden rise to a position where she could really bring about change, Elly scrubbed the shelves herself, listing her requirements, which included a supply of paper pads for reports and some facilities for making a hot drink. She expected to spend a good deal of time in this tiny space, keeping a finger on the pulse of the wards.

Today, beyond the wall, the usual noise swelled, although kept within reasonable limits by Elly's carefully timed appearances. Despite closed windows, the all prevailing drains forced themselves upon her notice. The breakfast oats had been burnt and she'd thrown them away, so she was ravenous; and, worst of all, she'd hardly slept, having spent the night pursuing frightful hordes of vermin which emerged in the darkness to attack every living thing in the hospital. Rats could be driven off, but the bugs marched in loathsome armies across the beds, biting and tormenting to madness, impervious to any counter-attack. Something would have to be done. Soap and water to scrub down walls and floors, fresh whitewash wherever possible, incoming patients' clothes steamed over burning sulphur before being stored away, and the patients themselves scoured from crown to heels and back again. There was not one bath in the whole of the hospital, while all water had to be carried in great casks from the bore in Hyde Park. Perhaps she could dunk the patients in the casks!

Elly stifled a yawn then set to work drawing up her plan of action. The board of directors would be the focus of her campaign to improve nursing training and status, but she had to move carefully. There'd been no mention of change on the day she had been formally instated, shaking hands with the Honourable Edward Deas Thomson, Colonial Secretary and Board President, then with the vice-president, Captain Dumaresq. The resident surgeon and apothecary, Mr Hugh Houston, who had almost knocked her down in the corridor that first day, had wished her well then rushed away again. There were other physicians and surgeons present, as well as the majority of directors, all male; yet Elly was conscious of one pair of eyes in particular, dark brown liquid eyes in a swarthy face, fixed on her with uncomfortable intensity. When the business of the meeting had been concluded, Elly had left the room as quickly as she could and hadn't met the owner of that disturbing stare, although the memory of it went with her.

And now she had what she'd wanted, a challenge which had begun to resemble Hercules's Augean stables. Each day at five she rose from her thin, lumpy mattress to wash and dress in a room no larger than a cupboard, breakfasted with the other nurses in a draughty hall distressingly near to the privies, then began her day with a ward inspection. She retired at night after the last patient had settled, which could be any time up to midnight, too weary to do more than wash her face and hang up her clothes, then put out the candle. The days raced by, full and hectic. Only in those early waking moments before she forced her feet out of bed onto the floor did she allow her mind to wander. Sometimes she thought about Paul Gascoigne, yet more often his quizzical regard faded in the memory of a darker, more intrusive gaze that had so disturbed her in the boardroom, and whose owner remained a mystery.

A knock sounded at her office door and Nurse Jenkins sidled in, her thin mouth surly as she began a litany of complaints.

'That Sarah Hodges has taken to her bed with the quinsy and now there's only me and old Betsy to look after the two wards. The kitchen's had another fire so there won't be no dinner today. And what about the black cordial? Matron Box—'

'There will be no black cordial, as I have already told you. I am Acting Matron now, so you will kindly remember your orders.' Elly held Jenkins's impertinent stare coolly, until the nurse's eyes dropped. 'As for the dinner, if it's anything like yesterday's or the day before's, we're better without it. I've put on a boiler with beef bones and vegetables and another cook will start tomorrow, after that appalling kitchen has been cleaned out. It's no more than a lean-to, set far too close to those even more dreadful privies.'

Jenkins smirked, and Elly pressed her lips against any further complaints. 'Get back to your work please. I am reminded that the commodes left in the wards overnight were not emptied this morning until eight o'clock. This should be done by six at the latest, with any spillage cleaned up immediately. I'll see Nurse Hodges and decide what might be done for her. Meanwhile, please be so kind as to relieve Betsy Haybrook of any liquor she's carrying on her person or has secreted in the wards. You may warn her I shall conduct a thorough inspection later today before the official committee rounds.'

Jenkins flounced out, leaving Elly to investigate Nurse Hodges's claims of illness. Elly had already met opposition from the so-called nursing staff, male and female, who appeared to have the merest smattering of medical knowledge and little commonsense between them. What they lacked in training they made up in goodwill towards the patients, but their clumsy efforts often caused pain and difficulty while contributing little towards the patients' recovery. Elly had already dismissed two maids—both of them dirty, light fingered and no loss to the hospital—but the nursing staff was no better. Of the three women, one was elderly and feeble and fond of gin, and the other just plain lazy, while Jenkins herself clearly intended to be as obstructive as possible within the bounds of dismissal. The wardsmen, coming under the superintendent's control, resented any suggestions from Matron and could not be compelled.

Nurse Hodges sat up in bed in the cramped, airless nurses' quarters, sipping from a brown bottle which she hastily hid under the blanket when Elly entered. Her cap had fallen over her forehead and strings of hair hung across her face.

'Mornin', Matron,' she wheezed. 'I got the quinsy real bad. Can't swallow a morsel. Can't hardly get a word out.'

'Indeed, I'm sorry to hear it Mrs Hodges. Be so good as to open your mouth.'

Sarah gaped and a little wooden stick appeared in Elly's hand, flashing in to depress Sarah's tongue. Elly turned the woman's face to the window, peered down her throat, then withdrew the stick, placing it in a bag at her waist.

'It's not quinsy, you'll be glad to know. A small amount of inflammation with mucous, nothing serious. You may get up and dress. Be ready to resume your duties within twenty minutes, if you please.'

'But ... me throat. 'Tis raw as a whore's arse—'

'That's enough. There's nothing wrong with you except laziness.' Elly stripped back the blanket ruthlessly. 'Out you come.'

Sarah slid her legs over the bedside, glaring. If she was a cat she'd spit, thought Elly, smiling despite her annoyance and pointing to the brown bottle.

'Come along. I'll give you a cup of tea before you start. It will do you far more good than mother's ruin.'

She left Sarah struggling into her patched woollen gown, sweat and food-stained and bursting at the seams, and made a mental note to order decent, washable uniforms. Her mind dwelt on staff deficiencies, and she knew she'd have to approach the committee about an increase. Three nurses simply couldn't do the work. Also, Elly wanted someone on duty in her wards during the night. But where could she find reliable women?

Only four members of the twelve appointed to the weekly committee made their appearance, full of self-importance and more interested in the refreshments awaiting them in the boardroom than the inspection. They had no desire to view the wardsmen's or servants' quarters above the ruinous kitchen, nor any other outbuildings. They would inspect the wards and, possibly, the theatres. They were busy men, Acting Matron Ballard must understand that.

Only too well, Elly thought as she led the way upstairs. The warm day had encouraged effluvia from the drains to seep through the floorboards, causing handkerchiefs to be clapped to noses. The men's wards were inspected, the patients questioned as to their treatment by the staff, and their answers forgotten almost as soon as they were given. Nobody mentioned the obvious fact that someone had failed to reach a privy in time, although the party left in some haste to inspect the female wards.

The first seemed orderly enough. There was a distinct lurch about Nurse Haybrook's walk, while the fumes of spirit wreathing her head would have made lighting a match inadvisable. But to Elly's relief the nurse managed to stay upright until the party left for the second female ward. Here Elly's eagle eye swept ahead, detecting no fault. Nurse Jenkins stood at attention at one end of the room while those patients who could sit up, did so, with smiles pinned on their faces. Yet Elly felt uneasy. It was unusually quiet.

Suddenly the ward erupted. Every mouth opened, every woman and child screamed. Missiles flew from bed to bed, blankets were flung back and patients began to dance half naked, shouting and singing lewd ditties. Elly surprised a satisfied expression on Nurse Jenkins's face before she recollected and, with a frown at Elly, plunged into the fray, hitting out and making matters worse. The stunned committee departed en masse to confront Elly in the corridor.

'Disgraceful' … 'Lack of control' … 'A serious error made' … 'A report to be submitted' … 'Utter madhouse.'

These words and more filtered through to Elly, only to be

swamped by her rising rage. Jenkins! That sly little snake! She'd planned this uproar to discredit Elly, and succeeded. Why the patients had cooperated had yet to be discovered, although Elly suspected threats or bribery.

Elly drew herself up to face her accusers. 'Gentlemen, pray excuse me while I deal with this emergency. If you have completed your inspection, I invite you to partake of refreshments in the boardroom with Mr Houston, who awaits you downstairs.' She nodded coldly, opened the door and stepped back into anarchy.

Chapter Eight

Jo-Beth stood on the quarter deck and watched the captain take his sextant from its case, handling the instrument carefully. Sunlight flashed on the brass fittings, dazzling her.

'You see the sun is almost at its zenith,' he told her, 'which determines noon "ship time". We measure the angle with the horizon to compare the ship time with Greenwich time as per the chronometer, then convert the difference to degrees. Each hour equals fifteen degrees, and thus we determine our longitude.'

He turned to the mate, who also had his sextant raised to meet the horizon. 'Ready?'

'Aye, sir.'

The two men lowered their instruments at the same time, and the captain said, 'Then make it noon.'

The mate raised an arm to signal the striking of eight bells. The ship's day had officially started.

'How do you determine latitude?', asked Jo-Beth, anxious for any excuse to stay by Ethan's side. He was circumspect before his men, but his eyes rested on her at this moment, bright with desire, following her slightest move. Her lips tingled as if kissed and she had to look away, unwilling to reveal the turbulence he could arouse in her.

'Latitude?', Ethan repeated. 'That also is dependent upon the noon sun-sight, with a reference to tables. A simple enough matter with clear skies, but a problem in bad weather. Excuse me while I check a course alteration.'

With his hot gaze removed, Jo-Beth moved away restlessly, stopping to watch the sand run through the half-hour glass, then walking on. She'd never felt like this before in her life. It was exhilarating. New sensations, erotic thoughts crowded out commonsense. She wanted nothing more than to be in Ethan's arms, shut away from the rest of the world. How painful strong emotions could be; and how easy it would be to lose control.

The call at Singapore Island had been a disappointment to Jo-Beth, with sultry weather and loneliness spoiling a trip in an open carriage through the picturesque tropical scenery, studded with exotic flowers and alive with birds that looked as if they'd fallen into paint pots. Pearl had not been allowed ashore, but Jo-Beth had brought her back a tiny monkey on a chain as consolation. Now they were sailing down the Australian coast, and the smell of the land came wafting out, spicy and sweet with blossom scents.

Finally they changed course, coming in sight of the two headlands guarding Sydney Harbour, just as the weather blew up. Since midday, clouds had been building ahead of the north-easter, yet the wind stayed merely fresh, driving the ship in the right direction. But as the sun descended the clouds grew heavy-bellied, reflecting an odd greenish light, eerily beautiful yet foreboding. Jo-Beth overheard Ethan's discussion with the mate. They were close to port. The South Head lighthouse shone reassuringly, while enough daylight remained for a pilot to put out. Should they run for harbour or ride out the coming storm at sea?

Even while they debated it became evident it was too late. With snakelike speed lightning forked down into the sea. The stiff breeze quickly escalated to a gale as the heavy cloudbank whirled in on itself to form a maelstrom of conflicting air currents, tearing at the sails and rigging and threatening to drive the ship under. Thunderclaps cracked the sky and rain sheeted down. The vessel plunged and bucked under the lash of wind and sea. Captain Petherbridge grimly ordered all passengers to their quarters with lamps extinguished, while sailors scurried aloft to reef in canvas. Others battened the hatches, securing all loose items as they drove through the wild waves, striving to put distance between themselves and the cliffs of a dangerously close lee shore.

Jo-Beth peered anxiously through her streaming window, then back at Pearl, acknowledging her fear. A wave hit the ship broadside on and for two terrifying minutes the vessel heeled right over, throwing the women into each other's arms.

'What's happening?' cried Pearl.

'I think Ethan's trying to turn the ship but the wind's against him. Those poor sailors up there in the rigging.' Jo-Beth shuddered.

The ship returned, then fell away sharply to the other side. Books and nick-nacks flew from railed shelves, raining down on the two women asprawl on the floor. Jo-Beth lay with her ears covered against the appalling clamour as the tormented ship creaked and plunged through the heavy seas. Something smashed through the window, letting in a solid sheet of water. The floor was awash, carrying the fallen articles from side to side of the cabin as the ship tossed. Pearl cried out when her head hit a metal basin, and Jo-Beth grabbed and pulled her, crawling, over to the bunk.

'Hold onto the leg so we're not thrown around!'

Pearl obeyed her, staring wide-eyed at the surrounding chaos. Lightning illumined the false night, giving bright white glimpses of a world gone mad. The cabin door had come unlatched and began to smash itself to pieces against the wall, while more water poured through the doorway, floating the women's skirts around them.

Jo-Beth fought her fear, sustained by the thought that Ethan would save them. He was the line's most skilled captain. And soon it seemed she might be right. The reckless rolling and plunging seemed to ease off as the ship slowly changed direction in response to the crew's practised seaman-ship.

'We're saved. We're moving out to sea.' Jo-Beth grabbed Pearl and hugged her. 'He's done it. He's turned the ship around.'

But even while Jo-Beth rejoiced there was a grinding, tearing howl then a massive crack overhead, followed by a crash as if a hundred trees had landed on the deck. The ship heeled over dangerously. She heard voices screaming and thought some poor soul had been crushed by whatever had fallen. Her skin prickled in horror as the screams faded and the ship began to wallow heavily, out of control.

Pearl thrust herself away from the bunk and dived for the corner where she kept her old clothes. Braced between the walls, she began to struggle out of her wet skirts.

'What are you doing?' Jo-Beth shrieked above the noise of men running and shouting and the pounding of the sea's assault.

'We're going to end up in the ocean. Our skirts will drag us down.' Pearl, now in her baggy trousers, slid across the wet floor to wrench at Jo-Beth's petticoats. 'Take them off. There might not be much time.'

Jo-Beth plucked at the ties half-heartedly, her fingers stiff and cold. It couldn't be true. Ethan had so nearly saved them. They'd been heading away from the shore, safely out to sea. What had gone wrong?

As if in answer a bulky shape appeared in the doorway, holding himself steady against the torn timbers.

'Jo-Beth. Miss Pearl. Listen carefully. The main mast's gone, along with the rudder, so the ship's no longer under control. You must be ready to go to the boat in two minutes.'

'Ethan!', cried Jo-Beth, but he was gone, his duty first to his vessel, as she knew. She tore at the last of her wet skirts until free of all but the outer layer of silk, which she refused to abandon.

A flash of lightning revealed Pearl's white face close to hers, calm as usual, but the eyes big with apprehension.

Suddenly another wave flung itself through the open doorway and Pearl lost her grip, sliding towards the opening. Jo-Beth plunged after her, grasping her jacket as she was dragged by the wash out onto the deck into a tangle of gear and fallen rigging. They ended hard up against a hatchway where they clung grimly until the vessel recovered from her roll. She did so but sluggishly. Jo-Beth felt the difference, then realised they were slowly being dragged over and down by the weight of fallen timber and canvas. On one of those rolls, perhaps the very next one, the ship would not return but go right over to dip her decks into the sea.

It was lighter outside, despite the storm. Jo-Beth could see the waves looming as much as thirty feet high to smash down savagely on the ship. Wind-whipped wavetops changed to flying spray, while the rain gave no respite, drumming painfully on exposed skin, pouring into eyes, nose, mouth, choking the breath in the lungs. Overhead, torn canvas thrashed and wrapped itself in shreds around the remaining masts, tearing at the men who clung there frantically. Others rolled about the deck like rag dolls, following the ship's motion, their limbs limp and broken. Several boats had been stove in, but Jo-Beth could see a group struggling to launch another. Even as she watched, two crewmen leapt aboard, ropes were payed out and the boat sank out of sight, with two more caped figures huddled in its stern. At the rail above, Ethan Petherbridge gesticulated, his voice lost in the roar of wind and water.

That's our boat, thought Jo-Beth, nudging Pearl, who sagged against her. She put her lips against the other girl's ears. 'Pearl, what's happened? Pearl?'

'I hit the hatch cover. I think I've broken some ribs. Go to the boat, my friend. I must stay here.'

Jo-Beth shook her head violently. 'I will not leave you. Anyway, the lifeboat's gone.'

Ethan had disappeared. Had he searched for them before letting the boat leave? Had he spared them another thought amongst so many other responsibilities? There was a roaring in Jo-Beth's ears. Her hair had come loose, streaming in wind and spray to knot around her throat. She had to keep her head turned aside to breathe, and her arms ached from gripping the hatch cover and Pearl. She didn't know what to do. Had Ethan decided to abandon ship? Were there any more lifeboats? Were the figures in the first boat her parents, who hadn't even tried to secure their daughter's safety? The deck tilted over slowly, inevitably, taking them with it. Men screamed. A wave hit Jo-Beth in the back and she could feel her fingers unlock their hold on the hatch as she began to slide. The roaring in her ears had become the boom of breakers hurling themselves ashore. They were headed for the rocks.

And then Ethan was there, his arms about her and Pearl, his massive bulk sheltering them from the Niagara of water. He put his mouth close to Jo-Beth's ear and shouted: 'She'll go over and break up, but there's still a chance for you. I'm going to lash you to a spar. It will keep your head above water.'

Jo-Beth clutched at him, shouting back, 'What about you? You can't stay with the ship if she's going down.'

He didn't answer, but set about tying her to her spar. Pearl was conscious but quiet. She gave a little scream as Ethan passed a rope under her arms, tightening it across her bruised chest. Her jacket bellied out and a tiny monkey's head with questioning, terrified eyes gazed up at Jo-Beth.

'It's Peanut,' she exclaimed. 'I forgot her, but you didn't.'

The monkey darted back into Pearl's pocket as Ethan swung the two girls up onto the deck rail just above the water. It must have taken all his strength, thought Jo-Beth, peering anxiously into his face, which was now level with hers. A flash of lightning revealed too much—the almost unbearable strain of a man about to lose all he held dear in life. Beneath the dripping moustache his lips were twisted, and the livid scar had never been so obvious.

'Ethan, my parents ...'

'Safely away. We couldn't hold the boat for you any longer or she'd have broached in this sea, but this will keep you afloat.' He patted the spar, then took Jo-Beth roughly into his arms. His kiss was frantic with pain and longing. 'My beloved girl, don't forget me.'

She heard him but couldn't take in his words. Battered senses were telling her the scene was real, but she couldn't believe in it, not even with the physical misery of salt stung cuts and cold, saturated clothing to prove this was no nightmare. It wasn't the end. It couldn't be. She opened her mouth to reassure Ethan and he lifted her and flung her into the sea.

Pearl was drowning. Something was dragging her down through the choking darkness, the rope about her chest unbearably tight. It was caught, tangled up with a weighty object, and plunging Pearl down to the sea floor. So far beneath the turmoil, in the depths the sea moved with a slower rhythm, peaceful, narcotic ...

She choked, tasted the sea rushing into her mouth and closed it tightly. Her hand went automatically to the hidden pocket and a second later her blade was sawing at the constricting rope. Her heart hammered mightily in her chest and pain blossomed there, growing rapidly, forcing her to breathe. She had to breathe. The pain ...

The rope strands parted and she kicked free, clawing upward, straining every muscle. Then her head burst through the surface and she coughed and gagged, spitting out saltwater, drawing in a blessed lungful of air before the next wave crashed over her, sending her under again to be tossed like a bundle of rags; then thrusting upward again, arms flapping, trying to keep her afloat, her salt-rimmed eyes striving to catch the phosphorescent crest of the next wave, to time her breath to the last second before being hit again. Cold. So cold. Numbness sapped her last bit of strength and she slipped beneath the surface. Then something bumped her head and she flung out an arm, grasped a floating spar. It dipped under her slight weight and she realised it already supported Jo-Beth, face down in the sea. Pearl grasped a handful of hair and dragged her friend's head back, resting it on the timber, realising that the sea had calmed slightly as they drifted into the lee of the doomed ship. Tucking away her knife she carefully balanced her weight on the spar and peered into Jo-Beth's face. Was she alive? Had she hit her head going overboard? If so, Pearl could do nothing about it. The important thing was to get clear of the ship, now a great dark whale wallowing on her side with masts and rigging dragging her lower by the minute, while the waves continued to buffet her to flinders.

Pearl began to kick, talking to herself to keep herself going.

'I don't want to expose us to those waves again, but I'll soon lose my grip with the cold ... then there'll be no-one to hold Jo-Beth's head up ... and I want to get to the shore ... I have to find Li Po ... I will not drown just a few yards from the land I've come so far to find.'

Filled with a mixture of dread and determination, the pain in her ribs numbed, Pearl kicked off towards the shore, towards the roaring breakers that could easily mean death yet represented their one chance of life. Beyond the shelter of the ship the waves hit her once more, and again she tried to time her breathing to their rhythm. She could see cliffs outlined against the boiling clouds and spume flung up from the rocks. But a little further away to the north there was a beach. It appeared intermittently between crests and troughs, a curve of shelving sand, a possible landing place if she could guide the spar past the rocks, if the current ran in the right direction, if the wind didn't push them onto the cliffs first.

Miraculously the storm had ceased. The wind lost its force and the thunder and lightning rolled on inland, leaving a wrack of cloud and a fitful moon to light the damage left behind. But Pearl had turned her back on the wreck. Her inner voice fell into rhythm with her kicking legs. Concentrate. Push. Kick. Grip the spar with unfeeling fingers. Check Jo-Beth's face is out of the water. Peer over the next wave. Concentrate. Push. Kick.

Her cold hands slipped from the spar and she floundered, thrashing about wildly until she could hook her arms over the piece of wood that was all she had. She peered despairingly ahead, see-ing only the ravening waves falling upon the rocks. Her head, so heavy. Her face, cut and stinging. Her throat raw with salt. Were her legs still there? She couldn't feel them. Surely she'd drifted in a little more. What was that ahead in the waves?

A moment later she identified the object as a cask, bobbing madly, with three men clinging on while attempting to climb upon it. But it couldn't support their combined weight and now they were bat-tling for life, one with an arm around another's throat while the third man took advantage of the throttling to raise a marlin spike and strike. Pearl's spar tumbled with her down into a wave hollow and when she emerged there were only two men clutching the cask. Two heads turned towards her, their expressions frighten-ingly blank. Suddenly Pearl could feel her legs again. She kicked hard, trying to steer her unwieldy spar away from the men.

'Hey! Wait! Help us!' The voice was rough, urgent.

Pearl wanted to say she had no energy left to help anyone, that the spar couldn't hold a third person, but her voice wouldn't come.

'Chink bitch. Get her.'

A pair of naked arms stretched out to grasp the spar, dragging it dangerously down in the water. Pearl felt her braid gripped and jerked as the sea closed over her. The next moment she was afloat again, in her ears a furious chattering and the man's curses as he struggled to free himself from Peanut's clinging paws. Pearl's hand snaked under her jacket. A second later the man gave an anguished howl and floundered backward, his bloodied knuckles to his mouth. Peanut leaped to Pearl's shoulder as she raised her knife, waiting. But the man was already two yards away making clumsily for the keg, his curses swamped in the seas breaking over him. His companion waited with the marlin spike raised. Then a wave hid them from Pearl's view.

She checked that Jo-Beth was safe, then slid the knife back into place, utterly exhausted. She touched Peanut's shivering body, too weary even to be glad the monkey had survived. It was too hard, too far to go. She had nothing left in her. Yet when she next craned her neck over a wavetop, the shore had risen up to meet them. Rocks menaced to the left but a trick of the current had taken the spar closer to the beach where sand sloped up to rough grass. Pearl kicked feebly, feeling the undertow suck at her body. The waves had flattened and lengthened into combers, building to a peak as they entered the shallows. She felt herself lifted and flung forward, her toes scrabbled on shingle, then she was dragged back. So near, yet beyond her reach. She couldn't make it.

Again the spar with its burdens was lifted and thrown onto the shore, then hauled agonisingly backward. Pearl could only lock her arms around the timber and moan as she saw safety slip away from her. It was so pointless. She'd escaped the sinking ship, battled her way back to the surface, found Jo-Beth, fought off the desperate sailor, eventually to reach the shore—and it was all wasted effort. She couldn't make it without help.

And then the gods reached down to pluck her from the gates of death. People were running down the beach—men with lanterns and ropes and grappling hooks, rushing into the surf to grasp her, to lift the spar and Jo-Beth with her lolling head and closed eyes and race them up onto the land. Pearl let her own eyes close. Hard hands under her armpits squeezed her battered ribs and a scream rose in her throat. Through fading senses she heard voices exclaim, 'What's that around her neck? It's a bloody monkey. A monkey! I ask you.'

Chapter Nine

N ew methods are always unpopular. It was Elly's axiom, and she went ahead with her changes, ignoring any opposition that was not founded on sensible argument. One of her first decisions was to stop scrubbing the ward floors. Meeting amazed stares from her staff, she explained how such methods only allowed the organic matter from feet and breath to be absorbed into the floor. By planing the timbers and saturating them with linseed oil, then polishing with beeswax and turpentine, the floor could be cleaned daily by using a brush with a cloth tied over it. Any spillages could be washed off immediately with soap and water and the place dried.

To Elly's great surprise, the Board approved the expenditure on materials, probably in the hope that she would cease her constant petitioning over the drains. The only difficulty was housing patients from a whole ward during the alterations. She was still pondering the logistics of tents in the courtyard when she received an unexpected visitor.

Paul Gascoigne paused in the doorway to survey the cramped office; then, at Elly's invitation, he wedged himself into the chair opposite her desk. Morning sunlight fell across it, burnishing the scarred wood to honey gold, highlighting the piles of documents and journals pushed to one side. It also highlighted the bleakness of the room. Elly herself had a no-nonsense image she cultivated for the benefit of her staff, helped by a severe uniform of dark serviceable twill with stiff collar and cuffs and a bonnet with a deep frill covering her neck at the back, hiding her cropped golden head. She aimed at neatness and propriety, hoping to overcome the disadvantages of youth and the good looks often remarked upon by others.

'So this is your lair, Madame Fox.'

Elly, suspecting she was being patronised, and annoyed at the way her pulse had leapt at his appearance, smiled sweetly. 'You compliment me. Wiliness is a necessary attribute for a woman seeking any kind of office, and as you see, it's achieved its purpose—almost. I plan to be fully installed as Matron by the end of the year.'

'I do mean to compliment you,' Paul said swiftly. 'Such a demanding post is not easily achieved, but I believe you will do it.'

'Thank you.' Elly was dismissive. 'Tell me how your campaign progresses. I see the *Empire* is busily deriding Mr Wentworth's schemes for a colonial aristocracy.'

Paul shrugged. 'He and Henry Parkes have never agreed on any point, so I fear the warfare can only escalate. Parkes is for the common man, wielding his newspaper in the common man's service—and his own, of course. He wants to enter the Legislature as a member for one of the Sydney districts.'

Elly who, despite her avowed lack of interest in politics, kept herself abreast of local matters, was thoughtful. 'His editorials show him to be forthright yet possessed of a good understanding of what goes on in the Colony. He also has influence.' She turned her vivid blue eyes on Paul with deliberate persuasiveness. 'You said he was your friend. Might you not induce him to apply pressure on the Legislature to help the hospital?'

'Ohhh, no.' Paul held up his hands in mock horror. 'We're not trying a fall with the gentlemen of the board of directors. They're far too powerful. They're also known as the stagnant barons. You'll never shift them, no matter what pressures you apply.'

Elly scented real possibilities here and would not be put off. The changes she wanted could only result from pressure on the

Board, and somehow she had to find the means of applying such pressure. She'd use anybody or anything that could help. 'Your Mr Parkes might be a match for them. Stagnant pools may be stirred up with the right sticks.'

Paul shook his head. 'There are so many more vital matters needing our attention. Henry Parkes is a busy man.'

'What could be more vital than the common man's health?' Elly's mildness hid a spark of irritation. Who in this world wasn't busy? What kind of an excuse was that?

She thought Paul's smile condescending.

'You don't understand. It's the vote that will give the common man power to change all the other ills in his life. We must channel every ounce of our energies into the fight for universal franchise, no matter how long it takes. Once we can get our men in next door the changes will come.'

His reference to the northern building which housed the Colony's Legislative Council Chambers failed to impress Elly, who had little faith in the goodwill of legislators. 'While in the meantime the males you intend to enfranchise may watch their families suffer and die for lack of the most basic health care. If that's your idea of a brave new world you may keep it. Now, I have a great deal of work to do, so if you'll excuse me ...'

Paul put out a staying hand. 'Wait. I didn't mean to argue with you the minute we met again. What is it between us?'

Elly would not be mollified. Her cause was too dear to her. 'We're simply as diametrically opposed as Mr Parkes and Mr Wentworth. We will never agree.'

'I don't believe it.' Paul paused, then said slowly: 'I will be honest. There's another reason for my reluctance to become involved in your battle—my career. In order to gain my objective—a seat in the Legislature—I need the support of influential men. I must align myself with popular causes, those which have some hope of success.'

When her lip curled, he flushed. 'Don't look like that. I truly believe in the causes I fight for. I simply can't afford to take on one which will be viewed by my patrons as time-wasting.' He shot up from his chair and began to pace the narrow room, hands thrust deep in his pockets, his mobile face alight with purpose. 'Do you realise Wentworth has been appointed head of a committee to draw up the new draft constitution? Do you know what that means?'

When Elly frowned his voice took on an edge. 'No, you neither know nor care that the whole future of this colony lies in the balance. The decisions made in London in the next year or so, based upon the committee's recommendations, will determine whether we become a modern, vigorous example to the world or merely mirror the old, class-ridden societies of Europe. We have to fight for what we want. We have to fight the Wentworths and the Macarthurs and your own Deas Thomson. I haven't the time for anything else.' He halted before her, spreading his hands, saying in a more reasonable tone, 'Your board of directors is powerful and entrenched. They're not to be taken on lightly. Perhaps, later ...'

Elly rose and moved to the door. 'You don't have to explain. I understand your position perfectly.'

Cursing under his breath, Paul said, 'Look, will you come downstairs to meet a friend of mine? He's waiting for me in the hall, not wanting to intrude.'

Elly hesitated. 'What friend?'

'A newspaper journalist, a radical. A man who disregards convention and says what he believes ... Aha. I see that interests you.'

She pondered the options, frowning. Her overfull schedule versus the possibility of some public support. She had intended approaching a newspaper herself, but if someone could speak for her ... 'Very well. I'll spare ten minutes.' She swept out ahead of Paul.

Down in the hall she held out her hand as Paul said, 'May I introduce Mr John George Patterson, commonly known as JG, or, in certain circles, that ruffian bloodhound. JG, you have the honour to meet the Acting Matron of the Sydney Infirmary and Dispensary, Miss Eleanor Ballard.'

Elly saw a slightly built man in his mid-thirties who walked hunched, his thin neck thrust forward as if in eternal quest for information. The casual observer would have named him nondescript—pale hair, pale eyes, pale freckled skin made raw by the sun. But the impish expression in those eyes commanded attention. Humour twinkled there, plus a fine disregard for accepted custom. Not your commonplace man in the street, thought Elly. He's like a leprechaun, spry and sharp, full of mischief.

Aware of Paul watching, she said immediately, 'I believe you're a journalist, Mr Patterson.'

His voice was light, an Irish brogue with a chuckle lurking behind the most ordinary words. 'I am indeed. I started in Melbourne but the *Argus* disagreed with my policies so I escaped to this fair city, where the *Herald* promptly blackballed me, so I had to settle for the well-known clarion of the people, the *Empire*.'

Elly glanced sideways at Paul. 'Indeed. So you work for Mr Parkes.'

JG grinned. 'I allow Mr Parkes to support me, in return for the privilege of printing my expressed views on whatever topic might arise.'

She had to smile. 'I was told you were an individualist, Mr—'

'Don't be saying it now. I'm JG to everyone. And never listen to the rascal there beside you. I'm not a real journalist at all. What I am is a gadfly to sting the politicians and gerrymanderers into behaving themselves. I'm the colony's conscience.'

'A solemn responsibility, Mr JG.' Elly repressed a laugh. 'How do you feel about stinging a hospital board of directors?'

He looked thoughtful. 'An appetising thought. All those fat rumps ....'

'Do you have twenty minutes to spare, JG?'

He cocked an eyebrow at Paul, who shrugged, saying, 'I'd be glad if you could accommodate Miss Ballard, JG. Unfortunately, I have business to attend to. Shall I see you at the rally tonight?'

'Barring an accidental meeting with a creditor, I'll be there.' JG turned to Elly. 'How may I serve you, Miss Ballard?'

'Come. I'll show you.' She said a brief, cool farewell to Paul and prepared to conduct her captured journalist over the hospital's worst features, determined to win his support and, through him, the support of newspaper readers all over the colony. She needed publicity to create a public outcry against the conditions she could do so little to change. Of course, it would not increase her popularity with the Board; considering her dependence upon them, it might be as well to have JG modify the tone of his reports. That is, if he agreed to help her at all. Paul was useless to her, just another blow-hard ignoring real needs in favour of his own pet fancies. He had disappointed her. She'd do far better with the irreverent JG.

After the journalist had departed, shaken and expressing his belief that the place should be blown up and begun again, she recalled certain other more personal remarks he'd passed. He'd been complimentary to her, applauding the changes already made, as well as those planned. Then he had met her staff, commenting so vividly and scurrilously, fortunately in an undervoice, that she'd had trouble keeping her composure. In hearty agreement with him, she nevertheless asked him to moderate his reactions in print, since she needed to keep what support she had.

Paul Gascoigne had also been mentioned.

'The man's a hard one to understand, Miss Ballard. He's my friend, but I'm only allowed so close and no further.'

'He's stubborn and afflicted with myopia,' she'd replied. 'We clash whenever we meet.'

He cocked his head at her. 'Now wouldn't that argue a similarity of nature?'

'You mean I'm stubborn and myopic, too?' Surprised, Elly thought about it. 'If you mean single-minded, I agree. One has to be, to achieve anything.'

'Paul is single-minded and passionate about legislative reform. He can't afford to be sidetracked, any more than you can.'

Elly shook her head. 'The cases are different.'

'They are indeed. Paul's background has made him a fighter. He's paid his dues in pain and poverty and the sneers of lesser men. There aren't many who'd deride him today.' He dropped his serious tone and grinned. 'One more thing. Paul can't abide managing women. He's had a surfeit of them.'

Elly gasped. 'You ... you're calling me a managing woman?'

'Aren't you?'

She exploded into laughter. 'Oh, go away, you detestable gadfly. Go and sting someone else. But be sure and write a column to galvanise your readers.'

That evening heavy clouds rolled in from the sea, glowing eerily green, their bellies laden with torrential rain blotting out the sunset. Trees tossed in sudden wind squalls and black night descended, yet lit periodically by lightning. Snug in her small sanctum with the thunderclaps shaking her window shutters, Elly pitied those caught out in the storm. When the porter's bell rang she went down to answer it herself, feeling a disturbing premonition.

The man on the step poured with water. His teeth chattered and his face had the pallor of shock.

'Ma'am, ye'd best make ready for casualties. There's a great ship gone on the rocks, with men risking their lives to save the poor souls aboard her. Any they do fetch ashore will be brought here, dead or alive.'

Chapter Ten

'Lie down. You are safe, I promise you.' Elly had to use her weight on the girl's thin shoulders as she struggled desperately to get up. 'You're safe, in a hospital and I'm taking care of you.' Elly wiped the sweaty forehead with a cloth dipped in her own lavender water. She knew the value of simple things in a moment of stress, and there was something reassuring about the common garden fragrance of lavender.

Her patient stiffened then fell back against her pillow, the dark hair spread there damp and dull, the darker eyes narrowed as she silently studied Elly.

'You are a nurse?' she asked.

Elly jumped, and Pearl's lips twisted.

'Yes, I'm the Matron in charge.'

'And you took me for an ignorant savage who could not understand you.'

Elly shook her head. 'I make no judgements of a patient. I took you for a woman half drowned, with two cracked ribs and in danger of contracting a congestion of the lungs.'

'But you were surprised that I understood you.'

'Yes,' said Elly, honestly. 'The Asian people we see in the colony rarely speak good English.' Elly laid a hand on her brow, detecting no sign of fever. 'Now try to rest.' As she rose, Pearl grasped her arm.

'My friend ... Jo-Beth. Is she ... ? Has she ... ?'

'She's safe beside you in the next bed, unconscious when brought in but peacefully asleep now.'

The tension left Pearl's face. 'At least she's alive. My name is Pearl. We were together on the ship.' She hesitated. 'Was there ... ? Have you seen a monkey? I had her in my pocket ...'

With a laugh Elly pointed to the windowsill where Peanut sat grooming herself hard up against the warm glass of a lantern. 'Your rescuers could not detach her without getting bitten, but she came when I offered her food. She can stay there tonight.'

'Thank you. Thank you.'

Elly patted her hand. 'I'll leave you now. Sleep. We'll talk to-morrow.'

She paused in the doorway to see Pearl craning towards the next bed, then closed the door quietly behind her.

The next morning Elly was wakened by her new young trainee hovering anxiously, dripping hot tallow on Elly's chin. She sat up hurriedly.

'What is it, Nurse Rachel?' She swung her legs over the side of the cot, seeking her slippers, her mind preparing for an emergency.

The girl's candle dipped. 'Oh, Matron, you'd best come to Ward One. A woman brought in from the shipwreck is hysterical and her friend wants her to have laudanum.'

One of Elly's strictest rules gave her, alone, control of all medications. In the bumbling hands of at least two of her inherited 'nurses', these were as dangerous as anarchists' bombs.

'I'll come at once. It's nearly time for me to rise, anyway.' She dressed rapidly, adding a shawl to her warm worsted gown and pinning on her watch and chain, noting that it was already five o'clock on a fine, chilly June morning. Hurrying along the corridor to Ward One, her ears alert to the early stirring of her hospital, she watched the black hordes of bedbugs scurry ahead of her light to disappear into cracks in the walls. The last scouring down had

obviously had little effect. She sighed, determined to approach
the Board once more for permission to replaster and whitewash,
although the only real solution might be the one proposed by JG—
to blow the place apart and rebuild. The whole hospital structure
was unsound and insanitary.

Ward One was wide awake. Faces shadowed and distorted by
lantern light turned greedily to the occupant of one bed. Jo-Beth
sat with her arms locked rigidly across her body as she rocked
back and forth, howling her misery. Tears ran down her cheeks
and into her mouth, stifling her, but still she cried the one word
over and over: 'Ethan. Ethan.'

The toneless lament fell on Elly's nerves like droplets of ice
water. She darted forward to tug at Jo-Beth's arms, trying to unlock them, trying to make the girl look at her.

'Jo-Beth. Jo-Beth. Listen to me.'

'It's useless. She won't hear. Her friend here tried to help and
got knocked half senseless for her pains.' Nurse Rachel pointed to
Pearl sitting on the floor, holding her ribs. Her bedgown had been
torn from neck to waist and there were scratches on her throat.

'See to her,' Elly ordered, 'Then take the key from my waist and
fetch the laudanum.' Her arms went around the rocking figure,
holding, rocking with her, trying to impart her own warmth to the
girl shut away behind her wall of despair. She rested her cheek on
Jo-Beth's auburn hair, crooning wordlessly, and watching the nurse
as she resettled Pearl in her bed, checked the strapping on her
ribs, soothed her obvious anxiety over her friend's condition. Rachel
had the right mix of compassion and dexterity. She'd make a good
nurse, if she stayed.

Detecting a slackening in the rigid muscles under her hands,
Elly was ready when quite suddenly Jo-Beth collapsed against her,
burrowing into the comforting human warmth. Elly raised her head
to glare at the rows of staring faces. Some had the grace to turn
aside while others continued to watch as Elly soothed and, when
Rachel returned, administered the drops of opium extract. She
then sat patiently until the sobbing ceased and Jo-Beth drifted off
to sleep.

Elly drew Rachel aside. 'Have you heard whether there are any
other survivors? Did you ask the porter?'

The girl bowed her head. 'All lost, poor souls. This Ethan was the ship's captain, so Miss Pearl says, a giant with golden hair and beard, but—'

'He hasn't been found. I see. All the same, I'll check the mortuary to be certain.'

The young nurse shuddered then bravely set off in Elly's wake out into the cold yard behind the hospital building. She held a lantern for her while she found the key to the padlocked shed which did duty as mortuary and post-mortem surgery. Elly paused a moment, drawing her shawl tightly around her shoulders as she gazed out towards the coast, now faintly outlined against the coming dawn. She took the lantern from Rachel.

'Wait for me, if you please. There's no need for us both to forgo our breakfasts.'

She opened the door, propping it wide with a piece of rubble, unable to endure the thought of that place with the door closed. Inside, the darkness closed around her and her feeble lantern, and her nostrils filled with a dreadful smell like the fetid breath of a carnivore. Rats scurried into the corners, trailing evidence of their feast—shredded skin and muscle, holes torn and gaping in the faces and bodies of the two dead sailors lying on trestles. Beyond them lay other bodies brought in before the wreck: a man killed in a drunken brawl, another who had simply lain down in the muddy road to die. Gases escaping from their rotting flesh, and the thought of the feasting rats, made Elly gag. She covered her mouth and nose with her shawl then raised the lantern, forcing herself to observe the two newcomers carefully. They were only partially clothed in seamen's slops, but their feet were hard with calluses, and what remained of these seamed faces could never have belonged to the vigorous giant described by Pearl.

'No beard,' muttered Elly, racing out the door and locking it behind her.

Twenty-four hours later the two young women survivors came to the matron's room to discharge themselves and thank Elly for her care. Pearl was holding up her borrowed gown three sizes too large—she had utterly refused to don a corset—and carried her damp jacket and pants beneath her arm. Jo-Beth wore her heavily stained and torn silk that would have shamed a guttersnipe.

Elly rose from her chair behind the desk. There was an idea forming in her mind. 'Ladies, before you go I have something to say to you. I suggest we repair to the boardroom where we can sit in comfort.'

She led them downstairs, ushering them into the Board's sanctum where a comfortable fire burned in the grate and cushioned chairs were available. Sunlight poured through the unadorned windows to glimmer on polished cabinets and gilded frames. Hospital benefactors stared down their painted noses at the intruders.

'Please be seated, ladies.' Elly arranged her skirts, laying her clasped hands on the large cedar table provided for meetings. 'I believe you were unable to save any belongings from the shipwreck. Nor do I think you have any contacts in Sydney Town.'

Pearl nodded gravely. Jo-Beth's lip trembled. Both young women had been marked forever by their terrible experience, thought Elly. It showed in their eyes. Heaven only knew what scars they carried within. She said gently: 'I'm afraid no other survivors have been found. Your ship broke in two and sank within a few minutes.'

Jo-Beth stifled a sob.

Pearl said, 'I had no-one aboard who mattered to me, but Jo-Beth has lost both her parents and her future husband.'

Yesterday's hysterics were understandable then, thought Elly. Poor, poor girl. But she made her voice brisk and businesslike. 'In that case, you may be interested in a proposition I'll put before you. You will forgive me for alluding to private matters, but I gather from your questions to the staff, Miss Pearl, that you have nursing training.'

'It is true I am skilled in nursing and dispensing,' Pearl replied. 'I was trained by a missionary doctor.'

Elly leaned forward. 'I am in dire need of trustworthy nurses. Would you be willing to stay, to work for me, to help train other young women, even for just a short while, until you have settled your future plans?' She hesitated only momentarily. 'Miss Loring— Jo-Beth. I don't know how you would feel about such work, but you are welcome to stay here until you've fully recovered. You have suffered a terrible shock, as well as physical trauma. Perhaps, if you wished, you could help in less demanding ways. There's always so much to be done.'

Pearl glanced at Jo-Beth. 'I need money saved before I can seek out my brother. I would be willing to stay if Jo-Beth agrees.'

While the two young women conferred, Elly watched them, thinking, I know so little about them. They've been blown onto my doorstep by a storm and left to lie like flotsam from the sea. However, their character is written in their faces. The small one, Pearl, I shall never truly know, yet she's capable of unselfish love for her friend, and mission trained, besides. She's a fighter to the last drop of her blood. The other has too-white hands. I doubt she's ever scrubbed a floor or carried slop pails, but she could learn. There's strength in her. She's already covering over a ghastly emotional wound and thinking about the future.

She leaned forward. 'I won't attempt to hide the difficulties, not the least of which is the hospital's board of directors. We disagree upon most matters, and since they hold the purse strings, we have some lively clashes. Yet I'm gradually achieving small victories. The wards have been cleaned up, the worst abuses done away with, but there are many changes still to be made. The great need, above all else, is for good staff to demonstrate to the Board and to the community that nursing can be a fine career. Suffering is endemic in this world, but we, as trained persons, can alleviate it. There can be no greater reward than to see our efforts transform a sick or injured person into a healthy one.' She stopped and smiled. 'Well, that's my speech. Has it convinced you?'

Pearl and Jo-Beth exchanged glances. Pearl spread her hands fatalistically. 'This is no gift you offer. It's a challenge. Yet I have found all of life to be a challenge. There would be a salary?'

'Twenty pounds per annum, with uniform provided.'

'Then I accept.'

'Good. Miss Loring?'

Jo-Beth answered slowly: 'I have family back in Boston, but I was never happy there. I thought I had escaped when Ethan ...' She choked on a sob, then continued more firmly. 'I don't believe he died in the sea. He will return to me one day, and I must be here, waiting for him.' She met Elly's amazed, compassionate look with one of fierceness. 'I mean it. I know he's alive and will seek me out. Tell me what I must do to earn my keep and I'll stay until he comes.'

'My dear ...' Elly couldn't go on. In the face of such belief, what could she say?

Pearl took her friend's hand and offered the other to Elly. 'We *both* accept your offer.'

With a mental sigh, compounded of satisfaction and pity, Elly rose and collected a silver tray with crystal glasses and decanter of madeira from a side cabinet, bringing it to the table. 'I want to thank you both. Your help will be invaluable to my future plans. And what better way to celebrate than with the Board's own private stock?'

She handed around the glasses, raising hers. 'Ladies, this is an historic moment. You may not have realised it, but you have helped to lay the first brick in the structure of career nursing in the Colony. Nurses of the future will look back to this day and see when it all began, the foundation day for an eminent profession.'

She looked at the two doubtful faces watching her and laughed. 'You will see, I promise you.' She flourished her glass. 'Let us drink to the future, to nursing ... and to the confusion of a most obstructive board of directors.'

The two raised their glasses dutifully to hers, swallowing any doubts they might have, along with the directors' best madeira.

PART TWO

Chapter Eleven

Elly had escaped for an hour. She felt wonderfully liberated as she closed the door in the hospital's surrounding wall behind her and set off north along Macquarie Street towards the harbour. She hadn't realised how burdened she'd been by her responsibilities—not that she'd consider for a minute giving them up when the struggle had barely begun. Nevertheless, this break gave her a welcome chance to breathe in air untainted by drains and carbolic fumes, to see a little of Sydney Town.

She paused at the brow of the hill to view the town laid out around her like a colourful chart. The spit of land dead ahead on the eastern side of the Quay was a defence station known as Fort Macquarie; while behind her stretched Macquarie Street ending at Hyde Park, a venue for saunterers, cricket players and the occasional military manoeuvre. It was also the outlet point for Mr Busby's bore, the source of water for the whole of Sydney, including the hospital. At present the supply coming from the sandhills to the south could be termed barely adequate for a community of some sixty or seventy thousand souls, but Elly foresaw problems ahead in summer. She'd been told the Tank Stream, the freshwater creek which had originally supplied settlers and which still ran down into Sydney Cove, had become irreparably polluted with sewerage and other waste.

A sharp breeze enlivened the sunny day, and Elly wrapped her cloak around her. Looking eastwards, beyond the Public Domain, she could follow a pattern of scalloped bays all the way to South Head and the white finger of Mr Francis Greenaway's lighthouse; then back again along the heavily forested line of the Northern Shore, still sparsely settled, although there were ample ferry services across the harbour and people crossed on daytrips to ride and picnic. They'd realise soon enough the advantage of living away from the town, with its influx of crazy gold-seekers clearing the shops of goods to be carried over the mountains to the mining camps. But the traffic was two-way, with the lucky strikers pouring back into town to fling their nuggets about and proclaim their good fortune. It brought joy to the merchants, but made for a rowdy passage down George Street at night.

To the west, beyond the main streets of the town, rose Flagstaff Hill, the signal station for the arrival of overseas vessels; while beyond that lay Darling Harbour and the western reaches of the great Port Jackson. If Elly squinted she could see for miles, across the flat plains flowing out past Parramatta to a range of blue misty mountains bounding the colony. One day, she promised herself, she'd take the paddle-steamer up-river and visit the town second in importance to Sydney. She might even go beyond to the foothills of the range, but never north to the cedar country at the back of Port Stephens. Never again.

With a tug at her wayward cloak, Elly abandoned her bird's-eye viewpoint and set off down the hill, past the Governor's crenellated palace, past the Botanic Gardens with their winter-bare trees, to turn west along the crowded quayside. Here was a scene of frantic activity, with ships and ferries arriving and departing the Colony's gateway.

I like this place, Elly thought. It's so alive, so unashamedly a rowdy frontier town evolving into a city. One day, despite itself, it will be a sophisticated metropolis, but until then it can enjoy itself like a growing child, testing and tasting along the road to the future. I'm glad to be a part of it all. I'll set my mark, however small, on Sydney Town. With the help of friends, and luck and determination, the people will one day have a hospital to be proud of.

She punctuated her thoughts with a decisive nod, and was startled when a deep voice behind her said, 'Now there's a strong decision just come to life. I trust the persons involved will survive its implementation.'

Paul Gascoigne stood hat in one hand, his other wrapped around a leash restraining Pepper, who bounced and yapped, clearly delighted to encounter Elly again.

She bent to pat the little brown dog. 'Good day to you, Mr Gascoigne.'

'What, no rising to the fly?' Paul's lips curved in his usual half smile. 'I was sure my cast would draw you.'

'I'm too happy this morning to allow my mood to be destroyed. What brings you and Pepper down to the Quay?'

Paul tugged on the leash and commanded the dog to sit, with no appreciable effect. 'This is one of our favourite daily walks. Pepper likes the smell of the sea and the various cargoes unloading, although, when I have time, I prefer the shore where he can chase gulls along the sand and be free as a dog should be.'

Elly looked around her at the bustling quayside thronged with porters and carriers servicing the ships; at the piles of goods— lumber, wool, spices and silks—waiting on the wharves; the ferryboat passengers lined up; clerks and servants hurrying on business; the horse cabs, omnibuses and private carriages; and understood the need for a leash on Pepper.

The little dog barked furiously at a passing mongrel, and Paul tightened the leash, admonishing Pepper to mind his manners before a lady, adding: 'We also have a problem with packs of halfwild dogs roaming the streets, along with the pigs and goats and hens. Pepper's mighty courage doesn't fit his small frame. He'll take on any challenger.'

Paul offered Elly his free arm and, scarcely hesitating, she took it. They strolled along the quayside, skirting piles of boxes and casks and removing their toes from the path of the heavy wool drays. Elly was very conscious of the muscular arm supporting hers, and annoyed with herself for being even the slightest bit effected. Paul Gascoigne meant nothing to her, that was certain.

At George Street, the main thoroughfare, they turned south to mingle with early shoppers patronising the stalls and emporiums so dear to the heart of Sydneysiders. The fashionable parade would not turn out until afternoon, and drunkards from the taverns some hours later. By night the streets would be thronged and rather more dangerous, with thieves and pickpockets abroad.

'How did you fare with my friend, JG?' Paul asked. 'Did he offer to help you?'

'He's a charming man, and yes, he did agree to mention some of the hospital's problems in the *Empire*. He agreed with me that the shocking conditions should be brought to public notice.'

'I see.' Paul's voice was dry. 'Did he indicate the, er, tone of the article?'

'How do you mean?' Elly stopped and stared at him, suspecting him of irony, exasperated by his ability to ruffle her within a few minutes of their meeting.

'I mean, I know JG rather better than you do, and he can be unpredictable. Did you ask him for a total exposé, a revelation of the staff's general ineptness and the Board's intransigence? Did he promise a trumpet call to action?'

'No, no. I asked for none of those things. He wouldn't, he couldn't imagine I'd want such a disastrous public airing ... 'Elly swallowed, unable to go on, her mind in a whirl. The journalist had been horrified by what he'd seen and heard on his tour of the hospital, but she'd made it clear that she must still tread warily, that the Board must not be alienated, with no actual accusations levelled ... No. He wouldn't ...

Paul's smile had disappeared. 'The *Empire's* a daily publication, but so far I've read nothing in it about the hospital. Let's see if the relevant article is in today. If not, maybe we should pay a call on JG.'

'Yes.' Elly's lips felt numb. 'Will you look?'

Waiting for Paul to buy the paper and scan the pages, she clasped her hands to hide their tremor. Paul grunted, and she started, searching his face for verification of her fears. He folded the pages and handed them to her, pointing.

'There it is. You may make your own interpretation.'

Elly began reading.

Hold High the Flame

A DISGRACE TO OUR COLONY. How many residents of Sydney Town are aware of the parlous conditions obtaining in their only hospital for the poor and indigent? While the Benevolent Society offers asylum, it cannot provide the medical care which is the province of the Sydney Dispensary and Infirmary, a crumbling ruin of a building founded on the vicious rum trade and historically associated with an iniquitous convict system which has only recently been done away.

Nowadays, this temple to healing is open to the needy upon recommendation of decent members of society. But when they enter its doors, what do they find? Not the calm and expert attention of skilled nurses in wards that are havens of rest and recovery, but a raucous parrot house where abuse is hurled above the screams of the insane or those driven half mad with pain, where vile legions of insects crawl over helpless patients, and from open drains and cesspits an army of rats emerges nightly to feast upon the dead.

The recently appointed Acting Matron, a skilled and selfless nurse, has charge of some fifty beds, with often more than two patients to a bed, and a meagre staff of slovenly, feckless women; whilst males are left to the tender mercies of untrained wardsmen. Drunkenness is rife amongst the staff and those patients who can procure liquor through bribery. The lack of a water supply creates enormous problems in the wards and operating theatres, as well as in the infamous kitchen and unspeakable mortuary, where bodies are left to rot until a member of the overworked medical staff can find time to perform an autopsy.

These outrageous conditions are presided over by a board of directors who represent the most prestigious members of our society, including its president, the Colonial Secretary himself, members of the judiciary and the Church.

We must ask ourselves whether this state of affairs can be permitted to continue. Where is the voice which speaks for all those without a voice? The Empire is that organ. It fights for the rights of the small man, the man without influence, and exposes the discrimination to which he is heir through no fault of his own. The Empire will continue to reveal the injustices in society as long as it exists ...'

Elly crumpled the paper between her fists. 'How could he have done it? I asked him to lead in gently. We want to attract public interest, yes, but not to invite a scandal.' She turned away, struggling with her emotions.

'JG has always been answerable only to himself. He's a crusader at heart.'

'He's an anarchist,' Elly returned fiercely. 'This article is a bomb that has probably destroyed all I've worked for. How will I face the Board? Will I have any staff left when I return? He's your friend. Why didn't you warn me?'

Paul's brows rose. 'I thought you'd appreciate his style of help. You were so fiercely determined to clean up the hospital and its administration. The system has to be destabilised before you can sweep it away to replace it with another.'

'I didn't want an earthquake. A few warning tremors would have started the reaction. I thought people would read about some of the difficulties and begin to pay attention. They'd seek out the next article, then talk amongst themselves, gradually concluding that they should take an interest. Perhaps questions would be asked by influential men, causing the Board to look more closely at our needs ...' She paused. What was the use? The damage had been done. Not even the pleasure of wringing Mr JG Patterson's neck would mend matters. She glared at Paul. 'I wish I'd never asked you to help. I almost wish I'd never met either of you.'

Pepper, sensing her distress, gave an anxious yelp and flung himself at her. She clutched his warm, wriggling body for a moment, gazing into his worried eyes. A wet tongue rasped her cheek.

'Down, Pepper.' Paul tugged the dog away and deposited him firmly in the dust.

'Don't be angry with him. He was only offering me comfort.' Elly brushed dust from the front of her cloak.

'Pepper always had more sense than any human being. Allow me to be his deputy. We'll have a drink and sit down and talk the matter over. Something might be done to mitigate the effects of JG's bomb.'

'What?' asked Elly, baldly. 'A retraction would be useless. The Board could sue but, as the accusations are based on fact, it would only draw further adverse attention. The newspapers would glory in it. It seems to me journalists are able to say absolutely anything they please without fear of reprisal.'

'I'm afraid that's true.' Paul steered her towards a teashop advertising the finest Lapsang Souchong freshly imported from the Far East.

Elly pulled her arm away. 'Where are you taking me? I should go back to the hospital at once and begin damage repair, if I can.'

'There's nothing you can do that couldn't be put off for an hour. Why let this ruin your free morning? We'll have a cup of tea—'

'I hate tea.' Elly heard the petulance in her voice and amended, 'Buy me a beer instead.'

'Done. Just down this alley into Pitt Street there's the Metropolitan Hotel which has a spacious garden at the back. Let's go there.'

Beneath shop signs clattering in the August wind, the three hurried down to Pitt Street, to the shelter of the Metropolitan's garden and a seat at an iron table in the sun. Elly, whose lifestyle decreed a modest number of petticoats with no crinoline under everyday clothes, had today dressed in a favourite green and blue tartan bodice and skirt supported by a small cage and with ruffles about the collar and balloon cuffs. She basked in her companion's obvious admiration as he took her cloak, laying it over the back of the chair. It was good to feel young and unfettered for an hour. Paul had been right. There was nothing she could do immediately about the article, so she might as well enjoy her small holiday.

Declining the waiter's offer of a Stone-fence—ginger beer and brandy—or a Madame Bishop—port, sugar and nutmeg, recommended for a lady on a cold day—she settled for a beer, the drink she'd learned to like during the drought last summer. Pouring half into a bowl for Pepper, she relaxed and let the sun filter through to her bones while the conversations of the other patrons formed a murmurous backdrop to her peace. Then, with a sigh, she began to discuss the article with Paul. Several ideas occurred to them but no firm conclusions were reached, Elly preferring to await the Board's reaction before she made any move. Paul promised to ask JG to write a less vitriolic piece on the hospital and, if possible, to find some aspect to praise. It was a poor enough suggestion, but all they could think of.

Despite Elly's demur, Paul ordered more beer, pointing out that Pepper was particularly thirsty.

'He's growing *particularly* rotund,' Elly retorted, 'and if beer is regularly included in his diet, I'm not surprised.' She patted Pepper in case he should be offended, wishing once more that the Board would permit animals in her quarters. Pearl's monkey was an open secret amongst the patients, but it would only take a word from some ill natured person such as Jenkins to have her ejected.

When Elly finally rose to leave, Paul surprised her by speaking with unusual hesitation. 'Please, stay awhile longer. I want ... I have something more to say.'

'I must go back, Mr Gascoigne. It's not reasonable for me to load my duties onto the others. None of them is fully trained, although "feckless" and "slovenly" does not apply to them all.'

'Please. I'd like the opportunity ... That is, I don't believe I explained fully about my work last time we met. I must have appeared like some cockscomb, so self-assured, self-interested ... Miss Ballard, will you come to supper one night and meet some of my friends who are involved in the political scene? It won't be a heavy discussion or speech-making. Nothing of that kind. But if you could just understand what it is we're fighting for, perhaps you would be interested.'

Elly stiffened. Not this political rubbish again. Then the memory of a recent conversation resurfaced, herself saying, 'He's stubborn and afflicted with myopia,' and another voice with a teasing lilt, 'Now wouldn't that argue a similarity of nature?' Was JG right; had she become so single-minded as to be blind to other interests just as valid as her own?

Under Paul's insistent gaze, she temporised. 'Where were you suggesting we sup? At your home?'

'No, indeed. There's a tavern in Bathurst Street, the Earl Grey, perfectly respectable, where people meet to argue and exchange ideas of all kinds, a sort of artists' cafe, if you like. Thursdays are the popular times.'

'I'd like to come, next Thursday.'

His face lit. The half smile broadened. 'May I call for you at seven o'clock?'

Elly said graciously: 'That will be suitable. Thank you for the beer. I must go.' She gave Pepper a final pat, picked up her cloak and whisked out of the garden into the street. Heading uphill to the hospital with the westerly wind at her back, she asked herself why her attitude towards Paul Gascoigne had so suddenly changed—and had no answer. Was it the sincerity that underlay his often teasing manner? JG had said he was ruled by a passion for justice, and that appealed to her. Perhaps there *was* more to the man than mere ambition.

The hospital's entrance lobby had become a dramatic stage, with the porter an open-mouthed audience of one. Backed up against the stair newel, JG had his arms raised protectively before him, his expression a mixture of amusement and apprehension. Inches away Pearl hovered, wasplike, a diminutive fury with hands crooked into claws, her pretty voice shrilling invective. Her bonnet had come off and her braid hung down, swinging with her every movement like the tail of an angry cat.

JG welcomed Elly's appearance. 'Thank God you're here. I can't make out a word she says, but I've no doubt it includes wanting to tear the eyes out of me head.'

Elly said sharply, 'Nurse Pearl, what does this mean? Why have you left your patients?'

Pearl didn't appear to hear her. She made a sudden dart at JG, who ducked and danced aside with an impish smile.

'Sure now, you'd best watch yourself, girl dear, or you'll be taking an apoplexy.'

Spitting furiously, Pearl launched herself at him, only to find herself held around the waist by Elly, who shook her hard. 'Calm yourself, Pearl. Tell me what's wrong.' She glared at the journalist who had dissolved into mirth.

'Your attitude is not helping the situation.' Leading Pearl to the stairs she sat her down and stood over her. 'Now, tell me.'

Pearl clenched her quivering fists in her lap. 'He has dishonoured us all. He has told the world we are drunken women, uncaring, living in filth. He is a liar, a pig—' She choked in fury.

'Oh, I see. You've heard about the *Empire* article, although its content seems to have become a little muddled.' Elly turned on JG. 'So, what have you to say for yourself? I doubt whether any epithet I could apply to you would surpass Pearl's efforts, in Chinese or English. But I had thought better of you, Mr JG Patterson.'

His dismay was almost comical. 'But ... I hoped you'd be pleased. You wanted publicity. You wanted all the deplorable conditions here exposed.'

Elly drew on her patience and the shreds of her temper. 'That's true. However, at the same time, I asked you to make it a gradual process, an undermining, not a direct attack. Your intemperance has probably caused irreparable damage and, rather than thank you for it, I ask you to abort the campaign entirely. I made a terrible mistake. I thought you were to be trusted.'

'Miss Ballard, I assure you—'

'Son of a diseased monkey!' Pearl sprang up suddenly and was restrained again by Elly, who was a little surprised by the girl's vehemence.

'Miss Pearl,' began the hapless JG.

Her lips curled in a snarl. 'I would hide bamboo slivers in your food. I would deliver you to the Death of the Thousand Knives. I would—'

'Here! Before God, I believe you would. Just hold her there a minute longer, Miss Ballard, and I'll be relieving you of me presence. But I'll be back and we'll sort this out like Christians, I promise you.' Cramming his hat on he hurried outside, where the wind promptly snatched it and whirled it away over the wall.

Elly began to laugh. 'Oh, Pearl, what a little fury you are. Would you really stick bamboo slivers in his dinner?'

Pearl's stiff muscles relaxed, her face softened. There was a suspicion of laughter about her lips. 'He thought I would do it. I would have scratched his face if you had not prevented it.'

'I know. I know. Oh, dear, what a day.' Elly dropped down on the stairs and rested her head against the rail.

The Earl Grey Tavern, with its welcoming yellow-paned windows aglow, while lively enough, was not the rowdy drinking place Elly had half feared it would be. Its benches and tabletops had seen hard use but were well scrubbed, while clean cushions covered the window seats. The polished mirrors behind the bar reflected a cheerful crowd and, as she soon found out, these patrons were more inclined to forget their wine in conversation which could quickly turn to spirited argument.

The smoky air, thick with the warmth of many bodies, the smell of pipe tobacco and frying sausages, the soft glow of lanterns hung from beams and a crackling log fire welcomed Elly openly. In her cushioned corner, a mug of beer before her, Paul at her side, she felt herself to be on the fringes of a foreign and fascinating world. It was primarily a world for men, although there were women present—a half dozen birds of paradise, with at least three more soberly dressed, like herself—and Elly found she envied the cama- raderie that men could find in such a place. It was more a club than a tavern, its members there to air ideas and ideologies, to discuss new ways of thinking and measure them against the old.

She listened to the exchanges taking place around her, a jum- ble of politics, art, religion, science, plus other topics she could only glean in snatches. She longed to join in, yet a part of her remained intimidated by the pace and the elliptical references in- trinsic to this world where everyone knew everyone else or at least met on the same level of knowledge. It didn't surprise her to see JG across the room, arguing vociferously, using his hands to dem- onstrate a point, but most of the faces were unknown to her.

A young man with the untamed hair and beard of a pirate and the body of a dancer threaded his way between the tables, hailing Paul in heavily accented English.

When Paul waved to him, he grabbed a bottle of wine from the waiter and continued to their table.

'Elly, allow me to introduce Edouard Chevrel,' Paul said. 'We don't stand on ceremony here. Frenchy, this is Elly Ballard.'

The newcomer bowed, eyeing Elly thoroughly and apprecia- tively. 'Mademoiselle Ellee, I kiss your hand.' He turned immedi- ately to Paul. 'What's the latest news? I was going to the meeting at the Royal Hotel but the press is so great I could not get in. To- night it is a *véritable* powder keg, with Wentworth and Henry Parkes the match and flint to ignite it.'

Paul shrugged. 'Henry knew how it would be and warned me

not to get involved. He has to speak against Wentworth being cho-sen to head the constitutional committee in London, but he knows he can't win. All he can hope to do is undermine the opposition while putting our case for the kind of upper house we want.'

'We should be there to rally around him.'

'No. He's stacked the audience, as has Wentworth. It'll end in a shouting match, that's all. You know how easily Wentworth loses his temper.'

Frenchy shook his bushy head and poured the wine.

'Why were you warned not to get involved?' Elly asked Paul.

He grinned, looking every bit as piratical as Frenchy. 'Some of us have to stay out of gaol to continue the work, particularly those who can make public speeches. As Frenchy said, the powder keg could go up very easily and end in half the audience finding them-selves before a magistrate in the morning.'

'Are your meetings always so volatile?'

'It depends ...' Paul broke off as a wave of laughter swept the next table, and a big man with a shock of violently red hair and nose to match, rose to stand before the chimney piece with his mug raised. His voice matched his large girth and filled the room easily.

'Speech is still free to all men, and I have something to say. Ladies and gentlemen, let us drink to freedom of thought, of pur-pose, of action, to our day of liberation and secession. Friends, I give a toast—the new Republic of Australia.'

Frenchy shot up, flourishing his glass, but Paul pulled him back by the tail of his elegant coat. 'Sit down, you fool. You can't drink to treason. This isn't France.'

Already there was an outcry and several men descended on the giant who had proposed the toast, forcing him to the floor and holding him while a dozen glasses and tankards were solemnly emptied over his head. Sputtering curses, he raised his eyes to a little bald man standing over him, swathed in a grease-spattered apron and wielding a long toasting fork.

'Mr Benjamin,' the bald man said. 'you know the rules of this tavern. No-one speaks against Her Majesty the Queen or the Brit-ish Empire. Will you leave peaceably or be pricked and added to the other sausages in my pan?'

Benjamin shook his wet head like a spaniel, counted the opposition, then meekly departed.

Elly joined in the general laughter, saying, 'Is Mr Benjamin one of your sympathisers, Paul?'

'He's a damned revolutionary, like Frenchy here, but a good fellow at heart. He just doesn't believe we want freedom to govern ourselves without breaking away from our mother country.'

Frenchy picked up the wine bottle and scrutinised the level within, saying morosely, 'If you're not careful you'll find yourself with a House of Lords running the Colony to suit a handful of squatters, and Wentworth the first to grasp a ducal coronet.'

'Rubbish. He only just scraped in at the last election. Next time ...'

Puzzled, Elly interrupted: 'What's wrong with an aristocracy? It's always worked well in England, if not in your country.'

Frenchy threw up his hands. '*Mon Dieu*, can she not see?'

She turned to Paul, who explained: 'Elly, there's great social injustice in England and the oppressors have always come from the titled class or the very rich. But now, in this new land, we have the opportunity to form a more equitable government, truly representative of all men and not merely the privileged few. We want to retain the Westminster system but adapt it, to use the brains and energy of men who would otherwise be denied their chance by virtue of their birth.'

Drinkers at the next table had turned to listen, and one put out a hand to shake Paul's. 'Well said, my friend. And it's men like Henry Parkes, from the ranks of the working class, who will help to mould this new parliament of ours.'

'Right. Right.' The current of agreement swept around the room. Other conversations ceased as more people began listening to Paul.

On his feet, flushed and eager, he continued, 'There are plenty of others like Parkes. We have the goodwill of men articulate enough to stand up to our Botany Bay aristocrats, those self-seeking scoundrels who would carve up the wealth of the Colony amongst themselves. Against their opposition, we've rid ourselves of convict labour and we now pay our workers. There'll be no slaves in this democracy. *And* we'll unlock the land so that anyone who wants to work can raise his children in plenty, without the need to send them into factories and mine pits and smelters to ruin their health. This country will raise a new breed of men and women, strong, independent and free.' He looked down apologetically at Elly. 'I promised you no speeches, tonight.'

'Don't apologise. It's stirring talk. I'm making discoveries.' Elly meant it. These people were alive, generating their own energy, trying to get things done. While some of it, no doubt, was air dreaming, there was purpose behind the discussions and an intention to work on the problems. These men were builders, not destroyers. Their lives were go-ahead, as she wanted hers to be.

Frenchy gazed at Paul with admiration. 'That is the spirit of the barricades. You have the heart of a true Frenchman, *mon ami*. I salute you.' He grabbed Paul by the shoulders and kissed him soundly on both cheeks. Paul jerked back out of range, cuffing his friend lightly on the jaw. Elly had never seen him so passionately alive, so happy with himself and his company.

'You should know, Frenchy. You've thrown a few cobbles in your time and had to run for your life.' He turned to Elly. 'Do you think we're all mad?'

'Yes, wonderfully, excitingly mad. You're all so unafraid to try to change the world.'

'Youth and a dream, always a powerful combination. But it must be accompanied by commonsense. There are older heads involved, experienced fighters who will be with us on the long haul to victory.' He raised his voice again to address the crowded room. 'Victory won't come overnight, we know, but come it will, if we have anything to say. Eh, friends?' He flung up his arms and was answered with an approving roar. 'Then join me in a toast to our new country, to self-government, to universal suffrage, to equality for all. To victory!'

Elly raised her glass, joined in the cry, 'To victory!' and drank deeply. As her gaze met with Paul's, a thrill ran through her body, bringing with it an odd, tingling awareness. Paul stiffened, his triumphant expression vanishing, to be replaced by a look of stupefaction.

For a long moment the tavern, with its noise and smoke and press of people, faded into the background and there were only the two of them, poised on the edge of some great revelation. Elly held her breath in the expectant silence. Then, like a thunderclap, the world rolled in again on a wave of sound and sight and smells to smash the fragile moment. Other people surged forward to claim Paul's attention, leaving Elly wondering whether she'd imagined it all.

Much later, when the tavern keeper had come around and turned down most of the lamps, Elly and Paul stepped out into a cold starlit night and hailed a cab. Elly's head reeled with words, so many words, so many ideas, so much enthusiasm. She felt drunk with it all. It seemed only natural to turn to her companion with her question.

'Paul, when you spoke of children in mines and factories, I heard something like pain in your voice. Do they mean so much to you?' She waited, trusting that the intimacy they'd shared with his friends would, for once, be enough to bring down his barriers.

His voice, when he finally answered, sounded distant, but not unfriendly, more questioning, as if he needed an answer where there was none. 'Have you stood on a hillside before dawn on a bitter morning, with the moon peering over your shoulder at a line of women on their way to the mills, frost biting their bare toes and their ragged backs bent into hoops, their faces shrivelled and yellow pale? Have you seen starvelings of seven and eight struggling along at their mothers' sides, heading for a work day of thirteen hours, with no hope of any future beyond crippled limbs, rotted lungs, stunted minds?'

Elly's hands tightened on her reticule.

He went on. 'Do you know what it's like to suck on a leather strap to ease the hunger ache in your belly, or strip a drunken man for his rags, leaving him in the gutter to freeze? Do you know what it's like to see hope fade from the eyes of loved ones?' Paul sighed and leaned back further into the shadowed interior of the cab. 'I'm a poor companion tonight. The wine has bred melancholy. Forgive me.'

'There's no need.' Elly sensed that, with the mood of the evening destroyed, he wanted their outing to end, and she remained silent until the cab drew up at the hospital gate. As he handed her up the steps to the front door she turned to him. 'Paul, I'm so glad you asked me to meet your friends. They're a wonderful band of people. Perhaps I may come with you again another Thursday night.'

He smiled noncommittally, thanked her for her company, then left. Standing with her hand on the stair newel, Elly listened to the sound of fading hoofbeats and thought she had just spent the strangest, most interesting evening of her life in the company of the most enigmatic and, yes, attractive of men.

Chapter Twelve

'It will be a simple amputation of the left leg above the knee, Matron, but as the child is so young, it would be wise to have a woman in attendance, to give reassurance.'

Elly glanced up from the notes in her hand and studied Dr Houston's increasingly worn face. He removed his spectacles, polishing them on a dirty handkerchief which he returned to the pocket of his equally filthy coat. She knew he'd been operating since early morning and probably wanted to go off duty.

The senior surgeon and apothecary was a kind man, Elly believed, but stubborn in his refusal to accept new ideas, of which antisepsis was one. Nor did he take kindly to suggestions from staff, however senior. Elly quailed at the thought of the imminent operation, to be conducted without anaesthetic. A child. A little boy, already terrified, torn from his mother, suffering a gangrenous infection of the leg, and about to be subjected to the horror of the knife and bone saw. 'Dr Houston …'

He hurriedly drew out his watch and examined its face. 'My goodness, can that be the time already? I must go. I leave all in your capable hands, Matron. Good day to you.' He raced off down the hall, coat-tails flapping about his knees.

Elly sighed and scanned her notes again. Simon Leonides, aged five. The surgeon would be Phineas Gault. Well, she could at least ensure that the theatre and instruments were scrubbed clean.

Half an hour later Elly stood beside the table where a child lay strapped down, unable to as much as wriggle his one good foot. Despite the effects of a dose of laudanum, panic-stricken eyes stared up at Elly from a tangle of wispy brown hair, and gaslight flickered over a face as pale as skimmed milk. The boy's breath came in uneven gasps as his thin chest pushed against the restraining leather. His infected limb had been stretched out away from his body, already looking like some alien attachment, a pulpy log of greenish-grey flesh, the toes starting to rot away. The clean instruments lay on a nearby cloth-covered tray, ready for the surgeon. But Dr Gault was late.

Elly tried to soothe the child, stroking his head and promising him it would soon be over and he would see his mam. She wiped his sweaty face and trickled a little water onto his dry lips, her own eyes shadowed with the knowledge of what was to come, her mouth compressed with anger at the unnecessary pain and danger, and at the surgeon's callous indifference to his patient's mental agony as he kept him waiting and waiting.

At last the surgeon bustled in brandishing a filthy, rust-stained saw. 'I found it at last. My favourite tool. I don't like to operate without it by me.'

A small man crowned with tight, dark curls, he had tiny pigeon-toed feet that carried him forward in a peculiar trotting gait. His face, set in discontented lines, had an unhealthy cheesy texture as though it rarely felt the sun. Elly concentrated on the awful saw and the small grubby hands holding it, the fingernails dark with encrusted blood.

'Doctor, I have already cleaned the instruments for you.'

'No thank you, Matron. I prefer to use my own. Ah, I see the patient is ready for me. Well, let's get down to business. I have a busy schedule this afternoon, and already I have delivered two infants and carried out a post-mortem examination of a most interesting case. The man died of syphilis as a primary cause, but he had these peculiar lesions ...' He prattled on.

Elly had ceased to listen, her gaze fixed in horror on those dirty hands. She hastened to a nearby table, saying, 'Doctor, here is a basin of water with chloride of lime, if you'd care to wash now.'

'Wash? Whatever for? I washed this morning. I also particularly dislike the chemical odour. Throw it away, Matron.' He stared around him. 'Now, I see the patient is well restrained and all is in order, so I shall not need your services after all. One of the wardsmen can take over when I've finished.'

'Dr Houston asked me to stay with Simon to comfort him and try to ease him over the shock.'

Dr Gault seemed nonplussed. 'The shock? Oh, you mean nerve pain.' He glanced at the boy's face for the first time. 'He'll probably faint when I reach the bone. But if you're worried about his screams, I can apply the gag.'

Elly swallowed her indignation and said firmly, 'As you know, Doctor, shock can kill, and your patient is very young. No doubt you have heard of the recent use of ether to anaesthetise patients undergoing radical surgery. I wonder whether you would care to try it in this case, since I happen to be practised in administering the drug.'

'Ether? Don't believe in it. Radical nonsense. We are meant to bear pain in this life. The Bible says so. And I must say I do not appreciate uncalled for advice from a mere nurse.' Gault's face had grown pink under its cheesy surface.

Elly disregarded the warning. 'Doctor, it can only enhance your fine reputation to increase the number of patients who survive your surgery. The death rate noted by my father in his practice improved considerably when patients did not have to contend with severe pain and shock—'

In what seemed like an echo from her last terrible day at the Settlement, she heard Gault say: 'I have absolutely no interest in your father's practice, nor in your advice, Matron. I now propose to proceed with the operation.' Gault strode over to the table, ignoring the child's terrified whimpering.

Elly moved swiftly to the other side and leaned protectively over the child. 'For God's sake, will you not wash your filthy hands? You've attended two births and handled necrotic tissue this afternoon, and now you're preparing to cut into healthy flesh. You will be passing along infection.'

Gault's voice trembled. 'Get out. Get out now. I don't want you here. I shall report your insolence to the committee.'

'Report it to the full Board, if you like. I'll be doing battle with them anyway.' Elly, flushed and trembling herself, placed a hand on the boy's shoulder. 'I won't leave this child until you've finished your butchery and moved on to your next victim.'

In answer, Gault picked up a knife from the tray and sliced straight across the boy's thigh, splitting skin and tissue to the bone. Elly closed her ears to the boy's shrieks. Her hands flashed to the clamps as she moved into the familiar rhythm of surgery, praying for Gault to be swift. When he grasped the filthy saw, she swallowed the bile in her throat and tried to prepare herself. An unearthly scream was wrenched from the boy's throat as the blade bit, dragged across bone and nerve and back again, hacking once, twice more before the severed leg dropped away. Elly glanced at the boy's face and saw he had, indeed, fainted. She measured his pulse while Gault busily sewed away at severed blood vessels, then prepared a flap of skin to go over the stump. The pulse beat faintly and the cloth beneath the child's body was saturated in a crimson tide.

'He has lost a great deal of blood,' she said.

Gault ignored her. If he prided himself on his speed, Elly thought, he had every right to. Within minutes the job was done and the surgeon stepped back, wiping the blade of his saw on his coat. The little eyes bored into hers.

'The patient is now in your care, Matron.' He moved with his peculiar gait to the door, then turned and added, 'I shall not forget this. You will regret your words today.'

Elly ignored him. She placed a pad saturated with a solution of chloride of lime over the wound and bound it up, then released the straps and lifted the child onto a wheeled stretcher. Under no circumstances would she allow him to be thrown into the chaos of a male ward, with only wardsmen to watch over him. Little Simon would go into the exclusive care of Nurse Pearl.

Simon Leonides never recovered consciousness. In the early hours of the morning, while Elly and Pearl and his mother watched helplessly at his bedside, his small heart gave up the struggle.

The following day Elly received notice to attend a special disciplinary meeting of the board of directors that afternoon.

Having already attended three monthly board meetings, Elly knew what to expect, although the faces around the table varied from month to month and there had never before been a full attendance of the twenty-four directors, four major office holders, medical officers and district surgeons. The room, wreathed in smoke from expensive cigars, was crowded, with extra chairs brought in for those who could not command a seat at the table. At its head presided the Honourable Edward Deas Thomson, Colonial Secretary and intimate of the Governor himself. Beside him, his vice-president, Captain Dumaresq, tapped a pencil impatiently, and next to him, the treasurer and secretary sat with solemn faces.

As Elly entered, the chatter died and thirty-seven pairs of eyes focused on her. She was wearing her best woollen gown in midnight blue, severely cut and edged with simple braid, which she hoped gave an impression of style and dignity. Her matching bonnet framed her face charmingly, she knew, and made a good substitute for the braided coronet she could no longer display. It took more than seven months to regrow hair which had, in places, been cut within two inches of the scalp. Vanity aside, she needed all the ammunition she could produce for this encounter.

Searching the room for a friendly face she saw Dr Houston watching her, but he glanced quickly away. Phineas Gault, on the other hand, pinned her with a dagger glare, his discontented mouth primmed and ready to accuse. Her skin prickled as she felt again the peculiar sensation of being watched very closely. Was it the same man, the owner of the brown eyes in a face she couldn't remember? But there was no time to search for him. Already the meeting had been called to order. Elly took the chair held ready for her, and proceedings commenced.

Deas Thomson cleared his throat. 'As chairman of this special gathering I have to announce that it has been convened at the request of several members following a most scandalous and scurrilous report on this hospital printed recently in the *Empire*. There is also the matter of a complaint against the matron, Miss Ballard, put forward by one of our medical officers, Surgeon Phineas Gault. In the first matter, since it is known that Miss Ballard conducted a certain journalist through the hospital with a view to commenting upon its standards, I believe we should ask her for an explanation.'

Elly rose. 'Gentlemen, I am perfectly prepared to explain and apologise for the extreme attitude adopted by Mr JG Patterson of the *Empire*. I have here a letter of apology addressed to the Board and signed by him.' She'd had a devil of a job getting JG to agree to this, but with pressure from Paul and the realisation that Elly would almost certainly be dismissed without it, he had finally relented. She handed this letter to the secretary. 'It's true that I took the opportunity to show him certain deficiencies in the building and facilities well known to you all and which have been the subject of petition from me for the past three months. I believe that, as a member of the public who supports this infirmary and dispensary, he had a right to know the truth and to request the help of others who might be interested in improving our conditions.

'He did not have the right, however, to criticise my staff in such unbridled terms, nor to impugn the work of this board of directors. I specifically asked him not to do so and, at the time, made clear to him that I wished only to excite public interest, not to lay blame anywhere. Unfortunately, he paid no attention to my wishes, with the result that unnecessary offence has been given. The initial fault was mine, and I apologise most sincerely.' She sat down to hide her trembling knees.

Deas Thomson regarded her sternly. 'Your apology is noted, Matron. Nevertheless, you should be aware of having far superseded your role. Regrettably, your forwardness has only succeeded in bringing the hospital you purport to care for so devotedly into disrepute, not to mention the men who serve this institution without favour or reward.'

Elly bowed her head in apparent remorse, but she felt only contempt. Where was the 'service' from this group of men who met simply to hear themselves talk and who never by any mischance did anything to overcome the huge problems she had listed for them? As for favour and reward, their names gained the lustre of benevolence without a finger being raised.

'If I might speak, Mr Chairman?'

The rich voice carried through the room. Elly turned quickly to see a man of middle height but great presence rise from a back corner. Beardless, his smooth face was lined about the temples and mouth to show at least forty years of living; he had a broad, high forehead, strong straight nose and black hair curling thickly and grey only at the temples. His dark gaze had a compelling quality that she immediately recognised as the anonymous surveillance she'd experienced as strongly as a physical contact at that first board meeting. Conscious of the strength of this man's personality, she was strangely heartened. He would help her. She knew it.

The chairman inclined his head. 'We should be glad of your views, Mr Cornwallis.'

Cornwallis bowed and produced a folded paper from his jacket. 'I have here a copy of the article in question and, with the greatest respect, would point out to my fellow members of this board of directors that there is not one untruth to be found in it. The writer has not misrepresented the hospital in any way. I have made it my business to delve into his accusations and can only say that "disgrace" is almost too mild a word to apply to conditions obtaining in the main buildings and ancillary structures.'

Protest rippled through the room but died as Cornwallis held up his hand. 'Bear with me, I beg. You know my reputation. I am not easily bamboozled or misled. Yet, to my shame, I have continued unaware of these deplorable conditions for months. This lady's courage and determination were needed to bring them to public notice, for which I believe she should be, not censured, but thanked.'

Tears of gratitude stung beneath Elly's lids. She had a champion at last. She smiled and saw an answering faint curve of his lips as he continued.

'There *are* vile legions of insects which crawl nightly from the woodwork. There are open drains and cess-pits harbouring vermin, and there is a shortage of water. I have seen all these things myself. I cannot speak for the staff or the situation in the wards. However, drunkenness is scarcely an unknown problem in the Colony, and not generally restricted to those in otherwise good health. Nor do I think we should expect perfection in the untrained. In short, gentlemen, I believe we should support our new matron in her efforts to improve the lot of her patients and suggest we immediately vote a sum towards this.'

To Elly, falling back in her seat and viewing him through a haze of gratitude and relief, he appeared almost a mythical figure,

Saint George without his armour, facing the dragon Board for her. The members, however, were clearly divided on his views. When the voices rose to something suspiciously like an uproar Deas Thomson rapped on the table for attention.

'Gentlemen. Let us have silence, if you please. Is there anyone else who would like to speak on this matter before a decision is made?'

Several gentlemen had plenty to say, although not always to the point; but at length it was agreed that JG's letter of apology should be given to the *Sydney Herald* for publication—which would lower his crest, thought Elly—and Matron admonished not to speak about hospital affairs to outsiders, especially not to journalists. In exchange, the Board promised to vote money for improvements and to discuss the provision of extra staff.

The chairman then referred to the second item on the agenda, Phineas Gault's complaint that Matron had asserted herself over him and tried to introduce her own measures into the operating theatre.

'What have you to say to this, Matron?'

'A good deal.' Elly girded herself. 'The members of the Board have seen from my application details that I was trained by an eminent physician and surgeon, my father, Dr Robert Ballard, of Edinburgh, Paris and Vienna. He was not only highly esteemed in his profession, but he also taught in the great hospitals and, after migrating to the Colonies, kept to the forefront of medical science through medical publications and through his correspondence with overseas colleagues.'

Elly turned to survey the row of house physicians and surgeons and the district physicians, all eyeing her with hostility. 'You medical gentlemen no doubt do the same, through the medium of journals and papers. And of course you will have heard of one of the greatest advances in medical history—the ability to anaesthetise a patient with ether and do away with the pain of surgery.'

Gault's unhealthy face turned bright red, while his confreres tried to appear knowledgeable but unimpressed.

Elly's voice gained an edge. 'When I made my *suggestion* Doctor Gault was good enough to inform me that he regarded this idea as "radical nonsense", although I explained how I had assisted my father in the use of ether many times with excellent results. My father never lost a patient through post-operative shock.'

Several of the faces in the crowd grew thoughtful, but the medical men preserved features of stone.

It's too innovative for them, Elly thought. They don't know about it and they don't want to know.

Nevertheless she went on. 'As long ago as 1845 a dentist named Morton was invited by the eminent senior surgeon at the Massachusetts General Hospital to try to anaesthetise a patient about to undergo surgery for a tumour of the jaw. He used ether, gentlemen, and the patient slept through the twenty-five minute procedure and woke saying he had noticed only a scratching sensation along his jaw. This case was written up in the *Boston Medical and Surgical Journal* two months later. The new method has been tested and adopted in London, France, Germany, all over Europe. Yet for some reason it has not reached the Colonies.'

'Utter rubbish.' Gault could contain himself no longer. 'I've never heard of Dr Robert Ballard, nor have I seen any evidence to prove this so-called anaesthetic does what is claimed. The woman's story of dentists and American surgeons is pure fabrication.'

'Hear, hear,' another doctor chimed in. 'Whatever experiments may have been carried out in Europe, I have yet to be convinced that there is anything in such an extraordinary notion.'

'Have you tried it?' Elly flashed back.

The man shook his head. 'Madam, if I tried every new idea hailed as the latest medical miracle, my patients would require a lifetime of treatment, provided none of these experimental notions killed them. I have no use for fads.'

'Nor I,' agreed another, older man, who rose to bow to Elly. 'Do you realise there are close to forty different schools of thought into which medical theory has been divided? Meta-physicians, iatrochemists, experimental physiologists, gastricists, infarct-men, homeopathists, hydropathists, phrenologists—the list goes on. Each of these schools has its own explanation for sickness and its own favoured methods of treatment—some most curious, most completely ineffectual. As my colleague said, we have not the time to try a fraction of these, nor the will to experiment on our patients.' He sat down to a patter of applause.

Elly refused to be moved. 'I agree, many ideas turn out to be worthless, but if we cease to try new methods we stagnate. Medicine is a science and cannot stand still. How many of you doctors would do without the stethoscope, now that it has proved to be such a valuable diagnostic tool?'

The first doctor nodded. 'We are not as hidebound as you may think, Matron. But we must be sure there is no danger before we adopt something as revolutionary as an inhaled anaesthetic. The recommendation of nitrous oxide for this purpose, for instance, has proved a costly failure. Not realising how greatly the substance increases the force of circulation, I tried it on a patient in surgery who subsequently bled to death. This so-called laughing gas has since been rightly relegated to the area of parlour tricks and side-shows.'

Elly began to feel helpless. The opposition was too great; the doctors were too afraid to step outside certain safe boundaries. Most of them were thinking of the welfare of their patients, and she couldn't argue with that, except that she *knew*, absolutely and positively knew that the greatest boon to those very patients was being denied them.

She rose again, slowly, placing her hands on the table for support and leaning earnestly towards the ring of surrounding faces. 'Please listen to me,' she begged. 'Forget I'm a woman and a mere lowly nurse. If this information came to you from a famous and skilled surgeon, would you not be impressed? Think of the little boy who died last night because his heart could not stand the shock of agonising surgery. Wouldn't it be worth the risk of trying this new treatment?' She saw the answer in their impatient expressions.

'My dear young woman, miracles only occur in Holy Writ.' The speaker was another doctor, a district surgeon attached to the Board. 'I've no doubt you have the best of intentions, but you really cannot try to teach professional men their jobs. The child's death was regrettable but unavoidable.'

'That's not all she did.' Gault added angrily. 'She tried to get me to wash my hands in some foul-smelling solution before I operated. Me, a man with twelve years' experience in the theatre. She treated me like a child.'

Elly marshalled her wits. 'Surely some of you have heard of

antisepsis, of the work of Dr Ignace Semmelweis at the Vienna Medical School?' She saw only blank faces. 'Oh, how can I convince you? Dr Semmelweis proved that the simple measure of washing the hands in chlorine solution until the skin was slippery prevented the transmission of contagious disease from one patient to another, from a cadaver after dissection to a woman in childbirth. He saved the lives of hundreds of women with this discovery. My father himself practised antisepsis with amazing results. He taught me to clean all instruments, furniture, swabs, needles and thread and, in particular, any hands which would touch the operating field.'

Gault stood up and shouted: 'Poppycock! Lunacy! We all know that septic infection is a miasmic contagion borne on the air.'

Deas Thomson ordered him to sit down, then said to Elly, 'What you are telling us is theory. Both this Dr Semmelweis and your father had a theory in which they believed. Where is the proof? What has been published?'

Elly looked at him hopelessly. It was true. She had only her father's word and her own experience to offer. It wasn't enough.

Cornwallis's smooth voice flowed from the corner of the room. 'It would appear Matron Ballard has once again intervened in the interests of a patient. Whether or not this was warranted is a matter for the Board to decide. I cannot agree that offering a surgeon the opportunity to wash hands no doubt filthy from the dissection room is an insult. Again, the offer of a new, if peculiar, technique in the interests of a patient's safety can scarcely be seen as interference. Gault remained within his rights to refuse the offer. However, his deliberate umbrage does him no credit. Miss Ballard, I should like to offer my personal apology for the slur cast upon you by Gault's intemperate reaction.'

Elly bowed slightly and sat down again, her head whirling as a further buzz of conversation broke out, which continued until Deas Thomson brought the room to order once again.

He addressed Elly coolly, but kindly. 'Matron Ballard, my colleagues and I have reached the conclusion that you are not to be censured in this matter.' He broke off to deliver a warning look to Gault, already halfway to his feet. 'However, we require you not to bring any further innovations to the operating theatre, and to comply at all times with the wishes of the surgeon in charge. Is that clear?'

'Perfectly clear.' The words stuck in Elly's throat, but she got them out.

'Very well. At the next monthly meeting the board of directors will decide upon extra funds to be allocated and their future use. Your advice will be invaluable, and we should like you to draw up a list of the most urgent repairs and necessities.'

'Thank you, sir. I am grateful.'

He nodded. 'The meeting is now adjourned. Miss Ballard. Gentlemen.'

Everyone rose and Elly headed blindly for the door, more than anxious to escape. A hand clasped her elbow and Cornwallis's voice said in her ear: 'Allow me to assist you out into the air. I'm not surprised you find it oppressive in here.'

Her feet seemed to glide above the floor as they traversed the corridor, then down the front steps and out through the gate into Macquarie Street.

Here Elly collected herself, saying, 'I can't leave now. I have duties ...'

'The Board adjourned earlier than was expected. Whoever you left in charge is still there. You can be spared for a few minutes longer.'

Persuaded by a voice with the consistency of honey, Elly allowed herself to be led down the street towards Hyde Park, and there, in the shade of a young Moreton Bay fig tree she found herself seated beside the man who had fought for her so strongly.

'Mr Cornwallis, I'm very grateful for your support.' Meeting the warm, dark eyes she realised they were only one striking feature of an impressive, statesmanlike face. A noble face, she thought, denoting the love of justice behind the physical facade.

'There's no need for gratitude. You had no-one else to speak for you, and those dolts would never have thought to investigate beyond their own prejudices had I not pointed out the obvious. I abhor stupidity.' His smile seemed to envelop her.

'Nevertheless, I thank you. And my patients will have cause to do so if the Board can bring itself actually to disgorge some money. It's a dear wish of mine to see each patient in a bed of her own, not forced to share with at least one other. And those cesspits ... Oh, don't let me start. I'd be boring you here forever.'

'I'm not bored. But, may I offer you some refreshment—a glass of wine before you return?'

'No, thank you. I don't need any stimulant. Quite the contrary. I feel I could walk back on air. The relief is enormous, I assure you.' She rose and held out her hand.

Cornwallis rose also. 'Allow me to escort you to the gate.'

'No, thank you again, but I shall do very well alone. Goodbye, Mr Cornwallis.'

He surprised her by taking her hand and carrying it to his lips, which just brushed her gloved knuckles.

'Rather, *au revoir*, Miss Eleanor Ballard.'

Chapter Thirteen

'I wish she had let me go with her to face the Board.' Jo-Beth scrubbed energetically at the stained sheets, then stretched to ease her aching back. 'It must have been quite an ordeal.'

Pearl, her arms bare to the elbow, her dark hair lank from steam, let her washload fall back into the tub which balanced on trestles in the courtyard, a makeshift affair set up near the kitchen water butt. There was no laundry outhouse as such, since Elly, in a fit of rage at its dark, dank filthiness, had ordered it torn down and its resident vermin incinerated in the rubble. A new one had been promised, but meanwhile the scrubbing and rinsing went on outdoors, with water discharged across the pitted sandstone slabs and down the nearest drain, amid prayers that it would not back up to overflow the yard.

'Matron is quite able to manage the Board. She's as competent as any ten men.' Pearl checked the load in the basket beside her then went back to her rubbing, an additional task laid on the nursing staff as the washer-woman had failed to arrive this week.

Jo-Beth surveyed her cracked, swollen hands, grimaced, then plunged them back into the scummy water. There was a nip in the early spring air, enough to redden her cheeks and remind her of her home in Boston where the leaves would be turning the same shade, along with others of gold and silver, falling to create a carpet only God could loom. She could almost smell the woodsmoke from farmers burning off, hear the skeins of geese clack across the pale sky on their way south for the winter. But she didn't miss the house, with its atmosphere so cold and repressive. She didn't miss her bullying mother and the father who never once supported his child against tyranny. Sighing, she dragged her attention back to prosaic present.

'You're an excellent nurse, too, Pearl.' The girl's tact and brisk kindness towards patients were admirable, Jo-Beth thought, as well as her thorough understanding of their needs. If she were withdrawn at times, this was only because of her longing to be gone to the diggings in search of her brother. 'I wish I could be more like you.'

'You have a compassionate heart; and although I know you find much of the work distasteful, you never let your patients guess it.'

Jo-Beth glanced at Pearl, then quickly away. 'So you've noticed. I am ashamed to be so squeamish, but sometimes the noise and smells and sights are too much for me. I had no idea how basic human needs could be.'

Pearl smiled. 'You've led too sheltered a life. I, on the other hand, have dealt with nothing but basic human needs since my childhood. Nursing is a natural ability in some people, I believe, and I take pride in my skill; while you are struggling against your nature, and that's hard. Yet you have courage and determination. You will endure.' She cocked her head inquisitively. 'Have you never thought of returning to Boston and claiming your inheritance?'

'More like a pittance.' Jo-Beth's voice was grim. 'My father's brother inherits the company and most of the money. I've no desire to be his pensioner, to be married off suitably and as quickly as possible.' She preferred not to discuss her most compelling reason for staying in Sydney—her conviction that Ethan would be returned to her.

She still had faith that Ethan would be returned to her, but as each day passed this was undermined by the unremitting toil, the inability to sleep through exhaustion and nightmares, and the lack of news, no matter how many people she buttonholed while she haunted the quayside at the end of the working day, questioning passengers and crew of incoming ships. Had they heard of someone rescued from the sea? Had they spoken to any survivors of a shipwreck? The coastline was littered with wrecks of all kinds, and survival stories were not unusual. But she never heard of a ship's master saved. She returned from such expeditions worn out and dispirited, yet unable to rest for more than a few hours before waking to another dawn of hope, soon to be eroded through the long busy day.

Jo-Beth let the sheet fall into the basket and stood gazing vacantly out through a gap between the buildings to the trees in the Domain. Above them rose a sky filled with painted clouds.

Pearl murmured sympathetically and put out a soapy hand to press Jo-Beth's rolled-back sleeve.

'I'm being self-indulgent, Pearl. Today I can't fight off the melancholy. I'm afraid that sometime in the future I'll have to reconcile myself ... But I can't, I won't believe he's gone forever.' Jo-Beth hung her head to let the slow tears fall into the washtub. 'Added to which, I despise myself. I ache for some of the comforts I left back home, my music, my books, a warm bath with scented soap. To me this is a mere existence, deprived of the small luxuries and social intercourse that smooth life's path. I took too much for granted. And I *hate* washing other people's linen.' She sobbed helplessly.

Softly Pearl said: 'You are a human being. Don't berate yourself for human weakness. I think the way you have adapted to new circumstances shows great courage. Now, leave the washing. Go walking in the Domain. You need grass and trees and sky to soothe your spirit.'

A few days later there were two new admissions, a Mrs Wynham with her youngest child, a girl of two years. They were accompanied by an imperative Paul Gascoigne demanding immediate assistance for them, beginning with a bed, an attending physician and Matron's own presence.

Elly being absent, Pearl placed the two patients in Ward One and called Dr Gault away from his dinner to examine them. He hastily did so, prescribing a paregoric draught, then returned to his meal, clearly glad to be rid of Paul, with his air of slight menace. Pearl, while washing both patients, discovered them to be frail, under-nourished and infested with fleas and lice. She was particularly concerned over the baby girl, Anne, whose hold on life seemed so tenuous. When they were settled she sought out Paul, who waited impatiently below in the hall.

'Who are they, Mr Gascoigne?'

'They're my friends.' His manner challenged her. 'Why? Are they not deemed suitable to occupy one of your beds? I've paid my two guineas, you know. I may recommend someone to the infirmary.'

'There's no need to be hostile. I place no boundaries on help. I simply want to know anything about Mrs Wynham's background which might help us care for her.'

Her spirited response brought out his familiar half smile. 'You sound just like Matron. My apologies, Nurse Pearl. I've heard tales of the difficulties experienced by some who seek help at the infirmary, particularly those living in poor circumstances, with no-one to vouch for their character. Mrs Wynham is unwed with three children by different men, and occupies a ruinous hut down at the Rocks.'

Pearl nodded. 'Then you must have lied to gain admittance for her. I don't blame you. The rules are nonsensical. What has morality to do with health care, and by what right do we turn away someone who is sick? Come up to Matron's office where you can give me the details you've invented for the sake of Dr Gault and any of the other moralists around here.'

Paul followed her upstairs, saying, 'When will Miss Ballard be back? I'd hoped to speak with her.'

'It's her afternoon off—the first in weeks—so I don't expect her until suppertime. Will you leave a message?'

'No. No, thank you. I'll call again to see how Mrs Wynham and the baby are.'

Watching him leave, Pearl pondered over his interest in the Wynham family. How much was altruism, how much political motivation, or even simply an excuse to call on Elly? Paul

Gascoigne's many-layered personality interested her. Which aspect was the reality?

In the storeroom, a stuffy cubicle lined with shelves and thick with the smell of chemicals, where, as a trusted assistant, Pearl was now permitted access to drugs and other valuable items, she paused in her work, ears pricked. A shadow fell over her and she sprang about, her arm raised with a bottle of ammonium ready to throw.

JG flinched, saying in a placatory voice: 'I mean no harm, I promise. Please put the bottle down.' He grinned as Pearl slowly lowered her weapon. 'I'm minded of a lass in a pub I know in Dublin. She always kept a bottle by her hand for emergencies.'

Pearl's heart still pounded. The old habits of vigilance and self-protection stayed long after the need had gone. Besides, it might have been the wardsman who had twice tried to corner her and take liberties, a creature with the eyes of the watchman who raped her in the grounds of her first owner. The terror of that victim lived on in the woman who could never quite drop her guard.

'What do you want?' she asked, knowing instinctively that JG would not harm her.

'I want to talk to you, when you can spare a moment.'

He's too mild, she thought. He's up to something. 'I'm very busy.'

'You're also off duty at present. I checked with Matron.'

Pearl replaced the heavy ammonium bottle on the shelf. 'You mean Elly will talk to you? After what you did to her, to us all?'

'Ah, now, there's a lass as doesn't hold a grudge. We've come to an understanding, Miss Elly Ballard and me, and all's well between us.'

'I hold grudges extremely well.' Pearl wasn't giving a fraction to JG's practised charm.

JG pulled up a drum of whitewash and settled himself on it. 'I, on the other hand, can't help letting grudges slip through me fingers like quicksilver. And I have the patience of Job.'

Pearl, now a superior few inches higher than the seated man, said, 'Very well. Say what you want then let me get on with my work.'

He glanced up obliquely, then down at his hands. 'Why did you do it, girl dear? Don't they feed you well enough in this place?'

Pearl stiffened. 'Why did I do what?'

'Steal my timepiece.'

There was silence in the tiny room. Pearl froze, unable to think clearly. He knew.

JG continued speaking to his hands. 'I've had me pocket picked enough times to know when it's happened again.'

'You ... let me do it?'

'I'm as curious as a billy goat. I want to know why you did it. You're no ordinary thief.'

Pearl knew the blood had risen to her face. A thief. Yes, she was a thief. What did others know of her struggle to stay alive, to gain her freedom, to make her way across the seas in the hope of finding her last remaining relative? What did this self-righteous scribbler know of hardship or abuse?

'Well? Why did you steal from me?'

She compressed her lips.

'Tell me.' The tone was firm but not vengeful.

Pearl paused, then said coolly, 'I needed the money.'

'You've already sold it, my dad's Tompion?' JG shot to his feet, and Pearl backed away, watching him warily.

'If a Tompion is your timepiece, no, I still have it.'

JG sank back, wiping his forehead. 'Well, the saints be praised. Look, girl dear, whatever your desperate need, you can return the watch to me and I'll give you money in exchange.'

The blood rushed away from Pearl's head, leaving her sick and faint. 'No. I can't.'

'You can't accept money freely given, yet you will steal. What kind of crazy code do you live by?'

Pearl couldn't explain. She only knew her personal pride was somehow involved. 'Let me fetch the timepiece for you.'

'I think not. We'll be getting to the bottom of this right this minute. Sit down on the cask so I can loom over you and browbeat you into telling me the truth.'

Pearl sat down, strangely heartened by his facetiousness. The man had great empathy and, as much as she didn't desire any connection with him, she responded to his warmth.

JG adopted a lecturing pose, thin legs in drainpipe trousers astride, one hand on his hip, the other wagging a finger at her.

'We have here, ladies and gentlemen, a young lady of taste and beauty, employed, housed and fed by another charming lady— oh, and dressed by her, as well.' He pointed at her sensible grey twill uniform. 'So why do you think she'd steal? To help someone else perhaps?'

Pearl shook her head slightly.

'For herself, then?'

Her gaze remained steady.

'Well now, she must have some great need. What could it be? Does she want passage money back home to China, or a house of her own, here in Sydney Town, or a carriage and pair to cut a dash in the Domain? Furs, jewels to trap a rich husband?'

To her horror, Pearl felt tears rising. How stupid. She didn't care what this man, or any other, thought of her.

He pressed his advantage. 'Is she simply a mercenary jackdaw out to line her nest with the best feathers at the expense of others? But then, she refused my offer of money. So, we have a mystery still.'

Pearl's lip trembled. She got up. 'I have to go now. I'll return ... return your ...' The tears spilled out down her cheeks. She stood petrified, unable to wipe them away.

JG gently reseated her on the cask, his touch as impersonal as she could wish. Producing a clean handkerchief, he patted her cheeks dry, then pocketed it before moving back to survey her with serious eyes.

'Now tell me what your trouble is, girl dear.'

Pearl told him. She didn't simply explain the carefully hoarded cache growing behind a brick in the wall of her room, but went right back to her years as a cast-off girl child sold for a few coppers to be used by her owners as they willed, then to her life in the mission in the Yangtse Valley. She relived her foster mother's murder, her own careful plot to kill the Triad who had enslaved her, the flight to a city about to be destroyed, then of her terrible disappointment upon discovering that her brother, Li Po, had gone.

'He is my family, all I have left. I must find him. That is why I need money, to reach the goldfields and search for Li Po. I need more than my wages at the hospital, much more, even if I eat little and walk the whole way.'

JG drew a deep breath. 'Mother of God, what a history. Not to mention a sea trip ending in shipwreck. But to search the diggings. It's out of the question. Do you know how many there are in the Colonies, and how far apart? Men have poured in from all parts of the globe, like ants to a honey jar. It would take years.'

'I have the rest of my life,' Pearl said simply.

'Which might not be so long if you set out on such a mad search. Look, why not try other methods first, such as an advertisement in the newspapers? Some of them would reach the goldfields. You could hire a man to make enquiries for you, someone setting off to try his luck. No, on second thoughts, he'd be altogether bent on making a fortune. But you must not go yourself. It's too dangerous, too full of hardship.'

Pearl's jaw tightened. 'I am used to danger and hardship, and I will go myself to find my brother.'

JG eyed her with frustration. 'Not with my Tompion, you won't.'

'Oh, to the bottom of the sea with your Tompion. I don't want it. I wish I'd never taken it.'

'Then there's one thing we agree upon. Now, be a good girl—'

'Don't speak to me like that. I am not a good girl. I am my own mistress. I'm sorry I told you about myself. I will not be so weak again.' She sprang up and whisked out the door like a small whirlwind, intent on retrieving the wretched timepiece then dismissing its owner.

But when she returned, Tompion in hand, JG had gone. She ran to the front lobby, then out into Macquarie Street, but there was no sign of him. Baffled, she returned the watch to its hiding place and went back to work in the storeroom.

That afternoon she was unaccountably clumsy, knocking flasks from shelves, stumbling over sacks. When a canister of precious sugar slipped from her hands and sprang open, dumping its contents all over the floor, she kicked it away from her then went in search of pail and scrubbing broom, freely cursing herself, JG and the whole race of men.

Chapter Fourteen

Elly picked up the ragged conglomeration of native flowers, the bushy cream and red bottlebrush foaming wildly over her hands and dropping fine hairs on the desk. She'd read the attached note from Paul Gascoigne asking her to accompany him to a political rally with a smile, shaking her head. The night at the Earl Grey Tavern had been fascinating, and at the time she had wanted to repeat it. Now, after consideration, she knew she could not allow herself to be drawn into Paul's world. She was far too busy with her own. And when he wished, he could be far too engaging for her comfort. She couldn't afford the distraction.

Inspecting the second offering, a magnificent arrangement of cultivated blooms, roses, delphiniums, and a dozen others, she was almost overpowered by their scent. She detached the note from its ribbon to find a quite different sort of invitation to dine and attend a concert with the man she now knew as the Honourable D'Arcy Lynton Cornwallis, son of Baron Gosselin of Gosselin Milton, Hertfordshire, and a rising power in the Colony.

Jo-Beth knocked and entered the office. 'Matron, can you help me? Nurse Irvine has gone down to the dispensary, leaving me to watch the ward.'

With a sigh, Elly replaced the flowers on the table. She couldn't

expect Jo-Beth to like the responsibility of the ward, untrained as
she was and, as Elly knew, finding the work distasteful. Yet she did
try to hide her lack of enthusiasm, showing compassion to her
charges, never shirking when asked to help. She had also become
the closest thing to a friend Elly had ever known. Jo-Beth, discard-
ing formality, had insisted on bringing her together with Pearl to
form a triune of support amongst the warring elements in the hospital; and Elly had happily released a small part of her burden into
the care of two people she could trust. She put aside the knowledge that the relationship must be brief. Pearl would leave as soon
as she could, while Jo-Beth—well, who knew what she would do?

Elly asked, 'Is someone ill, or giving trouble?'

'Neither. Mrs Porrett, the heavy woman with heart disease, has
slipped down flat on the cot and her breathing is impeded. I need
help to raise her.'

To Elly's ears, Jo-Beth sounded brighter, as though the mist of
sadness surrounding her had begun to dissipate. Perhaps she was
finding acceptance at last.

Jo-Beth noticed the flowers and her expression took on some
of it's old mischievousness. 'Well, how favoured you are, to be sure,
girl dear, as that rascal JG would say. Just which gentlemen are
battering at the doors of your heart with floral tributes?'

Elly laughed. 'None. Don't be ridiculous.' She pushed the flowers aside and left the office, Jo-Beth following. Together they heaved
the distressed patient up onto her pillows, setting a bolster at her
feet so she couldn't slip down again, then moved on to check a
new admission.

The careworn face of the woman hovering over the cot lit up as
they approached.

'Oh, now my little Lilly will be put right. I heard as how the new
nurses at the hospital were curing folk like magic. You'll fix up my
Lilly, won't you?'

Elly stooped over the little girl whose body was racked by constant coughing, each breath drawn with a distinctive whooping
sound. The soft brown hair was matted with sweat, and the child's
terrified expression wrung Elly's heart. With one hand gentling
the child's cheek, she took the pulse, while Jo-Beth spoke to the
mother, extracting what details she could.

'She's just turned three and she's not been right since she watched her daddy die a month back with the lockjaw.' The woman's eyes dulled in remembrance. 'It were a cruel way to go, with the awful pain and the convulsions. We broke his front tooth and all, to put a straw through to feed him some good broth, but it were no manner of use.'

Jo-Beth explained that Lilly's illness could not be attributed to this terrible experience. 'Has Lilly been near other sick children?' she asked.

'Oh, yes. My neighbour what come in to help had her three young 'uns sicken with the cough. One died only last week.' She looked frightened. ''Tis the hooping cough, isn't it?'

Elly glanced up. 'I'm afraid so. Lilly is very ill, Mrs ... ?'

'Smith. Is she going to die? You won't let her die?' She clutched at Elly, who sat her down on the end of the cot.

'Tell me what you've done to help her, Mrs Smith.'

'Oh, all the things. The minute she were born I had her passed under the belly of a donkey nine times; then when she started in to be sick I walked along the road until I met a stranger riding a piebald horse and asked him what to do, and went home and did it straight off.'

Elly schooled her feelings, saying gently, 'What advice did he give?'

'Why, to catch a mouse and fry it and give it her to eat. But the child couldn't stomach it no-how, so I give it to the other two just in case they was to sicken, like my Lilly.'

Elly refused to meet Jo-Beth's eye. 'Did you try any other remedy, Mrs Smith?'

'What else is there?' The woman looked at her helplessly. 'The Doctor here said to keep her warm and he'd send up a medicine for her, which the other nurse give her, but most of it spilled out of her mouth.' She began to sob.

Elly helped her to her feet. 'Mrs Smith, there are things we can do for Lilly, but I think you should go home now and tend your family. Lilly will be well cared for here, and you may visit her to-morrow.'

An order went down to the dispensary for a mixture of garlic, milk and honey to be made up, while Jo-Beth helped Elly to strip and sponge bathe the child to make her more comfortable, all the while soothing and promising she would soon feel better.

Jo-Beth's low-voiced comments on the mother's treatments were lightly turned off by Elly, long accustomed to the superstition masked as medical lore.

'She did the best she could, yet we may do better.'

'I'm certain of it.' Jo-Beth slid a glance at Elly. 'To change the subject, about your beautiful flowers, I imagine one bouquet was the gift of Mr Paul Gascoigne? I certainly haven't imagined his twice-weekly visits to his friend, Mrs Wynham, via your office. Which do you suppose is the greater attraction?'

Elly said composedly, 'It can't be me. I'm never available to see him for more than two minutes, to give a report on his protégés—a report which is becoming increasingly gloomy, I'm sad to say. That baby is so frail and she coughs all night through. I fear she won't reach her third birthday.'

Elly lifted Lilly up to support her through a spasm of coughing, then slipped a clean shift over her head. Although the child remained unresponsive, Elly continued to reassure her, promising to bring her mother back to her in the morning.

Jo-Beth's mind had remained on the Wynham baby. 'It's her lungs, I suppose? And her mother not much better. What's to become of the other children if she never leaves here alive?'

Elly shrugged to cover her distress. 'They're in care at the Benevolent Asylum at the moment. I suppose the people there will arrange something, perhaps send them to the new orphanage at Ormond House. Sometimes I feel so helpless, Jo-Beth. I wonder whether we make any difference at all. There were thirty cases of consumption admitted this month, nineteen of whom have died. The figures for syphilis are worse.'

'Of course you make a difference. Think how many would have died without proper attention. Think of the suffering relieved. It's unlike you to be despondent, Elly. Don't tell me you're about to sicken with some ailment.' Jo-Beth took the bowl brought up from the dispensary by a new trainee, Mary Malone, a fresh-faced girl with intelligence in her round brown eyes and concern for the exhausted child. Then, with Elly holding the little girl against her shoulder, Jo-Beth began spooning the mixture into the child's mouth.

Lilly swallowed obediently, her gaze now fixed on Elly, her formerly passive fingers clutching the matron's.

Turning to Malone, Elly said, 'You may assist in the dispensary while I'm on the ward, but return in thirty minutes' time.'

The girl bobbed then left.

Elly found Jo-Beth surveying her quizzically.

'Now, tell me, Matron, what of the second bouquet, the sumptuous arrangement that would not disgrace the salon of Government House?'

Elly looked self-conscious, and Jo-Beth pounced.

'Aha, it came from your white knight, your champion on the board of directors. Am I right?'

'Yes, although I don't know why it makes me so uncomfortable. After all, it's merely an invitation to dine and hear Toccarini sing. His name is Cornwallis, the Honourable D'Arcy Cornwallis.'

Jo-Beth dropped her teasing tone. 'You will go, Elly, won't you? It's time to remember you are a young, attractive woman, as well as an acting matron.'

Elly nodded at the bowl. 'See if the child will take more.'

'Elly?' Jo-Beth insinuated another spoonful of mixture between Lilly's slackened lips. The child seemed to be half asleep, except when racked by another spasm of coughing.

'No, I don't think so.' Elly wiped Lilly's mouth and gave her a sip of water.

'Why ever not? If he's the Cornwallis I've heard spoken of, he's gentlemanly, cultivated, personable, and could have his choice of all the unattached ladies in the Colony. Yet he's interested in you.'

'Perhaps I don't wish to be added to a list of conquests.'

'I think it's more like fear. You see yourself as a country girl, too homespun for the likes of the Honourable D'Arcy Cornwallis, without conversation, without the allure he expects in his women companions. Well, I can tell you you're wrong. Men like him seek below the conventionally lovely surface for intelligence and wit, and the charm conferred by these. You have them in abundance, Elly Ballard, plus the loveliness, as it happens.'

''Goodness! You've kissed the Blarney Stone, or else you've been taking lessons from JG' Elly laid the sleeping child down and covered her warmly. 'I don't know, Jo-Beth. It would be such an effort.'

'You must make the effort. Drag yourself up from the rut you've laboured in for months and take a peep at the outside world, if for no other reason than it will bind Cornwallis to you as an ally on the Board. Come along now, write the gentleman a polite note of acceptance. I'll post it for you. I've a letter of my own to send.'

Elly's interest awakened. 'Captain McAndrews? I heard you had a follower in a red coat.'

'Hardly a follower.' For a moment, sadness veiled Jo-Beth's vivid features. Then a smile broke through and she tilted her head cheekily.

'Well, a discreet admirer, then,' Elly amended. 'Has he invited you out?'

Jo-Beth primmed up her mouth. 'Oh, dear me, yes. Having daringly attended divine service together at St Phillip's Church, we actually ventured a drive in an open carriage through the Government Domain to admire the flowerbeds. I scarcely dare tell you of the delights in store next week.'

'Let me guess. Bathing at Woolloomooloo baths, perhaps?' Elly looked demure.

'How can you be so improper? No, we are to join a picnic party to the oyster beds out in the bay.'

'Where you will gorge yourselves and have a perfectly lovely day. I'm so glad you've found a companion, Jo-Beth. You must live in the present, not the past, however much it pulls at you. Will you introduce me to your captain when opportunity arises?'

'Of course. If you will make me known to the great business entrepreneur, after he has wined and dined you. Do go, Elly. There can be no harm in it.'

Elly stood up. 'Very well, I *shall* go, if only for the pleasure of a meal which has not been scorched in our depressing kitchen. Meanwhile, you, Nurse Assistant Loring, may find me two jars for my "sumptuous" arrangements. We'll put them in the wards and see whether they cheer our patients.'

One of Elly's particular joys was midwifery. Helping new life into the world made such a change from disease and death, and she eagerly emulated the Viennese doctor, Semmelweis, whose mothers and babies thrived while in other hospitals the fatality rate expanded at a horrifying rate. To this end Elly scalded or chemically cleaned any item likely to come into contact with her mothers; also, while barred by the Board's orders from actively persuading attending doctors to wash in chloride of lime, she always had this ready, and some did use it. Nor was she above locking the mortuary and losing the key on days when women expected to deliver, thus preventing doctors from dissecting cadavers before examining the mothers.

Soon word spread through the community that mothers in her care had a far greater chance of leaving the hospital in good health and with a living child. Women who were neither poor nor indigent, some of whom had lost several children in home births, queried the possibility of lying in at the Sydney Infirmary, thereby causing some embarrassment to Elly plus a good deal of indignation on the part of the divisional doctors. Eventually the Board agreed to let her accompany divisional doctors to private homes, upon request and upon payment of a fee to the hospital. This added to Elly's workload, yet gave her an opportunity to see how the upper echelons of the Colony lived. She also learned how nursing generally was regarded—as a lowly living unsuited to any woman with pretensions to gentility.

Elly continued to worry about Mrs Wynham's baby. She'd called on Dr Houston's expertise and he'd responded with all his knowledge and experience, but the child was clearly failing. Added to this worry was Paul Gascoigne's accusatory attitude. She couldn't understand it, when the staff had done their utmost for the child. She caught him on the hospital steps one afternoon after visiting hours and insisted on explaining to him each part of the treatment, adding an assurance that his friends were receiving the best available care. Yet he was obviously bitter.

'You've stated often enough how poorly the system operates in this hospital,' he said. 'Why should I believe it's changed merely because you say so?'

His words hurt, but Elly would not retaliate. For some reason

he cared deeply about this family and their lack of progress. 'You
don't have to take my word for it,' she said. 'Just ask Mrs Wynham.
Both Pearl and I have sat up at night with little Anne, trying to
ease her struggles, yet the baby can't thrive. I believe her lungs
were defective from birth. Such children never live long.'

Paul turned away. 'I'm sorry. I expect too much of you. It's so
unjust.'

Elly sighed. 'If you're thinking Anne would have had better
care had she come from a rich family, you're wrong. The district
physician would have called at her home and she'd have lain in a
silken cot, but the treatment would have been the same—and the
end result. I'm terribly sorry, but the baby will soon die. You'll
have to accept it, along with her mother.'

Paul faced her again, meeting her gaze. 'You must wonder at
my interest in this family. I … It's awkward to explain. You're partly
responsible, you know.'

'I?'

'It was something you said to me, about men fighting for their
rights while their women and children died for lack of proper health
care.'

'I remember.'

He shrugged. 'It stayed in my memory. Then one night Sophy
Wynham stopped me in the street, tried to beg money from me.
When I would have brushed her aside, she offered herself to me.
Her actual words were: "For God's sake, don't refuse me, sir. My
children must eat. I'll do anything you want. Just give me a trial."
Then she put on this travesty of a smile and thrust out her bosom,
and collapsed on the paving stones.'

'What then?' Elly had heard too many such stories to be
shocked.

'I gave her a meal and escorted her home. My God, what a place.
That whole Rocks area should be razed and rebuilt. When I saw
the conditions her children lived in I wanted to slap poor Sophy.'

'You blamed her for the men who ran off and left her.'

'I did, and I'm ashamed of it. It didn't take me long to realise
what little choice she'd had. Thrown on the street as a child, she'd
survived as best she could. Do you know she's only twenty years
old?'

Elly caught her breath. Twenty! The girl appeared forty. She said, 'So you decided to help her.'

There was no sign of his usual half smile and his voice had deepened to a growl. 'Someone had to. They were all near starvation. I found laundry work for Sophy where she could keep her baby with her, and I kept an eye on them. Then she and the babe fell ill, so I brought them here, to you.'

'So now you feel I've failed them.'

'No. I shouldn't have blamed you. I apologise.'

'What other reason did you have for championing the Wynhams? You said I was only partly responsible.'

Paul walked to the foot of the steps and stood with his back to her, hands in pockets, his shoulders hunched. He said bleakly, 'Poverty and malnutrition cost me my whole family, through no fault of my parents, I might add, except for my father's too easy trust in the word of a so-called gentleman. He was a proud man, John Gascoigne, giving others credit for the same honesty of character as his own. When that trust was betrayed, he found himself transported for a crime he could never have committed. I left school and went into the mills, but could not earn enough to feed us. Then Mother decided we must go to Australia and try to be near my father. Without money for fares, we sailed steerage. I shan't detail that particular circle of hell, only say the conditions were such that when typhoid swept through the ship, Mother, weakened by grief and lack of decent food, died, along with the babe she carried. My sister followed within the week, leaving me to bring the news to an already broken man. He was … killed soon after. I became self-supporting at fourteen. There's little I don't know about street life and the struggles of the poor.'

He turned to Elly. 'So those are my reasons for standing by Sophy and her children—a mixture of quixotism, shame and childhood memory.' He sketched a bow, rammed his hat on and left swiftly.

Elly watched him go, musing over their conversation, hardly able to equate this Paul with the one she thought she knew. She could easily imagine Paul as a tough little street-arab, and she ached for the child he'd been, wondering that he'd done so well. Someone other than his father must have taken an interest in his upbringing. She'd have liked to know more, but doubted whether Paul's reticence about his personal affairs could be probed. Besides, to get close enough for such intimate questions could be dangerous. She'd already made up her mind on that subject.

Elly sighed and walked back up the steps, thinking of all the things she must do before she would be free to dine with D'Arcy Cornwallis tonight.

That evening Elly found herself at the Cafe Restaurant Francais, delighted with the delicious food—an eye-widening array of seafood, viands, vegetables and side dishes such as she'd never tasted before. Her earlier misgivings now totally dispelled, she was able to appreciate her escort's attention to her comfort and entertainment. Cornwallis's behaviour, whether assisting her from the carriage outside the Prince of Wales Theatre in Castlereagh Street, or laying her cloak about her shoulders, was scrupulous. As for the entertainment, Toccarini's magnificent tenor voice had sealed the night forever in her memory. Music had never touched her before, never had the chance. But tonight it had awoken something, and the glorious soaring notes were locked within, to remind her that amidst the pain and drudgery of life, there was also great beauty.

Cornwallis escorted her home in an open carriage for all the world to see that her good name remained uncompromised. It was the long way back, of course, through the Domain, yet plenty of people were about, either driving or strolling in the balmy spring night. The gentle clop of hooves, the jingle of harness, the swaying motion of the carriage, all combined like a lullaby to soothe Elly into a state of utter relaxation. Knowing the outing had almost ended, she leaned back with a regretful sigh, the rustle of her silk gown an almost forgotten pleasure to her ears. Her jade earbobs, borrowed from Jo-Beth, dangled against her neck, and she could smell the perfume of the rose tucked into the bosom of her evening gown, one of Cornwallis's roses.

Cornwallis. What did she really think of him? Earlier at dinner, a barrier of starched napery and silver separating them, she had been conscious of his magnetism. Not precisely handsome, his features were striking in the dark Byronic mode, although without the brooding manner associated with the poet. She'd describe them as strong, even heavy, with an expressive mouth which could by turns become arrogant or persuasive. Yet his conversation had been impeccably impersonal until she had questioned him about his interests. He'd been willing enough to inform her.

'One of my principle interests is in land ownership. There has always been a desperate hunger for land in this Colony, ever since men spread out beyond the confines of the Sydney Basin. Most of the best pasture was taken up by the squatters, who had the means to afford to keep themselves and stock the holdings until they made a decent return. Their leaseholds run from the edges of the heavily settled areas right out to the dry west, and they currently hold these until 1862 at the latest. One leading subject of public debate is who uses the land after that date.'

Elly took a sip of wine. 'It hardly seems fair for one small section of the community to hold so much land. I've heard it said these squatters, having paid a pittance for their leaseholds, now make huge tax-free profits.' She didn't mention Paul Gascoigne as her source of information.

'True. Yet they were pioneers. Don't they deserve consideration for all the heartbreaking labour they've put into what were often wastelands? For the risks they ran?'

'I can see justice will be difficult to ensure when the time comes. A lot of little people will want to take up a selection and spread their roots in their new country.'

Cornwallis flicked a finger towards the waiter and ordered more wine, saying easily, 'The little people, as you call them, have always lost to wealth and influence. It's the way of the world.'

'Do you think that makes it right?'

He leaned forward, smiling. 'By no means. I have the utmost respect for anyone prepared to battle his way above the crowd to take what he wants. Such men are all too rare.'

Elly's thoughts went to Paul Gascoigne, prepared to do battle not for his own advancement alone, but for all the little men whose only strength lay in combining against a wealthy autocracy. She was discovering unsought socialist sympathies in herself.

Cornwallis watched her, amused. 'I see you believe me to be one of the plutocrats, or at least a sympathiser.'

'Are you?'

'The answer is yes, to both indictments. I am of my class and naturally support it. I own land which adjoins Mr MacArthur's property at Camden, from which I derive profits and which provides employment for twenty men and women. In the days of convict labour, so bitterly regretted, there were some fifty or more engaged in clearing and building for me. I paid a small enough sum for the land. However, I've also added such improvements as a homestead, housing for employees, fences, wells and dams. I stocked the pastures then put in a manager to free me to live in the town and pursue business activities here. One day I shall have to leave the colony when I inherit my father's estate, but I shall leave these shores richer for my having been here.'

He paused and amended: 'I mean the shores will be richer, as well as my own coffers. I'm one of that band of entrepreneurs who will develop the Colony, not merely exploit it. With our wealth and background we are in a position to do this. The little man is not.'

Elly frowned, but remained silent. Then their talk drifted into wider cultural avenues where Elly, although inexperienced, held her own. She turned aside any attempt to discuss her own ambitions, resolved to leave the hospital behind for one night. However, unexceptionable as their words might be, she noticed a subtle undercurrent to their exchanges, a delicate emotional probing on the part of Cornwallis which she knew she must withstand. It was flattering and delightful, but hazardous, given her firm plans for the future.

And now the magic night had almost ended. Elly felt, rather than saw Cornwallis's head turn towards her in the dark, the white frill of his shirt front reflecting the moonlight.

'Why do you sigh? Are you weary?'

'Not at all. I sighed because the evening is almost finished and I don't know how long it will be before I enjoy such another.' Realising how ambiguous this sounded, she added: 'Because I can't get away from my duties. We're still so short-staffed, even with the addition of Malone and Irvine.'

'Surely you can delegate to others. The competence of your training has been noted, believe me. And you must long for more in life than a never-ending devotion to duty. You're too intelligent not to want more.' His voice, so warm and interested, played on her like music. She felt his shoulder sway against hers with the motion of the carriage, his hand press hers before he moved back.

For a moment Elly was tempted to give way to the spell of the night and begin to weave fantasies of a life which included more than hard work and ambition. Did she want to wear herself down to a taper in the service of others, only to flicker and burn out at the end, never having known the joys and heartbreaks of marriage and children?

She answered her own question immediately. She knew what she wanted, and it was not this present singing in the blood—a mere physical attraction, a pointless indulgence when measured against her great ambition. She'd already decided she had no time for romantic attachment, not even a deep friendship which might sap her will to fight and draw her away from the battlefield. Yet this man's magnetic personality pulled, not just at her senses, but also at her intellect. He challenged her to meet him on a level few women were expected to reach. Only Paul Gascoigne had come close, with his ability to burrow beneath her calm facade and goad her into opposition. D'Arcy Cornwallis didn't burrow or goad. He asked her opinion, then argued a different viewpoint with tact and a sweet deference all too soothing to someone accustomed to having her opinions swept aside as negligible. A *very* dangerous man, Cornwallis.

She sat up straight, banishing the insidious languor. 'Look, over there. It's a rally of some kind.'

'A speaker on his box, with the usual crowd in attendance.' He sounded bored.

'Oh, I'd love to hear him. I've never listened to a speaker in the Domain. Could we not go closer?' Unable to see his face, she sensed his displeasure.

'Of course. If you wish it.' He directed the coachman to draw up and assisted Elly to alight, then escorted her across the grass to the fringes of the crowd. They seemed a happy enough group, although interjections forced the speaker to raise his voice. In the light of a nearby lantern Elly recognised Paul Gascoigne, in the middle of an impassioned argument with his listeners.

'I know that man,' Cornwallis said. 'He's one of Parkes's tribe of iconoclasts. You won't learn much of value from his speech.'

'What does he usually talk about?'

'The rights of the common man is his favourite topic, which can be stretched to include every kind of entitlement imaginable, including, if you can believe me, a common labourer's right to vote for a representative in government.'

'I suppose one could call it iconoclasm.'

'It's madness. Wentworth has to stop it.'

Elly looked at him. Shadows flickered across his face, altering the noble profile and twisting the strong features into something quite satyric. Elly must have gasped, for Cornwallis turned, shattering the illusion with his smile.

'I've talked enough politics for one night. Do you want to move in closer to hear what this fellow has to say?'

Elly shook her head. 'It's late. I'd better go back.'

She climbed wearily into the carriage, her marvellous mood dissipated. Why did politics have to enter into everything? She couldn't escape it, inside the hospital or out.

Five minutes later she stood at the infirmary's main door which Cornwallis opened for her. He bent suddenly and brought her fingers to his lips.

'Miss Ballard, I cannot recall having enjoyed an evening more. Thank you for your excellent company.'

'Sir, I can only return the compliment and wish you a good night's rest.' Regaining her hand, Elly stepped inside and closed the door.

A candle had been left ready for her, but the sounds from upstairs warned that others were still about. She hurried up to the landing to be met by Pearl, an amused quirk to her lips.

'Come quickly. We have had a disaster.'

'What sort of disaster? Where?'

Elly accompanied her into one of the men's wards where her senses were immediately assailed by noise and an overpowering stench of scorched linen. Patients had left their beds to group together, some almost hysterical with laughter, others wailing in dismay. Nurse Malone and Jo-Beth, clutching empty buckets, stood on either side of a drenched, blackened cot, while four burly wardsmen sat on two other men on the floor. The persons being sat upon protested loudly, their yells mingled with those of the patients.

Grasping Jo-Beth's pail, Elly flung it into the middle of the room, where it landed with a mighty crack and split open. The din diminished instantly, to the point where she could be heard. 'Be silent, all of you.'

The two men pinned to the floor continued to shout words unintelligible to Elly. She could now see they were native islanders, their glossy brown limbs splayed and kicking, their faces beneath their crowns of woolly hair distorted with rage.

She turned to Pearl, who had her sleeve across her mouth. 'Kindly tell me what's going on here.'

Pearl pointed to the wardsmen. 'They have to sit on them. Otherwise they will start the fire again.'

Elly approached the cot, grimly surveying the smouldering mattress and the scorched sheet covering a suspiciously motionless patient, also an islander. Jo-Beth met her gaze.

'It's all right. He was not burned alive.'

'You relieve my mind.' Elly turned on the wardsmen, heaving under the struggles of their prisoners. 'How did these men get in? Visitors are never permitted at night.'

The wardsmen shuffled sheepishly and did not answer.

'You were bribed, I suppose.' Elly turned to Nurse Malone who was clutching the bucket to her apron. 'Why did these men set the bed afire?'

The girl put down the bucket, answering dazedly, 'I think … They say they were conducting a cremation.'

Elly hoped her jaw hadn't fallen open. 'A cremation! In the ward, on the bed?'

Jo-Beth nodded. 'It seems it's their custom. Something to do with sending the spirit onward as soon as it leaves the body. It … It does seem an hygienic method of disposal.' She disciplined her expression, but her voice verged on horrified laughter.

Pearl's snort was immediately drowned in a roar from the floor and a surge of words which most certainly would not have translated politely. Dismissing an urge to throw up her hands and leave, Elly issued her orders, which included sending for Dr Houston and more wardsmen to replace her nurses, who were rapidly becoming the focus of lewd attention by the male patients. Nobody focused on her, except to try to avoid her eagle eye.

By the time Elly could go to her own bed, the romantic trappings of her evening had dissipated entirely, and she had reverted once more to the real core, Elly Ballard, Acting Matron very much in charge and responsible for just about everything.

Chapter Fifteen

Despite having yielded the once, Elly was now determined to dispense with a social life and threw herself into her work, refusing all distraction. Elegantly worded invitations from D'Arcy Cornwallis were politely declined in notes as formal and elegant; and while Paul Gascoigne's agenda clearly kept him busy, he found the time to knock on Elly's door on two further occasions with an invitation to walk with him and Pepper. After several unequivocal refusals, Paul ceased to ask. Even JG, bouncing in with his usual verve to try to drag Elly out for a drink at his favourite pub, had no success. She simply refused to socialise.

Baby Anne Wynham died, as predicted, with the mother following soon after, much to Elly's distress. She hardly knew how to tell Paul, but he laid no blame on anyone, saying he believed Sophy to have given up on life long before her illness. The sad loss of the baby had been the final blow.

To add to Elly's troubles, the pinpricks from the less loyal members of the staff had escalated into defiance, forcing her to draw on all her tact and patience to hold off open warfare. She knew her position was not yet strong enough. Her appointment had not been fully confirmed, nor would it be if she disregarded the Board's warning not to antagonise the medical staff. The pity was *they* seemed bent on antagonising *her.*

The situation had reached a ridiculous point, she thought, when for the third day in a row a patient had been admitted with the attending physician refusing to give staff any indication of the patient's condition or illness. Notes were withheld and the confused nurses later accused of not giving proper care. Worse, they were not being informed when a patient had been listed for surgery, which meant certain essential preparations such as the administration of castor oil, were not carried out in time, with the blame again falling on the nursing staff. Elly's requests for this situation to be rectified were noted by the visiting weekly committee, then dismissed. Her anger swelled. Her patients were not being treated well in this petty battling for superiority.

Matters were not improved by the Board's delay in supplying money for essential repairs, and their promise to provide training facilities had not been fulfilled. Just about all Elly had achieved in the past eight months, it seemed to her, were a few coats of white-wash, a new stove and two extra unfledged nurses.

Her ire reached a peak on the day when a child of no more than twelve was refused admission on the grounds that she did not have a good moral character, having come from a brothel in Durand's Alley, an area as notorious as the Rocks for filth and depravity. Despite an argument with the physician on duty, which almost descended into a physical battle with the child torn between them, Elly lost.

Jo-Beth found Elly in the storeroom kicking a flour bag and swearing—something she'd never have done a year ago.

'Elly, this isn't like you.' Jo-Beth urged her to sit down. 'Why are you so distressed? We've seen worse cases turned aside.'

Elly paced the tiny space, her arms tightly folded, her voice thick with rage. 'I'm tired of running into brick walls, tired of boards and committees and superior professionals whose aim in life is to thwart me. If it were just me they injured it wouldn't matter so much. But did you see that child's face? Did you? Just an abused waif, sick and terrified, and I'm prevented from helping her. One day soon, through no fault of her own, she'll die in a gutter of her venereal disease and not one soul will care.'

'We know you care very much, Elly. I care too. Until I came

here I never knew the world held such misery. But you of all people must know it does no good to batter yourself emotionally when you have no power to overcome such problems.'

'I *should* have the power. Who are these men to tell me whom I may nurse? Who are they to say one person shall be helped and another turned away?' Elly ground her teeth.

'They're the medical officers appointed by the Board which runs this hospital. They and their overlords may be arrogant, penny-pinching, moralistic and totally lacking in empathy, but they are in charge. You have to come to terms with it, Elly.'

Elly stopped pacing and faced her. 'You're absolutely right. I know I must work deviously, not confront them as a man would, but, oh, Jo-Beth, it hurts me.'

Jo-Beth put comforting arms around her friend. 'I know. I know. But there is a solution you have overlooked. Have you forgotten the nuns who sometimes visit in the wards?'

'The Sisters of Charity from the refuge. How stupid of me! Of course they'd take in the child. I'll visit them this evening.' Elly straightened up. 'I'm back to normal now, thanks to you, my dear, and heartily ashamed of my fall from commonsense.'

'Nonsense. You just need a cup of tea.'

'There isn't time. I've sent for a supply of leeches for little Lilly Smith. Dr Wykeham wants her bled slowly, rather than cupped. It's not a pleasant process, even for an adult who can understand the purpose, and I'm hoping she'll sleep through it.'

'I'll come with you. We can talk while we work. I doubt whether little Lilly will pass on any secrets, asleep or awake.'

Fighting down the disgust that the voracious little worms always engendered, Elly accepted the jar of leeches from the porter, lifting them one by one, black and dripping, from the fresh water and lying them on a cloth. Their slimy segments contracted at her touch, curling up like snails without their shells.

Jo-Beth shuddered at the sight. 'Horrible parasites. How do we attach them?'

Elly put a finger to her lips, indicating the sleeping child. 'They'll do it themselves, with their sucker mouths. But we lay them over a bone so that, if necessary, pressure may be applied.' Elly carefully wiped Lilly's forearms with a few droplets of milk, then laid three of the leeches on each arm. They attached immediately and began to gorge. The child stirred without waking.

White-faced, Jo-Beth pressed a hand over her mouth and swallowed. 'When do you remove them?'

'That, too, the leeches decide. When they've drunk their fill they simply let go and roll off. We can't pull them without tearing the skin. However, a little sprinkled salt will encourage them to release it.' Elly smiled bleakly. 'You will grow accustomed.'

She had drawn a screen around the patient's bed—an innovation of her own about which the Board had not been consulted—and felt as private with Jo-Beth as it was possible to be in this communal life of theirs. She took time to study her, finally saying, 'Jo-Beth, what's amiss? I know you're not happy and that's understandable, given all that's happened. Yet I feel there's more.'

Jo-Beth dragged her fascinated gaze from the swelling leeches. 'Very little escapes you, does it? However, I've decided I must not add to your burdens. It's unimportant, I assure you.' She rose and walked away to the window overlooking the courtyard.

Elly was struck by her grace. The brown uniform gown, an honorary distinction from the trainee nurses, could not mar her elegant carriage, her features refined by grief and hard work, draped by the red-gold hair drawn back from a centre part and confined in a roll at the nape. Just the hint of white ruffle at throat and wrist demonstrated an innate femininity, even in work dress. This woman, however kind-hearted, would never be suited to a nursing career. Yet with her good mind and background, she might have gone anywhere, to the salons of Europe, even the royal courts; as the wife of a diplomat or career officer she'd be invaluable.

Elly said on impulse, 'Captain McAndrews is growing most attentive. He's highly connected, I believe?'

Jo-Beth turned. 'That's so. He's also quite modest concerning his family, a refreshing change. Yes, I do enjoy his company, and no, I have no intention of encouraging him to make any advances. How could I put him in Ethan's place?'

'Of course not. The idea is unthinkable.' But was it? Jo-Beth couldn't grieve forever. She had youth and beauty, and when she forgot her sadness, a vitality which drew others to her. She'd certainly captivated Captain McAndrews, a perfectly nice man, as Elly had been assured; a man who could offer Jo-Beth the kind of life she was always intended to lead. Elly heard a sigh and a yawn, and leapt up to lean over her small patient, covering her arms with a sheet.

'Hello, darling. Did you have a good sleep? I have a surprise for you if you will lie quite still while I fix your arms.' She called Jo-Beth to hold the sheet in place across the girl's chest, while Elly herself raised the other end and removed the engorged leeches. As she had predicted, most of them had rolled off Lilly's arms onto the cot, and when encouraged with salt, the last one released its hold to join its fellows. Elly replaced them in the jar, which she hid under the cot.

Elly staunched the bleeding with wax and olive oil plasters, then removed the sheet. She smiled, patting the child's thin cheek, surprised to receive a wan smile in return.

'S'prise,' Lilly said hopefully.

'You shall certainly have your surprise, my dear. Jo-Beth, do you suppose our little friend would like a visit from a real monkey?'

Christmas loomed on the horizon and the hot weather blasted in from the deserts, driving a dry westerly wind across Sydney, flinging up stinging particles in faces, sifting beneath doors and windowsills, scraping nerves and generally creating misery. In the hospital Elly dragged the weekly committee mercilessly through wards heated like ovens with the windows closed against the wind and stench, inventing reasons to keep the members sweating into their unsuitably heavy jackets, even denying them the comfort of the boardroom and a glass of sherry by arranging to have the room redecorated for Christmas. The operating theatres were hellholes. If she could, Elly would have locked the committee in to experience vicariously every moment of terror and pain suffered there; but they made good their escape, then found reasons to send others in their place the following week.

Elly's expression grew more and more grim as she went back to battle with raging infections and fever-induced delirium with no ice available and the water supply to the Hyde Park bore now regularly cut off between the hours of three p.m. and six p.m. Any patients admitted between those hours, even those for emergency surgery, remained unbathed.

When Pearl knocked at Matron's office door late one night, she found her buried in paperwork. Elly raised a weary head in question.

'Matron, I have to tell you I will be leaving soon after Christmas.' Pearl stood formally, hands clasped.

Elly sighed. 'We're off duty now Pearl. Sit down and give me more details.'

Pearl relaxed and sat down. She surveyed the pile of reports, receipts, submissions. 'You work so hard, Elly, and I'm sorry to leave you like this. But I did warn you that I intended to go to the goldfields when I had enough money saved.'

'And now you have enough?' Elly thought how worn Pearl looked, like everyone else on staff; however, light glowed beneath the translucent ivory skin and she had an air of hope and excitement.

'I believe so. I don't want to wait any longer. I need to find Li Po.'

Elly nodded. 'Pearl, have you considered that you'll be hundreds of miles away in a bleak, comfortless area where strong men die of the conditions? You're not robust and you will have no protector in a brash and lawless society. The risks are enormous.'

Pearl's face set in stubborn lines. 'I have to go. I have to find Li Po.'

'Do you have any idea of where to begin?'

'I shall go to each camp in turn, starting from the town of Bathurst over the ranges.'

'Can I help? Do you need food, medical equipment?' Elly didn't waste her breath with further talk of danger, and she certainly wouldn't point out her own need for Pearl's trained hands and mind. Letting her go without argument was part of their agreement.

Pearl graciously accepted a medical kit and a canvas satchel. 'Also, would you return this package to JG when you see him? It's something he loaned me which I promised to give back. Only, please wait until I'm gone.'

Containing her curiosity, Elly put the package away in her cabinet then began to discuss possible dates, with Pearl agreeing to wait until mid-January to book a place on a wagon going over the mountains to Bathurst. Elly agreed, somewhat reluctantly, to take care of little Peanut, still technically under official banishment but in fact living in the nurses' new quarters over the large storeroom, sunning herself on the windowsill by day and enjoying the nuts and fruit supplied by Pearl at night.

At the door Pearl turned. 'Elly, you have been kind.'

'That's what a friend is for. You owe me nothing, Pearl, although the hospital owes you a great deal. I'd like to thank you for your unstinting help.' Elly added earnestly, 'And, Pearl, if you will be advised by me, on your travels you'll wear your Chinese trousers and jacket and revert to being a young man.'

Pearl smiled. 'I intend to. They served me well before and, ragged as they are, they'll serve again. Goodnight, Elly.'

'Do you like elephants?'

Elly, immersed in yet more paperwork on a hot December evening, raised her head to blink at her reflection in the glass-fronted cupboard opposite. Elephants? Why did she imagine she'd heard such a question?

'If not elephants, perhaps kangaroos and emus?'

She swivelled towards the door and saw Paul Gascoigne's tall frame leaning against the jamb. Something in her leapt at the sight, which made her stiffen and eye him with cool enquiry.

'I thought they might be more enticing than just Pepper and me,' he explained. 'As an inducement to an outing, that is.'

'I don't go on—'

'Ah, but it's Christmastide, or almost. Everyone goes on outings then. It's a commandment.'

Elly relaxed into a smile and beckoned him in. 'Whose commandment?'

'Mine. I just brought it down as number eleven.'

'Don't be sacrilegious.'

'Madame! Nothing could be further from my mind. Anyway, if it isn't a commandment, it ought to be. We should be made to celebrate the birth of the Christ Child. It's a joyous occasion, whatever else we believe.'

This was a new Paul, thought Elly, more light-hearted, intent on cajoling her with the same methods used by JG.

He seemed to catch her thought. 'Don't dare tell me I sound like JG. He's already swollen-headed over his success with the ladies, even daring to offer me lessons.'

'I don't think you need any.' Elly indicated the chair opposite her desk. 'But if you wish to prick the bladder of JG's self-importance, just mention a certain lady named Pearl.'

Paul laughed as he carefully lowered himself into the chair.

'Have you hurt yourself, Mr Gascoigne?'

'A bruise from a badly aimed brick. It's little enough. Can't you bring yourself to use my Christian name after all this time?'

She said slowly: 'I suppose I may. Paul, then. At least in private.' Her expression was as mischievous as JG's. 'My name is Eleanor.'

'What a strict, corsetted name. Lovely for introductions to the Governor, yet hardly to be used by a friend. I shall call you Nell.'

'You dare!'

'I won't, of course, Elly. Now, to celebrate our new mutual status, friend, will you accompany me on an outing to see the elephants?'

Elly stared. 'You really mean it? Where?'

'Botany Bay. Have you never heard of the Sir Joseph Banks Hotel's Annual Boxing Day Gala? It includes a circus, menagerie, dancing and dining, and a walk along the beach to follow.'

Despite her resolution, Elly was overwhelmed with longing at the thought of such festivity. How wonderful to get away from the eternal tensions under this roof, just for a day. And elephants! She had a momentary vision of a set of scales, with the hospital balanced on one side and a heap of ponderous grey pachyderms on the other, tipping the scale downward.

With the air of playing a trump card, Paul added, 'Of course, one travels by sea, down the coast on the most magnificent steamer in Port Jackson. It even has a bar and quadrille band for entertainment aboard to while away the tedium of the voyage.'

Tedium. Elly thought of the sea wind blowing in her hair, of music, laughter and companionship, and she succumbed.

'Thank you. I'd love to come, as you must well realise. I'll arrange with the others for my time away to be covered.'

Paul showed no elation. However there was a hint of self-satisfaction there, enough to cause her a few qualms. Her doubt turned to annoyance. But she'd accepted the invitation; she'd go and she would enjoy herself. To compensate for her inner turmoil, she abandoned her intended enquiry into the incident of the brick. It might be childish of her, but if Paul wanted to play at political pattacake with opponents who reinforced their arguments with violence, it could remain his own affair.

Christmas Day passed swiftly in the usual duties, combined with snatched attendance at divine service as and when staff could be spared. Fortunately, there were no new admissions to the women's wards, and by the following morning Elly knew she could leave her nurses with a clear conscience.

Pearl and Jo-Beth saw her off joyfully, assuring her of their ability to handle all conceivable problems.

Paul led her up the gangplank of the *Sir John Harvey* with an admiring glance at her striped blue and white cotton gown and her frilled parasol adjusted to shade the new straw bonnet.

'Oh, how I've dreamed of this trip,' Elly exclaimed as she stepped onto the deck. 'I haven't been on the water since our excursion down from Port Stephens, when I behaved so rudely to you.'

'We've agreed to forget our differences. Come up to the bow for the best view of our progress down the harbour. If you're extremely well behaved I might even buy you a beer.'

For Elly, the trip was all she had hoped for, enveloped in a halcyon blue and gold aura of sunlight, fresh air and freedom. As they passed between the sandstone cliffs, emerging into the ocean and turning south, her cares fell away. She took off her bonnet to feel the breeze, confident that the false coiled plaits she wore pinned over her ears covered the tips of her hair, hiding its true length. Strolling about the deck on Paul's arm, she exchanged greetings with fellow passengers all dressed for festivity. They were a living reflection of Sydney Town: tradesmen and their wives, apprentices, butchers' boys, milliners and maids, clerks, booksellers, waiters, teachers and even the poulterer who supplied the hospital's needs. Elly bowed sedately when they met and passed on, her eyes twinkling as she confided to Paul that she scarcely recognised Mr Scrubshaw without his apron.

Paul whispered how he'd already exchanged greetings with his wine merchant. 'And over there, the exceedingly well-turned out gentleman with the flower in his lapel, he's Hanslow the director of our fashionable obsequies.'

Elly cast a critical eye on the lady accompanying Mr Hanslow, deciding she could not be his wife. In fact, several of the ladies aboard had the sort of dashing air seldom seen in consorts.

As before, Paul caught her thought. 'It's mixed company. I thought you'd rather enjoy it. The stuffier carriage folk will be at the Gala, but they'll go by road, through the heat and dust.'

'You're quite right,' Elly agreed. 'I wouldn't have missed the boat trip for any money. I couldn't have thrown off my bonnet and kicked up my heels with the "carriage folk" on the watch. Oh, I'm as carefree as one of those gulls.' She pirouetted lightly, pointing to the cluster of birds wheeling overhead. 'Thank you for bringing me, Paul.'

'The gratitude is all mine. Christmas is a lonely time for me.'

Elly's attention was caught by a note of more than ordinary sadness behind the words. Snapping open her parasol and leaning back on the ship's rail, she chose her response with care.

'It can be lonely without someone to share our celebrations. Have you no-one left at all, Paul?'

His profile revealed little. 'No-one. Oh, there is a remote cousin with a wife and child living up near Maitland on the Hunter River. I have no contact with them. They migrated in '48 then immediately sought employment on the land.'

'I don't have family either. But I have friends, and some happy memories.'

Paul gripped the rail. 'Memories!' The word might have been an oath. 'But today is for sunshine and laughter, not bitter memories. Come on, the bar is open. Let's get a drink.'

For a few hours Elly forgot her responsibilities entirely, stepping onto the sandy shores of Botany Bay ready to fling herself

Chapter Fifteen

into whatever was offered. As effervescent as a child, she clapped
wildly at the circus performances, commiserated with the caged
animals in the menagerie then forgot their plight in the excitement of seeing a gentleman well in his cups mount one of the
elephants and take it for a bathe in the sea. She dined on crab and
drank champagne, and whirled around the great dance floor in
Paul's arms, the strings of coloured lamps, lit even in daylight,
swinging dizzily around her, her feet trapped in the rhythm of the
band playing on and on.

Late in the day, sated and light-headed from the music and
dancing, Elly allowed herself to be led down through the groves of
trees towards the beach, a wide curving horseshoe dwindling away
south into sandhills already topped with sea mist. To the west the
Blue Mountains had darkened against a sky streaked in gold as
brilliant as any to be dug from the soil and riverbeds. Elly walked
right down to the edge of the shallow surf creaming in from the
bay and raised her arms, letting the air lift and press her skirts
against her body, rippling her hair, cooling her hot cheeks. For-
getful of time and place, aware only of a sense of repletion, she let
herself drift.

The next moment she was in Paul's arms being thoroughly kissed.
Astonishment held her motionless, followed by a sudden jet of fire
throughout her body, stunning her with its force. Afterwards she
thought of it as a lightning strike, flashing along each nerve until
her whole being vibrated with an extraordinary joy. Paul's warmth
and firmness were an intense delight. Beneath the pressure of his
mouth she opened her lips to him, shivering and clutching at his
shoulders, giving herself over to her first experience of passion.

Then Paul pulled away, keeping a firm hold on her waist. She
saw his confusion, echoing her own. 'Elly ... I didn't know this
would happen. Elly, what have you done to me?'

Her senses swimming, she couldn't have answered him if she'd
had any answer to give. She only knew that the pressure of his
breast on hers, of his hand slipping down her back to hold her
more firmly against his body, was necessary and right and vital to
her happiness, increasing her longing to recapture the delirium
his lips could create.

Gazing into his green eyes, she saw golden flecks dancing there, growing larger, filling her vision as he claimed her mouth again. His fingers travelled down her spine, loosening buttons as they went; her gown slipped, exposing her shoulders, the skin glowing, scorched by his caresses. Her hands were in his hair, letting the dark silky strands slip through her fingers in an intimacy both thrilling and frightening. She pressed his face to her breasts and heard him groan. Her hips arched against his, feeling the rigidity of his erection through the layers of petticoat. She cried out, and his arms relaxed, then tightened again. With a gasp he said, 'Forgive me, Elly.'

Elly rested her head on his chest, the extraordinary excitement ebbing slowly, leaving her limp and unfulfilled. Still held fast in Paul's trembling grasp she tried to calm herself, feeling his heartbeat racing under her cheek.

With his lips on her hair he whispered, 'I've never known such an upheaval in my life. What kind of force lies in you, Elly, that you can tear a man's control to shreds and draw him irresistibly down into such scarcely dreamed of passion?'

She looked up shyly. 'Is it like that for you? I never knew. No-one ever told me ...'

Paul released his hold and drew back, but when Elly staggered he held her up and led her to a nearby rock. 'Sit down, Elly, and I'll button your gown. Don't say any more just yet.'

Elly sat down. Her legs quivered and her breasts ached, sensitive even to the brush of fabric as Paul adjusted her gown. A sudden pain thrust deep in her loins, and she shivered. She wondered if she had started a fever. Then she turned her head and saw Paul's strained expression, saw the hunger there, and knew she was indeed suffering from a fever in the blood which could only be assuaged in this man's embrace.

'For God's sake, Elly, don't look at me like that. Don't hold your mouth as if waiting to be kissed.' Paul abandoned the last button, then turned his back on Elly and walked the few yards down to the water's edge.

All her senses were heightened as she absorbed the sibilant sound of the surf, of the sand sinking back after Paul's passing, of the leaves in the casuarina trees sifting in the wind. She heard a gull's sharp cry and watched it float by on an invisible current, its breast like snow, its wings the colour of moor mist, its beak a dot of blood against the darkening sky. The harsh smell of the eucalypts blended with a wild honey scent from boronia and other native blossoms. Elly breathed deeply, saturating her memory with the aromas of this moment, fixing them in amber, captured and held until she died. The rock beneath her was cold and hard, and she knew the time had come for her to return to reality. She rose and went to stand beside Paul, not touching him, drinking in the strong profile silhouetted against the sky.

'Paul, we have to be sensible.'

He laughed, without amusement.

'No, listen. We're not heedless young ones to tumble headlong into love and think the world well lost for it.'

He took her face between his hands. 'Is it love, Elly? Is this overwhelming need and pain and joy what love really is?'

'I ... think so. I only know I want to show you tenderness, as well as desire, I want—' She broke off.

'Elly, I love you, too. I want to spend my life with you, caring for you.'

The tenderness in his voice moved her unbearably, yet her resolve stiffened. Gently she released herself, saying: 'Do you, Paul? Or do you mean you want me to run your home, entertain at your political parties, be your helpmeet, give up my ambitions?'

'I'm talking about loving and caring. I want you to be my wife. Yes, it would entail these things—'

'And sacrifice, Paul. *My* sacrifice. Would *you* give up your ambitions if I asked you to?'

His brows rose and there was a twist to his mouth as he countered, 'Would *you*, Elly?'

They stared at one another, Elly appalled at the swift dashing down from the sublime heights she'd just experienced, and at the knowledge that she'd done it to herself. 'I'm so sorry,' she whispered.

'As am I.'

The torment shadowing his face made her want to take back her words, to tell him she couldn't hurt him like this, that she'd love him forever, be whatever he wanted her to be. Instead she held his gaze steadily, imposing on herself the strongest, hardest discipline she'd ever had to employ. There could be no room in her life for the kind of love she'd just awakened to. It was all-consuming. It would eat up her ambition and leave just the shell of the real Elly Ballard, which would be no good to her or to the man who wanted her.

'It could never satisfy either of us to bring only half of ourselves to a marriage,' she told him. 'We're so much alike, Paul, so centred on our ambitions. I must honour a trust, while you ... you are driven by something more, a bitterness with its roots in a past you can't relinquish. In such a climate our love would eventually be destroyed.'

He turned to stare out over the bay. 'I'm afraid you're right, my love. You will always be my love, whatever else may happen.'

And you will always be mine, Elly said in her heart, but not aloud.

They walked back to the hotel in heavy silence.

Chapter Sixteen

A wave hit the wharf, shaking the planks beneath Pearl's feet. Between the cracks she could see water, dark green and oily, with tendrils of weed sucking around the piles just below the tideline. The backwash of passing ferry boats sent a fresh series of waves, rippling and slapping. The wharf shivered.

Inside, Pearl shivered too. This was the moment she'd long been planning for, when she set off alone once more. Beside her a small paddle-steamer with bright red wheels and white superstructure bobbed like a child's toy, tugging against the ropes bound around the bollards. It had an eager air about it, as though anxious to be on its way. As she was, at last, on her way to find Li Po and the kinship that would heal the inner wound dealt by the Taiping just a year ago.

She had left the hospital early to avoid any emotional farewells. The break should be made cleanly, she thought, like a knife cut. Detachment focused the mind, and to create detachment one must be alone, without ties of relationship, or even friendship. Elly Ballard had achieved this admirably, with her total focus on her ambition. However, Jo-Beth remained a puzzle, professing to believe that fate could be changed by will alone and her dead lover returned to her, even while she accepted the homage of her military admirer. She might have come from a distant star, with her outlook on the world so opposite to Pearl's. Jo-Beth had only recently learned what it was to fight for survival. Raised in a cushioned environment, she had this soft underbelly, an invitation to the rippers and kickers of the world. How long would she endure her present circumstances before having to accept Ethan Petherbridge's death? How long before she escaped back to family support in Boston, or into marriage with someone who would take care of her?

Dismissing these perplexities, Pearl picked up her canvas satchel, a present from Elly, as were the stout boots peeping incongruously from beneath her padded trousers. She'd go aboard now, grateful for the ticket upriver to Parramatta, a parting gift from her friends. From there she would find a cart crossing the Blue Mountains to Bathurst.

'Pearl, wait! Don't go yet!'

What seemed a carriageload of nurses tumbled out onto the wharf and ran towards her, while from another direction two men pounded up from the Customs House waving their hats and hallooing. Pearl hesitated, flushed to the hairline, unsure whether to be delighted or distressed.

JG reached her first, puffing like leaky bellows and forced to lean on a bollard to fan himself with his hat.

'You might ... have let a fellow ... know the departure time.'

Pearl frowned. 'I gave Elly your watch to return to you. I told you I would not sell it.'

'Be damned ... to the watch. You've been avoiding me, girl dear.'

'Sit down before you fall down, you silly man. You should not have run so hard.'

Paul, only two steps behind, shook his head at her, grinning. 'Ungrateful girl, when he simply wanted to say "Godspeed". It's why we all came.'

'Yes, indeed.' Jo-Beth rushed to envelop Pearl's slight frame in a hug. 'You wretch, to slip away like that.'

The two trainee nurses, staunch admirers of Pearl, nodded shyly in the background.

Pearl set her teeth. She would not be the victim of her emotions. She would stay in control. Her eyes suspiciously bright, she scanned the faces in the group, seeing the love and goodwill for her there.

'Thank you. I didn't want to trouble anyone ...'

'Trouble!' mocked JG. 'Girl dear, it's a lying tongue you have in your pretty little head. You wanted to slip away on the quiet, keeping to yourself, as ever. Well, we're your friends and we won't allow it.'

'Hear, hear.' Elly surged forward to kiss Pearl's cheek. 'I'm afraid you'll have to put up with us. We need you, even if you think you don't need us. Also, we expect to have regular news of you, wherever you go.'

Jo-Beth beamed as she handed a small parcel to Pearl. 'This is for you. I hope you find it useful.'

Unwrapped, the gift was revealed as a hinged sweet tin which, when opened, emitted a strong eucalyptus aroma.

'It's an antiseptic grease made up to a recipe I found in the dispensary. Very useful for cuts and abrasions and for colds when rubbed on the throat, and, oh, all manner of things.'

Pearl couldn't trust her voice. Handling the tin as if it contained emeralds, she put it in her satchel alongside the medical kit, food and linen. The paddle-steamer gave a toot, making them all jump, and steam poured from its funnel.

Paul thumped JG on the back, almost knocking him off his feet. 'She'll leave any minute. Go on, man.'

JG drew his thin frame erect, bowed, then presented Pearl with a folded sheet of paper. 'A parting gift from the two of us, girl dear. It's a mere sketch, but the best we could put together. Maybe it will help you.'

She stared at the paper through a blur, gradually distinguishing the markings. It proved to be a roughly drawn map of the established goldfields, with tracks, distances and useful information on transport, stores and accommodation. To a prospector it would be worth a good deal. She wondered how the men had obtained it and at what cost. Meeting JG's eyes, she saw their merriment quenched, for once, by an unaccustomed sadness. But it couldn't be. Her going would only lose him a sparring partner, not even a friend. She deliberately shifted her gaze to Paul. 'Thank you, both. It will be a great help.'

The steamer gave another warning toot. Pearl thrust the map in her pocket. 'Thank you all, my good friends. I'll think of you every day. Goodbye.' She turned and hurried up the plank onto the deck.

The others crowded forward to the edge of the wharf as seamen untied ropes and removed the plank. Imperceptibly a gap widened between wharf and vessel. The great wheels began to turn, paddles flashing wetly as they dipped and rose, churning the oily green water to foam. The engine thundered, a shudder rattled through the body of the ship as it slowly turned towards the west.

Oblivious of the gulls screaming overhead, of wind pulling at her braid, Pearl stood watching the wharf and the group of people on it dwindle into a speck on the horizon.

Elly moved briskly back to the carriage, avoiding Paul's eye. 'Come along, ladies. I'm uneasy with Nurse Jenkins in charge, even for an hour.'

As a voice hailed the group, she glanced around to see Captain McAndrews, whom she'd met several weeks ago, hurrying along the wharf, dressed in full regimentals.

Whipping off his cap, he bowed. 'I'm sorry to be late. I've just come off duty and hurried away as soon as I could. I see I've lost the opportunity to farewell Miss Pearl.'

His pleasant face only irritated Elly on this occasion. She was in no mood for socialising. But she instantly regretted her peevishness. The captain couldn't sense her anxiety; nor should he be blamed for placing his duties as a governor's equerry before his personal desires. She gave him a warm smile as Jo-Beth greeted him composedly.

'Good morning, Captain. Yes, unfortunately the boat has left and we shan't see Pearl for a long time, I fear. Let me make you known to these ladies and gentlemen.'

While introductions were made Elly tried not to tap her foot, avoiding looking at Paul, although very aware of his close proximity. Her skin tingled and she thought she would always know when he looked at her—it was so hard to be resolute when nature fought against her, reminding her that she was young, female and responsive to males. To a particular male, whose lips crooked in a half smile evoked an immediate response in her heart whenever she thought of them; whose wit and intelligence ignited a spark in her mind, usually one of opposition, she admitted, but the argument was half the fun. She felt so alive in Paul's company, as though a part of herself, kept buried most of the time, emerged into daylight. But it was *not* to be. She had made her decision to devote all her time and energies to nursing. The opposition was so great; the work so draining. Paul didn't really understand. That was the difficulty. He could not accept that her undertaking might be as important as his own.

She sighed and paid attention as the captain, with a sideways glance at Jo-Beth, issued an invitation to the ladies to take a light luncheon at a nearby hotel. Elly refused firmly.

'*We* have work to do, gentlemen.' Letting the implication that they did not have work to do hang delicately, then she smiled to take away the sting. 'Also, we must not keep you from your affairs.'

The three men exchanged glances of mutual solidarity and took their leave. They set off down Pitt Street, dodging the heavy delivery drays and carts of produce on the way to the markets. Street vendors shouted above the clatter of hooves and wheels as a stream of cabs, omnibuses and private vehicles joined the throng. Cries of 'Pigs trotters', 'Fresh rabbits', 'Muffins new baked', mingled with the shrill voices of urchins earning a penny by sweeping crossings or holding horses. A man passed by with a basket balanced on his head calling 'Watercresses! Watercresses!', and a dustman rang his bell on his rounds collecting rubbish from the shop yards.

Jo-Beth waved airily to the disappearing figures, remarking: 'I'll warrant they've gone off quite happily to some tavern to discuss the next cockfight, or Governor Fitzroy's latest scandalous escapade. Look, here comes the pieman. Do let's buy some of his wares for the noon meal. My stomach quails at the thought of hospital food.' She darted over to the little iron box with the smoke belching from its chimney, and made her purchase, returning to waft hot pies under Elly's nose and make her stomach gurgle in anticipation.

Back at the hospital Elly found all calm and orderly. Jenkins marched the length of her ward like a prison guard, welcoming the two trainees with snarled orders that sent them scurrying. Even the mentally disturbed women who made a habit of disrupting the wards most days, merely picked at their sheets, one talking to herself, the other bawling the usual lewd verses. But everyone had grown used to Mrs Lyddie and Old Rose by now, everyone except Elly, who petitioned the Board in vain for separate accommodation for the 'mental' cases.

Munching her pie secretly and guiltily in her office, glad not to be hearing Jenkins gulp her greasy soup in the communal dining room, Elly questioned whether she worried unnecessarily, seeing herself as indispensable. So her finest trained nurse had gone. It wasn't a calamity. She still had Jo-Beth—a willing, if unorthodox, helper—while Malone and Irvine added daily to their experience. Perhaps she'd been unfair to Jenkins, as able a nurse as Pearl, although lacking in initiative and untested in a real emergency. Yet Elly didn't trust her. She would not promote Jenkins just yet.

A few weeks later Jo-Beth cajoled Elly into accompanying her on a shopping trip down George Street, and Elly soon found herself in unaccustomed surroundings watching Jo-Beth's metamorphosis into a lady of fashion. The room had been lined from waist height to ceiling with polished cedar shelves stacked with rolls and bolts of fabric, bonnet boxes, feathers and fans, plus many other aids of apparel to delight the female eye. Below, deep drawers held buttons and laces, artificial sprays, clips, hooks and belt buckles, handkerchiefs, turbans and scarves. The counters were heaped with colour, an indiscriminate patchwork waiting to be sorted out, for choices to be made. The air hummed with feminine indecision.

Urged by Jo-Beth, Elly obediently fingered the striped fabric then let it slip back onto the counter in a pool of silver grey, her thoughts entirely divorced from shopping and dresses. She disliked dallying through the various emporia lining George Street as much as Jo-Beth enjoyed it, and would far rather have walked a beach with the sea breeze in her hair. Yet she valued her friend's company too much to complain. It made her happy to watch Jo-Beth emerge from her grief and enjoy being frivolous once again. Around them the noise level rose as assistants ran to serve the more affluent women of Sydney Town, whiling away an agreeable hour in Mr David Jones's establishment before lunch and an afternoon drive in the family carriage. Elly fidgeted, sighed, then smiled dutifully as Jo-Beth turned to her.

'Look, Elly. This ribbon is a perfect match. I could use it to trim my bonnet and create a completely new ensemble. What do you think?' She laid the ribbon against the taffeta, her head to one side, considering.

'I think you will grace the day in it,' said a male voice. Captain Alan McAndrews appeared at her side. 'Good day to you, Miss Loring, Miss Ballard.'

Elly gave him her hand while studying Jo-Beth's reaction. No-one could doubt her pleasure in the encounter.

McAndrews swaggered a little and touched his moustache. 'Fortune's tide flows with me today,' he said. 'Ladies, will you honour me by taking some refreshment before continuing with your arduous expedition?'

'Hardly arduous, sir,' said Jo-Beth. 'So far we have visited only two shops and purchased nothing.' She smiled coquettishly, lifting a corner of the taffeta. 'Then you approve this?'

'Most certainly. It will suit your striking colouring most admirably.'

'Elly?' queried Jo-Beth.

'It's very pretty. Buy the ribbon as well.'

'Well I will. And if you wish it, we'll drink tea with Captain McAndrews before we go back.' Jo-Beth turned to the shop assistant while Elly conversed pleasantly with McAndrews.

He found a chair for her then stood at his ease, cap under arm, each glossy strand of fair hair in place, no doubt aware of the fine figure he cut. Hiding her amusement, Elly said, 'It's uncommon for us to be found dawdling the morning away in idleness. Only recent additions to our staff have made this possible.'

He nodded. 'I heard the Board had increased the numbers of nurses, and why. You, Matron, are a notable combatant. We could use you in our ranks, by Jove.'

Outside the sunny April day had brought people into the street, which rang with the cries of pavement sellers and touts for custom, from goats milk cheese to a mining lease from a disillusioned digger standing between the grandiose pillars of the Savings Bank. Further up George Street a tea house advertised itself with a sign on an awning, and there the two shoppers and their escort made the most of several buns, along with the fragrant brew. All the while Elly covertly studied the demeanour of her companions. Certainly Jo-Beth showed little sign of infatuation, whether as the result of her upbringing or simply because she felt none. McAndrews, on the contrary, used the slightest opportunity to touch Jo-Beth's hand, to perform small services for her—cutting her bun, retrieving a dropped parcel. His hot gaze devoured her to a point where Elly began to feel uncomfortable. Lost in thought, she found she had missed some of the talk, which had turned to war. McAndrews was excitedly sketching a map on the table with a teaspoon.

'This is the Crimean Peninsula, the area in question, which Russia is determined to control, along with the rest of Turkey. It's my belief Britain will go to war over it, may even be at war by now, if we but knew the truth. We await confirmation with every ship.'

Jo-Beth drew in her breath. 'War! Would you have to go, Captain McAndrews?'

'I might. Would you care greatly if I did?'

Jo-Beth dropped her gaze. 'Of course. We must all deplore our friends running into danger. Tell me more about the Turks' wish for independence.'

'It's a myth, independence. Any one of the major nations would like Turkey to come within their sphere of influence. The Tsar, as head of the Orthodox Church, disguises his aggression by declaring himself protector of the many Christian subjects in Turkey. He doesn't seem to believe we'd go to war to stop him.'

'But you do.' Jo-Beth's expression clouded, obviously with a vision of the misery to result from such a war. Impulsively she turned to McAndrews. 'You must not go. Promise me you will not go.'

'My dear ...' He put out a hand to hers, then swiftly withdrew it. But the message was unmistakable.

Summer panted into its last month, bringing with it storms which thundered down on the town each afternoon to saturate the heated air to an unbearable level of humidity. Houses grew mould indoors and it seemed half the population arrived on the hospital doorstep suffering heat exhaustion and either gastric or respiratory problems. The staff stretched themselves to the full over impossible hours; tempers shortened as the mercury climbed and sweat failed to evaporate from clothes and bedding. The misery factor multiplied when windows could not be opened above the drains and the water shortage grew desperate. But for Elly the worst torment was the mosquitoes which hatched in thousands in stagnant pools to descend like angry clouds on bare skin.

On one of the hottest, louring days, little Charlotte Perkins was admitted, once again the victim of a grand mal seizure. Elly had her placed in isolation in a screened section of Ward Two and watched her until the fitting ceased and the girl lapsed into coma. She then called in Jenkins who, about to go off duty, energetically resisted Elly's request for her to stay with Charlotte until she recovered.

'It's not my job. I've finished my work for today.'

'I know, but it's not for long. The girl must be watched while she's so helpless, and I can't spare any more time. I have to meet the inspection committee in ten minutes but have still to finish my report. The water cart hasn't arrived so I must send for another, and Dr Houston wanted to see me half an hour ago. If you will just stay for thirty minutes more I'll relieve you then and allow you extra time off tomorrow. Will you oblige me in this?'

Jenkins folded her lips and glared. 'No. I want to get off my feet.'

Selfish hag, thought Elly. We're all tired out and wringing wet and wishing we were elsewhere. But in this hospital the patients come first. Oh, to have Pearl back again.

She schooled her emotions. 'You may sit down while you wait. All I ask is for you to see no harm comes to this child until I can relieve you. Well, Jenkins?'

Something in her tone seemed to penetrate Jenkins's wall of rejection. Her gaze flickered to the patient then back to Elly.

'All right. Thirty minutes.' Arms crossed, she flung herself down on the end of Charlotte's cot.

'Thank you.' Elly brushed her fingers over Charlotte's knotted curls, pulled the sheet straight under the girl's chin. She seemed even more frail than when last admitted almost a year ago. So many of the children she saw were undernourished, uncared for, running wild in back lanes amongst piles of filth and dead animals, exposed to all forms of vice and disease. But this one had spirit. She'd bitten Jenkins on that far-off day when the black cordial was being forcibly administered. Elly smiled at the memory as she hurried away.

Dr Houston had left without waiting for her, so Elly finished off her report, tidied her hair then descended to the front hall to meet the committee members as they arrived, sweltering in their fashionable broadcloth and beaver. She led them to the theatres, the first item on today's inspection agenda. They were on their way upstairs when screams broke out overhead, rising into high pitched shrieks as Elly raced ahead, ignoring the outraged comments from the men puffing along behind.

Elly burst into Ward Two to find half the ambulant patients gathered at one end in a sort of scrum, women piled on top of one another, bare legs waving from beneath their shifts, the shrieks issuing from somewhere within the pile. The partition around Charlotte's bed had fallen down and the cot was empty. There was no sign of Jenkins.

'What's wrong? Tell me what's happened? Where is Charlotte?' Elly tore at the heaped bodies, forcing her way through. Her heart beat so hard and fast her head swam. This was no ordinary ward uproar. She feared something terrible had happened to the helpless Charlotte.

A moment later she knew the truth. Old Rose lay spread eagled on the floor with bodies sitting on her arms and legs and even on her stomach. Her eyes had turned up in her head; her lips were drawn in a grinning rictus. She continued to shriek with laughter until Elly thrust a corner of sheet into the nearest pair of hands, saying, 'Gag her.'

She turned to Charlotte, thrown in the corner like a crumpled doll. Gently Elly smoothed aside the tumbled curls to reveal a face swollen almost beyond recognition. A bubble of froth hung on her blue lips and the girl had the fixed stare of a statue. The marks around her throat clearly demonstrated how Charlotte's coma had come to end in violent death.

Elly swallowed. 'Where's Jenkins?'

One of the older women replied, 'She went off just after you did, Matron.'

A chorus of horrified gasps behind her told Elly the committee had pushed their way through the scrum.

'She went off.' She whispered the words to herself. Then she straightened Charlotte's shift around her pathetic limbs and rose to face the committee. She trembled, but her voice did not.

'Gentlemen, you now see the results of your policy of keeping the mentally afflicted in the general wards.' She pointed to Old Rose. 'That woman is quite deranged, and has just murdered an innocent child who lay helpless in a coma.'

'Good God.'

'Shocking.'

'Appalling.'

'All of those things, gentlemen, including criminal. It's your criminal irresponsibility which has brought about the tragedy. I've begged and pleaded for special accommodation for such patients, but you would not listen. This is the outcome.'

'How dare you!' The speaker, a stout, red faced man with stringy hair, drew himself up. 'Why is there no nurse on duty here to keep order?'

'There was. She abandoned her post. I'll deal with her myself. However, she had been on duty all day without respite. There is simply not enough staff to have individual patients watched. I would also point out that the combined efforts of five people are needed to keep this deranged patient in check.'

With this Old Rose gave a mighty heave, dislodging two of her keepers and tearing the gag from her mouth as she struggled to sit up. The men retreated hastily when she spat at them and began to bawl one of her outrageous ditties.

Elly chased after them, bailing them up in the doorway. She raised her voice above the clamour. 'Don't you dare leave! There's more to being a member of the committee than a ten-minute traipse around the building once a week. You have a responsibility, all of you, and I hold you to it. Send for whomever you like to take over here, do what you must. But until *something* is done, I will no longer act as matron in this hospital.'

The inevitable special meeting of the board of directors convened
the following day. Elly presented herself, well-prepared, knowing
what to expect, but with a sore heart and a core of anger within,
ready to be fanned to a conflagration. She had sent an explanatory
note to D'Arcy Cornwallis, begging him to be present, and was
relieved to see him rise and bow as she entered the boardroom.
She took her seat, comforted to know she had at least one supporter. Her staff had been excluded, as they were not witnesses to
the events under investigation, and the Board apparently dis-
counted the testimony of patients.

Anyone with any right to be there had crowded in. Already the
room stank of compressed humanity, not always particularly clean,
plus another smell not immediately recognisable. Then she saw
the sea of faces, avid, prurient, and knew she could scent the hunt-
ers' excitement as they drew in on their prey. Repressing a shudder, she held herself erect before that collective stare.

Chairman Deas Thomson came quickly to the point, charging
Elly with neglect and dereliction of duty. His manner hinted
strongly at firing squads and, despite her misery, Elly was entertained. The worst they could do would be to dismiss her. But in
the event of such an outcome, she wouldn't go quietly. The *Empire* pages would scorch with her comments.

Not bothering to disguise her scorn and anger, she rose to meet
the charge. 'Mr Chairman, members of the Board, this is not a
court of law and I am not on trial. Nor are you conducting a military tribunal. You are here to investigate the unhappy events of
yesterday, which I shall recount and which may be verified by the
six members of the weekly committee who were also present. I will
add that it was their insistence on my presence to conduct them
on their cursory tour of the hospital that forced me to leave the
patient, Charlotte Perkins, in the care of Nurse Jenkins.'

She paused to survey the six gentlemen mentioned, all of whom
looked uncomfortable, then continued. 'Jenkins had been on duty
in Ward Two all day, with occasional help from Malone, who assisted in both wards. We currently care for sixty-five women and

children. Assistant Nurse Loring oversaw Ward One until my one
other available nurse, Irvine, could relieve her; I planned to do the
night duty in Ward Two myself, after the inspection.'

Cornwallis rose and begged leave to pose a question. Deas
Thomson nodded.

'Matron Ballard,' said Cornwallis, 'at what hour did you commence your own duties yesterday?'

'At five a.m.'

'And you planned to stay up all night in Ward Two. Was there
no-one else to take your place?'

'No-one, sir, since the Board has seen fit to restrict the number
of nurses I may employ. My staff frequently take on a double load
when the wards are as crowded as they are at present.'

Deas Thomson interposed. 'The members will recall the Board's
decision not to have nurses on duty at night. The wards were to be
locked and the patients confined until morning.'

Cornwallis honed his voice to a fine edge. 'With yesterday's inevitable result: an assault on a patient and no-one in authority
present to succour her. Which brings me to another point, also
stressed by Matron Ballard at previous meetings, the need to seg-
regate the mentally impaired from other patients. Clearly, if this
had been done, the child Charlotte Perkins would still be alive.'
He resumed his seat.

Phineas Gault rose to address the Board, ignoring Elly and speaking directly to the chair. 'Sir, the point in question is surely whether
Matron Ballard, the person in overall charge of the women's wards,
should be held responsible. It was she who insisted upon a weary
nurse who was physically unwell staying with the patient. Nurse
Jenkins waits outside this room to attest to the fact that she left the
patient because she herself became ill. She believes she has been
mostly unjustly accused and dismissed. Also, there is more to her
testimony which I believe you should hear.'

'Very well, let her be brought in.' The chairman drummed his
fingers on the table, impatient yet not dissatisfied. Elly saw him
glance at Cornwallis and realised there was antagonism between
the two men. Just what she needed, to be embroiled in a personal
quarrel with the powerful Deas Thomson. As for that lying
Jenkins ...

Jenkins swam into the room in a sea of lace and feathers, her elaborate costume far from the neat uniform she'd worn at the infirmary. Invited to give her version of the facts, she fixed her marble-blue eyes on Elly and began.

'I were worn out from running the ward all day with little enough help from Malone, the lazy skelp, and I got this gripe in the innards. It's this terrible weather and all the heavy work. Matron wouldn't listen when I told her I needed to lie down and she made me stay on duty. 'Twern't fair, I say. All right for some people to give orders and sit in an office with their feet up. Mine'd swollen something cruel. Then I had to go to the privy in a hurry. What could I do?'

Gault said quickly, 'What *did* you do, to see to the welfare of your patient, I mean?'

Jenkins assumed a virtuous expression. 'I called in at the nurses' quarters to ask Irvine to take my place for a few minutes, but she'd skived off somewhere. So you see, 'twern't my fault. I had to go.'

Elly turned on her. 'Jenkins, you're a liar. You no more had the gripes than I had. You made no mention of it to me. Nor, I have discovered, did you issue the calming dose I had ordered for both Mrs Lyddie and Old Rose. In consequence they were both in a dangerously agitated state by the time I left Charlotte in your care.'

'That's not true! You've always had in for me—'

'I've always distrusted you, and with good reason, it seems. Nurse Irvine was not in her quarters, if indeed you did go there. She had spent the afternoon in the dispensary and was about to go on night duty in a ward with at least fifteen seriously ill patients needing constant monitoring.' She whirled on Deas Thomson. 'You can't lock people in like animals, leaving them in pain and troubled mind. They need nursing, day *and* night.'

He frowned. 'Let us return to the point. Nurse Jenkins avers she was ill and could not remain on duty.'

'Then she should have come for me. I remained in my office for ten minutes, not with my feet up, but finishing the weekly report. She knew I would then go downstairs to meet the committee. I never left the building and could be easily found.'

Attention fixed on Jenkins, who scowled. 'She's the liar, the stuck-up bitch. She wouldn't listen when I told her I were sick …'

She trailed off as Cornwallis stepped forward to concentrate his considerable personality on her.

'Miss Jenkins, I warn you there are witnesses prepared to refute your statements—patients in the ward who overheard your conversation with Matron. We also have the evidence of the porter, Will Tripp, who saw you with two of the wardsmen drinking in a nearby tavern soon after you went missing with, er, the "gripes". Is ale a common cure for such an ailment?'

Jenkins paled. 'You can't believe them. They're all lying, those cows upstairs and Tripp. They've all got it in for me. It's not fair …' She began to snivel.

Cornwallis's gaze moved from Jenkins to Gault then on to Deas Thomson. His sonorous voice filled the room. 'I suggest the testimony of this witness is a tissue of falsehood, designed to injure the woman who dismissed her and to absolve the real culprit, Nurse Jenkins herself, who cared so little for a helpless patient as to go off drinking in a tavern while the child Charlotte Perkins was murdered.'

Jenkins's screech of protest could barely be heard above the general hubbub of approval, with only a few dissenting voices, notably Gault's.

Cornwallis's voice rose above the others. 'Also, gentlemen, you will recall a previous occasion when Nurse Jenkins incurred censure for inciting riot in the wards. I am disinclined to believe anything said by such a proven troublemaker.'

Obviously irritated, Deas Thomson rose from his seat to call for quiet. He asked members of the Board to vote on the charge against Matron Ballard of neglect and dereliction of duty, and was then able formally to dismiss the charge. He ordered the former Nurse Jenkins to leave the hospital, never to return. Jenkins promptly went into a fit of hysteria and had to be carried out, stiff as a paling, heels drumming. Elly wondered what her unwilling porters would do with her—leave her propped up in the corridor, perhaps, for Will Tripp to deal with? It was a pleasant thought. Still, she couldn't leave her unattended. With the chairman's permission she had Jo-Beth sent for to take Jenkins to the dispensary, then returned to her seat.

Deas Thomson had recovered his temper. 'Matron, you have

been vindicated and your actions approved by the Board. Do you have anything more to say?'

'I do. Gentlemen, I beg you, don't let this terrible thing happen again. At the very least, will you provide separate accommodation for deranged patients, with appropriate carers? Charlotte Perkins wasn't an important person, but she had a right to her life. It's our moral duty to see patients like her protected.'

The chairman was grave. 'You point us the way, Matron. It shall be as you wish.'

Elly bowed, as grave as he, then left the boardroom, victorious yet fully aware that the opposition had been merely knocked out for the duration. How many more battles were to follow? And how could she ever consider abandoning the war and its victims for any reason at all?

Chapter Seventeen

With an hour to spare, Elly stepped out of the hospital gateway and raised her face to the sun, its warmth a benediction on her pale cheeks. She knew she needed to get out into the fresh air more—the home visits hardly qualified when she moved from hospital to carriage to overheated bedrooms then back again. It would be a welcome change to go on foot, even on this short errand.

Macquarie Street was rapidly gaining favour as a plum residential area, with its remarkable views and proximity to the shops. It seemed to Elly that each week more attractive terrace houses sprang up, their balconies adorned with iron lace work, the low sandstone fences neatly railed. A horse trotted up beside her and she stepped back as Cornwallis dismounted to block her passage down Macquarie Street. He swept off his hat and bowed, his eyes searching her face with an uncomfortable intensity.

'You've been avoiding me, Miss Ballard. What have I done to deserve such treatment?' Although his tone was light, Elly heard the note of pique, and regretted it. He had supported her when she most needed help, and deserved her civility.

'Not avoiding *you*, sir, but anything which takes me away from my duties. I'm aware how greatly I am in your debt—'

'Nonsense. Please abolish the thought. If ever a fighter deserved to win, you did, with such an army of slow tops and gubernatorial boot-lickers arrayed against you. I thoroughly enjoyed the engagement. However, you really should have allowed me to celebrate victory with you.'

'Of course you are right.' Elly thought for a moment. 'Allow me to make amends. Will you be my guest for dinner one night soon? I'm afraid circumstances don't permit me to entertain here at the hospital, but I'm told Tattersall's Hotel fare is not to be despised.'

'Delighted, dear lady. An excellent choice, if I may say so, especially as I've not yet seen the more recent additions to their private art gallery. You will permit me to fetch you in my carriage and see to the wines.'

His eagerness made her uneasy. However, she'd committed herself, so she named a date a week away, hoping no emergency would arise to spoil the arrangement. She would not mind, but he would take a postponement as rejection.

Elly held out her hand. 'You must forgive me. I have an errand, and my time is limited.'

He glanced at the parcel of books under her arm.

'You're on your way to Piddington's Bookshop? May I escort you? I have business in the same direction.'

Salvation appeared over his shoulder in the form of JG, sauntering down the street twirling a gold-topped cane like a bandsman with his drumstick.

'Thank you.' She gave Cornwallis her best smile. 'However, I've arranged to go with Mr Patterson to the subscription library.' Side-stepping, she moved quickly to intercept her friend. 'JG you're late. I had almost given you up.'

JG neither blinked nor paused, but bowed extravagantly over Elly's free hand, cane extended at an angle to support his doffed hat, his whole manner aping a Regency dandy.

Elly said playfully, 'You need a third hand for your hat, Monsieur Macaroni, unless you abandon your delightful cane.'

'It serves a double purpose as a hatstand, thus freeing me to greet a lady with style.' JG glanced at the vexed Cornwallis, grinned mischievously, then deliberately kissed Elly's fingers. He then straightened and put his hat back on at a rakish angle. 'Good day to you, sir.' With a nod to Cornwallis, he swept Elly about on his arm, saying out of the side of his mouth, 'Where are we supposed to be going?'

'To the library,' she hissed back, twisting around to say good-bye to Cornwallis.

JG took her books and hurried her away at a brisk trot.

At the corner of Bent and Macquarie Streets where the imposing library building rose like a Greek monument, Elly, breathless, pulled him up. 'Thank you, JG We can now moderate our pace. He's not following.'

'It'd be beneath his dignity, since we didn't ask him to join us. What a rude pair we are.' He glanced at her quizzically.

'I haven't run away from him, precisely. I can't explain. It's … it's his air of proprietorship that worries me. He's so accustomed to power, to swaying others. He sweeps me along without giving me time to think.'

'He's a power in the Colony, to be sure, with a finger and just about every toe in any pie worth the baking. Some say he has too many interests.'

'What do you mean?'

JG shrugged and guided her up the steps under the archway, swerving past a number of other citizens bent on the same errand. 'I've heard talk of him being a remittance man, banished, at least until he comes into the title. Still, in business, as in politics, there are always voices to denounce the rich and powerful. Sometimes there's truth in rumours of chicanery and false dealing. Sometimes it's mere envious spite. In this case, I've not yet discovered which.'

Elly said in a troubled tone, 'I don't like to listen to tales about other people. I've always found Mr Cornwallis to be honourable in his dealings with me. However, I'll keep your warning in mind. Now please, let's talk about something else.' She added more cheerfully, 'I expect you attended Mr Wentworth's departure for London in all his glory?'

JG held the door open for her. 'Yes, indeed, I saw the great man off, just to be sure we were rid of him and his recommendations for a colonial House of Lords filled with rosewater Liberals. He'll make the spring sitting of Parliament with time to spare. The

Chusan's the fastest steam packet we have.'

' "Nasty-smelling tin cans afloat. Give me a clipper any time." I quote Jo-Beth, who fell victim to the charms of a great sailing ship during her voyage from China.'

'Which just about drowned her in the end. You don't catch a "tin can" breaking in two from worm rot. No, steamships are the coming thing. They'll sweep the seas clean of sail before long. That's progress, girl dear.' He flung out an arm, and almost knocked the hat off a bewhiskered old gentleman. 'I beg your pardon, sir.'

Glaring at JG, the man clutched his low-crowned beaver, whispering hoarsely, 'Kindly remember this is a library, sir, and moderate your voice.' He stomped off, leaving JG affronted.

'Ye'd think I'd brought in a brass band,' he complained, placing the books on the desk. 'So, how goes the campaign to improve the hospital? And don't be thinking I'm after another article. I just want to know.'

'It goes at snail speed,' Elly confessed. She began to inspect the volumes in a nearby bookstand. The combination of smells in a library pleased her, a pot-pourri of ink and paper and paste and a fustiness that went well with high ceilings and walls lined with gilt-lettered spines, books by the yard, information by the hundred-weight, entertainment for years to come. 'We're training new staff,' she explained, 'yet the number of improvements has been small. Nothing major has been attempted, like the drains. Thank heaven winter's on its way, to kill off flies and mosquitoes.'

'I thought, with the Honourable D'Arcy Cornwallis's support ... ?' JG paused delicately.

'He can only do so much as one board member. He's championed me twice already. Besides, I don't like to be indebted to him, made to feel he expects repayment.'

JG's brows rose. 'Surely not.'

'Oh, I can't be specific. It's just ... he likes my company and ... apart from all else, I'm simply too tired these days to socialise.'

'Hmm. You are quite pale and Ophelia-like.' JG studied her a moment. 'I think perhaps I should drop a warning word in your ear. Whatever his business methods, the Dishonourable D'Arcy has a sizeable reputation with the ladies, as well as with women of another order. Take care, girl dear.'

Elly discarded the book she had been examining, saying in a carefully lowered voice, 'I know you mean well, JG, but as I've told you, Mr Cornwallis's behaviour towards me has been most proper. A reputation for gallantry is hardly unusual amongst men of means, and until I've good reason to question his behaviour, Mr Cornwallis will remain my friend. Now, will you abandon this topic, or must I abandon you?'

JG clutched at his heart, well concealed beneath a grass-green striped satin waistcoat. 'You couldn't be so cruel.' His eyes danced.

'I could, you know.'

'Then I won't risk it. Cornwallis as a topic of conversation is now dead, coffined, entombed and surrounded by churchyard yews.'

'That could have been better put. However, if you will fetch me a volume just beyond my reach—yes, that's the one, *Wanderings Through New South Wales*—I'll forgive you. Thank you. And now, JG, I think you should continue your interrupted stroll, with my sincere thanks for a timely rescue.'

JG's brows went up. 'Dismissal? Oh well, I should be slaving over my next column. By the way, did you know Paul is due back this week?'

Elly's grip tightened on Mr Bennett's *Wanderings*. 'Back from where? I've not heard from him since we saw Pearl off on the river steamer almost three months ago.' Her level tone concealed her true feelings. She had tried so hard to drive Paul from her thoughts. He too had agreed they should not allow a lightning passion to interfere with either of their goals. When they met on the wharf to farewell Pearl he had stayed aloof, and had made no effort to contact her since. Despite knowing she had brought it on herself, his changed attitude hurt. So she had built a high, thick wall around her hurt, hardening it into indifference. She told herself she no longer cared what Paul Gascoigne did, and had believed it until this moment.

The grievance in JG's voice penetrated her thoughts. 'Don't I know it's all of three months. The spalpeen left on one of his no-madic campaigns up country, after depositing his dog with me. So far I've lost five pounds exercising the mutt, not to mention a bed-room slipper and as nice a ham as ever graced a board. I'll give him three months when I see him.'

Elly's clutch on the book loosened and she smiled. 'Is Pepper misbehaving? I expect he misses his master. He's been gone all this time?'

'Either he's travelled much further than planned or been delayed by an accident.'

Her heart banged against her ribs. Accident! She knew so well what it meant to be alone in the bush, injured, with nowhere to turn for help.

JG grasped her arm. 'You're not going to faint on me, are you? You're the colour of a Gloucester cheese.'

She gathered herself. 'No, I won't faint. I shall go to the desk and ask for *Pickwick Papers* plus volume three of Sir Walter Scott's *Waverley* series. Goodbye, JG. Thank you for your escort.'

He let her go reluctantly, took two paces, then turned back again as she said, 'You will let me know if Paul—Mr Gascoigne—arrives home safely?'

'To be sure I will.' He waved his cane at her then went off, to work, Elly supposed, watching him disappear through the heavy door. But her thoughts were with Paul, wondering where his travels had taken him, whether he was safe, whether he ever thought of her.

Dinner with D'Arcy Cornwallis had been a mistake, Elly thought, a week later. Despite being her guest he had, without her knowledge, secured a table in a secluded bay of the restaurant which gave an appearance of privacy and particularity, then proceeded to turn the evening into something she had not intended.

Sauté of goose and kidneys *aux champagne*, with side dishes of partridge and truffles, were not enough to leaven a situation which called for the greatest tact. JG's warnings should have been heeded. For, while playing the gentleman still, Cornwallis had succeeded in discomforting her with his gallantry, and his conversation had become loaded with innuendo, acceptable perhaps to ladies of a different order, but not to Elly. Still, she hesitated to speak her mind, restrained by gratitude for his help, and the need to retain the goodwill of at least one hospital board member. She wriggled and manoeuvered the conversation away from personal topics, yet as often as she succeeded he would angle it back with a compliment or an intimate glance. He used his eyes as a weapon. She felt like an animal being gently, inexorably herded into a pen. If he had touched her she thought she must have risen and left him; but he was not so crude.

Smothering her anger at his familiarity, Elly refused dessert, impatient for him to end his meal. Finally she asked him to take her home.

Cornwallis called for a liqueur for the lady.

'No thank you. I'd like to leave now, if you please,' Elly repeated pleasantly but firmly, drawing her wrap around her shoulders to cover the low neck of her gown.

'But Eleanor—I may call you Eleanor?—the night has scarcely begun. I had plans—'

'So have I plans, which include a great deal of work to be done before I can sleep. I apologise for cutting short this pleasant interlude. However, I did say dinner, not a full evening's entertainment. So, Mr Cornwallis, if you don't mind ...'

His hand shot out to grasp her wrist, holding her in her chair. She stared at the square, polished nails, at the dark hairs springing above the knuckles.

'But I do mind, very much. I had anticipated a great deal from this "interlude". When a charming woman issues an invitation to join her for dinner, I expect to enjoy her company for several hours. Nothing was said about an abrupt termination. I protest, Eleanor. I have been ill-used.' His voice had an unmistakable edge which warned Elly, even as it added to her anger.

She pointedly waited until he released her, then leant towards him, injecting warmth into her tone. 'I'm extremely sorry if there's been a misunderstanding. I thought I'd made it clear that at present we are so inundated with work I can't be spared for long. I've been on duty in the wards all day and have several reports to fill out, accounts to be checked, inventories ... You see how it is? I doubt whether I'll be abed before one o'clock yet I must rise again tomorrow at five.' She drooped a little at the prospect.

Cornwallis frowned then settled back, his stare disconcerting. 'A pity, indeed. But I see you are weary and console myself with the anticipation of future meetings. There will be such occasions, will there not?'

Elly inclined her head with a smile. 'Indeed, I hope so.' She gathered her skirts and he rose to draw back her chair.

Having arranged prior payment for the meal, she moved quickly to the stairs, accepting his arm as support, but careful to maintain distance between them. She climbed into the closed carriage waiting outside, trusting her escort would keep to his own seat. During the short journey up hill to the hospital Cornwallis spoke of commonplace matters and Elly would have dismissed him when they arrived at the gate in the wall, but she somehow found herself accompanied out of the carriage to the main door.

When she held out her hand he folded it between his own, saying deliberately, 'I shall not conceal from you my disappointment at the loss of your company, especially as you have not been averse to spending a whole day in the company of Mr Gascoigne.'

Astonished, Elly replied, 'That was weeks ago. I've had no social engagements since the New Year, although I fail to see what concern it is of yours, Mr Cornwallis.'

His gaze intensified while he tightened his grip, almost crushing her fingers. 'You cannot fail to be aware of my regard, my deepest admiration. You're a lovely woman, Eleanor, and I must know you better. No more avoidance. I will not accept a refusal.'

She looked at the closed door with longing, knowing her key lay buried in her reticule and the porter had gone off duty. She tried to tug free. 'Mr Cornwallis, pray … You embarrass me. I had no idea … Of course I have a regard for you, but—'

'You're most attractive when you're provoked, my dear. I'm all admiration.' His arm went around her waist, pinning her to him. His face, distorted with sudden passion, loomed far too close for comfort, his gaze burned with an almost tangible heat. Warring emotions held Elly speechless. The satyric mouth smiled and, overcome by sudden loathing, she struck at his imprisoning arm.

'Let me go. How dare you treat me like some street drab!'

His grip tightened. His full-lipped mouth hovered over hers, their breaths mingling. His voice, also, had changed, harsh, stripped of deference, thick with menace. 'You mistake me, my dear. I treat whores quite differently. You, I fancy, are more than a cut or two above such creatures.'

Straining her head back, Elly said with as much dignity as she could, 'I had hoped that a gentleman would recognise a lady by her behaviour, Mr Cornwallis. Kindly release me at once.'

His laughter jeered at her. 'A lady doesn't dip her hands daily in filth and disease. No, my dear, you make a brave show, but you've stepped down into the lower echelons of public entertainers and working-class women. You're available and, believe me, I'm more than willing to make our liaison worthwhile to you.'

Elly gaped. A moment later he had tilted her chin and fastened his mouth on hers, hard, hurtfully, allowing her no opportunity to protest. Elly was suffocating. Restrained by a strength such as she'd never imagined, she was powerless and afraid. When he suddenly let her go she fell back against the door, fingers to her bruised lips, too breathless to find words to hurl at him. A second later he landed hard against the wall beside her, his grunt of surprise followed by an oath.

Before he could straighten up, Paul was upon him, gripping him by the coat lapels as he dragged him down the steps into the courtyard.

'You bastard! How dare you touch her!' Paul's fist met Cornwallis's jaw with a terrific crack and he went down, sprawled across the flags to lie still. Paul bounded up the steps to Elly. 'Are you all right? Did he hurt you?'

Elly shook her head. 'My self-esteem is wounded, nothing else. Thank heaven you appeared when you did.'

He turned her to the light above the door and examined her face, his eyes blazing. 'He did hurt you. Your lip is cut.'

· Frightened by his expression, she said hastily, 'It's nothing. Paul …' She began to tremble and was grateful when his arms came around her in comforting support.

'It's all right. Just a reaction, Elly.' He glanced down at Cornwallis, still lying on the pavement. 'I must have hit him harder than I thought.' He sounded quite happy about it.

'I'd better see—' Elly began, but Paul held her back.

'Let him lie for the moment. I'd have intervened earlier if I hadn't been some distance away, enjoying a pipe while I waited for you. JG said you were worried about me.'

Elly gently withdrew from his hold. 'I was concerned because you'd been gone for so many weeks, with no word. I'm glad you're back safely.' She glanced down at Cornwallis, now struggling to his feet, supporting his swelling jaw. Her anger flared up, cooled only slightly by the spectacle of Cornwallis's humiliation.

But the man who stood glaring at her was not a figure to be mocked. Violence emanated from him in almost visible waves. His shoulder muscles bunched under his coat as he lurched forward into the light. Elly shrank against the door, while Paul moved in front of her, his fists clenched. Cornwallis maintained his gaze for a long moment, then turned and limped out the gate to his carriage.

Elly turned to Paul in horror and said: 'Did you see his face? It was evil.'

'We've made a bad enemy there,' he agreed. 'Guard your back from now on at the board meetings.'

Elly decided not to think about that until she had to. She'd borne enough for one night. 'You be careful, too. Don't go down any dark alleys alone. I'm not being melodramatic. I truly believe he's capable of anything.'

Relaxed now, Paul took her reticule from her and extracted her key. 'I'll keep it in mind. Now, you've had a trying evening and should be in bed. I called only to reassure you of my safety. I'll bore you with my traveller's tales some other time.' He opened the door, giving her the key. 'Sleep well, Elly, and don't trouble your head over that brute. We can deal with him.'

'I hope so. Thank you for the rescue, Paul.'

He kissed her cheek then left, collecting his hat at the bottom of the steps and closing the gate in the wall behind him.

Elly bolted the door, taking the stairs slowly, determined to do her last round of the wards before going to bed. Her lip stung, her bruised ribs protested and her brain felt battered by a jumble of thoughts and questions, too much to sort out tonight. She'd think about it all tomorrow.

Chapter Eighteen

Elly's contact with the male wards remained limited, but she had introduced a strategem of her own for patients about to undergo surgery, ensuring that once delivered to the theatre she bathed them in carbolic solution and rendered them as clean as possible before the surgeon arrived. However, this, together with her increased hours outside the hospital, meant she was badly overworked, and Jo-Beth decided to offer her services for preparation in the theatre.

She surprised Elly at her desk, chin on hands, staring out the window at a vista of ragged cloud. The sun had played hide-and-seek since dawn, and winter had laid its finger on the town. Children scuffed through the fallen leaves, playing running games to warm themselves, while their elders moved briskly along the street below.

Elly spoke without turning her head. 'Look out there. The year's turned and we're into our second without having achieved anything worthy of notice. It's been such a struggle, for so little.'

Jo-Beth patted her friend's shoulder. 'You've achieved more than you realise. The whole atmosphere of this hospital has changed for the better. You've banished dirt and slovenliness, and introduced hope, Elly. People don't come here as a last resort;

they know they'll be cared for. That's something to be proud of.'

'I suppose so. You're right. I must banish depression before it blights anyone else.' She rose. 'I'm needed in the theatre in ten minutes.'

'I'll come with you. Let me help, Elly. Surely I can carry out the preparation if you instruct me.' Jo-Beth searched her friend's worn face with concern.

Elly hesitated only a moment. 'I'd be very glad of your help. But ... are you sure? It would involve handling male patients.'

Jo-Beth said airily: 'Sedated male patients. I can manage them.'

Down in the theatre the man waited, buckled to the table. He regarded the two women with the terrified eyes of a bolting horse, every muscle in his body straining against the straps. Jo-Beth's gaze, however, was rivetted to his naked body. Her face hot, she moved quickly to the bench to pour carbolic into a bowl of instruments. Elly, who always knew the name of the theatre patient, tried to reassure him while she raised his head to help him drink from a flask.

'Mr Brown, I see you've already imbibed rum. Now here is laudanum to further dull your senses. Try not to be afraid. Mr Wykeham is a good swift surgeon. The tumour will be removed from your groin and you'll be back in the ward in no time at all.' She beckoned to Jo-Beth to fetch a bowl and cloths to the table.

Jo-Beth obeyed reluctantly, keeping her head averted.

Elly said, surprised, 'What's wrong?'

'Nothing. Will you wash the patient?'

'We'll both do it. I want to demonstrate how thoroughly this must be done, particularly in the operative area. You begin with the head.'

I must not be silly, Jo-Beth told herself. He's only a man, a human being in need.

The two worked together down the man's body. As the sedative mixed with the alcohol already in his system, it began to take effect. He gave a loud snort and Jo-Beth looked up to see a maudlin smile replace the terror in his features.

'Pretty hair,' he said suddenly.

Jo-Beth jumped. The flaccid lump under her hand twitched and began to swell. She hurriedly let go, watching in growing horror as it rose even higher, until it seemed to point straight at her, a great red finger of lurid flesh. She stepped back from the table, dropping her cloth.

'Elly.' She swallowed then tried again. 'Elly, something's wrong.'

'What is it?' Elly's quick glance appraised the situation. After an obvious struggle, she dissolved into laughter. 'Oh, Jo-Beth. Have you never seen a naked man before?'

Hanging her head, Jo-Beth whispered, 'Never.' Her cheeks felt like beacons. The patient tittered then began humming tunelessly. But when she forced herself to look at him, Jo-Beth realised he was unaware of her, wandering in a half-drunken world where his fear was masked, if not laid to rest.

Elly controlled her laughter, although her eyes still sparkled. 'I'm sorry, Jo-Beth. Under the circumstances, naturally the patient's tumescence has come as a shock. However, you have to understand that it's a natural reaction to your touching him, even when he's only half awake. A nurse who works out in the community grows accustomed to dealing with the other sex. It's one of the reasons why nurses are so lowly regarded, because we will put aside our gentility and see the patient as someone in need, not a particular man or woman.'

She's right, thought Jo-Beth. This is not the time or place for maidenly modesty. Steeling herself, she picked up the fallen cloth, dipped it in the carbolic solution and wrung it out, then set to work resolutely. This would be the cleanest patient ever to pass into Mr Wykeham's not so clean hands.

As she worked, Jo-Beth suddenly burst out, 'Elly, I need to talk to someone.'

Elly merely nodded and began cleaning instruments, while Jo-Beth continued. 'I feel such a fool, as well as disloyal to Ethan. Yet I can't go on forever marking time in the hospital, waiting, hoping, fearing. It tears me in two.'

'You wanted a miracle, Jo-Beth.'

'Yes. I wore out my knees pleading with God to restore my love, but He's failed me. Maybe I'm simply not worthy.'

Elly turned on her. 'Never say that! Never. I forbid you to denigrate yourself in the name of religion. You are as fine a friend as anyone could hope for. You're compassionate, you do your best for the patients, you've survived all your difficulties with dignity. You *deserve* happiness.'

'Why, Elly, thank you. You know what I'm about to tell you, don't you?'

'Alan McAndrews has asked you to marry him. I approve.'

'He's not Ethan, not in any way like him. But he's kind and thoughtful, and he says he loves me. Of course, his wealth and position are not to be sneered at.' Her self-derogatory tone evoked an immediate response.

'You're doing it again, decrying a perfectly natural desire to return to the life you've always known.'

Jo-Beth sighed. 'I don't know whether I could marry without love.'

'There are other considerations, such as respect.' Elly paused. 'Not to mention the opportunity for a full and useful life. You could use your influence in society to advance the cause of nursing, raise funds, provoke discussion, exert political pressure. You'd never be happy idle, but you could create your own happiness in such service.'

Jo-Beth was thoughtful as she bent to wash the patient's legs.

The *Empire* offices were scarcely overwhelming, thought Elly, unless she adopted noise level as the criterion. Seated in the tiny space reserved for visitors, she covered her ears against the machines' assault, feeling the vibrations rise up through the floorboards. People rushed in and out of doors, waving papers, attending machines, shouting to one another above the incessant din in a pattern of controlled hysteria. Odours peculiar to the printing trade—ink, chemicals, machine oil—made her wrinkle her nose, while she thought the battered furniture and general sparsity of the newsroom more suited to a poorhouse than a successful newspaper. Was Henry Parkes unable to afford better? How could he get anyone to work in such an environment, let alone detach himself sufficiently to produce the roaring diatribes that galvanised half of Sydney Town?

A comparison with the more staid *Sydney Herald*, the organ of squatters and men of wealth, had quickly decided her in favour of the *Empire*'s vitality and willingness to take risks. She'd long forgiven JG for the trouble his hospital article had caused her, and now counted him as a good friend. It was as a friend that she now needed his help.

He bustled in within a few minutes, striped shirt-tails billowing from beneath his waistcoat, an ink-stained hand held out to her.

' 'Tis a fine day when the lady of my heart calls to interrupt my work,' he bellowed.

Elly shouted back, 'It's a wonder you can lie straight in bed, JG. How many hearts do you have and how do you keep track of them all?' She leapt as an almighty crash shook the building and the clatter of machinery stopped. She lowered her voice. 'What's happened? Has it blown up?'

'More than likely. Now, girl dear, come into my little sanctum and tell me what brings you here.' He ushered her through a doorway into a minute cell furnished with a table, a tall cabinet and two chairs that seemed to have survived a kicking with hob-nailed boots. The window overlooked a malodorous lane between buildings, and JG hastily pulled down the sash.

Elly sank into the nearest chair, her ears ringing with the sudden silence. 'I need your help, JG. I've had a letter from Pearl, written weeks ago, saying she'd found no trace of her brother so she intended to travel overland to the Victorian goldfields. She's promised to maintain contact through the Melbourne Post Office. I want you to help me influence her to abandon her search.'

'Me influence Pearl!' JG's brows hit his hairline and his jaw dropped ludicrously. 'It's mad you are. The minx is more likely to do the opposite to any advice I might give her. Who was it wanted to feed me bamboo slivers in me dinner?'

'JG, we've got to do something. I'm afraid she'll come to harm if she persists with this perilous expedition.'

JG's expression was as grim as his merry face would allow. 'Don't think this crazy notion of hers hasn't bothered me, too, but I couldn't dissuade the girl. She's hell-bent on finding her brother, and on that subject she's about as malleable as the Sphinx, and as conversational.'

'Then will you give me any published material on the Victorian diggings for me to send her? Anything emphasising how dangerous it is there, especially for a woman alone?'

'Indeed I will. What's more, there are reports of a recent riot against the Chinese, who're much resented by the other diggers for their industry and just plain foreignness.' He rummaged in his cabinet, emerging with a sheaf of papers which he handed to Elly.

She scanned them quickly, frowning in consternation. 'My heavens, this is terrible. The place is a hell hole—little food or water, no habitation, no law, and awash with rum. She can't go there. It's impossible.' She let the papers fall. Stooping, she clutched at the table for support, then gathering the papers together, she thrust them into her shopping bag and rose.

JG said abruptly, 'Are you quite well, Elly? You seem tired.'

'Thank you. I'm well enough. I'll send off the information immediately and hope for once Pearl will let herself be influenced by others.' As she walked out of the building she heard the crash of machinery starting up. The particular hullabaloo and frenzy of a newspaper world had begun again.

After visiting the post office, she finished her shopping, then turned wearily for home. The climb back up the hill to Macquarie Street seemed steeper than ever. She took it slowly, drawing on all her energy. In the hospital lobby Jo-Beth met her with excitement.

'Elly! Elly! Such a wonderful thing has happened. Oh, how I wish you'd been here.'

Behind Jo-Beth, Dr Houston and two other medical officers came striding up the corridor, their expressions animated, their voices raised as each interrupted the other without apology.

Dr Houston stopped to beam at Elly. 'Matron, once again you've proved yourself to be ahead of us in the matter of patient care. I congratulate you on your foresight. A new era in surgery has dawned.'

Confused, Elly simply stared after him as he bustled off in his usual style, his confreres in tow. She turned to Jo-Beth. 'What on earth has happened?'

'Well, I'd say our revered board of directors is about to go down on its collective knees and beg you to assume the mantle of Matron in perpetuity. Come up to the office and I'll tell you all about it.'

Elly took one step then sank down heavily on the stairs. Her knees had simply given way. She shivered continually, yet was burning up inside.

'Elly, what is it? Are you unwell?' Jo-Beth rushed to her.

'I'm all right, I think. Just let me rest here a moment to catch my breath. That hill is steep. What were you saying about the Board?'

Jo-Beth eyed her uneasily. 'It's about the operation performed by Dr Alleyne. You know him. He's the Liverpool coroner and highly thought of. And, Elly, he's amputated a girl's leg using an anaesthetic, chloroform! She didn't feel a thing!'

Elly straightened her weary back. 'At last!'

'I know. What's more, he had the staff surgeons there to observe. They were overwhelmed. You've been proved right in the face of their opposition. Ether or chloroform, these inhaled gases will revolutionise surgery in Australia, and you're the one who foretold it.'

A tear overflowed onto Elly's cheek.

'Elly! You're not crying?'

'Don't worry. It's mere relief and joy for all the souls who will benefit from this day. Dr Alleyne's reputation will force the change.' She focused beyond Jo-Beth, seeing only little Simon Leonides' face twisted in agonised terror, thinking how he might have been saved.

'Of course the Board will apologise to you.'

'I shouldn't rely on it. An apology is only words. I want to see action. Thanks to Dr Alleyne, and our personal publicist, JG, we should get it.' Elly hunted for her handkerchief to wipe her cheeks. 'You don't know what this means to me.'

Jo-Beth seemed mystified at her reaction. 'I would insist upon an apology myself. However, your status is clearly much improved. You may even squeeze extra money out of the Board while they're amenable.'

Elly shook her head. 'We've barely scaled the foothills of our medical Everest. Money is only the first of our needs.'

'It'd be a wonderful start, you must admit. Now, I think you should rest before going back on duty.'

Rest, Elly thought, as she struggled to her feet. What's that? I could sleep for a hundred years. My head feels like a drifting balloon and my feet are made of stone. How strange. Jo-Beth's face is surrounded by mist.

She clutched at the stair rail, hearing her friend's voice winding away from her down a long tunnel.

'Elly! Hold up. I've got you.'

I'm actually ill, she thought. Oh, my heavens, what will happen to the hospital now?

Chapter Nineteen

The weather had broken and wild storms raged over the town while Elly tossed and burned with fever and her mind ranged through its own private tormented world. Nursed devotedly by Jo-Beth, attended conscientiously by Dr Houston himself, she sometimes surfaced far enough to recognise them, but only briefly, before dropping back into unconsciousness.

Only much later did she learn of the *Empire*'s report on the huge surgical breakthrough by Dr Alleyne, who in vain denied the novelty of anaesthetics or himself as their inventor. She learned, also, of the hospital board's decision to appoint her in absentia as full Matron, with increased salary to one hundred pounds per annum, plus voting her a sum of money for the most urgent repairs and equipment.

'All of which is about as much use to her now as a case of stuffed ornithological specimens,' Paul said savagely.

His voice penetrated the shallow mist of sleep as Elly felt herself emerging finally into the real world. She wanted to respond.

Jo-Beth answered him, saying she had an errand but would soon return, and Elly moved her head on the pillow and opened her eyes. 'Hello, Paul.' She began to cough.

His broad figure stooped over her to slip an arm under her shoulders and add another pillow. 'How do you feel, Elly?'

'Better, thank you.' Something worried her. What had he said? Oh, yes. 'We don't have any space to display them.'

'Display what?' Paul looked anxious.

'The ornithological specimens.'

His half smile appeared and she heard the relief in his voice. 'It was just a joke. Do you know this is the first time you've been lucid since you were struck down three weeks ago?' He drew the one available chair close to the bed and sat down.

'Three weeks!'

'You've been extremely ill with a fever. Patients, friends and well-wishers have stormed heaven with pleas for your recovery, which seem to've been heard.'

Elly flushed with pleasure. She tried to raise her hand to Paul and was astounded to find it so heavy. What had happened to her muscles?

'Don't try to do anything yet. Would you like a drink?'

She nodded, letting him assist her to sip from a glass of barley water by the bedside, enjoying his touch as much as the quenching of her thirst. When she lay back her gaze went to the window, black and streaming and buffeted by a wild wind. It was as if only chaos existed outside this tiny peaceful room. An oil lamp stood on the bedside chest, the glass bowl shedding a soft golden glow, and someone had placed a new knitted shawl around her shoulders. She fingered its softness, then glanced back at the window. 'Is it night-time?'

'No. It's not yet four o'clock. The storm has brought early darkness.'

Darkness! What about the patients? Had the lamps been lit? She didn't trust the trainees with the newly installed gas fittings. She struggled up, filled with a sudden overwhelming anxiety. 'The hospital. Who is in charge? What's happening in the wards? There's a bad leak in the roof over Ward—'

Paul pushed her gently back on the pillow. 'All's well in your world, Elly. Jo-Beth is coping; not, perhaps, with much pleasure, but she knows how to command staff. The place is running like well-oiled machinery. And the committee had the leak mended after the first storm.' He laughed. 'You never saw a posse of men so eager to please. They've positively searched out defects to re-

pair, even building a bathroom on the back landing. You're regarded as somewhat of an oracle around here now. JG's eulogy in
his paper might have had some bearing on that, plus the consequent public interest.'

'Oh, dear.'

'It was tastefully done, I assure you. Also, Dr Alleyne's admiration and approval of your methods did nothing to detract from
your reputation. How does it feel to be coupled with a celebrated
surgeon?'

'I'm not. Don't be silly.' She moved her head aside.

'All right. I won't tease you. I'm the first visitor allowed past
the door, but when you feel strong enough, JG would like to call.'

'I'd be glad to see him.' Elly's colourless tone had an obvious
effect, and Paul studied her gravely, as if concerned about a re-
lapse. How could he know it was his own friendly, unemotional
attitude that upset her, as much as her own inconsistency? Hadn't
they agreed to stifle their passionate involvement before it could
take over their lives? Wasn't that what she'd wanted, insisted upon?

Paul got up. 'I've wearied you,' he said. 'Rest now and recover
your strength. I'll call again later, by your leave, to see how you
do.'

Jo-Beth brought in a pot full of winter roses, placing them on
the windowledge where they burned like cream and pink flames
against the dark glass. While Elly admired them Jo-Beth bustled
Paul from the room with a brisk, 'Out with you, sir,' then hurried
back to straighten the counterpane. She felt Elly's forehead.
'You're so much better, my dear, God be thanked.'

'I feel rather insubstantial, Jo-Beth.'

'Food will fix that. Did Paul tell you what's been happening?'

'Yes, he did. But what about you?'

'What about me? I've never been more energetic. You have no
need to worry about me.' She sounded almost too positive, Elly
thought.

'I'm sorry you have had to take over all my responsibilities.'

Jo-Beth was dismissive. 'We're managing. Don't worry. You've
been our greatest concern, Elly. At first we feared the glandular
swelling meant lung disease; however, Dr Houston is now more
inclined to think it a virulent fever associated with the glands.'

'Thank you for all your care, Jo-Beth. I'm blessed with your friendship. I know it can't be easy for you.' Feeling suddenly exhausted, Elly closed her eyes and heard Jo-Beth quietly leave the room, freeing her to think over Paul's visit. She turned her face into the pillow, unable now to avoid the painful truth that while Paul had taken up residence in her heart and would not be banished, he, it seemed, had been more successful in ridding himself of her.

As Elly grew daily stronger and could dress and sit by the window, the number of visitors increased. She was touched to find small gifts left for her by patients she'd cared for, but embarrassed and annoyed by the cornucopia of fruits and flowers delivered daily with D'Arcy Cornwallis's card attached. The cards were immediately torn up, the gifts sent to the wards, and a puzzled Jo-Beth instructed to keep the sender away, if he should happen to call.

Elly filled her days of convalescence by mending the hospital linen and reading the daily papers, in particular their details of Britain's entry into the war against Russia in the Crimea. It had turned out as Alan McAndrews had predicted. The Tsar, having attacked Turkey in October 1853 and almost destroyed the Turkish fleet, was reportedly astonished to find himself by January at war with Great Britain and France.

Together Elly and Jo-Beth read of the carnage and the casualties resulting not only from battle, but from unattended wounds and disease. One morning Elly's unthinking speculation as to Captain McAndrews's possible involvement provoked an outburst from Jo-Beth, who clearly feared such an event. Jo-Beth stormed off, leaving Elly appalled at her own stupidity, her weakened nerves in tatters. Paul found her hunched over the windowsill in tears.

'What is it? Are you in pain?' He dropped the armful of flowering shrub he carried and rushed over to kneel beside her chair. 'Tell me, Elly. Shall I fetch someone?'

'It's nothing. I'm perfectly well. Oh, go away, please do. I'm making an exhibition of myself and I can't hel ... help it,' she sobbed, burying her face in her shawl.

Paul hugged her. 'You're being emotional, which isn't any wonder. Convalescents are allowed to shed tears, didn't you know?'

Elly sniffled and sat up, searching for her handkerchief. His arm around her shoulders felt like a hot brand. She wished he'd remove it.

'You're flesh and blood, Elly, not cast iron, despite any notions you may have to the contrary.' He let her go and stood up. 'Now, tell me if there's a difficulty I or Jo-Beth, or any number of others who would climb mountains for you, can deal with.'

Warmed by his concern she said: 'I'm just wretchedly weak and unaccustomed to having my emotions overflow without warning. I'm sorry, Paul.' She peeked at him over the handkerchief. 'I've hurt poor Jo-Beth, after she's been so good and self-sacrificing. I feel like a worm.'

'She'll forgive you. Your friendship is strong enough to stand a small contretemps. Jo-Beth is not a person to hold a grudge for long.'

'I know. But I must apologise as soon as possible.' Elly sighed and tucked the handkerchief in her sleeve. 'I so dislike unbalanced females, yet here I am wobbling like a child's top. Pay no mind to it, as my little Irish maid says whenever I point out something she's missed.' She indicated the chair especially brought for visitors. 'Sit and tell me what you've been doing, Paul.'

He gathered up the bush flowers, leaving a spray of shed petals all over the floor, then plunged the remainder into a nearby water jug and sat down.

'I've been trying to persuade JG to take Pepper as a boarder once more.'

'You're going away?' She couldn't hide her dismay.

'I must. It's a family obligation.'

'But I thought you had no family, or only remote cousins up in the Hunter River district.' Her voice had risen noticeably.

'My mother's cousin, Rob Whatmough, and his wife and daughter. Sadly, it seems Rob lost his wife soon after they settled, so he decided to move on further west to Bathurst. I visited him a few weeks past and found him congenial.'

'So, why must you visit him again?' She searched his face, unable to repress a twinge of jealousy.

He looked grave. 'I've had a letter from a Reverend Barton of Bathurst. Rob Whatmough was killed by a falling tree limb when riding in the forest, leaving his daughter, Lucy, an orphan. It seems that on his deathbed Rob commended her to my care.'

'A child? A little girl?'

'A young woman. Lucy is seventeen. Oh, I know I can scarcely take her into my bachelor household. I don't intend to. Lucy is skilled in the making of machine lace, as was her family, and while she has no equipment to do such work here, her nimble fingers will, I'm sure, be well suited to employment in a millinery establishment. I've found a place in Sydney where she may be apprenticed. I'll keep her under my eye and see she's cared for by the Widow Brockenhurst, who will house and feed her and see to her welfare.'

'Well, I've no doubt the poor girl will be glad enough to have a cousin left to her. She must be so lonely in her grief.' Elly's emotions threatened to overwhelm her once more as she thought of the forlorn young woman in Bathurst.

'Which is why I must leave by the end of the week. The Reverend Barton's epistolary style is curt to the point of rudeness. I'd say he wants to be rid of Lucy.'

'I'll miss your visits. Will you call again before you leave?' Elly tried to keep her disappointment under control.

'Of course I'll come. I'm happy to see so much stronger, although you must not return to your duties just yet.'

Elly hated to admit it, but he was right. She couldn't face the wards just yet.

That evening, Jo-Beth, who had long forgiven their quarrel, found Elly despondent and questioned her about it.

'I'm tired, that's all. I'm tired of these four walls, tired of fighting … oh, tired of everything.'

'We're all tired and overworked, but you've driven yourself beyond sense. Although you may be physically well again, your spirits have not yet caught up with your body.'

'That's as may be. But the malaise is so draining. It's like being at the bottom of a well with a ladder to climb, but the rungs are so far apart and I haven't the will to pull myself up.' Elly laughed unhappily. 'Take no notice of my whimpering. I'm not proud of myself.'

Jo-Beth was thoughtful. 'You won't thank me for saying this will pass. You know it will, in time. However, I can suggest a way of making it happen more quickly.'

'How? Tell me.'

'A holiday. You need a holiday, Elly.'

Elly's face fell. 'It's impossible.'

'No, it's not. Paul and I have had a discussion behind your back, for which we hope you'll forgive us. We've decided you should go with him to Bathurst to chaperon young Lucy Whatmough on the return journey.'

Elly stared, open-mouthed. 'You're not serious.'

'I am. The coach service over the mountains is good, and the passes are clear. There's been no snow for weeks. You will enjoy the trip, I'm sure. I hear the mountain country and the western slopes are beautiful.'

Oh, if I only could go, Elly thought. But it's a ridiculous notion, for many reasons. 'Just who would chaperon *me* on the outward journey?'

Jo-Beth laughed. 'The coachman and passengers.'

'Your argument isn't logical.'

'It isn't meant to be. Come, you know you'd love to go. The change would do you so much good. I can continue to run the hospital perfectly well for a few more days, with the help of two excellent young nurses and the two new trainees. You know you're not yet fit to go back to work.'

'But Paul ... Did he really suggest this?'

'He approached me with the idea this morning, asking me to persuade you into agreement. Now, don't be difficult Elly. Paul is not just anyone, he's a friend, the longest standing friend you have in this town. He can be trusted to care for you. After all, it's not as if you haven't travelled together before—unchaperoned.'

The unbidden thought flashed through Elly's mind—perhaps, if we're thrown together for days on end ... Caught between hope and duty, she wavered, finally raising her hands in surrender. 'Jo-Beth! What will I do with you, and how can I do without you? I'm positively beset with goodwill. All the same, I intend taking my life back into my own control quite soon, I give you due warning.'

Jo-Beth wasn't noticeably cast down. 'We'll defer to you in all ways, once you're back from your holiday. Until then, I'm in charge, Matron.'

Four days later, Elly and Paul boarded the paddle-steamer going up-river to Parramatta, a thriving town surrounded by farms, orchards and lush market gardens. There they joined the coach for the one hundred and twenty mile trip to Bathurst. The coach's huge body, painted tan with elegant black scrollwork and shaped like a large egg flattened at the top, hung on leather straps above the undercarriage; while the team of four strong horses harnessed to it appeared quite capable of dragging the eleven people with sundry goods up and down mountainsides. Elly, excited by the bustle of departure and the new scenes, felt stronger by the minute.

Paul handed her up to join the other four passengers inside, then took his seat beside her.

'The baggage is secure, but I'm sorry for those poor devils up top. They'll freeze, even in their greatcoats.' He tucked a rug around her knees, checking that her feet were placed on a stone footwarmer.

She thanked him, then leant from the window to watch the coachman spring up to his seat to take the reins. With a shout and a whip crack, the coach rolled out of the inn yard onto the hard-packed street, past St John's Church to join the pike road westward. Ahead of them the plain stretched towards a haze of blue-ridged mountains, and puffs of dust marked the passage of drays and carts carrying merchandise for the diggings. They passed these slow vehicles and bowled along at an exhilarating fifteen miles to the hour past farms, mills, orchards and, closer to the foothills, rows of grapevines snaking down to the river. From the outpost of Emu the road sloped sharply upwards in long hairpin bends, affording stupendous views back to the coast. There was also the added excitement of negotiating a passage past spring wagons laden with travellers and their goods; mobs of sheep being herded west to a squatter's domain; horsemen and men on foot with all their worldly possessions upon their backs, undaunted by the miles to be covered over disheartening terrain.

The three-day trip was a delight to Elly, despite the appalling road. In places, rocks protruded up to two feet above the surface of the track. However, the coach crashed hardily up and over to roll on undamaged through the forest towards Springwood, where they stopped for refreshment. The grandeur of the mountains, their magnificent stands of trees and fern-filled glens, the constantly changing vistas of valleys and peaks and red-rock canyons continued to fascinate Elly. Then the scene turned to a bleaker, more alpine terrain, with stunted trees, their bark webbed in silver-green lichens. Yet even this had power to awe with its silence and the uninterrupted ranges marching away in splendid isolation towards the horizon.

The other passengers, an ex-digger returning to his farm, a husband and wife on a visit to their married daughter in Bathurst, and a tongue-tied young man about to join a group of surveyors, were pleasant enough company. But Elly longed for privacy with Paul, for an opportunity to discover whether there was still a chance for true intimacy between them. It was such a joy to have him beside her, within touching distance, but tantalising, too.

At King's Tableland, where they would spend the night at an inn, the temperature dropped sharply and Elly gladly left the coach for a log fire and a cup of hot cocoa.

'The fleas were thrown in as an extra,' she quipped the next morning to Paul as the coach moved out onto the mist veiled track. There had been no opportunity for them to be alone together at the inn. She could only look forward to their day together in Bathurst before taking the coach home. Surely Lucy Whatmough could wait a few hours longer.

Her spirits rose with the sun. The change of surroundings had done its job; despite chilled feet and a bruised and shaken body, with Paul beside her and her responsibilities left behind, Elly was happy for the first time in months. As the coach slipped and slid down the steep pass, brakes hard on, with a great log chained to the back to slow them so as not to overrun the horses, she gazed out at the vista of rich pastoral lands and downs sloping out to the horizon and knew it for a rural paradise. No wonder men fought to have their share.

The following day they crossed the sparsely treed plains marking the most westward of the nineteen counties and rolled into Bathurst after sunset, muddy from stream crossings, the horses hanging their weary heads. At the inn, a verandahed two-storey stone structure as fine as any in Sydney Town, Elly found herself so stiff she had to be lifted down. Held briefly in Paul's arms, she allowed herself the luxury of pressing against him. Then she was on her feet looking up at the inn lanterns burning in the frosty air, with the tingle of circulation returning to her limbs, and recognising one of those rare moments of complete happiness.

'Thank you for bringing me, Paul. I'm so glad I came.'

'I'm every bit as glad. But I hope you feel the same way on the return journey.' He raised his head. 'Those clouds are ominous. There's snow coming.'

Elly tensed. 'Oh, no.'

'I'm afraid so. Elly, I think we should fetch Lucy immediately and take the morning coach back.'

Chapter Twenty

Pearl crouched on the back of the laden dray, swaying and lurching with each jolt, cocooned in a bone-deep weariness that masked both physical discomfort and the interminable length of days measured by the walking pace of a bullock.

Pearl knew the inertia she was feeling had its roots in disappointment after long-sustained hope. More than hope. *Knowing* that Li Po would be found in one of the miners' camps beyond the mountains, she had trudged the weary miles from Ophir to Hill End to the more far-flung diggings, through dust and dung, buoyed by this certainty. Over the next rise, at the next creek he'd be there, sifting sand through his pan, rocking the miner's cradle, plucking out gold from dross.

There were days when, parched by a merciless sun, she scrabbled in creek beds and sieved grit between her teeth to extract moisture; nights she spent rolled in a ball under the roots of a fallen tree, plagued by hunger and pain, prepared for an uncertain reception at each new camp. She questioned Chinese men who worked the abandoned tailings of more impatient westerners, but none had heard of Li Po. Others treated her variously with hostility, derision or simple indifference as she followed the tracks marked on her map, earning food by cooking or binding up wounds, enduring soaring temperatures and summer storms that cracked the forest giants and toppled them around her. Without shelter or friendly company to ease the rigours of her journey, she combed the hills and plains of the western goldfields until her certainty crumbled into a despairing admission. Li Po was not there.

Then, like a trumpet call to arms, news of another great strike in Victoria swept through the camps, bringing hope to spirits ground down by months of toil and disillusionment. Victoria's the place to go, boys. Let's pack up and try our luck further south. Pearl managed to attach herself as cook to a party of four with an ox-pulled dray to carry their equipment—decent enough men beneath their rough, bearded exterior—who treated her with an offhandedness which suited her well. She ran to their cries of 'Chinky, boil up the kettle', baked their mutton chops and damper and kept her distance.

Through rough mountain terrain, down to the dry grass plains following the stock route, fording creeks, ferrying across the last great river dividing the two colonies, they reached the high gum forests of Victoria. There they joined the stream of travellers between Sydney and Melbourne, along with other gold seekers and stockmen droving cattle from the north to feed the miners already established in their thousands throughout the land. Pearl left her party when they turned off east to the Ballarat–Bendigo diggings. Having lost her pack of medical equipment when fording the Murrumbidgee, she needed to replace her stock in order to earn a livelihood. Cooks could be found amongst the weak or disabled, but a person with medical skills was prized beyond gold itself by men living in conditions ripe for disease and accident. She also wanted to honour her promise to Elly and visit the Post Office in Melbourne, as well as to seek traces of Li Po amongst the burgeoning Chinese community in that city.

She arrived on the outskirts one afternoon to find herself in a town gone mad. Inpouring migrants scoured the stores to set themselves up for the diggings, while those who had made their pile but lost all commonsense whooped it up on the spending spree of their lives. Wild-looking fellows in cabbage-tree hats and moleskins galloped the streets on gold-shod horses, firing off pistols at will. Others had gathered flashy companions of both sexes' in shiny new carriages and whipped through town at reckless speed while downing the best champagne and lighting cigars with five-pound notes.

Amazed, Pearl stood well back on the boardwalk of Collins Street. There were no saunterers, no people going sedately about their business, only men scurrying with purpose across the traffic to avoid being mown down by the roisterers. Gaudy street-women, chattering like macaws, clung to their escorts and screeched with laughter as men reeled from a nearby hotel to empty champagne bottles into a horse trough, inviting passers-by to drink with them on pain of assault.

Pearl slipped away from the brawling streets to find the Chinese immigrant quarter, a cluster of shops, laundries and vegetable gardens, where Li Po's name evoked no response, although she did learn that most men of her race favoured the goldfields at Forest Creek, Bendigo and Ballarat. She sheltered overnight in the home of an ancient apothecary who gave her his own brand of salve to rub on her blisters; then she sallied forth with renewed vigour to visit the post office, buy new boots and medical equipment, and book a place on the stage to Castlemaine, Forest Creek. The fare of four pounds would deplete her hoard, but it would take her so long to walk the eighty-five miles. She feared her brother could move on to the new fields being opened up each week. Also, she had been warned of the dangers on the track, from ex-convict plunderers to snakes to sudden violent storms filling potholes deep enough to drown a horse. There had been adventures enough getting this far.

At six the next morning a coach run by Mr Cobb's American Telegraph Line left the Criterion Hotel in Collins Street, with Pearl perched behind a pile of baggage thirteen feet above the wheel hubs. She had not expected to be allocated an inside seat. Crimson plush was not for scrubby oriental boys. The heavy booking of all roof seats had left her no option but to wedge herself between luggage and the iron rail running around the roof and hold on tight as the Yankee Whip on the box, once clear of the city, picked up the pace on a track knee-deep with dust. This rose to hang like fog over the drays and carts toiling along the ruts. Horses and bullocks strove under the whip, barely avoiding running down men on foot with swags on their shoulders or pushing wheelbarrows laden with tools. Pearl saw children harnessed to carts, women trundling prams piled high with camping gear, their babies tied to their backs. A packhorse went by laden with a portable iron bedstead, then came a carriage pulled by a team of large white dogs. Every imaginable stratum of society was represented—runaway servants and seamen, ticket-of-leave men fresh from the penal settlements in Van Diemen's Land, men who had abandoned business or profession, prostitutes, gentlemen, clergymen, the hale and the weak, plus whole families scrambling out of the slums and onto the rutted highway to riches, north to the goldfields.

The journey turned into an endurance test, with the six-horse team being changed at ten miles so expertly that the passengers barely had time to register that motion had, blessedly, briefly ceased. At fifteen miles an hour they whirled past the grog shanties which had sprung up along the route, where many travellers stopped for a dose of oblivion. Pearl's heart was wrenched by the sight of children left untended and exhausted beside the track, along with the carcasses of horses and bullocks pushed beyond tolerance then left to rot.

Rain had fallen steadily since they started the long steep climb up The Gap then plunged down the other side into Gisborne, thirty-four miles out of Melbourne. The worst stage of the journey lay ahead. Pearl sensed the other roof passengers' anxiety as they entered a thirteen-mile stretch of range country which included the gloomy Black Forest, notorious for the shocking state of the track and the number of attacks by bushrangers who hid amongst the dense thickets of ironbarks. Her own nerves tightened as they entered a cavern of trees where all sound ceased, save for the drumming of hooves and raindrops pattering on canvas. Commonsense told her the more obvious victims would be gold-laden miners returning to civilisation, or even, daringly, the gold transport under armed escort. Yet logic had little weight when the senses were oppressed by such sullen, lonely surroundings and the travellers' tales told with false bravado while eyes darted from tree to tree. Along with the other passengers, Pearl relaxed her taut vigilance only when the Wood End Inn at Five-Mile Creek came into sight, with its promise of food and rest and, above all, safety.

It poured all night and through the next day's travel north over undulating high country, but eventually they reached the turn-off to Castlemaine, Forest Creek. Soon the coach drew into a muddy market square lined with wagons drawn up outside a row of shopfronts. Shivering in her wet clothes, Pearl climbed stiffly down to survey the scene. The shantytown stores were outnumbered by weatherboard and canvas public houses, but signboards indicated a post office and bank, and even in such bad weather it was a bustling place.

Brown-faced men in moleskins and vests over their worn blue or red shirts heaved provisions into carts or slung sacks over their backs before heading off towards the tent town that mushroomed beyond the marketplace. Pearl followed, unable to believe what she saw—thousands upon thousands of dun-coloured tents extending through gullies for miles in all directions. Despite its name, there was no sign of a forest, only a few straggling trees left as a reminder of how the land had once been. The slippery clay, pock-marked with immense holes, had been chopped to a muddy slush, knee deep in places. Everything dripped, including the tents sprung up like some ugly fungal growth intent on swallowing the countryside. It was immense—impossible to search.

Pearl sat down on a tree stump, feeling her courage ebb. But she hadn't come this far to be defeated. Soon she rose again and set off for the nearest store. Meeting with rejection there, she continued around the square, asking whoever would listen whether they could direct her to a Chinese encampment, and eventually her persistence won her a response. Mentally repeating the rough directions given by a tavern keeper, she hurried off into the dusk, anxious to find the creek before full dark.

Luck was with her. Stumbling down the sandy bank, she turned right, following the almost dry bed down to a junction with another trickling stream. Half a mile further on she found the Chinese encampment, heard the familiar cadence of voices like her own, smelt the pungent aroma of spices in the cooking pots and incense rising from the tong leaders' tents as they knelt on their prayer mats and approached their ancestors on behalf of their people so far from home.

'Your brother was here, but two moons have passed since he departed.' Ah Fung stroked his beard with long thin fingers and examined Pearl's face for a reaction.

She knew she had betrayed her elation, quickly cut short by dismay, but she kept her voice steady as she continued to question the old tong leader. They squatted together outside his tent, Ah Fung enjoying a pipe, with an occasional sip from a porcelain jar beside him. A lone gum tree spread its boughs overhead, where a party of sulphur-crested cockatoos squabbled and screeched in the wintry sunlight. Around them the ground steamed like a kettle after last night's rain.

'Is it in the mind of the venerable grandfather to tell this lowly woman where to seek Li Po?' Pearl kept her gaze correctly averted and stared down at the creek banks, swarming with figures of all ages, size and description, digging, puddling in tin dishes, carting water buckets and wheelbarrows of dirt amidst the clacking of hundreds of cradles.

There were Englishmen, weedy products of Whitechapel alongside gentlemen's sons; perky Irish next to brawny Scots; experienced Americans from the California fields rubbing shoulders with new chums who hardly knew one end of a pick from another, blistering their hands and exchanging news on the latest finds with ticket-of-leaves still pallid from prison. Chinese, Indian, African and Middle-Eastern—all were represented in the melting pot of the rush, each man only as good as his word. Thick yellow clay overlaid everything, smearing clothes, tools and tents, colouring the water to a sickly gamboge. Hillocks of discarded yellow soil pimpled the barren landscape, creating an ugly alien world for inhabitants who concentrated only on digging more holes, shifting more gravel in their endless search for gold.

The old man closed his eyes and puffed on his pipe. He said: 'Once this land was green, the grass and trees rooted in rich black soil. Then men came to cut through the soil to find grey clay and red gravel. They dug further and found the yellow clay. Sometimes they worked down twenty feet to reach the thin layer of rich blue-brown clay that held the gold. They raped the earth, left it despoiled, then moved on to do the same elsewhere. Your brother is such a one.'

Pearl acknowledged the old man's disapproval with a nod, and waited patiently for him to answer her question.

He continued. 'I accompanied the men of my village, to be with them when they faced their struggles in a new and hostile land. They came because their families starved, and they send their gold back to China so that their wives and sons may be released from bondage to the rich men who paid the passage money. Your brother hoards his gold for himself, yet what he gains is never sufficient. He has been overcome by greed.'

Pearl bowed her head. The silence extended until the old man sighed and gathered his creaking bones to stand up. She rose with him, knowing she was about to be dismissed.

'Sister of Li Po, your spirit is as loyal and tenacious as a man's. Seek your brother on the field called Ballarat.' He entered his tent and closed the flap.

Ballarat! Another fifty-five miles to walk! Why couldn't Li-Po have chosen to go to the rich Bendigo diggings, just a little way to the north? Then, feeling she tempted fate with her ingratitude, Pearl hastily amended her thoughts, giving appropriate thanks to any gods who might be listening.

With her last coins, she replenished her stock of food at a store where Asian customers were tolerated; then, her bulging pack over her shoulder, she set off for the road to Ballarat. Along the way she saw trees signposted with misspelt private messages—*if This Meets the I of James Crakinton, He Will ear of His Frend Tomass fawke at mistre Snars Opposite The guvermint camp*—and placards shouting *No chains for free Englishmen,* a reference to the wave of rebellion against the licence fees swelling throughout the goldfields. Pearl shook her head over this, vowing to keep clear of the disturbances.

The weather stayed fine, although the nights were so cold Pearl found it hard to sleep on a bed of boughs under one worn blanket. But the third day saw her stepping out the last few miles of her destination. The road ran through a section of dense bush reminiscent of the Dark Forest near Five Mile Creek. Uneasy at the gloom and ominous stillness, she increased her pace, keeping to the middle of the track. Her apprehension was justified when three men sprang suddenly from between the trees and stood regarding her from beneath their wide-brimmed hats. They were dressed like diggers but with the addition of pistols which they pointed at Pearl.

She turned to run, but one man had moved behind her. He lowered his pistol, saying contemptuously to his fellows: 'It's just a scurvy Mongol. He'll have nothing worth the taking.'

Pearl was furious at the prospect of losing her precious medical kit once more, but she felt the stirrings of fear at the expression in the eyes of the red-bearded man who had come up close to stare at her. They were mud-brown in colour, with a spark at the pupil, like the eyes of an unreliable animal.

'I'll cut off his pigtail for a souvenir.' He drew a bowie knife from his belt and with the other hand swept Pearl's cap off onto the track. Before she could move, he had her by the plait, stretching it high, cruelly dangling her with the tips of her toes on the ground. Watching her face, he seemed angry when she didn't plead for release, and gave a vicious jerk that wrenched a scream from her.

A smile split the bearded features, revealing gapped and stained teeth. 'Well, well. I thought you were a mite tiny, even for a Mongol. Lookee here, lads.' He slit through Pearl's jacket, shirt and trousers, and ruthlessly tore them aside, exposing her woman's body.

Seeing Redbeard's companion lick his lips, hearing the surprised grunt from the man behind her, Pearl knew what awaited her. But her fears centred on Redbeard. She'd seen his like before, and knew she'd be lucky to come out of this alive. Her thoughts flickered incoherently. Could she wrench free without losing her hair? Could she hope to escape all three men, even if the chance came to disable her captor with a kick? The pain in her neck and scalp was excruciating; her skin was slippery with sweat. She brought her arms up, flailing, trying to grasp the man's wrist, but he held it too high above her head. She scrabbled, vainly, for her knife. The pieces of coat had fallen back from her shoulders, beyond her reach. Another tug tore at her scalp and warm blood trickled down her face. Pearl cried out in agony.

Redbeard released her so suddenly that she overbalanced and fell onto a rib she'd broken only last year in the shipwreck, hearing it snap as she hit a ridge in the track. Her teeth met on her tongue and blood filled her mouth. Dust rose in her nostrils as a breeze stirred, breaking the stillness.

The man behind moved her with his boot. 'I don't want no truck with no dirty Mongol. I say we leave her be and clear out. There'll be better game along.'

Through a red haze of pain Pearl saw him pick up her pack and begin rummaging through it.

'Clean or dirty, yellow or white, what's the difference?' asked the third man. 'They've all got a hole in the right place.'

Redbeard sniggered. 'You should know, Cato, out with the sheep all those years. Or didn't you choose between ram and ewe, eh?'

'Shut up, and let's get on with it before someone else happens by.'

Half senseless with the torment of her injuries, Pearl was dragged in amongst the trees and thrown down on her side. Her eyes rolled up but she fought to remain conscious, desperate to get to her knife. She slid a hand under her body, feeling for cloth, but it was too late. Her legs were thrust apart and Redbeard was upon her. She'd been right about him. He liked the refinements of cruelty, and for the next few minutes he practised his brand of sadism, using knife tip and fingers to exact the maximum satisfaction, leaning back after each attack to enjoy the results as portrayed in her face. Agonised, Pearl abandoned her stoicism and screamed, knowing his malignancy would only increase if she did not. But all the while she clung onto her purpose, holding off the pain with an enormous effort of will and edging her left hand along the ground, feeling for the torn fabric of her jacket.

Her courage almost failed when she felt the knife tip against her lips. Looking up into the cruel eyes holding hers she hovered on the edge of hysteria. Not her face! The knife tip glided so slowly, almost lovingly across her cheek and up into the hairline. The pain was nothing to her mental anguish. Her face! He was destroying her face!

The breeze had become a wild wind tearing through the treetops above. She fixed her gaze on the branches madly thrashing against the darkening sky while leaves showered down on her upturned face like ragged confetti. Almost delirious, she felt the earth shake from a stronger blast. In her fancy the trees gripped the soil with their roots, hanging on grimly while smaller branches were torn from their crowns and whirled away, gyrating madly in time to some unheard devil's orchestra. Her fingers closed on cloth and edged their way beneath.

'Here, when's it my turn?' The man Cato stood over her, looking disgusted. 'There won't be nuthin' left for me if you don't finish.'

His companion, standing some distance away, shouted above the noise of the wind: 'I don't hold with killin'. It sets the traps on. Are you two comin' or will I go on alone?'

A lull fell, and the earth seemed to take a breath. Redbeard's voice broke the sudden silence. 'What're you after there?' His hand descended, pinning Pearl's wrist. The bones crunched and her fingers opened involuntarily to release the bit of fabric. The torn lining fell away to reveal a pair of gold earrings.

Before Pearl's attacker could move, Cato bent and scooped up the glinting gold. With a roar, Redbeard surged up onto his knees. 'Give me that, you thieving swine. It's mine.' He teetered sideways, off-balance, as the other man stepped back.

It was all the time Pearl had, and all she needed. Her hand closed on the knife hilt. The gale struck again, blasting through the forest, drowning Pearl's cry as she plunged the blade with all her strength into Redbeard's belly. He gazed down in astonishment, his mouth gaping. Pearl wrenched the blade across, and hot blood and intestines spilled out over her hands and body.

'Bitch!' he screamed. Two great hands met around Pearl's throat and began to throttle her.

'I never seen anythin' to equal it, not ever. And in a Christian country, too.' The voice reached Pearl like an echo from a far canyon, reverberating, not quite clear.

Another, slower voice answered, 'Well, it happened to a heathen din't it?'

'A woman, Tom. If she was heathen as the Cham of Tartary, what's bin done to her is a disgrace to all men. Lucky for her we found that cap on the track and had a scout around.'

Pearl became aware of a jolting movement, racking her with each breath. It was almost unbearable. For a moment she lost track of the voices, then she heard the first man again.

'I reckon it was one o'them Vandemonians come over from Port Arthur to set up as a bushranger. The Geelong coach's bin bailed up twice this month, the driver and a passenger shot the first time; and a man was robbed and left for dead on this stretch o'road only a week ago. Now this. Do you think she'll hold out till we get to the Chinee doctor over Golden Point? He's her best bet, I reckon.'

The man named Tom must have expressed doubt, because his companion said vehemently: 'Well, she won't do a perish if I c'n help it. Come on, horse.' A whip cracked smartly and the cart picked up speed. 'And you, Tom Rudd, wantin' to stop to bury the flamin' mad dog what did it to her. I hope the dingoes have 'im for breakfast.' The cartwheel hit a stone, and a spear of agony went through Pearl and she fainted.

She awoke to a stinging sensation as if she'd been attacked by a swarm of mosquitoes from head to foot. A pungent odour filled her nostrils. Above her, lamplight flickered on canvas walls. The only sounds were external, distant shouts, the occasional shot, snatches of music accompanied by barking dogs. Her whole body flamed with pain; yet it was a strangely damped-down agony, as if she were detached from it, feeling it at second-hand. Her mind had gone mercifully blank. Turning her head she first noticed her arm, impaled with silver needles fine as filaments; and beyond, a thin, upright figure in blue blouse and trousers, his slender fingers outstretched to twist two of the needles. The fresh pain was negligible, although she did wonder why this stranger inflicted it upon her.

'What are you doing?' She knew she'd spoken, although no sound emerged. When she tried again, without success, she decided her throat must be damaged.

An egg-shaped head, smooth and brown all over, and a face embellished with a stringy moustache and beard loomed over her. A voice said in Mandarin: 'Lie quietly. Do not try to speak. You will recover if you obey my instructions. Here is a draught to ease pain and induce sleep. Drink.'

Pearl drank, then drifted off to sleep.

Hold High the Flame

This time, when she awoke, sunlight filtered through the canvas, revealing it to be a large tent lined with chests and a small cupboard fitted with many drawers. In one corner a brazier threw off a pungent herbal odour. A bowl of sand set beneath a hanging silk scroll held several burning incense sticks. A carpet had been spread and the tall Chinese who had attended her sat cross-legged on a pile of cushions, working a pestle and mortar. He looked up when she turned her head.

'I am Dr Hsien Lo. Your throat has been injured, but it will not be permanent if you do not attempt to speak for another day. I will endeavour to supply answers to questions which will be in your mind.' The high, twittery voice was strangely reassuring. She was in capable hands. She could afford to let go her vigilance.

But the moment she relaxed, memory swept back in, and she began to relive the scene in the forest. Sweat broke out on her forehead. A keening moan rose in her throat. With a cry she flung her hand over her eyes, trying to blot out the horror.

An arm slipped under her neck to raise her and a chirping voice penetrated her nightmare, demanding that she listen. Enveloped by a soothing odour of herbs, she began to take in the words.

'Know that serenity is the master of restlessness and an integral being is placid, never departing from the centre of his own being. The things of the world change constantly. There is a time for things to move ahead, and a following time for things to retreat; a time to withdraw internally, and a following time to expand. This is your time to withdraw, to centre your being and allow healing to take place.'

Needles pricked her flesh and a delicate pulsation flowed through her body. Calm enveloped her as the doctor's voice rose and fell in gentle cadence, the words sometimes familiar, sometimes imparting truths she thought she had always known. Drifting, awake and yet not awake, and now wonderfully at peace, she began to examine her life in depth, amazed to find how little it meant. Finding Li Po had been an excuse, she now saw. She had used it as a reason to escape the old pattern, without any plan beyond that moment of culmination. She had no path to follow. Had she really meant to hand over her future to a stranger, to abdicate her hard-won freedom and self-sufficiency?

Much later she noticed with amazement how her thoughts had turned away from her dreadful ordeal. In some way the agony of mind she'd expected to suffer had been pushed into the back of her consciousness, still there, yet diminished, leached of much of the terror and grief, and overlaid by a meditative calm.

During the following days Pearl watched Dr Hsien Lo closely. His unusual treatments, his detailing of ancient Chinese medical lore allied to the teachings of Lao-tse, interested her and she listened to him intently. When he treated other patients, she followed his activities closely; when he was absent he always left one of his servant assistants with her to explain the various contents of the herb chests and, as she soon realised, to give her a sense of security. The fear of being alone and vulnerable was the one thing she couldn't yet deal with. In the meantime her body and mind healed.

The doctor explained the rudiments of his profession, emphasising the importance of one element, *Qi*, the life force affecting the whole body, mind and spirit; then there were the yin organs deep within, and the more external organs, the yang. He discussed the origins of disharmony, the precipitating factors in illness, the ways to examine signs and symptoms, plus the use of the needle therapy to tap into the meridians or unseen channels that carry *Qi*, nourishment and strength throughout the body.

Pearl learned that every Chinese physician must have a complete grasp of the meridian system and the three hundred and sixty-five main points where these may be intercepted in order to rebalance disharmonies. She watched her mentor insert needles with unassailable confidence, saw patients relieved of localised pain by an insertion in seemingly unrelated parts of the body. Sometimes he burned a tiny portion of moxa, a herbal mix, sending heat into the pressure point to achieve his aim.

'Intervention with moxa or needles can reduce what is excessive,' Hsien Lo explained, 'increase what is deficient, warm what is cold, cool what is hot, circulate what is stagnant, move what is congealed, stabilise what is reckless, raise what is falling and lower what is rising. And then, there is the use of herbs.'

Pearl glanced at the chests. 'There must be hundreds.'

'More than five thousand, if we include animal ingredients and minerals. Herbology extends back to the Han dynasty. There are some five hundred common classical prescriptions with which to begin. However, since each patient's body is unique, these must then be adjusted to the individual.'

'It's a life's study.'

'It is so.'

One day Pearl asked the doctor for a mirror. He paused for a long moment before replying: 'The face you have now is altered, but not the being behind the mask. You have seen what was done to your body and you have accepted. It is time to learn whether you can accept another change.'

Pearl, knowing the bowie knife had been used on her face, braced herself and held out her hand for the mirror.

The almond eyes had not been touched. Her button nose retained its shape. But from the corner of her delicate mouth the knife tip had cut a line across her cheek up to the temple, splitting the skin like overripe fruit, distorting the curve of her upper lip into a permanent lop-sided smile. The wound was livid and raw, with the stitches showing like jagged teeth; it would heal with time, but her face could never be restored. Pearl stared impassively at her reflection, as if at a stranger, the anger and distress she had expected to feel surprisingly absent, as though this thing had been done to someone else.

'It could have been worse,' she remarked, giving back the mirror. She fingered the hole in her upper arm where the brand of a slave had been gouged out of her flesh. She thought about the damage done to the rest of her body.

Dr Hsien Lo looked grave. 'Later you will feel grief. Remember this time when you are grateful to be alive and able to function. Your face is scarred, but not hideously, and your mind is resilient. You were ready to know the Way.'

'I was taught to be a Christian and to use Western medicine. How can I reconcile these with the Tao teachings and the methods you use to heal?'

Hsien Lo spread his thin hands. 'I am a Buddhist. The Way is open to all who are willing to listen. It is not a religion but a philosophy of living, a pathway of subtle truth which allows us to perceive the gentle operation of the universe. As for the medicine, perhaps there is room for both eastern and western streams. However, I cannot see a way of bringing them into confluence. The western healer views the human body as a machine, governed by mechanical laws, a working system of separate components which can be treated in isolation from the whole, even removed. A doctor of the east views the human being as a microcosm of nature, a smaller universe in which a damaged part must necessarily throw out the balance of the whole. He is more interested in preventing disease than in treating it. In all my years of study I have acquired only a portion of the knowledge encompassed by this profession. I see the pattern, yet can follow only part.'

As the weeks followed, Pearl soaked up Hsien Lo's teaching, healing mentally and physically while absorbing the intricacies and seeming contradictions of the Taoist philosophy as he interpreted it. She was content, and not anxious to disturb the even passage of time.

Then one evening after the last patient had left and Pearl was packing away the herb chest, without warning, the doctor said: 'I have made enquiries. Your brother, Li Po, has been found at a place named Chinaman's Gully, on the western slopes of White Horse Range, but he has not been told of your search.'

Pearl sat down suddenly. 'How did you know about him?'

'You revealed many things when your mind wandered. Will you go to him?'

Faced with re-entering the world, unprotected, Pearl quailed inwardly. I'm like a turtle who has lost its shell, she thought. Still, I have to leave some time. It might as well be now. 'Tomorrow,' she said. 'I've hidden in your shadow long enough, venerable doctor.'

A smile cracked the smooth surface of Hsien Lo's face. His lips parted to show pointed, yellow teeth, and he made a hissing sound of pleasure. 'You should have been a son. Your father would have taken pride in you.'

Pearl responded with a grimace. 'My father addressed me only as Second Girl, and sold me when he could. I give my loyalty and respect to one who earns it. You, venerable doctor, I can never repay. You may ask of me what you will.'

'Ah. Then you will attempt to follow the Way, in virtue and self-mastery?'

'I will try.'

'And you will remember that one of natural, integral virtue helps all people impartially. Thus, no-one is abandoned. This is called "embodying the light of the subtle truth".'

'You're saying, forgive your enemies, turn the other cheek.'

'Only by cultivating the virtue of wholeness and by returning injury with kindness can there be true harmony.'

'I killed a man.'

'Who died trying to kill you. There is no law against self-preservation.'

Pearl sighed. 'I have such a long way to go.'

'Despair is unwarranted. The path of subtle truth of the universe always supports those who are wholly virtuous, and even those who simply try. Come, take this pack of the herbs whose properties you have learned. Use them as I have shown you, with care and with kindness towards all those in need.'

Chapter Twenty-one

The Reverend John Barton's cottage proved to be close by the Bathhurst coaching inn, but as far from its cosy welcoming aura as an ice house on the moon. Elly and Paul were not invited in beyond the hall with its bare scrubbed boards and smell of boiling sheets, while the minister himself, tight-mouthed and rigidly erect, greeted them with more relief than warmth.

'The young woman you have come to collect will require the strictest supervision. She appears not to have been taught the most basic principles of behaviour.'

Startled, Elly glanced at Paul, whose brows rose half comically.

'Is she a naughty lass?' he asked. 'I expect my cousin spoiled her.'

Barton snorted. 'If you call smearing the inside of my wife's best teapot with soap and cutting off the brim of my Sunday beaver naughty. I call it malice aforethought. She needs to feel a birch broom about her legs.'

'Surely not!' Paul and Elly found themselves in chorus, as the door at the end of the hall opened and a figure erupted through it in a flurry of skirts.

'Oh, Cousin Paul, how wonderful! You've come to save me.

Take me away from this horrid place. Do you know they locked me in my room on bread and water and threatened to whip me?' Lucy Whatmough threw herself into Paul's arms.

She was beautiful, a pocket Venus with the face of a flower and quite the most improbably long lashes Elly had ever seen.

Extricating himself from an embrace that brought colour to his cheeks, Paul set Lucy on her feet and held her off like an overwelcoming puppy. 'Lucy, you must not say such things. It was kind of the Reverend Barton and his good lady to take you in when you had nowhere to go.'

The girl's face set mutinously, and glossy brown curls danced as she shook her head. 'They were mean and hateful … '

Elly moved past the two, holding out her hand to the indignant minister. 'I see you have had your difficulties, sir, and on behalf of Mr Gascoigne I thank you for your Christian charity towards an orphan. I expect you made allowance for her grief, which might give the appearance of willfulness.'

Before Barton could reply, Paul had picked up the bag standing at the door and pushed it and Lucy outside. He returned to add his thanks and farewells, then bustled Elly out.

'This is your bag, Lucy?' he asked. 'Good. Now let's depart this mausoleum before the owner decides to air more grievances.' He grinned at Lucy. 'You really have been tiresome, haven't you? The Reverend Barton has my sympathy.' He hurried the two women up the street to the inn, not even giving Elly a chance to introduce herself.

The temperature dropped overnight, leaving the road iron-hard where the wheel ruts had frozen with ice as thick as a shilling, although it hadn't yet snowed. Paul eyed the threatening clouds and chose to gamble on the weather holding until they were through the mountains.

'I don't want to be here for a week or more. We'll risk it,' he said and went to arrange their seats on the coach.

They left early, without seeing much of the town. But although disappointed, Elly had resigned herself. There would be no chance of intimacy with Paul now that Lucy had joined them, but she couldn't dislike the girl, so bright and mischievous. She had taken a liking to Elly, peppering her with a thousand questions about

Sydney Town, which the girl had barely seen on her way from the ship to Maitland.

'It's a lively place,' Elly told her. 'I think you'll be happy there. Paul and I will introduce you to our friends and there will be the people where you work.'

Lucy's face, framed in a fur-lined hood, bore a frown. 'I don't want to make hats for other women. I'd like to have pretty clothes and ride every day in a carriage.' She fingered her plain woollen gown with distaste. Elly could almost see visions of silken furbelows dancing in Lucy's head.

'One day you shall. But most people have to earn these rewards. There's a lot of satisfaction in working towards a solid future.'

'Do you work? I thought you were a lady.'

So Elly explained about the hospital, and time passed quickly, with Lucy entranced by stories of minor disasters and funny happenings. In some ways, Elly realised, she was younger than her seventeen years, a little spoilt, and eager to taste life to the full. However, in appearance she was fully a woman, with a body men would notice and blue eyes big enough to drown in. All in all, Elly thought, Paul would have a lively time caring for his young cousin. While he sat in his corner seat and listened, looking positively patriarchal, Lucy made friendly overtures to a woman with a new baby and began to interrogate her. The woman's husband, a government agent, plus an elderly man with gout and a temperament to match, made up the remainder of the inside passengers. Elly pictured those on the roof as rigid as frozen dolls, their hands permanently tightened on the sidebars. For their sake she hoped the snow would hold off.

They spent the night at the foot of the pass, beginning the steep climb early the next day when the sun hid behind the crags and frost still lay in the shadows of the tablelands two thousand feet above sea level. Today the passengers huddled into shawls and under rugs; expired breath hung like a mist in the air, and the crack of the driver's whip rang like shattered crystal above the clatter of hooves.

Halfway up the pass they caught up with a bullock dray from the inland laden with wool destined for English mills. The sixteen great beasts heaved and strained against the yokes, their strong

necks stretched under the tremendous weight, their hooves slipping on the icy slope. The driver cracked his whip and bellowed,
pulling his team against the cliff face so the coach could edge by.
Elly peered out over a dizzy drop to the valley floor, closed her
eyes, refusing to open them until Lucy told her they had the road
to themselves again.

The sun eventually appeared to drive away the mist and the
forest echoed with the crazy call of the laughing jackass, who had
frightened many a settler into reaching for his gun before he realised it was only a bird. The day dragged out, even for Lucy, and
Elly looked forward to the final lap, down the eastern slopes onto
the plains, with a clear run through to Parramatta.

The public nature of their travels had scotched Elly's plan to
draw closer to Paul, although she believed he could have arranged
it somehow, had he tried. He simply hadn't wanted to. He seemed
happy to retreat into friendship; and clearly for him the incident
at Botany Bay was not merely closed, but erased.

Elly slept badly that night at King's Tableland, waking to a silent, white-blanketed world compressed beneath a canopy of snow-
laden cloud. The ostler and coachman cursed as they poled up
the team, carefully checking all the equipment. Elly didn't blame
the coachman for downing a couple of rums against the cold before he heaved himself onto the box seat, but she watched doubt-
fully as he pocketed a whole bottle. The government agent queried
the chances of them getting through, but their driver was san-
guine.

'It's downhill all the way, and Jack Tyler and his team have
never been stopped yet.' He wound his muffler around his chin
and picked up the reins. The passengers scrambled aboard and
they were off.

Paul fastened the leather window covers carefully, winking at
Lucy. 'I'd sooner not spend another night with the fleas. What do
you think?'

She smiled at him sleepily and snuggled her head into her hood,
prepared to join the rest of the passengers in catching up on their
broken rest. By the time the carriage reverberated with snores, Elly
knew by Paul's manner that he had something particular to say to
her. Her pulse beat faster and she clasped her hands in her muff

to hide their tremor.

Eventually he brought his head down near hers, saying softly, 'I want to speak to you about D'Arcy Cornwallis.'

Stabbed with disappointment, she took time to control her voice. 'Yes? I haven't seen him since that regrettable incident, although he's written to apologise, many times.'

'How much do you know about him, Elly?'

She said ruefully: 'Only that I'll miss his support at the hospital board meetings. He's a powerful orator, able to sway the other members as he wills.'

'I know a good deal about him. In his capacity as a landowner, a business entrepreneur and lobbyist, he gives generously of time and money, presenting an altogether admirable figure to the world.'

Elly waited.

'However, there's another side to his character which is not so well known, and which you've seen.'

'JG did hint as much to me. I refused to listen, to my regret.'

'He's dangerous, believe me. There are stories of what goes on in his town house and down on his Camden property, although he pays heavily to hide the truth. He also deals in fear. His business activities are questionable, at the very least, while his character with women is appalling. A man has ways of knowing these things.'

'That's monstrous, Paul. Surely some of these tales are jealous gossip spread by his business opponents.' Light and shade, she thought. Putting aside her own experience, how much of the originally courteous and intelligent Cornwallis was the real man, how much the villain painted by report?

'There's always gossip about prominent men, I'll admit. But this is something more. I have definite knowledge of this man, Elly, and I beg you not to have dealings with him, no matter how apologetic he is, no matter how many hospital matters he may wish to discuss with you privately. You have seen him humiliated. He won't forgive that.'

Elly, disappointed that he did not wish to discuss a more intimate topic, yet pleased by his care for her safety, could only thank Paul and promise to be particularly watchful, assuring him she had no wish to see Cornwallis again.

Yet after Paul leaned into the corner, composing himself for sleep, she found she couldn't dismiss the subject. He had opened a closed box in her mind, recalling her last meeting with Cornwallis and his expression before he limped off into the night. A shiver of apprehension ran through her. Something inhuman had looked out of his eyes, something she'd never seen in any other person, however angry or humiliated. It had challenged her with its promise of vengeance, and she had quickly buried the knowledge, closing it off while she went on with her busy life. Now Paul had forced her to remember, bringing fear sweeping back in like a dark wind.

By midafternoon snow gusted past the windows in icy veils, bringing early night with it. The forest on either side of the track had formed impenetrable walls, hemming the coach in, enclosing the passengers in a silent deserted world. Where had all the other travellers gone? Surely the horses picked their way by instinct alone. Could they be trusted to bring them all safely home? Elly saw her misgivings echoed in her companions' uneasy faces, while the baby, clearly sensitive to the atmosphere, began to wail.

'Should we not, perhaps, turn back to wait out the storm?' the government agent suggested. A small man, a sparrow to his wife's mother hen, he fussed agitatedly over his family.

If Paul was anxious, he hid it well. 'I judge it would be as far to go back as forward to shelter, and it would mean the team straining uphill. It's best to conserve their energy.'

'Those poor men on the roof. Could we not squeeze up and let one or two share our shelter for a time?' Elly gazed around questioningly.

The gout-plagued passenger frowned, while the mother of the baby smiled dubiously, no doubt opposed to wet snow being brought inside.

Again Paul answered. 'It might not be wise to stop the coach, even if we could attract the driver's attention. The men do have a canvas to pull over them—inadequate, I know, but—' He broke off to clutch at the door beside him, his other hand outthrust to hold Elly as the coach lurched to the right, swerved again, then began to tip. It stopped, righted itself. Then, wheels locked, it began to slide.

Outside, through the swirling snow, Elly heard muffled shouts.

'We've hit ice!' cried the government agent, grasping his wife. The baby wailed even louder, and Lucy clutched at Elly, crying, 'What is it?'

'I don't know. We seem to be slipping.'

'Hold on!' shouted Paul. He threw himself across the two women as the coach rocked and slid, gathering momentum. With a terrific crunch the front wheels struck some rigid object, the coach tipped to the left, hovered on the brink of recovery, then crashed over an incline to bump its way downhill, tearing out rocks and brush, until finally it came to rest against a large tree.

In the ensuing silence a horse screamed, a terrible sound. Dazed, Elly tried to thrust herself up against the weight pinning her between the seat and another body; her right elbow vibrated in agony and she'd bitten her cheek. It was Paul's knee in her stomach. She heard him struggle with the coach door above his head, mutter that it had stuck, and tear away the leather curtain over the window. The weight on her stomach lifted as he scrambled out through the gap; snow leaked in to fall on her face, cold and stinging. Her head cleared and she remembered they'd come off the road, overturned, smashed into something. Was everyone all right? She felt around in the darkness. The soft body beneath her must be Lucy. Her fingers found a fur-lined hood and a cold face within.

'Lucy, can you hear me?'

'I ... hear. Can't breathe ... '

Elly moved aside, dragging Lucy into a sitting position against the upended squab. She could hear heavy breathing somewhere in the coach. The baby had fallen silent. There were no further sounds from outside. Then the door above her head was wrenched open and Paul said, 'Reach up, Elly, and I'll lift you out.'

'Take Lucy first. I'll give her a push up to you.'

Lucy, who, with Elly off her chest, appeared to have recovered her breath, said, 'The baby ... '

'I'll search for it. You go ahead to make room for me to move.' She boosted Lucy as well as she could in the confined space and the girl disappeared through the opening, her skirts flapping in Elly's face. Only a few flakes of snow sifted in, for which Elly thanked providence. The wind, also, had dropped. Nearby someone groaned and she groped her way to another body in male clothing, too heavy a body for her to life. It must be the older man with the gouty leg.

Paul leaned down again. 'You next, Elly.'

'I can't leave the others until I know how badly they're hurt. If only we had some light.'

'I'll see if the candles are still in the coach lanterns. Hold on.' He disappeared again and the cold drifted down through the gap. Elly could see a faint square of lighter sky.

'Help me,' whispered a voice almost under Elly's foot.

She reached down to touch the woman's bodice, feeling a racing heartbeat beneath. 'Where's the baby?' Elly scrabbled about frantically until her hands closed around a soft, yielding bundle under the mother's arm. The bundle squeaked when she picked it up. Thank heaven! The baby was alive.

An upheaval in the dark nearby and two voices cursing signalled the survival of the other inside passengers. Relieved, Elly took charge. In her calmest matron's manner she lined up her patients, examining them as best she could by touch. No-one appeared to be badly hurt, although her hands were sticky with blood welling from a head wound above a bearded face—the older man with gout. Elly was glad to hear Paul climb up the side of the coach. His body filled the opening and his face glowed eerily above her in the light of two candles fixed to a piece of board, which he handed down.

'Will this help?' He also passed down her small bag with the travelling medical kit.

'Oh, yes. There's just a superficial head wound here, plus shock, of course. What about the others?'

He waited before answering, then said steadily: 'The driver jumped into a snowdrift. He's unhurt. Two of the roof passengers are dead, thrown into the trees to break their necks. The others have various cuts and bruises. I'm very much afraid there's a broken leg, a bad multiple break, I think. Will you come and see?'

Despite the circumstances, Elly was galvanised by the contact with Paul as he helped her to climb through the gap then lifted her down. For an instant, clutched in his arms, she melted against him, her face pressed to his chest, inhaling his familiar odour. It was like a homecoming. Then she was on her feet and the needs of the moment claimed her.

Half an hour later Elly had set the leg, with the help of a wide-eyed Lucy who'd trembled as she held the candles, and settled the shocked mother to feed her baby in the shelter of a canvas torn from the coach roof. The able bodied men had put the coach back on its wheels so the injured passengers could be placed inside. It seemed to have suffered no structural damage, despite gouged paintwork and baggage strewn widely through the trees.

To Paul had fallen the sad duty of despatching the badly injured pole horses which had been dragged down the slope with the coach. Their driver, pulled from his snowdrift, proved to be hopelessly drunk, unfit to use the shotgun carried under his seat. Elly flinched as the reports echoed through the trees, then went calmly on with her work, while Paul and the government agent set off to find the two leaders, who had broken their traces and escaped the accident. When Elly finally repacked her medical bag and washed her hands in some snow, Lucy put down the candles to hug her.

'Miss Ballard, you're so brave and strong. I wish I could be like you.'

Elly smiled tiredly and squeezed her back again. 'It's all in knowing what to do. I'm used to emergencies, Lucy. You've kept your head well. I'm proud of you. Do you think, as we're already intimate, you could call me Elly?'

Lucy beamed.

Out of the darkness came a tall figure, leading two horses in dangling harness. 'Your father would be proud of you, also, Lucy,' Paul said. 'Now, would you hold the candles for me while I cobble together these bits of leather and, with any luck, we'll get these nags to drag the coach back up to the road. It's not far.' He glanced at Elly. 'I saw cheeses loaded aboard for the market. If you can find one we'd all welcome some sustenance—oh, Lord! That's all we need.'

'Where's me whip? Got to keep up with the time sheet. All aboard now.' The driver staggered towards the coach, tried to climb up to the box seat, then fell back heavily into the churned mud and snow, swearing.

Handing Elly the harness, Paul bent to grasp the man under

the arm. 'Shut your mouth. You're not driving anywhere.'

'Me legs've gone,' the driver muttered in a surprised tone as he collapsed against Paul.

'Paul shook him. 'And so've your wits. God, what an idiot. I suppose I'll have to tie you on. There's no room inside.'

'No-one but me drives my rig,' the man blustered, swinging an ineffectual fist at Paul's head.

'Wrong, friend. You just watch me. Come on, up we go.' With help from two men, the driver was hoisted to a roof seat and tied there to keep him from toppling off. The bodies of the two dead passengers were secured behind.

All available hands pushed and dragged the coach away from the dead horses, in deference to the sensibilities of the live ones. Then a large cheese was found and broached, along with Paul's hipflask of brandy. When the harness had been mended to his liking and the remaining horses poled up, he addressed his companions.

'The snow has stopped and we should make it down from the mountains safely if we're careful, even in the dark. With only two horses and injured people aboard, the pace won't go much above a snail's. Still, it's the best we can do. So, all aboard, as they say, ladies. You men who can walk will have to push us up the slope as far as the road, but once there you can climb up top.'

There was a murmur of general consent. Elly, preparing to mount into the coach, her mind on her patients, spared a glance for the man who had taken charge. He seemed rock-like, indomitable.

Lucy stared at him, rapt in admiration. 'Isn't he marvellous?' she whispered. 'I think he could take care of anything.'

Elly smiled in absolute agreement.

Their journey down to the plains, while slow, remained uneventful. From the way station a team of fresh horses carried them on to Parramatta where the injured travellers could receive medical attention. Elly would have pressed on to town, if she could. The old fear that some disaster would befall *her* hospital if she were not there to somehow forestall it occupied her mind. She also wished to leave Paul's company as soon as possible, now she was sure he no longer cared deeply for her.

Chapter Twenty-one

However, Paul pleaded exhaustion, making a determined effort to appear drained by the cold journey down the mountainside in the dark. Undeceived by Lucy's insistence that she too needed to recover, Elly yielded to persuasion, and they spent one more night at an inn. The loss of their baggage was a minor inconvenience and Elly, in her shift, slept dreamlessly alongside Lucy for ten full hours. The following day the three boarded the river steamer with Lucy in high fettle and anxious to regale the other passengers with her adventure.

Elly was standing alone at the rail, watching the farms and orchards slide by, when Paul joined her. She avoided looking at him, saying brightly: 'Our journey is almost over. Despite all the drama, I've enjoyed it.'

'So have I. Oh, not the accident or its aftermath, but being with you. Your friendship means a great deal to me, Elly.'

Her smile slipped. 'My friendship?'

'Yes. I don't deny it's been a struggle to overcome my deeper feelings for you. That day at Botany Bay you wrenched the heart out of me, and it's never been the same since. Yet you were right to say our loving each other would be a mistake. There are so many reasons why we should agree to remain just good friends. I've finally come to terms with this and I'm happy again. I wanted you to know.'

'I … see.' Elly turned away, unable to control her expression. However, her voice remained steady. 'Of course, you've made the right decision, and friends we shall be, always.'

He patted her arm. 'Wonderful. Now, I must find Lucy. That young lady is ever ready to slip away at the first chance.'

Chapter Twenty-two

'Chinaman's Gully's down there quite a ways,' said the digger, pointing a dirty callused finger southwards. 'It's on the other side of the range, one of the fields opened up late last year. Just about cleaned out by now, I reckon.' A slit in his grizzled beard revealed a grinning, toothless mouth. ''Cept, a'course, for the Chinks, who'll find pickings in a kiddy's sand box. You hoping to try your luck, youngster?'

Pearl shook her head. 'I'm hoping to find my brother down there, Mr Coffey.' They had met up earlier in the morning as the digger ambled down from the northwest hills and the two discovered that both were headed in the same direction. She was pleased to have company on the tramp.

'Call me Ezra. And this here's Polly Doodle.' He flipped the reins on the mule trotting beside him, loaded with tools and camp equipment, ropes and canvas flapping in the wind. 'We're from the States, both of us. We've covered a lot of ground, and ocean, together.'

'And have you found much gold yet, Ezra?'

'Nope. I been up in the hills for months without a strike. So now I'm off to try one of them surface drifts around the White Horse Range. A lot of new leads've been found, but at the same time the surface deposits and the old river gravels are worked out. It's easy enough to find gold under a thin layer of clay or sand, but you mark my words, there'll be deep reefs under the rock.'

Pearl said: 'I've seen the shafts at Ophir where the gold had sunk into the clay. The men there brought the dirt up in buckets and washed it on the surface; but I haven't seen anyone digging through rock.'

'They can't. Not till they've got machines to do the work up top. But the crushers'll come soon enough, when the reefs are found. I seen it all in California.' Ezra broke off a piece of tobacco from his pocket, popped it in his mouth and, despite his lack of teeth, began to chew. 'You tired, gal? Want a ride on Polly Doodle?'

In pity for the overloaded mule, Pearl declined, shifting her pack to a more comfortable position. Thankfully her attackers had taken fright when she knifed Redbeard and had left her pack beside the track, where it was picked up by her rescuers. Her kit, supplemented with the herbal remedies she had been studying, weighed like a rock, while the mud under foot sent her sliding in all directions. Fortunately, the rain had ceased for the moment, although the sky loured and a sharp wind cut through her wet clothes.

Pearl's surroundings were depressing, a desolate landscape in sepia and black, barren and heaped with ten-foot high clay hillocks. Everywhere water lay in pools. The men throwing up clay to add to the mullock heaps worked hip-deep in a slurry of wet mud; hundreds of men, with hundreds more working cradles, windlasses and wee-gees—the long poles balanced by a stone at one end and a bucket at the other, used to pump out water. It was an ant heap, and to an outsider it would appear mindless, perpetual motion without visible purpose; unless, of course, one saw the gold peeping through the slush and heard the cry of delight from a man who had worn himself down to a rheumaticy bundle of bones in search of it.

When Pearl and Ezra reached the Chinese encampment, it looked no better and no worse than the tent towns of the western men, although there were some queer structures made of packing cases and kerosene tins held together with saplings. The ground here sloped sharply into gullies as barren as the rest of the camp.

Ezra pulled Polly Doodle to a halt and pointed to a large tent at the northern end. 'That'll be the head man's place. He'll be able to tell you where your brother's claim is.'

Pearl put out her hand and, after a small hesitation, he took it carefully in his grubby paw.

'Thank you, Ezra. I hope you find a mountain of gold.'

'Wouldn't know what to do with it if I did.' He grinned. 'The fun's in the search, you see? Good luck, gal.' He gave the mule a light tap on the nose and moved off southwards, his gaze already turning to the horizon, seeking a likely spot to stake his claim and start work.

The tong, when queried, directed Elly to an area a hundred yards down the gully where a party of Chinese worked around a long wooden pipe about six inches square with a wheel attached at the upper end. As she drew nearer, she saw it was like a paddle wheel, its canvas band fitted with pieces of board which drew up water and discharged it down the pipe and out the other end. It was, in effect, an elaborate baler, keeping a pit dry enough for men to work.

Pearl approached a man clearing an obstruction at the pipe mouth. 'Do you know Li Po?'

He straightened up, a slender, brown-skinned figure whose thinning hair hung in a rat's tail braid. His long blue blouse, faded and patched, was smeared with the ubiquitous clay, his knee-high boots the same. His gaze bored into her, sharp, almost hostile.

'What do you want with Li Po?'

'He's my brother.'

'I am Li Po, and I have no brother.'

Momentarily shocked, Pearl finally said: 'Look closely. Have you never had a sister, Li Po?'

Her excitement edged with a sensation of disappointment, Pearl studied the stranger as he studied her. She didn't remember him. With no conscious picture of him in her mind, she had somehow fallen into the trap of imagining a benign, brotherly figure opening his arms in welcome, but the reality could not have been more different. Li Po had the stringy, exhausted aspect of so many diggers, with lines of bitterness around his mouth.

'You could be Younger Sister. How do I know you speak the truth?'

'Do you remember playing with me in the fields, lifting me over the ditches? I cried when I was sold away as a servant and you comforted me. You told me that one day I would attract a rich man and have servants of my own. I would wear fine silk clothes and never be hungry again.'

He waited impassively for Pearl to continue.

'When I cried, our father beat me, and you took the stick and broke it. Do you remember?'

Some of the tension went out of Li Po, although there was still no welcome in his tone. 'You are Younger Sister. How did you come here? Why did you seek me out?'

'Because you are all the family I have left. Because I thought you would welcome me.'

'You thought I had found much gold.'

The emphatic statement sent Pearl's chin in the air. 'I'm not interested in gold. I've travelled from the Yangtse Valley to find you. I've been enslaved, shipwrecked, attacked; I have used all my ingenuity and all my strength in my search for a brother I thought I could love. Now you accuse me of wanting your gold.' Her anger sustained her, but she was appalled at this outcome to her long journey. It had never entered her mind that Li Po would reject her.

At a shout from above, she raised her head and saw two men waving. Li Po lifted an arm in reply, saying to Pearl: 'I am needed. I must go back to work. Wait at the tong's tent and I will speak with you after the evening gun.' He sped away up the gully without a backward glance.

Pearl settled her pack and turned away. She felt numb and hollow. For it to end like this, with suspicion instead of the glad reunion she'd carefully constructed in her imagination for so many months. Her numbness gave way to deeper misery. She climbed the gully away from the tong's tent, finding her way through a salty blur, unable to make any plans beyond escaping to hide somewhere alone with her unhappiness. She didn't see the loose stone until her boot slipped and she fell heavily. Throwing out her arms to save her battered ribs another break, she landed awkwardly on one knee. Pain shot up her leg. She sat in the wet clay hugging her knee, and for the first time in her life considered giving up.

Li Po must have been watching, after all, for he arrived within minutes to stand over her.

'Where are you going?'

Pearl shook her head. If he couldn't see how his reception had affected her, she couldn't be bothered to explain.

He put a tentative hand on her shoulder. 'Are you hurt? Show me.'

When she didn't move, he squatted down and pulled the leg of her trousers above the knee, which had already begun to swell. Clicking his tongue against his teeth, he swept her up with a deceptive wiry strength and carried her up the steep slope to one of the packing case huts she had seen on the ridge.

Inside, he placed her on a mattress on a shelf of mud bricks, then lit a candle, revealing a compact space that was surprisingly comfortable if one stood no higher than five feet. Pearl regarded the woven mat on the earth floor, the slab table and bench, the tin chest hanging from a rafter to keep food out of reach of animals. Li Po had taken the trouble to construct a home in the wilderness. While she watched in silence, he built a small fire in the dry stone hearth to boil water for tea, then brought it to her in a tin mug. Finally he sat down cross-legged on the mat, saying: 'Will you stay here and rest? I have much to say to you, but not until the day's work is finished.'

Utterly weary, in pain from her throbbing knee, Pearl hadn't the energy or the will to set off again just yet. Here she was protected from the weather, while Li Po's softened attitude demonstrated some sort of interest in her. Despite her disappointment, she still wanted to know him better. They were still the same blood. However, pride must be preserved. She appeared to give his request thought, then said coolly: 'I will stay until you return.'

Pearl stayed a lot longer. By the time she had helped Li Po cook the evening meal and sat over their tea well into the night, exchanging life stories, Pearl felt she had been accepted. Her brother was a lonely, withdrawn man whose manner repelled any close relationship. However, she had seen beneath to his real need and was glad she had come.

Settled in one spot for the first time since leaving Sydney, she allowed herself time to acclimatise before tackling the future, content to keep the camp tidy and learn her way about the vast Ballarat diggings.

In many ways it resembled all the others she had visited in her search; however, there were differences, particularly in the weather, which had turned bad enough to disrupt the Cobb & Co coach service, discontinued until there was some hope of the horses getting through. At night temperatures dropped below freezing, and by morning a light dusting of snow frequently frosted the ugly surroundings with a deceptive beauty. But, it only added to the misery of the miners, forcing them to work in icy slush, often up to their waists, weakened by the lack of proper nutrition, since they existed mainly on damper, mutton and black tea.

Milk could not be had at any price, unless a family cow had been dragged up from Melbourne to be cherished and carefully guarded by its owners; vegetables were a rare luxury, with cabbages selling at half a crown each and potatoes at a shilling and sixpence a pound. The cost of cartage usually trebled the city prices. Even flour for damper sold at up to £200 per ton. All this resulted in a variety of deficiencies and skin diseases, usually dismissed with contempt by the miners but actually seriously draining their physical strength.

Because the creeks were polluted, fresh water, brought in by a few entrepreneurs willing to travel to distant streams, sold at a shilling a bucket—too dear for many miners, who then fell prey to dysentery, even in winter. Infections spread rapidly in the crowded, primitive conditions, and rheumatism, fevers, cramps and colds were endemic. The situation cried out for medical men, of which there were a few— mostly quacks.

Meanwhile, despite their difficulties, or perhaps to spite them, the diggers created their own entertainment. This ranged from camp-fire sing songs accompanied by harmonica, or squeezebox accordion, even bagpipes, to Saturday nights in the illegal grog tents where the favours of harlots could be arranged, and wild partying was accompanied by fights and gunshots until dawn. For the more sophisticated, dances were held in a purpose-built hall in Ballarat, or a concert by visiting players. Pearl found the township to have a settled, prosperous air, its thronged main street lined with shops, lodging houses, banks and hotels. Delivery drays vied with water carriers and shoppers, many of these women and children who accompanied their menfolk to the goldfields in increasing numbers.

One day Pearl witnessed a digger wedding, the bride in full satin and lace, the groom and his friends in silk hats, all racing from church to hotel to begin a week-long fiesta. She also witnessed the outcome at the end of the week: a drunken brawl in which the bride received a black eye and knocked her husband out with a bottle of gin before departing for fresher fields.

Pearl reported this with some amusement to her brother, who retorted: 'These western "marriages" are an excuse for licence. The bride will have offered herself at a price and when she tires of the situation will return to the town to seek another partner. Some women will enjoy six wedding feasts in the same hotel in as many months.'

Before long Pearl recognised the same rumbling precursors to rebellion as she'd seen in other mining camps. The ostensible problem—the miners' resentment of a licensing tax which fell most heavily on the poor and unsuccessful—only masked the true problem, which was their real hatred of the fee collectors, the gold commissioner's police. These sprang from the ranks of ex-convicts and bullies who delighted in exercising their power against those without redress. With bribery and standover tactics the norm, many diggers refused to pay for their licences, instead posting lookouts for the 'traps' then disappearing into hiding at the first warning. There were constant confrontations, and the local gaol became so crowded that men who could not pay the immediate fine, or had to wait for a magistrate to arrive on his circuit, were left chained to trees in all weather, to be mocked by their gaolers.

Pearl stepped uneasily around the indignation meetings and the raids by mounted troopers. Her people were resented for their lack of interest in the miners' rights as well as for their strange and, no doubt devious, ways.

She shopped for their needs with Li Po's gold dust, discovering a market where the destitute sold their clothes and valuables for food or a passage back to civilisation. She also found a school being conducted in a tent by a digger returning to his previous profession, but attended by all too few of the hundreds of children who swarmed through the camps. Most of them were unpaid labourers for their fathers and would never be educated. Sundays were observed by all diggers as a day of rest from their labours, whether they attended church or merely cleaned and mended around the camp or nursed their various ailments.

Dressing a blister on Li Po's foot one day, Pearl's restlessness stirred. This was her job. She should be getting on with it. However, she struck opposition at once.

Li Po drew himself up to his full height, which was in fact only two inches taller than Pearl. 'Our people are healthier than the *yi*. We eat more wisely and know how to use a variety of remedies. However, there are always accidents, and you are free to attend to those.' He added graciously, 'Your skill is not in doubt, yet we have little use for western medicine, which appears to consist of Holloway's cure-everything pills and the letting of blood. Content yourself with seeing to our camp and to our people when needed.'

Pearl was prepared for the confrontation. 'I understand how you feel. However, I have lived among the *yi*. My foster parents were westerners and the first people to care about me and give me a chance to better myself. Ada Carter was my true mother who loved me. It was a western woman who befriended me on the ship, and another who took me in, gave me work and respect.'

Li Po said harshly, 'And what of the men who attacked you and left you maimed?'

'There are beasts at all levels of nature. Not all western men are evil. In Sydney Town I met with many I liked and respected.' JG's irreverent, lived-in face came to mind, making her smile. 'I have had time to think while I recovered and listened to the wisdom of Lao-tse. Regrets are vain, brother. They stifle the present.'

'You forgive those *yi* dogs? You can forget that once you had beauty?' He was incredulous.

'It doesn't matter any more. I don't need a beautiful face to pursue my calling. When I set up my clinic for the sick and injured, they will be interested only in my skill to heal and my ability to quieten pain.'

Li Po's face twitched. 'You will not do this. It is unseemly for a woman of the Celestial Kingdom to put herself forward in such a way. I have already settled your future. A dowry has been arranged. I am a wealthy man, Younger Sister, and you are to marry Chan Yu-lan at the full moon.

'No. I'm sorry, brother, but I will order my own life.'

Li Po slapped her face. The blood rushed to her cheek where the scar still stood out like a badly mended crack in a porcelain vase. Her eyes flashed, then watered with pain, but she conquered her initial response, saying mildly, 'Li Po, you must realise that I am not a chattel. I am a person in my own right. Here in this country I have a freedom I could never have in our land.'

'A woman should be meek and hold herself small before a man.'

'Not so. The Christian holy book says "blessed are the meek", meaning all people, men and women, without one being greater than another. Lao-tse says: "How does the sea become the queen of all rivers and streams? By lying lower than they do. One who humbles himself, therefore, can serve all people." Until you are willing to be humble yourself, brother, to be equal with me, we cannot live side by side. So I must go.' She picked up her ready packed bag.

Li-Po said bitterly, 'You are not my Younger Sister. You are no true woman.'

'I was given a name, Pearl. It is the only name I have. Goodbye, Li Po.'

Chapter Twenty-three

Pearl didn't stop until she reached the tent of Dr Hsien Lo; there she found him supervising the packing of his goods. He explained that he intended returning to the land of his ancestors and fate had obviously meant Pearl to arrive in time to take over his practice.

'I'm not a qualified doctor,' Pearl objected, although they both knew anyone at all could hang out a shingle on the goldfields and be assured of plenty of custom.

'You are more qualified than most of the impostors who demand a sovereign in exchange for a mix of chalk, opium and brandy to cure dysentery, which instead induces prolonged, agonising constipation. You will dissipate much misery and save lives. One may always perceive the workings of the Way.'

With a touch of irony, Pearl asked, 'Will the Way provide me with a roof and food to keep me alive until I have paying patients?'

'I will do so.' Hsien Lo's indifference to his own generosity was so superb that Pearl could only bow her acceptance. 'Have you parted from your brother?

'Unfortunately, he does not subscribe to the Way and wants me to turn myself into a chattel. I can't stay with him.' Pearl concealed her hurt and began to question the doctor on herbal lore.

Hsien Lo left at the end of the week, having established Pearl as
his replacement, in possession of a neat tent divided by a curtain
into surgery and living quarters. With packing-case furniture, a
folding bed and a properly constructed fireplace, plus a chest to
hold her nostrums and herbs, Pearl was ready for business. Despite the prejudice against orientals, Pearl found herself inundated
with patients, and since her fees were small—nonexistent in the
case of hardship—she soon ran the risk of collapse through exhaustion.

At the beginning she concealed her sex, and by the time it was
known, too many miners had been treated for intimate complaints
for anyone to be overly concerned. Gunshot wounds were plenti-

cost of a better burial than the usual bark shroud. Their ominous mood was understandable. Pearl knew this was not an isolated event. Scarcely a week went past without a sly-grog tent being burned to the ground, the kegs confiscated by the police and any persons found on the premises dragged off to gaol. Since half the fines for successful prosecutions were paid to the arresting trooper, this led to blackmail and perjury on the part of the police, while the traffickers in spirits, who could afford the bribe continued to flourish.

The brutal officiousness in dragging men up from the bottom of a hundred-foot shaft to display their licences, twice weekly, was bad enough. But when it reached the point of men being left to die, Pearl's own blade had not been used previously for skinning a rabbit or cleaning out a pipe.

'But this doctor,' continued the miner, 'he said as how he'd cup him—for a bullet wound! And he cuts into his chest with this little metal box full of blades, then heats these little bell-shaped glasses and lays them on to burn the man while all the blood's sucked out and him screaming with the pain of the shattered bone, until we pulls off the glasses and throws them out the tent, along with the doctor. And then we thought of you.'

So kind, thought Pearl, her sense of humour tickled. Third on the list after the national panacea and the medical impostor. She knew the more conservative miners regarded her as a useful crank, a cross between a native witchdoctor and a miracle worker, to be called upon only in the case of dire necessity. But Pearl's amusement vanished the moment she stepped into the tent and saw her patient—the man she knew as Cato, Redbeard's partner in crime.

She paled and involuntarily stepped back. Her voice sounded like a stranger's, harsh and discordant. 'How was he shot? In an armed holdup?'

Her escort looked at her curiously; but Cato's eyes widened at the sight of her. His lips moved soundlessly.

Pearl fought down the urge to run, to put the greatest possible distance between herself and this man who had taken part in her degradation. She dug her nails into her palms, feeling sweat break out on her forehead as she battled her emotions. Then, from some recess in her mind a voice emerged. She could hear Dr Hsien Lo as clearly as if he stood beside her exuding calmness and detachment.

'One of natural, integral virtue is good at helping all people impartially. Thus, no-one is abandoned.'

No one is abandoned.

'He is good at protecting and preserving ...'

Protecting and preserving.

'A centred being is placid ... never loses his poise ... if one's root is lost one's self-mastery could go with the wind.'

Pearl drew in her breath and said quietly, 'Please place my bag there on the floor then fetch me a bowl of water which has boiled.'

The man lying on the rough bundle of branches, thrown down

directly onto the dirt floor, watched her, his pain-filled expression haunted. 'What … what … ?' was all he could manage.

'What am I going to do to you?' Pearl knelt beside him, putting all the assurance she could into her voice. 'I'm going to help you, if I can. You needn't fear me.'

He watched her in obvious trepidation as she worked steadily over him, cleaning the terrible wound in his right shoulder as gently as possible and binding his arm to his body, then attending the smaller wounds inflicted by the self-styled doctor.

When she had done all she could, she washed and repacked her bag, then got up saying: 'You must have realised your wound is serious. Your shoulder joint has been shattered and you will lose the mobility of your arm. However, if we can prevent infection, you should not lose the arm itself. I'll return tomorrow. Rest now, and have your friends make a mutton broth for you.'

She picked up her bag and hurried outside. A few yards from the tent nausea overtook her. She bent over, retching until physically and emotionally empty.

The man who had summoned her waited at a decent distance, approaching only when she straightened up and wiped her face. He said awkwardly: 'You know Cato then? You know what kind of man he is?' When she didn't answer he pulled at his beard, obviously choosing his words. 'He was on the duff and got caught. He's my brother. When he come to me for help I couldn't turn him away. I know he's no good, but there it is. He's my kin.' He hesitated. 'Will you inform on him? It was only a few head o'cattle.'

Pearl couldn't see his face. Little moonlight penetrated the streamers of cloud and he held his lantern low. 'Once I would have had your brother thrown into gaol. But now I think he's had his punishment. He'll never steal cattle again—or worse—with that arm. I'll see to him until he's recovered, but I want no payment. This is something I must do in my own way.'

Surprisingly, Cato's brother seemed to understand, or at least was prepared to humour her. 'Right. Then I'll take you home. You'd never find your way alone,' as she shook her head. 'And men with rotgut in their bellies mightn't recognise the Chinese witchwoman flitting without her broomstick.' He gave a grunt of amusement, then sobered. 'Whatever Cato done to you, I'm sorry for it, and I thank you for helping him. Come along then.' He hefted her bag and set off with the lantern swinging by his knee.

Pearl slept very little that night. Instead, she lay pondering the changes in herself since she'd left her homeland. Never could she have envisaged such a complete about-face that would see her abandoning vengeance to succour her enemy. It was contrary to all she had ever been. Her western mother had deplored the idea of an eye for an eye, had gently tried to inculcate the Christian ideal of forgiveness, which Pearl could only see as feebleness and lack of spirit; but it had taken Dr Hsien Lo's vision of the Way to reveal to her the truth of religious teaching. Pearl now understood that to be sufficiently centred and self-reliant to forswear vengeance was not a weakness, it was actually strength in disguise. She could have hugged herself with pleasure and pride at her new-found strength. Neither emotion typified the humility encouraged by the Tao, but she decided to be lenient with herself. No-one could achieve perfection in a few weeks—or even a lifetime.

'Powdered seahorse,' Pearl muttered, shutting the drawer of her herb cabinet. 'Where can I get some without going to Melbourne?'

A voice behind her made her jump. 'Have you tried the China Sea? What's it for anyway?'

Pearl turned. 'Goitre,' she said automatically, and then, 'JG!'

'In the flesh, girl dear.' JG's grin faded slowly as he took in her ruined face. 'Jesus, God! What happened?'

Pearl's welcoming smile trembled, although her voice remained steady. 'An accident. It's healed. Don't fuss, JG.' She couldn't stand the shock in his eyes and moved away to continue restoring various herbs to their places in the cabinet. 'What are you doing here?' For one fraction of an instant her heart had leapt at the sight of him, and she had realised in that moment how important he was to her and had hoped he had come for her sake. Then he saw her face.

JG turned her firmly to face him. 'This was done with a knife. Who did it, Pearl?'

'A stranger, a devil. I killed him.' Her gaze didn't flinch. Nor did his.

Chapter Twenty-three

'I'm glad, or I'd have done it for you. Are you all right now?'

'Perfectly.'

His hands shifted to cup her face, the long, mobile fingers holding her steady while his thumb moved over the scar, tracing the line from her upcurved lip to her temple. 'Your face was perfect. Now it's a work of art with a small imperfection.' His voice roughened. 'God curse the hell-hound who did this to you. May he fester in an unhallowed grave for eternity.' His hands dropped and he moved away, idly pulling out one of the drawers in the herb cabinet then pushing it in again.

Still feeling the touch of his warm thumb on her cheek, Pearl wondered whether JG's reaction was simply that of any decent person faced with an obvious outrage.

'You asked why I've come. Simple curiosity, girl dear. Rumours abound concerning the rebellious miners' fight with authority. I happen to think it's coming to a head, and I want to be here to report on the outcome.'

Pearl thrust personal matters aside. 'I shouldn't be surprised if you were right. There has been an increase in disturbances, meetings at night down in the gullies with firebrand speeches. It began with the new twice-weekly licence searches ordered by the Governor. The traps seem to regard it as a new sport, hunting men instead of foxes, and they treat their prisoners abominably.'

'Hotham's a fool heading for trouble. Is it true the men are chained like common criminals?'

Pearl flushed angrily with the memory. 'Too true. Some of them have died of mistreatment.'

'But not if you get to them first, eh? Little Chinese witchwoman. I've heard the term in the town. It's how I found you so easily. Didn't you come up with your brother, after all, girl dear?'

Pearl became busy again. 'Oh, yes. I stayed with him awhile, then decided to set up my clinic in a more central position.'

She knew he had seen through the careful words to the truth, yet he simply commented: 'And a great thing it is, your clinic, from all I hear. Have you a cure, now, for a case of starvation? What do you prescribe?'

'Whiskey and dinner. You will be my guest, JG. Tell me how you performed the miracle of getting through to Ballarat when the roads have been closed since June.'

He accepted the dinner invitation with alacrity, explaining: 'I've set up a tent not far from here, with the basics, but no food as yet. As to my miraculous arrival, the coach service has reopened from Geelong so I took a place on the first one. I won't pretend I enjoyed the journey. Still, one suffers for one's art.'

Arguing happily over JG's claims to artistic representation of the truth in his columns, Pearl knew the initial barriers between them had fallen. She felt more comfortable with JG than she had in the past, and intensely thankful for his presence. She hadn't realised how lonely she had been for news of friends and the sense of support he gave just sitting across the packing-case table.

Later than evening, when they had finished their meal, JG settled himself with his pipe and began a faithful account of events back in Sydney, including his belief that Elly and Paul cared deeply for one another, without admitting it. Then he turned the talk to his interest in the brewing storm on the goldfields. He wanted to hear everything Pearl knew, plus her conclusions, before giving his own.

'I might not have been here long, but I've followed the reports since last year's little flare-up. It's more than the licence row, you know. There's a strong political upsurge, fanned by the republican element, while plenty of diggers have come from direct experience of revolution in Europe. They want representation in the Legislative Council so they can have the laws changed.'

'They have a right,' argued Pearl, 'when you see the contemptuous way decent men are treated by Commissioner Rede's bullies. There's no justice in these camps, except when the men take the law into their own hands.'

'Which only gives their enemies more ammunition. They can point to such lawlessness then come down in force on the protest meetings.'

Pearl was indignant. 'What other form of protest can the miners make? How else can they be heard?'

JG shrugged and knocked out his pipe before getting up. 'I'm going to one tonight over at Eureka. You heard about the murder of a man called Scobie ten days ago at the Eureka Hotel?'

'Yes. They spoke of charging the proprietor. But the magistrates found there was no case.'

'Well, Scobie's digger mates think the court of enquiry smells and they're to hold a meeting about it. This could be the spark to set off the conflagration.' He grinned slyly. 'Care to come along with me?'

Pearl agreed at once. 'I'll take my bag. There is bound to be a fight, so stay well to one side, JG. You don't know these diggers as I do.'

'Are they so belligerent?'

'With the drink in them, they are. And the goldfields are awash with liquor, whatever the law may say.' She damped down the fire then picked up her bag, which JG promptly took from her.

He looked around. 'Is is safe to leave all your goods unguarded.'

Pearl laughed. 'I'm the Chinese witchwoman, remember? No-one wants to touch anything in case they turn into a frog. Of course, they don't really believe it, but there's a sufficient element of doubt to keep light fingers out of my tent. You have the lantern, so lead the way.'

Over the past two days the weather had changed. A hot dry wind now blew over the camp, fraying nerves already strained. On the road approaching the Eureka Hotel, Pearl and JG found a milling mass of men, many of them armed, most of whom had oiled their throats well with liquor and were in a reckless mood. A speaker mounted a tree trunk to address the crowd, pleading with them to stay within the law while using all possible means to have the case against Bentley, the hotel proprietor, and his men, brought before a more competent jurisdiction. The diggers seemed amenable and began to disperse. JG showed his disappointment.

'Where are the hotheads? Are they all reasonable men here?'

Pearl pointed out a second man climbing up on the trunk. 'That's Henry Westerby, a notorious stirrer of trouble. He's drunk.'

Westerby began to bawl at the remainder of the crowd that the government camp was a hotbed of corruption and bribery, the magistrates in collusion with Bentley and his like. Shouts of approval urged him to greater heights of oratory. Bottles passed from hand to hand while the crowd's mood grew hotter.

'This is more like it.'

JG's satisfaction disgusted Pearl. 'You want trouble, don't you?

All newspapermen are the same, encouraging disturbance just so they can report it, no matter the consequences.'

'That's not quite true, girl dear. We go where trouble's expected and always to be found, mankind being what it is. And you can't deny the excitement in standing at the heart of things. Don't you feel it?'

'Yes, I do. But I don't think I like it. These men are being deliberately inspired to throw off restraint when they're not sober enough to know what they are doing.'

Westerby's shout of, 'We'll have the bugger Bentley out,' was met with a roar from a hundred throats, and cries of 'We'll smoke the bugger out. We want Bentley. We want Bentley!'

A detachment of troopers arrived to parade along the outskirts of the crowd, clearly hesitating to tackle such a number. Minutes later Westerby, with two other men, raced over to the canvas bowling alley attached to the hotel, their arms full of paper and rags which they rammed against the wall. A flame spurted and the hot north wind did the rest. A gout of fire rushed up, followed by an explosion of sparks which drove the men back. The wall of the hotel had caught alight and the diggers hailed this with glee, passing their bottles of rum freely while spreading out around the building in the hope of catching Bentley on the run.

Pearl grasped JG's arm. 'What will happen to Bentley? Those troopers won't stop the mob.'

JG concentrated on the burning hotel. 'When it reaches the liquor she'll go to glory. Don't worry about the proprietor. I saw him scuttle off while the firebrand preached his message.'

'Then let's leave. If there's a riot we can't do much except get caught up in it.'

'Not yet.'

Sheets of fire devoured the wooden walls, turning the verandah posts into flaming torches. An orange light played over the gleeful watching faces, while owners of nearby stores ran with buckets and billy cans and any other available utensils to fling water over their canvas and timber shanties. The crowd had grown quiet as the voice of the fire rose from a crackle to a roar; plumes of smoke and sparks shot into the sky to be blown like a comet's tail out into the dark. With the crash of a thousand tin kettles the roof fell in on the heart of the inferno. The windows blew out like shotgun blasts and, as JG had predicted, the liquor bottles exploded. Anguished howls greeted such waste and men began stamping on the flames, beating at them with branches or sheepskin waistcoats torn from their own backs, in a bid to save the kegs.

Despite JG's hopes for more action, little else happened beyond the ransacking of the ruined hotel by the mob, while Westerby and his crew fell down dead drunk. The troopers marched away to their barracks, and JG and Pearl administered to a few broken heads then went home, agreeing that it had been a mere flash in the pan, not at all indicative of the true diggers' spirit. There would always be wild men and brawlers, but it would be a pity if they were to spoil the chances of those seeking compromise with the government.

JG saw Pearl to her tent before he retired to his own modest shelter nearby. 'We'll see what tomorrow brings,' he said. 'Commissioner Rede is not the man to take this tweaking of the nose and say thank you. Meanwhile, I'm for my bed. It's been a long, full day. Goodnight, girl dear. Angels guard your dreams.' He lightly kissed her scarred cheek and closed the tent flap behind her.

Chapter Twenty-four

Spring had come to Sydney Town, launching itself on a fresh salt breeze blowing up from the harbour, scouring away winter's residue of stale odours. Spring rains had washed down streets, roofs and gutters, carrying away refuse, freshening buildings and yards, while blossoms burst from trees and bushes to scent the new-rinsed air. Housewives aired out mattresses and rugs; maid-servants polished door-knobs and whitened doorsteps; street-sellers and delivery boys whistled at their work.

Dressed in fresh muslin and carrying a pretty, frilled sunshade, Jo-Beth set out to walk through the Botanical Gardens out onto the promontory known as Mrs Macquarie's Chair. The water curving so closely around the point gave an impression of coolness. Surely, she thought, there could be no more lovely harbour view in all the world, with the naval ships bobbing at anchor and colourful ferries beetling between the green and gold foreshores. On the rocks below, a native fisherman stood with his spear poised as if cast in bronze, while his catch flapped sequinned scales in a pool at his feet. Behind Jo-Beth, below the brow of the hill, children played ball in the gardens, laughingly chasing one another around the trees, oblivious of the heat; to the east a bay lay edged in sand where gulls strutted and pecked amongst the tide wrack. In the

shade of a fig tree Jo-Beth furled her parasol and proceeded to think seriously about her position.

What she longed for with all her heart had been denied her, and it was time she accepted that Ethan was not coming back. She did not enjoy nursing. Yet there were other avenues of support open to her—assistant to a linen draper, perhaps, with her knowledge of fabrics, or a dressmaker. She'd always had a good eye for fashion and wielded a clever needle. Then there was the best opportunity of all—marriage to Alan McAndrews.

It probably wasn't fair to accept so much love and give so little in return. But life wasn't fair; she'd learned that lesson. She could make Alan happy, even without caring deeply for him. It wasn't as though she'd tried to deceive him or build false hopes. He knew all about Ethan and willingly accepted the friendly affection which was all she could offer. As chatelaine of his home and social adjunct to his career, she'd be superb. She had the background and training which she'd use in his interests. It would be a good bargain for them both. Because she needed to return to her own stratum of society. Elly had recognised this, even while praising Jo-Beth's good points—her compassionate sharing of the patients' fears and disappointments, her willingness to hide her distaste, to plunge into blood and ordure when asked. It was just the eternal scrubbing, and the endless hours spent in noisy, stuffy wards, she thought. And the ordeals witnessed in surgery. And the vermin.

Jo-Beth took off her gloves and inspected her hands, rough and chafed, despite all her efforts. She missed the comforts of a lifestyle she had undervalued when it was hers. She would have exchanged them all gladly for the freedom of the high seas with Ethan; but that brief glimpse of another reality had been cut off. Now, as Elly pointed out, she could choose a different way, easier, although not without responsibility. As the wife of Alan McAndrews her position in London society would enable her to raise funds and squeeze all she could out of the privileged classes, organising charities, supporting hospitals, pressuring for the endowment of institutions and changes in discriminatory laws affecting the underprivileged. With her new knowledge and experience she could forge unbeatable weapons, keys to the hearts and consciences and coffers of rich men and women who would wonder what whirlwind had come out of Australia to overset their comfortable British lives. It wasn't what she wanted, but it was the only offer available, and she'd keep her part of the bargain faithfully.

A chittering sound emerged from her large reticule and she opened it to release Peanut, her boot-button eyes darting in all directions.

'So you're awake, lazy one. Run about then, take your exercise. That leg is strong enough now. But no more tumbling into drains.' She tweaked the end of the bandage on Peanut's twiglike limb, feeling the monkey's tail wrap around her wrist and tug. 'No. I'm not coming. Be off with you.'

Head to one side, she regarded her, then sprang up onto her shoulder, pulled a strand of hair behind her ear then disappeared into the lowest branch of the fig tree.

'Mischief!' Jo-Beth straightened her hat, then pulled on her gloves, hoping once again that Pearl could be persuaded to relinquish her pet entirely.

The tall figure she expected loomed over the crest of the hill and she rose to greet Captain Alan McAndrews, who sweated in his hot uniform.

'Miss Loring—Jo-Beth.' His usual urbanity had deserted him. She saw his anxiety in his tightened mouth, his exaggerated low bow. The waxed points of his moustache quivered.

'I was watching for you.' She smiled, beckoning him to sit with her on the granite slab. This was the moment ... but for just an instant she allowed Ethan's features to overlay the paler, less decisive face before her. She pictured golden brown eyes narrowed against the wind, a firm bearded chin jutting, a mouth that could soften in a remembered kiss, so passionate, so adoring. Squeezing her eyelids tight, she forced the image away. It was useless. She had chosen her way, and would now put aside these memories forever while looking to the future.

Alan's voice trembled. 'Jo-Beth, you know why I asked you to meet me. I'm living in torment. Please, I implore you, give me my answer today.'

She opened her mouth to speak, but he hurriedly continued. 'You should know that my duty here ended with the departure of Governor Fitzroy. I intend rejoining my regiment in London. I may even be sent on to the Crimea.'

She paled. 'Oh, I pray not.'

'Do you, my love? Do you care?'

'I care a great deal.'

'Enough to marry me? To spend whatever time we may have together in my homeland?' His gaze trapped hers, pleading rather than demanding.

Jo-Beth took a deep breath, ready to commit herself. 'I'll ... I ...' The words would not come. Her gaze held McAndrews's, but unseeingly, blinded by a sudden, unexpected illumination. Then closing her parasol, she laid it carefully aside and stood up. 'I'm sorry, Alan, so very sorry to have misled you, but I can't accept your flattering offer—'

'Don't! Don't be so polite when you're stabbing me to the heart.' He sprang up and grasped her hands, so tightly that the seams of her gloves marked her for an hour afterwards. His eyes blazed, his voice was a throttled cry. 'Why? I've waited for months, and you never gave me cause to be discouraged.'

She met his rage and pain with her chin raised. 'I didn't know how much I'd changed during those months, Alan. I did intend to wed you and to be as good a wife as possible; but now the moment has come, I find I can't do it. It would be disastrous for us both.'

'You're wrong—'

'Hear me out, I beg you.'

'It's the memory of your sea captain, isn't it? You're trapped in a fantasy of what might have been.'

'No. You'd be justified in thinking so, if I was the old Jo-Beth. But I'm not. Please, let me try to explain.'

Releasing her, he turned aside, hiding his expression while ostensibly looking out over the harbour. 'Very well.'

'It's difficult to say just when I changed. I only know that I'm not that same wild, spoilt girl who took ship from China and was washed up on the shores of the Colony to begin a new life. I suppose I'm trying to say that I've finally learned to stand alone. In the company of two of the finest, most courageous women, I found a core of strength within myself and built upon it. Now I know I can't go back to dependence, to submission. You wouldn't enjoy marriage to the person I've become.'

'How can you know that?'

'I know. You need someone quite different, Alan, and I pray that one day soon you will meet the right woman to love you as you deserve to be loved.' She came to him, laying a hand on his sleeve, but he threw it off, his face still turned aside.

Sighing, she picked up her parasol and beckoned to Peanut.

McAndrews turned to face her. 'You will not reconsider?'

'I'm sorry.'

'Then I will bid you good day.' He clapped on his cap and bowed stiffly. 'Permit me to wish you happiness in whatever future awaits you.' Then he stalked off.

Her eyes followed him until he disappeared below the lip of the hill. She wanted to cry, to assuage her own guilty pain, but tears would not come. There would be no release for either of them except through the passage of time.

Chapter Twenty-five

Elly, poised on the footway outside the old Hyde Park Convict Barracks, sniffed the spring air and felt rejuvenated. On impulse, she bought a sprig of mimosa from a flower seller and pinned it to her collar, then crossed the street to the park, where other Sunday strollers paraded inside the railings. What little grass managed to grow here was regularly cut up by horses and vehicles, and the young trees had scarcely reached the proportions necessary for a park. Still, it was the hub of the city, the meeting place for all classes, not just the residents of mansions lining Elizabeth and Macquarie Streets. Shop girls and clerks strolled arm in arm or sat close together on one of the many benches; military men showed their paces on horseback; families took the air in their carriages.

Elly expected, rather than hoped, to see Paul riding with his ward, knowing that Lucy practised her new skills as a horsewoman at every opportunity. Elly told herself she approved of Paul's interest in the girl. After all, Lucy had no other family to rely upon. It was good, too, for Paul to escape his involvement in politics and remember that he was still a young man in need of exercise and diversion. Nights spent at meetings in smoky taverns and beer halls; days of visiting prospective constituents, listening to complaints, arguing, pleading and explaining, must wear him down.

In the near distance a pair of riders drew off the carriageway and stopped. Elly recognised Paul and Lucy straightaway, both mounted on handsome bays, both in the highest spirits. Lucy glowed with youth, thought Elly, contrasting her shabby old tartan gown with the gloss on the girl's smart blue velvet habit. Paul looked a born horseman, holding his mount easily in check while he coached Lucy in mastery of her animal. She dimpled and nodded, clearly inattentive, her gaze roaming to catch the glances of young military men, also exercising in the park.

A voice spoke above Elly's head.

'Persephone, you gild the spring. I particularly admire the touch of mimosa.' D'Arcy Cornwallis bowed from the saddle of a magnificent black stallion. He glanced ahead at the two approaching riders and Elly could have sworn his lip curled for a second.

Paul's welcoming expression froze and he yanked at his horse's mouth, while Lucy treated Cornwallis to a slumberous smile and an inviting glance. Her astonishment when Paul leaned over to grasp her reins, pulling her mount around, made Elly smile. But the way Paul stared at her, then deliberately looked away, was enough to kill any amusement. Without any effort at politeness, he spurred his own horse into a trot and dragged Lucy away with him.

'How impetuous.' Cornwallis laughed ironically, moving the stallion up closer to Elly, his hand on his hip, perfectly at ease. 'Have you forgiven me, yet, Eleanor? I've been most patient, I believe.'

Puzzled by his attitude, as if there had been only the mildest of differences between them, Elly answered: 'I've accepted your apology. But I don't care to continue our acquaintance, Mr Cornwallis, and I'd rather you didn't try to force your company upon me.' Her mind was with Paul and his obvious, hurtful conclusion that she had an assignation with Cornwallis. He should know her better.

When the black stallion lowered his muzzle to blow gently in Elly's face, she automatically put up a hand to stroke his velvety nose, catching an expression of tenderness on Cornwallis's face, as he patted the horse's neck. 'I apologise for Tartar's manners. Like his master, he's always had an eye for the ladies.'

Affection for an animal still did not alter the basic character, thought Elly. How would he react if the horse refused to obey orders?

Cornwallis continued, 'When have I forced my company upon you, Eleanor?'

Recalling the stream of notes, flowers and invitations which had continued weekly since her return from Bathurst, Elly replied, 'You refuse to accept dismissal.'

'I've never accepted dismissal from anyone, certainly not from a woman. You're too hot-blooded, my lady.' The black stallion fidgeted, dancing from side to side, a sure indication of his rider's restlessness.

Elly said disdainfully: 'For you, of all people, to make such an accusation. Now, please understand me. I don't wish to associate with you. You discomfort me, and you've certainly demonstrated your opinion of me. It would be better if we were not to meet ever again.'

'Very well.' The words were clipped, although his expression did not alter. 'I shall no longer importune you. But you've not heard the last of me, Miss Eleanor Ballard.' He raised his hat and rode off, leaving Elly uncertain whether she'd been threatened or reprieved.

She carried her ruffled feelings back to the hospital, her pleasant mood destroyed. An hour later she was called out with Dr Cooper, one of the younger district physicians, to attend a confinement at Darlinghurst Gaol. Mrs Burton, a thin lady of nervous disposition and wife to the gaol governor, had haunted Elly for months, declaring she would not survive the birth if the matron were not present. Elly, knowing the woman had lost three children in stillbirth, barely surviving herself, had readily agreed to help. This time she made her preparations buoyed by the thought that the stork-like Dr Cooper actually appreciated her help. He had even adopted her recommended practice of washing in carbolic solution, and passed on this modern attitude to the medical students under his direction.

They arrived to find Mr Burton in a panic and his wife on her knees beside the bed calling upon all the archangels for protection in her coming travail. Dr Cooper's examination showed the birth to be still some way off, so the stout little governor, reassured, excused himself on the grounds of duty.

Elly, having made the patient comfortable, strolled to a window above the prison yard and halted in shock. She was staring down on a gallows and the preparations for an execution. She watched as if in a trance as a prisoner was brought out, hands bound, he and his squad of guards marching in step to a drum. Other guards had lined up behind prisoners being paraded to witness a salutary lesson, while a party of onlookers had collected by the steps—Mr Burton, a clergyman and, of all people, D'Arcy Cornwallis. He stood bare-headed, tensely absorbed in the scene before him.

Drums rolled and Elly covered her mouth, unable to drag her gaze away from Cornwallis who savoured the poor condemned wretch's terror with a smile, before turning to speak to Burton. The gaoler appeared to expostulate, gold glinted in the sunlight, then Cornwallis stepped forward past the clergyman reading from his Bible, up the steps, and took the rope from the hangman. He fitted the noose around the prisoner's neck, drew it tight, all the while staring into the man's eyes, then stepped down from the gallows. The drum ceased, the signal came, the prisoner dropped. Elly could have sworn she heard his neck crack. Covering her face, she turned from the window just as her patient screamed and went into convulsions.

Elly forced from her mind the horrible scene she had just witnessed and went to work. Puerperal convulsions were a dreaded and serious complication occurring only too often, but Elly had never accustomed herself to it. Mrs Burton's paroxysms increased at an alarming rate until she was constantly wracked. Her face registered terror at her body's involuntary spasms; her arms and legs hit out as Elly and a maidservant fought to hold her down so she could be bled.

Dr Cooper panted from his exertions. He had taken off his coat and rolled up his shirt sleeves, appearing even thinner than ever. 'We'll try a cold douche to the head, Matron, and if that doesn't answer, a large foetid enema of turpentine.'

These, together with other remedies, including mustard cataplasm to the legs, having failed, Dr Cooper turned to Elly. 'The poor woman is unconscious, but I fear for the child if this continues. Her movements are too violent for me to attempt to use instruments for the delivery.' He drew Elly away from the bed, lowering his voice. 'Have you by chance heard of Dr Tracy, a physician to the Melbourne Lying-in Hospital?'

Elly shook her head. 'Does he suggest a remedy in such cases?'

'Chloroform, administered for two minutes at most. It acts most rapidly after bleeding.'

Elly glanced back at the writhing patient, drenched with sweat, her contorted face a reproach to them both. 'Then try it, Doctor. If it does nothing else it will ease her pain.' She bathed the sunken face and held the woman's head still as a pad with a few drops of the anaesthetic was placed under her nose. Elly could feel the muscles begin to relax and then, with an almost magical swiftness, the paroxysms ceased and Mrs Burton fell into deep sleep.

Doctor Cooper wiped his forehead. 'I wasn't sure of the effect on a pregnant woman, yet she seems easy. I hope to God it hasn't affected the child.'

'The baby's heartbeat is strong.' Elly put down her stethoscope. 'What if the convulsions recur?'

'We may have to repeat the exercise when she goes into second stage labour. According to Dr Tracy it does no harm to administer up to an ounce of chloroform. Beyond that, no-one knows.'

Twice more they repeated the dose, despite the doctor's obvious trepidation, and each time the incipient convulsions ceased. Labour proceeded normally until, five hours later, a lusty boy was born, his colour and his lungs testifying to his health. The placenta delivered easily and Elly cleaned the now conscious mother then placed the swaddled baby in her arms, the woman's face as she received him being all the reward Elly needed for her arduous afternoon.

'I knew we'd be safe if you were here,' whispered Mrs Burton, her mouth against the newborn's crumpled cheek.

Elly shook her head. 'You have a fine doctor to thank, not me. Your safety and your healthy child are due to his interest in modern medical discoveries and his willingness to try them.'

Colour rose in Dr Cooper's thin cheeks. 'I had excellent support. Matron, you may invite Mr Burton in to see his family.' He began to roll down his sleeves.

But seconds later Burton burst in unceremoniously. 'Doctor, you're wanted urgently. A gentleman has been set upon by thieves in an alley behind the gaol. They say he looks set to die.'

Elly grabbed the doctor's medical bag and accompanied him to the door.

'Where is he?' asked Cooper, taking the stairs at a run.

'In our parlour. Two of my men found him and chased off the attackers. This way.' He led them into a room at the left of the stairs, its heavily patterned walls and window draperies creating an under-sea gloom. Beyond the barricade of tables, chairs and screens stood a chaise longue with a still figure stretched upon it.

'Light the gas,' ordered the doctor, threading his way across the room with Elly close behind. He bent down as light flared suddenly, and over Cooper's shoulder Elly had a clear view of the unconscious victim's face. It was masked in blood, but the features were well known to her. It was Paul Gascoigne.

Elly held the sobbing girl in her arms, wondering what more she could say to comfort her. It had all been said. Nevertheless, she went on smoothing the dark head, repeating her litany as if it were some magic incantation.

'Lucy, he's not going to die. We won't let him. You will *not* lose the last person in the world you love.'

Lucy raised her head from Elly's shoulder and wailed: 'How can anyone help him? He's been brutalised. Did you see … ? Did you see … ?' Her face collapsed and she buried it again, her body shaking with sobs.

Controlling her own tears, Elly said softly into the girl's hair: 'Yes, I saw. But it's mainly bruising, my dear, not nearly as horrible as it appears. The head injury was more severe, yet he has recovered his senses. Only his leg gives us cause for concern, and the bone will eventually mend.'

Lucy wrenched herself free of Elly's hold and faced her, fists clenched, her voice rising. 'I don't believe you. I heard the doctors say it was serious. I know I'm going to lose Paul, like all the other people I ever loved, and I'll be alone again. It's not fair! It's not fair!'

Chapter Twenty-five

'Lucy—'

'Leave me alone.'

Elly caught Lucy's arm as she whirled to leave the room. 'I know it isn't fair for your life to be so disrupted again, but I'd expect you to display more maturity in such a crisis. Paul needs you. Now is the time to repay his goodness. He asks for you constantly, yet you refuse to go to him because your feelings are lacerated by his appearance, and you fear he might die. How can you be so selfish?'

'I can't help it. I can't bear to see him so ... so mauled.' Lucy's face paled at the memory, and Elly forced the girl down on the landlady's best parlour chair, holding her head between her knees.

'You're not to faint. I haven't time to care for swooning maidens.' When Lucy had recovered her colour, she was allowed to sit up, only to receive a lecture, delivered gently but firmly.

'I shall not ask you about your feelings for Paul. I do know he loves *you*, whether it is fondness for a young relative in his care, or something stronger. He's done all in his power to make you happy since you came to Sydney Town, taken you riding, dancing, shopping for clothes. He's not a wealthy man, yet he's done his best. He has been kind, Lucy, and you're repaying him with cruelty.' She gave the girl a handkerchief, waiting while she mopped her cheeks.

'Elly, don't berate me. I don't mean to be cruel.' Lucy hiccupped, swallowing her sobs. 'I love Paul, truly, but blood and injuries make me feel sick. That day of the coach accident I admired you so much for helping the people who'd been hurt, but I couldn't have done it. I shut my eyes when I held the candles for you, then afterwards I went behind the trees and vomited.' She hesitated, eyeing Elly diffidently, then went on. 'It sounds wicked, I know, but if I'm to lose Paul, I don't want to see him any more. I don't want to ... to invest any more of myself in someone who will leave me. It hurts too much.'

Elly had a short struggle with herself, and the better half won. 'I understand what you mean, although I can't accept it. My sympathies are always with the distressed, and Paul is suffering terribly, both in mind and body, while you try to protect yourself from future pain.' She sighed as she got up. 'I don't suppose there's much more I can say to change your mind.'

Lucy shook her head miserably. 'Please don't hate me, Elly.'

'I don't hate you. It's just ... Will you write to him?'

'I ... perhaps. Do you truly believe he'll live, Elly?'

'If I have anything to say about it, he will.' Elly left the room before she said anything she might later regret. Lucy would be well taken care of, she knew, with the Widow Brockenhurst fluttering around her like a mother hen, and Jo-Beth promising to take the girl on an outing to the Botanical Gardens that afternoon. Elly, herself, would be on duty until late, but she intended to call on Paul at his home before she retired.

Dr Hart, the district surgeon, remained cautiously optimistic about Paul's recovery, two weeks having passed without him succumbing to pneumonia, while most of his injuries had healed. On the evening when he was carried into the gaol governor's residence, Elly had believed, like Lucy, that he would die. His pulse had been almost indistinguishable, his clothes soaked in blood from his injuries. Elly had felt like dying herself as she worked alongside Dr Cooper on Paul's poor battered body. The head wounds had worried her most, but Paul had recovered his senses over a period of days.

It was assumed that his attackers were thieves who had been interrupted before finishing their work. However, Elly had a disturbing feeling that Cornwallis had arranged it. Having witnessed for herself the kind of sadistic enjoyment his nature craved, she knew it would be only a matter of time before he struck out again. She cursed herself for not handling the conversation with Cornwallis in Hyde Park more tactfully. All she had done was add to his desire for revenge, and Paul had suffered for it. He would go on suffering, too. Elly knew that. She was not as happy about his condition as she'd told Lucy. His gashed leg would not heal. Proud flesh had been cut away more than once and all possible remedies tried, but still the wound festered over the crack in his shinbone. Along with Dr Hart, Elly feared gangrene.

That night the hired cab dropped her outside the narrow brick cottage Paul rented; overlooking the water in Balmain, it was one of several new developments on half-acre lots, close to the city yet retaining a feel of the countryside. It had proved popular with merchants anxious to spend their wealth on houses worthy of their new estate, and with investors who saw the possibilities of increasing property values as Sydney spread into the suburbs. Paul's landlord, at present in London, occupied the ground floor.

When Elly arrived she found the door had been left on the latch. She let herself in quietly and climbed the stairs to a panelled door on the landing. As on the few previous occasions when she had visited Paul's sanctum, she was impressed. He'd taken an ordinary room and turned it into a tranquil haven, offering a wing chair by a fire, a convenient footstool nearby, glass-fronted bookshelves within easy reach, and a rack of pipes. A massive desk stood under the sitting room window; it was covered in papers, a cedar and brass inkstand, several pens and books of cuttings from journals lying loose, waiting to be glued in. The worn rug had faded to muted reds and turquoise, the walls to a dull dusky rose. Over the timber mantel hung a portrait of Pepper, and below it squatted a pretty green and gold lacquer clock. The only other object which could be classed as ornamental was an oil lamp on the desk, a large affair of brass and crystal with an elaborate painted bowl. This pooled light on the leather couch where Paul lay, his injured leg propped on a cushion. He sat up when he saw Elly, his smile weary but welcoming.

Elly's heart lurched at the sight of his worn, vulnerable face. Furrows between his brows and newly hollowed cheeks were indications of how much he had endured. But he had brushed his hair carefully and arrayed himself in a Chinese silk dressing gown which had seen better days.

'Paul, you are positively magnificent—a pasha upon his throne,' Elly teased him, laying her pelisse over the wing chair.

Paul's smiling response did not quite mask his wince as he sat up to greet her. 'My best *déshabillé*, donned in your honour, Elly. I knew you would call in, however late the hour. Does Hart know you're here?'

She shook her head. 'It's better not to tell him. He's so jealous of his status, unlike Dr Cooper. How are you feeling, Paul?'

'Oh, tolerable. Better, in fact.'

'I see. Perhaps I'd better inspect your leg.'

'There's no need, my dear. Hart dressed it this morning, and he'll call in again tomorrow.' A new note in his voice set off an alarm.

'What did he say?' Elly settled herself on a stool beside the couch, the rug covering his legs under her hand.

'Why, the usual. It's slow to heal, but there's no cause for worry.'

Elly leaned forward. 'Oh, Paul, why won't you tell me the truth? Or better still, let me see for myself.' Before her could protest, she twitched the rug onto the floor then pulled his nightshirt back to the knee. A bandage bound his leg from ankle to above the kneejoint, stained with the yellow salve smelling of comfrey which was favoured by Dr Hart.

'No, Elly.' Paul grasped her hands hard enough to hurt.

She held his gaze steadily. 'Let me go. I will examine your wound. It's my duty and my right.'

For a long moment their wills locked. In the silence Elly heard the mantel clock ticking, the fall of a piece of wood in the grate. Paul's eyes were hard as agate. Then he let go her hands. 'Very well. Have it your way.' He lay back to demon... his lack of interest as Elly unwound the bandage and remo...

the wound.

When a good two minutes had gone by...

...he said, 'We...'

'Because I've only ever heard of it once, from a patient who saw the natives use it. It's revolting, and I only suggest it out of desperation. For you to lose your leg would be to halve your usefulness in your cause. It could even mean the end of a career which matters more to you than anything in the world.'

'Not quite anything. But that's neither here nor there at this moment. Elly, what is this treatment?'

Elly swallowed. 'It means allowing maggots to eat away the dead flesh, as they would carrion.'

Paul released her and sank back. This time the silence had the intensity of utter stillness, echoing with unspoken thoughts. Elly kept her head down and continued to rebandage his leg. When she had finished she rose.

'I'm sorry, Paul. It was a stupid notion. Why should you take such a risk with an unknown native remedy?' She touched his leg gently, hesitating. Her voice trembled. 'Oh, Paul, couldn't you bring yourself to at least try it? You might equally die after surgery as from your septic wound.'

'Where would you get the maggots?'

She chuckled sadly. 'I'll get them, Paul. Will you let me try?'

He considered, then spoke out, and Elly was sickened. 'I will, and I'd rather die with my dignity at stake with your maggots than be cut up like a carcase on a block. Alive with crawling flesh or death to any man, who—'

Chapter Twenty-six

Elly finally returned to Paul's rooms late the following after
noon, accompanied by Jo-Beth, who had insisted on supporting her friends through this ordeal. Glad of her dis-
tracting presence for Paul's sake as well as her own, Elly erected a
rough screen across Paul's body which would hide her actions from
him. Unfortunately, she could not disguise her movements, and
she felt him stiffen as she began to unwind the bandage on his leg.
His fever had returned, an indication that the infection had wors-
ened.

'Did Doctor Hart visit today?' she asked him.

'Yes, with a portentous frown and an offer to operate this week.
I told him I wanted to give the idea more thought while I pursued
another form of treatment privately. He went off in a huff.' Although pale, Paul smiled easily at Elly then began chatting to Jo-
Beth, who handed him a large tumbler of whiskey.

'Start sipping, my lad. In no time at all you'll forget what's happening and be merry as a cricket.' Paul looked at the brimming
tumbler then placed it back on the table beside the couch. 'Good
God, do you want to knock me out cold? My thanks, but I'd prefer
not to embarrass myself before two ladies.'

Elly picked up the tumbler. 'Paul, you should drink it. Your

pulse is thundering. There's no shame in dreading this procedure, so why not make it easier for yourself?'

'No. I've never yet needed a crutch. I will not start now.' His
face closed against her, and she turned away.

She worked swiftly, having braced herself mentally for what
she must do. Her hands were steady as she picked the heaving
mass of maggots from their box and laid them on the suppurating
wound, watching to see them begin their work. There was a line of
demarcation between the healthy tissue and the ulcerated mass, a
red inflamed zone running into black, and the maggots fastened
upon the dying tissue. This was not Paul's body, Elly told herself,
and these were merely some of God's little creatures doing what
came naturally to them. She even said a small prayer, before remembering she no longer believed in Him. How strange, she
thought, recalling her father's strictures. Had he been mistaken?
Was there a divine plan after all? Had she not been victimised by
the Settlement dwellers she would never have met Paul, or the
patient who had witnessed this method of saving a limb. If Paul's
leg was saved.

Jo-Beth's voice penetrated her thoughts, the assumed Irish
brogue exaggerated as she embroidered one of JG's tales in an
effort to distract Paul. '… but Wentworth didn't like me calling
him a fool, so he told me I was drunk. "Sir", I said to him, "I may
be drunk, but I'll be sober tomorrow, and you'll still be a fool.".'

Paul smiled dutifully, although his leg muscles shivered un-
controllably under Elly's touch.

'Elly, I can feel them. I can … God! It's horrible.'

She saw the sweat break out on his brow and she picked up the
tumbler. 'Please, Paul, drink some whiskey to relax your nerves.'

Jo-Beth said, 'If JG were here he'd match you and say, "Here's
mud in one eye, lad, and a glint in the other".'

With only a moment's hesitation, Paul took the whiskey and
gulped half of it down, avoiding Elly's glance.

Hiding her anxiety, Elly watched him grow paler and more rigid
by the moment. His jaw had clenched tight enough for the cords
to stand out in his neck. He tipped the glass, draining it. Jo-Beth
caught Elly's glance and refilled the tumbler. Now Elly wished she'd
given Paul laudanum, although he would probably have refused

it, neither of them having realised how much mental strain would result from their experiment. However, with so much alcohol in him, she daren't add the opium. After another tumbler of whiskey his eyes were bright, but with the feverishness of an almost intolerable restraint. Paul was screaming inwardly, Elly was sure.

She leaned over him, screening him from Jo-Beth's view.

'Shall I take them off?' she whispered.

His eyes pleaded with her, but his lips formed the word, 'No.'

Elly's own nerves had tightened painfully. Paul's intolerable tension reached out to her, goading her to do something. What *could* she do to help? He was a proud man. His self-esteem might be wounded beyond bearing if he were driven to break in front of others. It would be better if only she bore the brunt of it, she thought grimly. On the pretense of wanting better light to check her work, she got Jo-Beth to set the large oil lamp on the floor below the screen, keeping Paul's face in shadow, and indicated with a meaningful glance that her friend should leave.

Jo-Beth shook her head, careful not to look beyond the screen, but evidently determined to stay. Then someone banged on the door and she went to it, holding it open only a few inches.

'Lucy! You can't come in. Paul is having a treatment—'

'I must see him.' Lucy's voice sounded high and strained. 'I've been terrible to him and I want to say I'm sorry and I'll do anything I can to help.'

'Not now. Paul wouldn't be able to talk to you. He's not well enough.'

'No. Let me in. I must see him.' Lucy pushed the door suddenly, violently, sending Jo-Beth reeling back. She ran across to the couch and, brushing Elly aside, knelt to snatch Paul's hands against her breast. 'Dearest Cousin Paul, I had to see you, to tell you how much I've missed you.'

Elly grasped her shoulder, but she twisted aside, saying sharply: 'Why are you here? I'd have thought you'd be needed at the hospital. Paul's doctor is caring for him perfectly well, I'm sure.'

Paul managed to produce a few, half-strangled words, 'For the love of heaven, get her out of here.'

Jo-Beth had her by the waist, lifting her away from the couch. As she struggled, her arm caught Elly's makeshift screen, knocking it down. Lucy stared at Paul's leg, at the box with its writhing contents. Her scream was shattering. Elly made a grab for Lucy's free arm then helped hustle her to the door.

'Take her home, Jo-Beth, and stay with her if Widow Brockenhurst isn't there. I'll call in later.'

Lucy had gone from white to red. She dragged her arm free and hit out at Elly. 'Don't touch me. What are you doing to him, you fiends?'

'We're helping him, Lucy. I'll explain it all—'

'No! You're lying! What you're doing is vile. I'll get the police … the Governor …'

Jo-Beth slapped her cheek, hard. 'Shut up, my lass, and pay attention to your elders. Paul has asked for this treatment. He's not drugged or restrained in any way, as you can see. But it's taking all his strength to withstand it, and the last thing he needs is interruption from a spoilt, hysterical brat who thinks the universe revolves around her precious self. Now, you come with me, and no more argument.'

Elly stared at the closed door, listened to the receding footsteps and the sound of Lucy's angry sobbing. She went back to Paul.

Sweat streamed down his forehead and his hands were locked, white-knuckled. Elly wiped his face as she sat down.

'Paul, it will help if your attention is distracted. Talk to me. Tell me about your childhood in Yorkshire. Was it on a farm?'

With an obvious effort he focused his mind, saying through clenched teeth, 'Yes, not far from Great Ayton. Good … land, it was, and we … made a good living.'

'You told me you went to school, so your father must have been prosperous if he could spare you from the farm. Did you have only the one sister?'

For an instant, the half smile appeared. 'Jessie. She had … hair like spun straw and a merry nature that could charm birds into the kitchen to feed from her fingertips.' The light in his face died, and Elly quickly asked another question.

'Were you happy at school? Were you a studious little boy?'

'When it suited me.'

She heard the breath hiss between his teeth, and knew she must goad him into anger if he was to forget his present torment. 'So how did it happen? What took you out of school into the mills?'

'I don't want to think about … that.'

'Yes, you do. Tell me, Paul.'

He held her gaze firmly. 'It's not your affair.'

She was just as adamant. 'I'm making it my affair. You're not the only person with a difficult past. Children have always suffered for their father's sins.'

'My father committed no sin,' he roared feebly. 'He was a wonderful man. If he hadn't been so innately good, he'd never have been cheated out of his land by a smiling villain not fit to wipe his boots!'

'Tell me what happened.'

'I'm damned if I will.' He sounded less like an enraged adult than a cross, sulky child, and Elly grinned.

Paul said stiffly: 'I beg your pardon. I shouldn't have shouted at you.'

Delighted that he had forgotten the maggots for the moment, Elly continued to prod him. 'Shout as much as you like. Who was this villain who stole your land, and how did he do it?'

Paul looked grim. 'He was a gentleman, so-called, a member of the railway company who knew our land would be wanted for a new spur line out to the coast at Whitby. When my father refused to sell, mysterious fires broke out in the hayricks, sheep were savaged by wild dogs, fences came down. Our workmen were bought off—' He stopped, stretching out towards the screen. 'Could we … No. Never mind. I'm sorry, what was I saying?'

'The farm had been under attack.'

'Yes.' He collected his thoughts. 'One night several sheep were found in a field with their throats cut. Two men lay against the stone wall: my father, unconscious from a bump on the head, and a stranger, dead with a billhook through his chest. My father was arraigned for murder. He'd no need to swear his innocence to me. I knew him for a man who could never kill another, whatever the provocation.'

Elly poured another small whisky and gave it to him. 'So your mother couldn't continue without help; the farm ran down, and the railway entrepreneur bought it at a low price. Where did your family go?'

'To a cottage in the village. Mam was pregnant and ill, so Jessie stayed with her while I went into the mill. The money from the farm swelled the purses of doctors with their useless medicines and the equally useless lawyers who failed to bring my father off. I slaved in that mill, drawing lint into my lungs with every breath, but the pay was pitiful. The babe came into the world sickly, and Mam never fully recovered. Grief for my father didn't help.'

He lapsed into gloomy silence, and Elly urged him to continue. 'So you took ship to Australia, lost your family tragically at sea, and found yourself alone in a strange country at ... what age?'

'Fourteen. I felt like forty, with the weight of misery and experience on my back. It made me very angry, very resentful.'

'I think you still are.'

His head snapped up and he gave her his full attention. 'Is that what you think? That I'm brooding over my losses, still?'

'Are you not?'

'In part, I suppose. I've thought of pushing the Yorkshire gentleman under one of his own trains.' He paused. 'Elly, the boy who'd gone on the streets, running wild, had the good fortune to be rescued, educated and stood on his feet by a philanthropist. I'll tell you about him some day. But the boy grew into a man determined to create a society of equal opportunity, where children are not enslaved through poverty, where men may speak for themselves without fear of reprisal. Where the law is the same for all and one man may not own another nor treat him as something lower than the beasts.' His voice had grown stronger, and at last he sounded like the old Paul.

'As the child of a convict father,' he continued, 'I should have been relegated to the underclass in our society. But I refused to be classified, branded. I've fought to be seen as the man I made myself. I've also waited a long time to avenge my father's murder.'

Shock rendered Elly immobile, searching for words. 'Murder! I thought he was transported ...'

'He was—' Paul thumped his thigh with a fist. His voice rose. 'Christ! Will those little buggers never let up? Elly, I think I'll go mad.'

She flew to him, holding his shoulders as he struggled to rise from the couch. 'No. No. You must go through with it. It's your only hope of saving your leg. Paul, tell me about your father. Who killed him?'

His eyes bulged with effort. She could see him being torn by a desire to knock her aside and rip away the bindings holding the maggots against his flesh, saw the self-restraint which allowed her to hold him down against the cushion.

'My father ... They assigned him to a country property,' Paul panted. 'The overseer was bad, but his master was worse. On his orders my father died on the triangle, his back shredded to ribbons by the cat. That man will die by my hand, one day.'

These last words seemed suddenly to release the alcohol into his brain and he went limp in her hold, his jaw slackening as his head fell to one side and he slept. But before long he began to moan and mutter, his fingers twitching, reaching down his legs towards the source of his restlessness.

The hours passed slowly as Elly sat with his hands locked in hers, her back and neck stiff with fatigue, listening to him rave in a half-drunken state about the itch, the awful, tearing, nerve-shredding itch of tiny mouths nibbling, chewing, gorging on his flesh. But when daylight filtered through the windows, Elly detached herself from his hold to inspect the wound, and there she saw what she had prayed for. Cleaning away the glutted creatures into the box, she found that the necrotic tissue had all but disappeared, leaving behind healthy pink granulated tissue, the beginnings of new flesh. If she wasn't so exhausted she wouldn't be crying, she told herself as the tears rolled down her cheeks.

Paul's cracked and weary voice recalled her. 'What is it, Elly? Has it all been for nothing?'

She beamed through the tears. 'My dear, it worked. It worked!'

He bolted upright and tore away the screen to stare at the wound where red and black flesh had made way for raw pink. 'It's true,' he croaked. 'You did it, Elly.'

'I'm not so sure. I seem to detect the guidance of another hand here.' Elly shook herself. Mysticism at dawn—impractical and misleading. She must pull herself together.

Paul seemed dazed. He sat staring at his leg, muttering: 'It's true. It's true.'

Elly wondered whether she had the strength to finish off here and get back to the hospital. A hot drink. That's what they both needed.

Yawning and stretching cramped muscles, she revived the almost dead fire then put water on to boil.

'Elly?'

Paul's voice, so tentative, made her shrink inwardly. He had remembered his loss of control during the long night and wanted her to leave. He couldn't bear to face the person who had heard and seen his humiliating disintegration.

'Yes, Paul?'

'Come here, please.'

She went slowly, not meeting his gaze as she sank down again on the stool beside the couch.

'Elly, I placed my trust in you, knowing you'd stand by me through whatever came, and you upheld that trust. I know I didn't suffer alone through those hours. There will never be any way to thank you. I simply want you to know I couldn't have held out without your presence, holding me together, giving me your strength. I owe you my life, Elly.'

It wasn't a moment to demur politely. Elly felt she *had* held Paul's life in her keeping for a time, or if not his life, his sanity. She never wanted to see anyone go through such an experience again. But it had been worthwhile. His leg would heal in due course—the cracked shin-bone was minor in comparison with the infection—and Paul would walk again without aid. His career and life were safe, but for how long, with Cornwallis on the prowl?

'Paul, do you have any idea who your assailants were?'

'Hirelings, thugs in the pay of Cornwallis. I've thought so from the beginning, when I woke up to find how close I'd come to being crippled. It's his style.'

Paul sounded so matter of fact, Elly was amazed, and then angry. 'How can you be so calm about it? What if ... what happens when he tries again?'

'I'll be ready, and more careful.' He drew her close beside the couch. 'Elly, it's you I'm afraid for. You're next in line.'

'I know it. But how can we guard against the unexpected? He won't try the same ploy twice. He's too clever. He's a sadist, Paul. He'll draw out the plot with twists and traps. Do you know he pays the governor at Darlinghurst Gaol to let him watch hangings, now they're no longer public? I even saw him set the rope around a poor man's neck.'

Paul stiffened. 'How in the hell did you see such a thing?'

'Oh, from a window. I was attending a patient at the time.' Elly dismissed this.

Paul relaxed and he lay back, exhausted, while Elly hurried to fetch a steaming mug of tea. She refused to let him talk until he had drunk most of it. Then, placing the mug on his table he said: 'My dear, we must make plans of our own. A creature who'll pay to participate in a hanging is, as you say, capable of any action.'

'I know it. But although I started this conversation, I want to put aside worry over the future, for just a few minutes longer. I want to relive the joy of our success.' She put her hand in his. 'Paul, you're whole and healthy, or will be again soon. It's a kind of miracle.'

His fingers closed over hers, tightening. A tide of exhaustion mixed with elation washed over and through her, as she gave silent thanks. Luck, or divine planning, or whatever—something much more powerful than either of them—had been with her and Paul that night, and she was grateful from the very depths of her being.

Chapter Twenty-Seven

For the next few days after the burning of the Eureka Hotel Pearl saw little of JG as he moved through the various camp sites, talking with the men, adding to his understanding of the situation. Pearl herself had more than enough work with an outbreak of sandy blight caused by wind-blown dust and a consequent call for her particular form of eye wash. This simple solution of boiled boracic and herbs acted like magic on the painful swelling, made worse by poor diet and the generally run down condition of the sufferers; but at least the warmer weather meant less rheumatics and pneumonia.

November was an uneasy month. The arrest of Westerby and two others charged with burning down the Eureka Hotel had caused an uproar amongst the miners. At a meeting on Bakery Hill a crowd of nearly ten thousand gathered to wave their banners and listen to moderate speakers plead for restraint and firebrands preach rebellion. A deputation went to the Governor demanding the release of Westerby, although the hotel proprietor, Bentley, and his two henchmen were convicted of Scobie's manslaughter and sentenced to three years' hard labour on the roads. Rumours flew that the Commissioner and the Governor were secretly planning to teach the diggers 'a fearful lesson', and a detachment of the 40th Regiment marched into Ballarat from Geelong, jeered by the diggers. There was some scuffling which led to a few injuries, and tempers were still running high that night when a troop of mounted police rode through the camp to the accompaniment of shots fired in the air, showers of sticks and stones and angry cries of 'Joe! Joe! Get rid of the bloody traps.'

Things remained strangely quiet around Golden Point during the next day. Pearl missed the background noise of the windlasses creaking, of digging, chipping, cursing, of water running. She knew a meeting had been called and felt uneasy, knowing the temper of the camp. She was also worried about JG, whom she had not seen for days. His activities had several times led him into trouble with men who resented his curiosity or feared his motives. The gold-fields already had their own newspapers. They didn't need some toffee-nosed city journalist poking around, misrepresenting their case. But the occasional black eye never deterred JG, and Pearl admired his courage and devotion to his calling. In fact, in JG's absence, Pearl realised she cared a great deal about him.

Thinking back on their encounters in Sydney Town, Pearl recognised just how long ago this caring had begun, even when she believed she hated him for his interference in her affairs. Was it because *he* had so obviously cared what happened to her, an insignificant little woman from a despised country, who flew at him in a fury whenever he approached her? But how much of that caring went beyond humanity and friendship? Would someone as restless and cynical on the one hand, and broad-mindedly inquisitive on the other, ever consider tying himself down to one woman, when he had always roamed the world freely and clearly loved doing it? It wasn't possible. She had to forget any notions of love between them and instead enjoy the friendship. This point settled, Pearl firmly turned her mind to a case of asthma aggravated by the patient's conviction that it could be cured by smoking stinkweed.

JG slipped into her tent later that evening after the lamps had been lit, while Pearl bent over her casebook, entering the details of the day. She raised her head as a shadow passed over her packing-case desk, and saw him transfigured. It was more than normal excitement there in his face, she thought, more like a solemn fervour, almost exaltation.

'What has happened? I can see it must have been something momentous.' She waited in some trepidation for his answer.

JG paced the tent restlessly. 'How can I explain? This meeting, it was the experience of a lifetime, a conversion. I listened to plain men address their fellows with an honesty and consideration for the rights of others that I've never before heard or seen. It was democracy and brotherly love and rage against tyranny, all rolled into one. And by all that's holy, it was magnificent.'

He has thrown himself in with their cause, Pearl thought. What would it lead to? 'What did they say?' she asked, her throat dry.

'Everything. A German fellow named Vern exhorted them to burn their licences, so anyone arrested for being without one would be defended and protected by his united fellow diggers. Then a fine-looking Irishman, a Peter Lalor, took a stand under the Southern Cross flag, the sun blazing down on him as he called upon us all to unite against oppression and tyranny. He spoke of true democracy; his words were inspiring, Pearl. 'If a democrat means opposition to a tyrannical press, a tyrannical people, or a tyrannical government, then I have been, I am still, and will ever remain a democrat'. And I knew he was right.

'It's time to change the balance in this Colony, to create a new society based on equality. You know, I always believed deep down that Paul and his friends chased an impossible dream, that the heavy guns of the squatters and their ilk would forever maintain the power. But here, on the goldfields, there's only the power of the police plus one army regiment against thousands who believe we can prevail. If we do, what an example it will set to the world. Don't you see, Pearl? It would mean the coming of a new era, such as civilisation has never seen.'

Where have I heard such words before, thought Pearl grimly. 'Did they burn the licences?'

'Did they! The chairman of the meeting got up—by that time we were all half drunk on excitement, and some on rum—and he shouted "Are you ready to die, men?" All replied "Yes", drawing their guns and firing. Then out came the licences to burn like the flames in the hearts of those brave men.'

'Those idiots, more like,' Pearl said bitterly. 'You see what you've done, all of you? Rede will never take such a slight to his office. They'll come for you, the mounted troops with their guns and swords and bayonets. They'll trample you and shoot you down with no more compunction than they'd destroy vermin. And you will have died for nothing—an ideal which can never have any reality.' She almost sobbed. 'The world isn't run on idealistic lines. It never can be. You fool, JG. Oh, you fool.'

JG put an arm around Pearl's shoulders and squeezed, saying comfortingly: 'It won't come to that, girl dear. When the authorities see we're in earnest, they will agree to compromise.'

Pearl removed herself from his hold. 'Have they ever done so before? This new governor is not like La Trobe. He needs to be in control. Besides, Rede already has his reinforcements. He'll act before any word comes from Melbourne.'

'Perhaps. But we'll be ready. It's gone too far, Pearl. The men are sickened by the treatment handed out to them. They want justice.'

In the glow of the lamplight Pearl studied him, realising she had never really known what moved this man to action, beyond the obvious demands of his work. Why had he so suddenly joined the rebels—he, the cynic who had seen it all before, who believed nothing without irrefutable proof? 'JG I didn't know you cared so much for the rights of man. You sound more like Paul Gascoigne, thundering against tyranny on his box down in the Domain.'

JG sat down on a packing case, as if suddenly weary, his face falling into lines that wiped away the illusion of blazing youth, fired with youth's energy and enthusiasm.

'I'll be forty before long—perhaps two thirds of my life gone, and what have I achieved? I earn my living sniping at others, paid for my nuisance value and merely tolerated in a society that has a wary respect for my tongue. My father, an unknown seaman, departed before my mother knew to expect me, and she contained her joy in my arrival sufficiently to hand me over to an orphanage as soon as she had strength to run off. I owe them nothing but an inherited streak of stubbornness plus a body which sometimes fails me at awkward moments. I am what I made myself, and lately I haven't been too pleased with the result.'

Pearl held her breath, not wanting to interrupt this rare confession.

JG looked up at her, then gazed off into the distance, his thoughts far beyond these four canvas walls. 'I suppose a time comes for every man when he takes stock and knows what imprint, if any, he'll leave behind when he departs this world. I have a fancy to make a mark worth remembering. Just a small mark, mind you, yet one which says JG stood up for something important. He might not have done any good, yet he tried.' He sighed, then smiled and brought his attention back to Pearl. 'It seems like this is my moment to make that imprint, girl dear.'

Pearl could think of nothing to say. She wasn't sure she wanted to comment. This was JG's decision and she had no right to try to influence him at such a time. 'I'll brew some tea,' she said. 'Planning a war is thirsty business.'

Before she climbed into her bed that night, Pearl opened a small silk bag worn around her neck and took out her foster mother's earrings. They winked on her palm like slivers of sunlight, more precious to her than any gemstone. She thought about the man who had returned them to her, shame faced, inarticulately grateful for her care, and only able to mutter a remorseful apology. But with that some of the grief lessened, and she could look back on her attackers without hatred.

At ten o'clock the next day a troop of mounted and foot police, swords and bayonets at the ready, set out behind Commissioner Rede for a major inspection of licences. The riot act was read and imprisonment threatened for those who resisted, plus instant shooting of any man who raised his hand to strike or throw a stone. The diggers grouped behind their Southern Cross flag and marched out, gathering reinforcement as they went, although not before one man had been mysteriously shot down on the road, increasing resistance and firing the diggers with the need to take up arms in their own defence.

Pearl stood beside her tent and watched them tramp past to their meeting place at Eureka, chanting slogans, those without weapons fashioning home-made pikes from sharpened steel heads attached to poles. JG paused to say goodbye, his face alight with excitement and zeal, a pistol through his belt and a double-barrelled rifle across his arm.

'We'll win through, never fear,' he said. 'But just in case, I'd like you to hold this letter for me. If I don't return, would you send it on to Sydney?'

Pearl accepted the letter, her calm expression hiding the tumult of emotions storming through her.

JG put down the rifle to cradle her face once more. His merry expression had disappeared, and the freckles stood out against his skin, giving him an almost bloodless pallor. But the blue eyes, shining with conviction, held a tender light Pearl could easily have mistaken for love. 'Don't forget me, Chinese witchwoman.' He kissed her scarred cheek then let her go.

She saw him join the band of marching men and disappear between the hillocks of clay, on his way to a destiny he could hardly have foreseen when he set off from Sydney a few weeks earlier.

The next two days passed in uneasy silence. All activity on the fields had ceased. Even the grog shops were empty. Over in the troopers' camp the men drilled, exhorted vigorously by their officers, and Pearl suspected councils of war were under way. On the second night of December, hot and breathless as though in anticipation of the coming storm, Ezra Coffey rode up to Pearl's tent and slid down from Polly Doodle's back. He carried only the smallest amount of equipment and appeared stripped down for a rapid journey. When Pearl's last patient had scuttled off into the dark, not anxious to be away from home in these uneasy times, she greeted her visitor with pleasure. But he grimly cut across her words.

'Gal, you gotta get outa here. There's big trouble coming, and you don't want to be caught in the middle. The troopers are near ready to move out against the diggers who've dug in behind a palisade like they're about to fight the Indian Wars all over again.'

'Have you come from Eureka, Ezra? What's happening?'

'I told you. They're readyin' for war up on their hill. A couple o' wild boys tried to rope me in, telling me I wasn't no patriot, but I give one o' them a close shave with a bullet and they changed their mind. But I decided to move on quick. Me and Polly Doodle like peace and quiet, so we're headed back beyond the range. Come with us, at least part of the way.'

In that moment Pearl made her decision. 'I can't, Ezra. I'm going to Eureka.'

'What! Now look, gal, I just finished telling you—'

'I know. But I'll be needed there. I can save lives.'

'Only if you hang onto your own.' His old eyes peered at her shrewdly. 'There's more to it, isn't there? Some man you're worried about. Right?'

'Right. He is a fool to get involved. Still, I know why and I love him because of it. He won't thank me for getting underfoot, but I've got my own path to follow. Thank you, Ezra, for thinking of my safety.'

'Hmph. Wasted my time, didn't I?' However, he smiled as he climbed up on Polly Doodle and picked up the reins. 'Good luck, gal, to you and your man. See you in heaven.' He kicked his heel in the mule's flank and rode off.

Pearl picked up her bag and lantern and set off north towards Eureka.

Chapter Twenty eight

It was still dark when Pearl arrived at the stockade, a crude palisade formed from pit props taken out of the mining shafts. The sentries who challenged her fell back, amused at the sight of the Chinese witchwoman with her bag of nostrums, a sight too well known to be suspect.

'You're early, dearie,' quipped one. 'No injuries yet. But you could have a squiz at me piles.'

'I will when I've sharpened my knife,' Pearl promised. 'Can you tell me where to find a newspaperman named JG Patterson?'

When the sentry shook his head, she moved on past figures clumped by the barricade, her path dimly lit by torches and a few camp fires with billies on the boil. Voices were low amongst the tents as the men discussed their chances in the imminent battle, although a few lay like logs, dead drunk and useless. Pearl wondered whether they had caroused to bolster their spirits, or simply didn't believe they would be called on to fight. The first faint light glimmered below the horizon, enough for her to see how small the numbers were. What had become of the hundreds who had marched out past her tent two days ago? There couldn't be more than two hundred here now.

A scuffle and a cry of pain made her turn. The sentries had a man pinned between them, his arms twisted behind him.

'A spy' called a voice, and a torch shone on a sweating oriental face.

Pearl dropped her pack to run back to the entrance, shouting: 'Let him go! He's no spy. He's my brother.'

One man shrugged and released his prisoner, but the other growled, 'How do we know he's not a spy?'

'Because I say he's not. You know the Chinese take no interest in the politics of the goldfields, and the troopers treat them worse than some of the miners. Let him go.' The last words were spoken so fiercely that the man wisely decided not to argue. Dropping Li Po's arm, he returned to his position, still grumbling, while Pearl confronted her brother.

'Why are you here? This is not your fight, Li Po.'

He rubbed his sore arms. 'It is not yours either. But I am not surprised to find you here, ready to tend those who will be wounded. You must listen to me this time, Younger Sister. You will recognise my authority.'

'Why should I?'

He answered slowly. 'There are only the two of us. I do not want you to risk being killed.'

Dumbfounded, not sure she had heard him correctly, she said, 'You mean you care what happens to me?'

'You are Younger Sister. I care for my own.'

She could not read his face in the slowly gathering light, but she had detected a tremor in his voice. 'Li Po, I am very happy that you cared enough to follow me, but nothing will persuade me to leave.

'What can a woman do in a battle? Come with me and wait beyond the hill until the fighting is ended. You can return to tend the wounded. Hurry. The soldiers are coming. I heard them in the woods, moving silently, without drums and bugles. They will attack at full light.'

'It's too late.' Pearl pointed to the sentries, sprung to life, shouting and gesticulating towards the north where a column of cavalry had appeared. Dust rose beneath the horses' hooves, and behind them an even greater cloud raised by the infantry and police on foot. The gap in the barricade was closed and people rushed to their defence positions.

Pearl found herself jostled aside, while her brother disappeared into a group armed with ploughshares and reaping hooks. She gazed around frantically, with little hope of seeing JG in the melee. Finding herself increasingly in the way, she scrambled up on the jumble of boxes and barrels to the top of the stockade to peer at the oncoming force.

The cavalry, having reached a point about a hundred and fifty yards away, now wheeled to the left, while mounted police formed ranks on the right flank. Behind them the infantry deployed, with supports in the rear. From the stockade a volley rang out, followed by sustained fire from the defenders. In answer, a bugle sounded the order to commence firing. The noise was like a New Year's celebration, with hundreds of firecrackers exploding, and the same smell of gunpowder in the air. A man standing beside Pearl slumped suddenly against her then slid headfirst down the barricade, leaving a smear of blood on her coat. Pearl knew she must help him, yet she continued to stare, mesmerised, at the army ranged against them. There must be four or five hundred, at least, she thought. What hope did the diggers have against such a trained force?

Out in the open field two men fell off their horses, their red jackets disappearing in the dust of a cavalry charge. Around Pearl men were hit, crying out as their weapons dropped from useless hands and they tumbled to the ground. Then the foremost troopers reached the stockade, abandoning their mounts to clamber over the top, their cutlasses reflecting the first rays of sunlight.

A bullet whistled past Pearl's head and someone dragged her down, thrusting her behind a barrel. A body fell on top of her, knocking her breathless. Her ears were filled with cries and gunshots. She choked on the smell of powder and smoke as tents were set alight, regardless of the drunken men within. Sudden loud cheers announced the taking of the rebel flag.

'Kill the bastards, every one!' a voice screamed above her head.

In answer another shouted: 'Give quarter! Give quarter! Any man who murders a prisoner will be shot on the spot.'

Pearl lay pinned, unable to move for what seemed a long time, listening to the screams of the dying. For the order to give quarter was largely ignored. Diggers were being chased down and bayoneted with brutal glee by a force of men brought to frenzy by the week of waiting to be attacked in their camp by a foe rumoured to outnumber them by thousands. The fact that their fears had been groundless meant nothing. They released their pent-up emotions in an orgy of killing, including innocent bystanders, acting more like a crazed mob than units of trained men. Told later that the bugle sounded the ceasefire only fifteen minutes after the attack had been launched, Pearl could scarcely believe it. During those minutes, and in the following hour, twenty-four rebels were killed, with another twenty wounded; while those not immediately taken prisoner spread out and ran for cover in the camps or down the road to Melbourne, chased by the troopers.

A woman searching for her husband discovered Pearl and called men to remove the body which pinned her down, staked to the ground itself by barrel staves shattered into swordlike pieces. Pearl, erect and swaying, gazed down at Li Po's face, contorted in his last agony. Her heart burned with pain. She would never be able to tell him how sorry she was to be indirectly responsible for his death. He had only wanted to protect her. He had cared for her, after all, but now she would never truly know him. Kneeling to close his eyes with gentle fingers, she addressed a brief prayer to whomever might be listening, commending a brave soul.

Desperate to find JG, Pearl found men willing to carry Li Po's body and accompanied it back to Chinaman's Gully, where she delivered it into the care of his compatriots. Then, at last she was free to begin her search. To her overwhelming relief, JG had not been counted amongst the dead. Nor, she noted, had the leaders of the rebellion, who had mysteriously disappeared, either escaped or hidden by their friends. The troopers returned to their camp, taking the wounded under arrest, while the police raged through the diggings, laying waste to tents and grog shops, and chasing frightened men into their holes. Pearl found her tent and everything in it burned to the ground. All she had left was her medical bag of supplies. She stood beside the smouldering patch of earth, her eyes smarting from the heat and ash, her senses bombarded by the misery of the dispossessed who had lost friends and family in what the soldiers cheerfully referred to as a skirmish.

For the rest of the day she wandered through the area between Eureka and Golden Point, stopping to help the subdued but angry diggers where she could, always asking whether anyone had seen JG. There were plenty of burns and injuries from clashes with the police, plenty of arguments as to whether the rebellion had been justified. Not until late in the evening did she receive a whispered message calling her back to Chinaman's Gully. Although tired out, Pearl left immediately, arriving at her brother's hut to find JG unconscious but tended by the tong himself.

'Why did you give him sanctuary?' she asked the old man, kneeling to examine the deep laceration in JG's skull. She had gone ice cold at the sight, before reminding herself that she was foremost a healer and had no time to indulge her nerves.

The old man moved back to allow her space. 'He used your name, Younger Sister of Li Po. He claimed to be your friend. Is that not so?'

'Oh, yes. He is my friend. Thank you, honourable sir, for taking him in. All prisoners are being transferred to Melbourne, whatever their condition, and I doubt if JG would have survived the journey with such a wound.' She examined the long gash running from below JG's ear across the base of his skull, finding it had been cleaned and the edges stitched together. But a great deal of blood had soaked into his shirt, and his skin was pallid. He hardly seemed to breathe, although from time to time he muttered unintelligibly.

Despite an age-cracked voice and severely bent back, the old tong was clearly experienced in dealing with wounds. He detailed the methods he had used on the patient, which included compression of the wound until bleeding had all but ceased and the use of boiled thread to sew it together.

Reassured, Pearl brought out an ointment of mouldy strained cream and applied it before bandaging, saying as calmly as she could: 'You have saved his life. I am eternally grateful to you.'

'You are one of us. Also, your fame as a healer has spread like an ocean wave across the land. It is known that you never refuse anyone in need. That is the way of an enlightened soul.'

Pearl, thinking of Dr. Hsien Lo, muttered, 'I try.' With the tong's help she undressed JG, searching for further injuries, thankfully finding only a few bruises. After wrapping him in a blanket, she cleaned his face where he had bled from the nostrils, moistened his dry lips and placed pads soaked in cooling herbs over his eyelids, then waited for him to come to his senses.

She waited through another day and night, with only snatched minutes of rest, growing more concerned by the hour. Close to dawn after the second night JG seemed to rise nearer to consciousness, his occasional muttered words becoming clearer. 'Tell her … no … must not … angel … stupid to care … send the letter … she'll know then … so sweet …'

Pearl, filled with a wild hope, grasped his hands and said urgently: 'What is it, my dear? Were you trying to tell me something?'

The mutters died away, and Pearl sat back on her heels, disappointed. Was she the woman he spoke of? Did he see her as an angel? Was the letter the one he had entrusted to her, and did it mention another woman after all? Jealousy burst into her brain, shattering her composure; then, just as quickly, died. What right had she to feel such an emotion? JG had never said a word to indicate a more than brotherly affection for her. She, like so many others, was just his 'girl dear'. She stroked his unruly hair, more thickly peppered with grey than she had realised, smoothed the frown from his forehead with her thumb, noting how beaked his nose had become, how his eyes had sunk deep into their sockets. He was so thin. If he didn't waken and eat soon …

To distract herself, she reviewed her treatment, examining each part to see whether she could have done more for him. But she knew she had done her best, given her limited supplies. His recovery now lay with the gods.

The old tong called in to see the patient and shook his head, obviously believing another coffin would be ordered before long. He explained Li Po's wish to go home, in the event of his death in Australia, and the arrangements made for his remains to be held with others awaiting transport to Melbourne and temporary interment before shipment back to China. Pearl thanked him absentmindedly and returned to her patient.

JG had begun to mutter again, no names, but a reiteration of his love for some woman, begging her to come to him, crying out his need for her comforting presence. Holding back emotion, Pearl bathed his face, smoothed his hair, tried to reach him with words, but in vain. He could not be comforted.

At last she could stand it no longer. If she was unable to help JG she might at least assuage her own need to know whom he summoned from the depths of unconsciousness. Taking the letter from inside her jacket, she read the superscription—to Messrs Tomlinson and Bryan of Pitt Street, Sydney Town. Could she violate his confidence and break the seal? There was a time when she would have been amazed at her hesitation. She put the letter back in her pocket and wept. Tears poured down her face, threatening to choke her with the violence of her sobs. Life had dealt her many blows, but none like this—to watch the man she loved, with a frightening depth and passion, die. To be unable to help, and never to know whether he loved her in return.

A weak voice penetrated her misery. 'Pearl, I feel sick.'

She rushed to the bed in time to help him turn his head and rid himself of the blood he had swallowed. When he lay back, exhausted, she found herself smiling foolishly at him. 'You're awake!'

'Haven't I just proved it? Brought up gizzards and all, I'm sure.' His own smile was a pale echo of the old one, yet it was there. He inspected her more closely and frowned. 'What've you been doing to yourself? Have you been crying?'

'Never you mind, you busybody. Drink this water then just lie still while I fetch you some good broth to get your strength up.' She darted away, all the spring back in her step, her misery dispelled like mist in the midday sun. Hurrying back, she felt almost afraid to look inside the cabin in case she had somehow been mistaken and JG still lay in a stupor from which he might never recover. But her patient waited, staring anxiously at the doorway, as if he, too, had his fears.

She fed him careful spoonfuls, not letting him talk while she gave him all the news she thought he would want to hear, about the removal of the wounded, the escape of the ringleaders and rumours that Governor Hotham would deal severely with the culprits.

JG shook his head. 'I don't remember the action at all. I can recall saying goodbye to you and marching off with the men to the stockade, and that's it. A blank.'

'That's not uncommon with such a head wound. You may never remember how you came to be hit. The tong says you were found wandering empty-handed, in imminent danger of falling into one of the pits.'

Chapter Twenty-eight

'I've lost my guns then? A pity.'

'That fact probably saved you from arrest.'

'We were let down, girl dear. Hundreds slipped away the night before the attack, their hot blood turned to ice at the thought of a fight. Some were the fiercest malcontents of all, the ones who urged us on, then left us.'

Pearl said gently: 'It couldn't have had any other outcome, my dear. We must just wait to see what action the Governor will take. There's talk of considerable support for the miners amongst the populace in Melbourne. Hotham might find he can't have his way after all.'

JG seemed to lose interest, falling asleep within minutes. He woke ravenous, and within two days began tottering about the immediate vicinity of the cabin with the assistance of a walking cane. He had been horrified to hear of Pearl's part in the uprising, attributing it to compassion for the wounded. He also shared her sorrow at the loss of her brother. Despite her belief in each person's right to make his own decisions, and to bear with the consequences, she still felt guilty; while the loss of her last family tie, the missed opportunity to know Li Po, added to her load.

Explaining her brother's appearance at the stockade, Pearl said, 'The same urge sent me there, to watch over—' She stopped, realising what she had been about to say.

JG's wits had not suffered from the blow on the head. He looked at her sternly. 'Go on. To watch over ... ?'

'I meant, to help the wounded.'

'I can always tell when you're lying, girl dear. You followed me, didn't you? Why? Did you think I couldn't take care of myself?'

The blood rushed to Pearl's head, then drained away. She sat down suddenly on a rock, dropping the kindling she had gathered on their walk. 'Don't interrogate me. I haven't done anything wrong.' She had meant to snap at him, but sounded merely piteous. She was disgusted with herself and terrified that she had revealed too much.

JG sat down beside her, threading her fingers through his. 'Look at me, Pearl.'

Never a coward, Pearl raised her face to find herself only inches from his. The blue eyes, deep-set amidst laughter lines, held hers.

'You followed me because you thought I might need you, because you cared about me.' His voice hardly rose above a whisper. 'What have I done to deserve this?'

Pearl sighed. 'You've just been yourself, JG. I could not wait back at Golden Point not knowing what was happening to you. As it turned out, I might have saved myself the trouble, and Li Po his life. But I could not have known. Nor could I let you go, perhaps to your death, then wait for some stranger to tell me.'

'You love me?'

'Yes. But you need not do anything about it.'

'The hell I needn't! Girl, haven't I loved you from the moment I set eyes on your cool little face so ready to suspect me of nameless things, so angry when I wrote the exposé of the hospital? Haven't I turned myself inside out trying not to take you in my arms and kiss you when you're spitting fire at me? Glory, hallelujah! I've come out first in life's lottery, after all.' He threw aside his cane and hugged Pearl to him, covering her face with kisses until she protested, freeing herself to fling her arms up around his neck and plant her mouth firmly on his.

JG's joyful shout echoed in her own heart, which seemed to swell with gladness, filling her chest to bursting. She *was* the woman in the letter, the woman he'd called for in his delirium.

It took her half an hour to come back to her senses. And then she remembered. Detaching herself from JG's arms, she got up. 'I forgot. I was so happy, I forgot.'

'What did you forget, dear heart?'

'Come back with me to the cabin. I will show you.' The light had gone from her face, and Pearl drooped as she led the way, her spirits utterly cast down at the thought of what she must tell JG.

Inside, she dropped the flour sack over the door and lit the lamp, then faced him, a sheen of tears blurring her sight. 'The man who disfigured me did more than just cut my face.' Pulling her jacket aside, she raised her shirt, exposing herself from the waist up. At the same time she released the cord of her trousers and, as they fell around her ankles, she watched JG's expression change to horror.

Pearl said, evenly: 'The scars are ugly, are they not? And a woman without nipples is not a pretty sight. But what you cannot see is worse. I have been damaged internally. I can still give a man pleasure, but I cannot ever give him a child.' Covering herself, she turned away from him. 'So you see, my dear, I will not hold you to your word. It would be unfair to us both. Pity would destroy us in the end.'

JG stood utterly still. She hoped he would not come to her. She couldn't have borne it.

Then he said in a broken voice: 'I don't feel pity. I feel an unutterable rage at the destruction of beauty, and the deepest respect for your honesty and courage. Pearl, you must know that love is based on far more than physical attraction.'

'It plays its part.'

'So it does. But I will tell you another thing. The act of love, the coming together of a man and woman whose hearts are attuned means the giving of pleasure to both. Who taught you to please a man and not think of yourself?'

She whirled on him. 'What chance did I have to learn of love between man and woman? Used from the age of six as a bed toy, a comfort pillow, a thing, an object. What do I know of pleasure for a woman?'

He moved then, taking her in his arms and holding her while she fought him, furiously, hopelessly.

'Let me go. Do not do this to me. You think I have no heart to be broken.'

JG kissed her hair. 'I think you have the greatest heart I've ever known, my beauty, and I'm honoured above all men to have your love. Now, let me show you what I mean.'

Having brought herself to the point of exhaustion, Pearl could only let him lift her onto the bed and submit to the gentle kissing and stroking that started a tingling response in her nerve ends. Every inch of her skin felt sensitised as JG removed her clothes with loving attention to each limb, to each fingertip and toe. Waves of pleasure rose and broke over her, generated by his lips and hands as they travelled over her body, kissing her scars, caressing her as she had never been caressed before, while he murmured his love, telling her how infinitely precious she was to him, how much more beautiful than any other woman he had known. And finally, on a crescendo of passion, her throat opening in a delighted moan, Pearl believed him.

Chapter Twenty-nine

Sunlight glinted off the harbour waters like splinters of glass, hurting the eyes, and new-laid asphalt melted into puddles in the streets. It was February's tail end, a day of blazing heat, and Jo-Beth was snatching a cup of afternoon tea when a message came that she was wanted in the lobby. Sighing at the interruption to her few minutes break, she smoothed her dress and went downstairs. In the doorway a giant of a man was outlined against the sunlit opening, his shadow reaching out to where she stood.

'Jo-Beth?' The voice, deep, unforgettable, trembled with emotion.

She stared up into brown eyes moist with tears, into a familiar scarred and bearded face alight with love.

'Don't you know me? Have I changed so much?' The man's voice cracked.

Jo-Beth's lips moved soundlessly. Her frozen throat muscles strove to move. 'Ethan,' she whispered, finally.

'My dearest.' The two words, so simple, held a world of longing.

She thought, he's aged. He's changed. But he's alive! He's really alive. Some miracle has happened and Ethan has come back to me.

Ethan held out his arms. Jo-Beth took one step towards him and was swept up into a crushing embrace.

She emerged from the maelstrom of emotion to hear Elly urging her to take Captain Petherbridge to her office where they could be private; and in a dream she led Ethan upstairs, his arm clamped about her waist, her feet seeming to skim the boards as she moved. The door closed behind them and she turned in Ethan's hold. The first shock had passed, and now she felt oddly hollow, almost panic-stricken.

'Jo-Beth?' His warm, familiar voice had an unexpectedly soothing effect, and she relaxed her rigid hold on herself. 'I should have given you warning, sent a letter. But I couldn't wait, my love. I just couldn't wait.'

Conflicting feelings surged in her. He *had* waited, more than two years. While she had kept faith, refused to believe he'd been lost, and suffered like the damned. Angry regret warred with an undercurrent of excitement building slowly, filling that hollow space, bringing a flush to her cheeks, a tingling in the fingertips, a vitality she hadn't experienced in years.

'My darling girl ... I can't believe it. To be with you again after so long ... to know I've not lost you.' His cheek muscles worked as he struggled for control.

Jo-Beth studied the lines of experience and suffering in his face, noted the grey streaking his hair and beard. He wasn't the same man who had radiated such blithe confidence when striding the quarterdeck of his small world; but then, she wasn't the same flighty Jo-Beth. How quickly fate changed people.

She moistened her lips and forced the words out. 'Where have you been, Ethan? For so long I endured ... I grieved for you.' Her voice shook.

His arm tightened around her. 'Oh, God, I'm sorry. If I could have spared you one moment's pain ...'

Gently detaching herself, Jo-Beth moved over to Elly's desk, giving herself space. Then she said, 'Tell me what happened to you.'

He paused, seeming to choose his words. 'The ship sank soon after you went overboard. I had time to shed my boots and grasp a couple of barrel staves before she sucked me under. Afterwards, it was all confusion.' He shook his head, unable or unwilling to describe his experience in the sea. 'The waves washed me ashore on a rocky islet far up the coast, where I was eventually picked up by a whaler heading for the southern ocean. I later learned that I was out of this world with fever for some weeks; and when I recovered they pressed me to work as one of the crew. We were gone months, slaving in a brutal climate, living like animals—' He bit off the rest of the words. Jo-Beth could only guess at the privations he had suffered. 'In port they took good care that I didn't escape ashore. They found me useful, you see.'

'But you were a clipper captain, Ethan. Didn't you tell them?'

His laughter had a bitter edge. 'I did more than tell, but they were too many for me. I spent more hours in the anchor locker than I like to recall, delirious much of the time, I think.'

Seeing his haunted expression, Jo-Beth's heart lurched with pity and love. She could only guess in what fantastic universe he had wandered during those days of delirium.

'It was the memory of your sweet face that kept me sane. My heart told me you were still alive, that the sea had not taken you. I prayed that one day fate would bring us together again.' Again he paused. 'Jo-Beth, there were times when I could easily have given up, yet I struggled to live, to find you again. I *knew* you would be waiting for me, somewhere.'

Her hands went out to him and he reached her in two strides to grasp and press them to his mouth. His voice came muffled from between her fingers. 'There's little more to tell. A few weeks ago the whaler came to grief on a promontory off Van Diemen's Land, the survivors being taken aboard a coastal trader and brought to Hobart Town. There I took ship for Sydney, to search for you, my own dear one.'

Pulling her hands free, Jo-Beth flung them around his neck drawing him down to her. She looked deeply into his eyes, letting him see the love there for him. 'You are alive and with me. That's all that matters now.'

Their lips met in a kiss which transported Jo-Beth back to the deck of the *East Wind*, to the precious moment when she had fallen truly deeply in love. And then she knew it was time to be honest.

'Ethan, I have something to say to you.'

He drew back to gaze at her. 'I know, my love. But you've no cause to worry. I've done with the sea. The day of the great sailing ships is ending; and when I saw my beautiful *East Wind* go to the bottom, her hull eaten with woodworm, her back broken, I knew it was the end for me. Nor will I risk your precious life ever again. The sea is a jealous mistress.'

'Oh, Ethan, don't give it up for me.'

'My dear, I've made my decision with a light heart. I've other challenges to meet, in the world of shipping commerce. I've made my packet trading and there's plenty of money to support us. Could you be the wife of a merchant here in Sydney Town? It's an exciting place, bursting with opportunity.'

'I'd be your wife if you were the poorest of men. But, my dear, what I'm trying to tell you is that I've changed. I'm not the carefree girl you knew and loved. I know myself better, and I can't resign my independence, even for you. There are things I want to do, decisions I must make on my own.'

Ethan laughed. 'Do you think I can't see that for myself? Or that you've grown more beautiful, with a sweet maturity in your face and the serenity arising from suffering overcome. No, you're not that girl from the past; you are a woman, proud and staunch, the one I need by my side to share whatever life brings, in storm and calm.' He claimed her lips once more, this time demanding a response to his rising passion.

Clinging to him as if her life depended upon it, her body moulded against his, Jo-Beth thanked God from a bursting heart, then gave herself up to her own desire.

As JG had telegraphed their arrival date to Paul, the Pattersons were met on the wharf by a reception committee consisting of Paul, Elly, Ethan and Jo-Beth. Pearl disembarked ahead of the other passengers, a diminutive figure in proper gown and bonnet, but still without the corsets—pelting down the plank like an excited child straight into Elly's arms.

Elly, hugging her until she squeaked that her ribs were cracked, felt a rush of emotion bringing tears and laughter and blessed relief that her dear friend had come safely home.

'Oh, I've missed you, Pearl.' She held her at arm's length and was struck with dismay.

Pearl's smile slipped a little. 'I know. My face. It doesn't matter, Elly dear, not any longer.' She beckoned to her husband. 'JG come, kiss Elly and be welcomed.'

'Do I dare?' Nevertheless, JG saluted Elly heartily on the cheek, his own happiness evident, despite his gaunt appearance.

'You've been ill.'

'Merely a clip on the head during the little affray at Eureka, girl dear.'

'How foolish to involve yourself. You're lucky not to have spent weeks imprisoned awaiting trial, along with the other accused men.'

He grinned at her severe tone. 'They were acquitted, weren't they? There was overwhelming public support for them. Besides, it would have been worthwhile anyway. The affair brought me my heart's delight.' His gaze went to Pearl, with such a light of love there that Elly caught her breath. Then he strode over to clap Paul on the shoulder. 'Take your hands off my wife, you cad, and give an account of yourself.'

When Jo-Beth introduced Ethan, JG's jaw dropped, but Pearl held out her hands immediately.

'This is the working of fate. You two were meant to be together in this life. I am so happy for you.'

Ethan's great laugh rumbled from behind his beard. 'Little Miss Pearl. I always knew you would win through, with all that determination.'

'Which she sharpens on me.' JG had recovered. 'Well met, Captain. It's not every day a man's privileged to encounter a ghost.'

Finding themselves the centre of a milling crowd of passengers with luggage, sightseers, clerks waving manifests, labourers waiting to unload cargo, the group took cabs to the York Hotel where Paul had hired a private room and ordered a celebratory lunch. Here all the pent-up news of months was exchanged, with many exclamations and requests for details.

Elly turned to Pearl. 'Tell me what plan you have for the future. I know you'll have one.'

A brief silence had fallen in the room. They all stared at Pearl, awaiting her answer. She glanced across the table at her husband, who nodded with a smile.

'We have been very fortunate,' she began. 'My brother died an extremely wealthy man, with much gold in a bank in Melbourne. He willed his fortune to me.'

When the exclamations died, Pearl went on. 'JG and I have formed a plan, and since it concerns you, Elly, I hope it meets with your approval.'

'Concerns me? But Pearl, it's your money—'

'Wait. Listen. We're going back to China.'

Elly felt her heart plummet, but JG said reassuringly: 'Wait until you've heard it all, Elly. Pearl has thought this out carefully.'

He grinned at his wife, who continued: 'I want to carry on the medical work of my foster parents. I plan to set up a clinic, to attract at least one Chinese doctor of medicine to help me, and to train local girls in nursing.' Seeing their amazement, she said earnestly: 'You can have no idea what the lives of unwanted girls are like in my country. I can rescue some of them, at least, from virtual slavery; then, Elly, I'll send to you those who wish a final polish, as you might say. They can then return to China to pass on their skills to others. The network of good nursing will thus be spread, gradually, over great distances. What do you think of my plan?'

Elly swallowed her disappointment. 'How could I not approve? It's a wonderful plan, my dear, and a worthy way of using your brother's money. I'll be happy to carry out my part.'

Paul shifted his attention to JG. 'Just what is your role in all this? I don't see you sitting on the verandah sipping gin while your wife saves lives.'

'I'll be setting up my own newspaper to give those colonial boyos a run for their money. One little matter I have in mind is the roaring trade in opium through the treaty ports.'

With a crack of laughter, Paul raised his glass. 'They don't know what they're in for over there. You'll undermine trade and reorganise the whole of their society if they don't watch out. I'd like to propose a toast to this marvellous new venture. To Pearl's clinic, JG's journal, and a brave new world, both in the east and west.'

The toast was drunk with solemnity. Then Pearl slipped out of her seat to place an arm around Elly.

'Don't be sad, Elly. I will miss you too. Yet we always knew we would go our separate ways in the end. You have achieved your purpose in pulling the hospital into order, making it a safe place for the poor. The Board is still difficult, I know, particularly as, as you say, Mr Cornwallis has withdrawn his support, but they dare not lose you.'

Elly smiled tightly. 'We walk a careful line, the Board and I, yet I agree there have been vast improvements over the past year. Of course, you're right. Each of us must take her own path, although I'll miss you both so much.'

Elly refused to dampen the occasion by detailing the difficulties of her life at present. Not only had the Board blocked all further plans, but she knew Cornwallis had stirred an undercurrent of feeling against her, evident in the attitude of the medical staff as well as in the myriad small frustrations met every day— problems with appointments and deliveries, broken promises, odd and inconvenient accidents. The list never ended. The pettiness annoyed her, but the consequences of disruption to the patients made her furious, sometimes bringing her close to despair. Then to cap all, she had just learned that the building housing the nurses and hospital stores would be handed over to the newly established government mint. Work had begun last year on conversion of the southern block occupied by the military as staff offices, plus construction of factories and staff cottages. Elly failed to see why her one small extra building should be reft from her, but needless to say she had not been consulted by the Board.

Pearl hugged her. 'We won't leave you just yet, Elly. It will take time for us to organise our journey, so I can come back to the hospital for several days each week until we go.'

'I'll stay on for a while, too,' Jo-Beth added. 'Ethan has much to do setting up his business and we must find a suitable home. You're not being deserted just yet.'

Smiling in gratitude, Elly put aside her bleak vision of the future to entertain Pearl with the story of her trip to Bathurst. This led to talk of Lucy Whatmough, with Jo-Beth confessing that lately she found the girl both wayward and difficult to talk to. Guiltily, Elly realised she hadn't given a lot of thought to Lucy in the past few weeks. Her anger with the girl over her attitude towards Paul's illness had passed and she and Lucy had re-established a rapport, or so she had believed. But her own preoccupation with the hospital's affairs, with Paul's protracted recovery, and the background worry over Cornwallis's plots, had taken up most of her time. Jo-Beth had befriended Lucy, since her dismissal from the millinery establishment for laziness and impertinence, but she had her own employment. So Lucy rode daily in Hyde Park, usually accompanied by an admirer or one of the young women met socially through Jo-Beth and Alan, and in general she enjoyed an unusual amount of freedom. The Widow Brockenhurst, in whom Paul had placed his hopes, had proved a pliable reed, quite unable to control Lucy's high spirits.

'I've been remiss,' Elly said. 'I undertook to help establish Lucy in her new environment. She's far too young and inexperienced to be left alone.'

Jo-Beth, delicately peeling a peach, said: 'She's Paul's responsibility, after all. If he can find the time for his own political interests, which he seems to have done, he can organise a proper chaperone for Lucy. She's had a taste of freedom and won't want to return to work, even if he can find someone willing to take her on.'

Paul broke off his conversation with the two men to plead: 'Don't forget the poor child has suffered the loss of everything in her former life. It takes time to adjust. Yet you are quite right. She needs occupation. I must find a more suitable situation for her where she will be carefully chaperoned. It's a pity she has no bent towards nursing.'

Jo-Beth and Elly were both amused at the idea, but gracefully guided the talk away to another topic. The lunch party broke up soon after, with the ladies preparing to return to the hospital. Standing on the street corner, Elly's attention was attracted by Mrs Burton, the gaol governor's wife, waving from the shelter of a doorway opposite. Excusing herself to the others, Elly stepped into the roadway, then hurriedly retreated as a pair of horses pulling a smart town carriage almost ran her down. She looked up to see Lucy watching her from the window with a mixture of defiance and triumph as she turned to her companion D'Arcy Cornwallis.

My fault, thought Elly. I was too proud to reveal my experience at Cornwallis's hands. Naturally Lucy, and Jo-Beth who introduced them, believe him to be a gentleman. Why didn't I keep a closer eye on Lucy's associates? He can ruin her so easily. Yet the affair may not have gone too far. If Lucy can be warned in time … No. She won't listen. I could see by her expression she believes she has brought off a coup. Poor, silly child. There's only one thing to be done. I must approach Cornwallis myself to warn him off. Paul mustn't know. There's enough trouble between them. But Cornwallis might listen to me if I threaten to spread the story of that night on the hospital steps. His reputation is precious to him. He'll be ropable, of course. How can I best protect myself at such an interview? I'll take someone with me—JG—and stay in his view the whole time. No, not JG. He'd be bound to tell Paul and it would all come out. Alan McAndrews would oblige me, I'm sure. He's still a friend, despite the break with Jo-Beth; and he's too polite to question me if I prefer not to tell him my errand. Oh, God, I hope I'm in time to save her. I could shake the little wretch. But it's my fault she has no idea how dangerous that man is.

Tangled in her chaotic emotions, Elly found it hard to carry out her duties until she could be relieved; but once free she put her simple plan into operation, running Cornwallis to ground at his club. The co-operative Captain McAndrews sent in a note requesting an interview, and soon Cornwallis emerged to peer about him, then follow McAndrews's summons to the mouth of a lane. There he found Elly waiting.

'What the devil!'

McAndrews said sharply: 'Watch your tongue in a lady's presence. Miss Ballard has something to discuss with you. I shall wait just beyond earshot.' Elly was glad to hear the menace implicit in his voice. His attitude showed he wouldn't move far off.

Cornwallis jeered at her. 'Well, Miss Eleanor Ballard, I believe I can guess your errand. It's effort wasted. I'm losing interest in the callow charms of your protégée.' He loomed unpleasantly close, but Elly refused to give ground. She looked up at his shadowed features, teeth and eyes gleaming like some beast.

'That's just as well since, if you were to injure Lucy, I would have no hesitation in spreading the story of your attack on me and your humiliation at Paul Gascoigne's hands.'

'Don't try a fall with me, my lady. You would be worsted. Besmirch my reputation and I'll inform the world that you are the daughter of a foul abortionist, forced to hide in the backwoods to save himself from public dishonour or worse.'

Elly clutched her midriff and reeled as if from a physical blow. 'You're lying. My father was devoted to saving lives.' It was a whisper, forced out by lungs suddenly short of air.

'It's a matter of record, which, incidentally, I hold safely. I've always found it useful to keep such things.'

Elly had recovered her breath. 'I don't believe you. My father was not a Christian but he believed in the sanctity of all life and fought for it unremittingly.' She saw him shrug.

'Perhaps he believed the lives of the women to be more important. Who knows how he reasoned? Yet he was a criminal, for all that, performing criminal acts. How does it feel, Eleanor, to be the daughter of a felon?'

'You shan't call him that!' She threw the words in his face, hitting out at him with her fists. Alan McAndrews came running. Seeing her apparently struggling in Cornwallis's grasp, he wasted no time thrusting the hilt of his sabre hard under the man's chin, knocking him backwards. He staggered and fell as McAndrews grasped Elly, pulling her away.

'Come on out of this. We can't have you involved in a public brawl.'

Elly tugged against his hold, trying to reach the man slowly gathering himself out of the filthy gutter. 'You are the lowest creature, to malign a dead man's reputation. But you don't frighten me. Make sure you leave Lucy alone or you will regret it.'

McAndrews thrust her out into the street and hurried her away.

Her visit next day to Widow Brockenhurst's house brought her no joy, as Lucy refused to appear until Elly forced her way into her bedroom. The girl then burst out with furious recriminations, accusing Elly of having broken her heart. She would not listen, but continued her hysterical tirade until eventually Elly had to leave, still unsure of the exact nature of Cornwallis's dealings with Lucy, yet fearing the worst.

A week later Lucy knocked on her door late at night, shivering like a forlorn puppy. Elly took her into her own room, now back in the main hospital. She chafed the girl's frozen hands and made her sit with the bed coverlet tucked around her.

'Tell me your trouble, my dear,' Elly encouraged sympathetically, giving her a hug.

The girl gulped, sliding her eyes away from Elly's. 'I've been so utterly stupid.'

'We've all been stupid at some time, my dear. How can I help? Tell me.'

Lucy struggled, but the words would not come out. Suddenly she slipped from the chair to kneel with her head in Elly's lap. 'Don't look at me, or I can't tell you.'

Elly stroked the dark ringlets. 'I won't look at you.'

Lucy gave a convulsive sob. 'You've got to help me, Elly. I'm going to have a baby, and I want you to get rid of it.'

Chapter Thirty

'**M**y poor girl. My poor, poor girl. But I couldn't do it, Lucy. You don't realise what you're asking.' Elly never understood how she found the right words, yet she knew she had to. Her own feelings must be subordinated to Lucy's need. 'You're carrying a new life inside you. You are responsible for it.'

'I thought you would say that. But I'm not responsible. I didn't know what could happen. Elly, you're my only hope. You have the knowledge, and you would never tell ... anyone.'

'You mean, Paul? He'll have to be told, Lucy. He can make arrangements for you to go away—'

'No!' Lucy sprang up and stood quivering before Elly, ready to hurl herself in any mad direction to escape her fate. 'I'll kill myself before I'll face him.'

'Don't talk so wildly. You're not capable of such a thing. Consider, Lucy. You're asking me to kill your unborn child. It's ... unthinkable.' She shuddered as Cornwallis's recent accusations against her father came back to haunt her. Had he been guilty of abortion? Unbelievable. And yet ... Why had they left Sydney for a place buried far into the bush? Why had a highly skilled surgeon and physician settled for general practice in some insignificant village when he could have headed a great hospital? She'd thought it was through grief at her mother's death, but such an explanation wore thin in time. Could he have done it?

Lucy's immature face hardened. Her skin had taken on a sickly yellow cast. She said harshly: 'Hundreds of women rid themselves of unborn children when they can no longer abide to produce litters. It's men who say we must. It's men who bring on the babies and what matter if the woman dies of it? There's always another to be wed and bedded and brought to bed with child. My mother was one such—a baby each year with myself the only survivor. Well, I'll not go down the same road.'

'You need not. I'd look after you and see you safely through the birth. There are ways of avoiding pregnancy, which I could teach you. None of this is your fault, Lucy. You're the victim of your inexperience and the wiles of a hardened rake. I blame myself for not having taken better care of you. You couldn't have known what Cornwallis is.'

Lucy began to laugh, the sound growing louder and higher, until Elly slapped her briskly, then rubbed the reddened cheek. 'Don't, darling. You're not alone in this. You have people who care about you.'

Collapsing in a sobbing heap, Lucy cuddled into Elly and let her emotions go. Elly held her, calming her as best she could.

Finally a murmur emerged from the head buried in her shoulder. 'It's not your fault either, Elly. I let him touch me, caress me. I wanted him to. It was so exciting, his hands on my body, the way he made me feel. He did things I couldn't begin to tell you, and I wanted him to go on doing it. He taught me how to give him pleasure. He took me into such a strange, wonderful world, Elly; and I believed he loved me. He gave me champagne to drink, saying it matched the sparkle in my eyes. It was all the magical things he said, as much as what he did that betrayed me. He lied to me, Elly.'

'He's the master of lies, my dear,' Elly commented sadly.

Lucy raised her face, damp and woebegone yet earnest as well. 'But it was *ecstasy*. How can I regret it?' Her expression crumpled. 'Then he threw me out, saying I bored him. I loved him, but he didn't love me.'

'He used you, Lucy. He's not capable of loving anyone apart from himself.' But he's very capable of hatred, she added silently, and of devising this revenge on Paul and me.

'I know what a fool I've been. Still it doesn't help me out of this trap. *You* must help me. There's no-one else.'

Elly stayed silent, her mind in a turmoil. While recoiling from the idea of abortion, she wholeheartedly agreed with the outburst about women being forced to bear children unwillingly. It was grossly unfair for them to be loaded with the stigma of having delivered an illegitimate child; it was worse to force them to undergo the danger and physical and psychological pain of an unwanted birth. Had her father thought this way? Had he decided to redress the balance in the only possible manner?

'Elly?' Lucy sat back, her gaze boring into Elly, demanding an answer.

'I … can't. I can't destroy a life, even one scarcely formed.'

'Please. Oh, please.'

Elly shook her head. Immediately Lucy sprang up and ran to the door. 'You don't love me. Your friendship has been a mere sham. Well, I don't want it, either. You can go to the devil, Elly Ballard. I'll take care of myself.'

'Come back, Lucy!' Elly followed her down the corridor to the stairs, tripping then righting herself, gasping with the pain of a ricked ankle. The girl fled before her across the hall, out onto the step. For a moment she paused under the lantern, a slight figure poised mothlike, ready to fly. 'Wait, Lucy.' Gritting her teeth, Elly hobbled through the courtyard gate and stared up and down the street. But Lucy had disappeared into the night.

The search began as soon as Elly could raise the cry, but although Paul and JG and their friends combed the most likely areas of the city, Lucy remained lost. A call at Cornwallis's house revealed that he had left to visit his Camden property hours before Lucy's arrival at the hospital; still, it took a lot of persuasion to keep Paul from following to confront Cornwallis. Only the need to find Lucy kept him with the searchers, and even they had to give in eventually and rest. Elly stayed on in her office, ostensibly to work, but in reality struggling with her conscience. Should she have violated her principles by helping Lucy to rid herself of the foetus? Where did the rights of an unformed child begin and rights of the mother end? If her own morally strict father had seen fit to help other women in similar situations, why couldn't she? Lucy had no-one except Elly to turn to with this dilemma. She felt she had failed the girl.

She would be eternally thankful that Paul had gone home to snatch some sleep before the message came, delivered by a bare-foot urchin in a gabble so fast she had to make him repeat it.

'Grannam says fetch Matron quick's I can, the lass's near gorn as wants 'er.'

'What lass? Lucy?'

'Dunno. Grannam says to come along of me. You comin'?'

In answer, Elly flung on her cloak, grasped her purse, then spun the boy out the door ahead of her. 'Call up a cab,' she directed.

The boy stopped short. 'Won't get no cabby to come down Durand's Alley at night.'

Elly shuddered. 'We'll go as close as he will then walk the rest of the way.'

What had happened? It had to be Lucy. Was the woman exaggerating who said the girl was 'near gorn'. When she questioned the boy she got only a blank stare. A minute later he offered the comment that there had been 'a lota blood when we picked 'er up. Like a pig killin', and she asked no more questions.

The cab pulled up in Goulburn Street, the driver having refused to turn into the notorious quarter where the boy lived; Elly paid the fare then set off after the small figure scampering ahead. The noisome lanes were unlit, save from an occasional shaft of lamplight from a tavern doorway. Elly's feet sank ankle deep in mud and refuse so foul she couldn't define the combination of smells. Backyard privies exuded their contents through fences to pool with garbage heaving under the sly onslaught of rats, while the night was hideous with drunken shouting and singing, even screams. A pair of yellow eyes sped out of the dark straight at her, but the boy flew at the creature, kicking and yelling, and the goat bounded away.

Elly tried to still her thundering heartbeat then shuffled on, careful to take small steps in case she tripped and fell into something unnameably dreadful. The lanes grew even more narrow, until her shoulders brushed against the shanty walls crowding in on her. The boy clutched her hand, saying cheerfully, 'S'black as a blind man's holiday, ain't it?' Still he led her unerringly through almost pitch darkness until they rounded a corner and saw a door standing crazily ajar, the glow of candlelight within.

Elly hardly noticed the poverty of the room. She made straight for the bundle of straw in the corner where a figure lay with blood-encrusted skirts drawn up, a wad of rags thrust up between her legs. A bedraggled old woman rose from kneeling beside her.

'You the matron?' Her voice was as rough as her appearance, but her eyes, flicking over Elly, were large and soft, sunk in a mass of wrinkles.

Elly nodded, dropping down beside Lucy to feel her pulse. That, with her pallor and shallow breathing, told the sorry tale. 'She's lost the baby. Has the bleeding ceased?' She gingerly moved the rags, unable to suppress her gasp.

The woman said grimly. 'Been butchered, ain't she?'

Elly's fury almost choked her. 'Who did this? Was it you?' She spun around, the blood rushing to her face.

The woman answered mildly: 'No, 'Tweren't me. Think I'd be fool enough to send for you if I'd a done it? Found 'er in the alley, we did, me and young Barty here. She'd been flung out to die in the dirt. Just a young 'un she is. Still milk on 'er lips.'

'I'm sorry. Thank you for taking her in and sending for me.' Elly looked back helplessly at the unconscious girl. 'She's lost so much blood. I'll have to get her to the hospital somehow.'

Barty's grandmother touched her shoulder lightly. 'It's too late, lass. I sent for ye because she called yer name, but I knowed it were no use.'

Lucy's eyelids fluttered and Elly leaned forward.

'Lucy, dear. Can you hear me? It's Elly.'

The faintest smile seemed to twitch the corners of the pale mouth. Elly bent lower to detect faint breathing. She touched one of the cold hands, lying flaccid like the hands of a doll, then took off her cloak to lay it over the girl.

'Elly.' She caught the faint whisper and leaned close again. Lucy's glazed stare seemed to go far beyond the crumbling walls of the room. 'I never meant to die, Elly. It's all gone wrong.'

'Hush, dear. I won't let you die. Save your strength.'

The faint voice persisted: 'He said I'd be all right, but he lied to me. Then he tied me down. He hurt me, so much. I screamed ... begged him to stop ... '

Elly bit her lip hard and tasted blood. She couldn't listen to this.

'Hold me, Elly. I don't want to go into the darkness alone ... '

Elly slid her arm under the girl's shoulders, gathering her against her bosom. With a sigh Lucy tucked her head under Elly's chin. 'So much blood,' she whispered. The breath rattled in her throat.

'Lucy?' Elly tipped the dark head back, watched as the girl's facial muscles smoothed out, leaving her little nose more prominent, slackening her jaw. With gentle fingers she closed the staring blue eyes. Lucy had gone on her long journey alone.

Elly stayed on her knees for a long time, cradling the slight body. Then, sighing, she laid it down on the straw and said to the watching woman: 'Who did it? Do you know, Mrs ... ?'

'Smith. Grannam Smith. I got a suspicion. The girls round here know where to go when they've taken a tumble too many, risky though 'tis.'

Elly got up slowly, feeling as though her energy had drained away into the dirt floor under her boots. 'Tell me where to go.'

Grannam Smith shook her grey head. 'Best not. This is no place for the likes of you. Let Barty here take yer back home to make arrangements for this poor lass. Yer can't do no good goin' for the butcher.'

'I can see him hanged.'

'No. You'll bring trouble on us. We don't want the law down in the Alley.'

Elly up-ended her purse on the one piece of furniture, a rickety shelf holding a heel of loaf and a few utensils. 'It's all yours if you will tell me where to find this person.'

The old eyes followed the coins rolling off the shelf onto the floor.

Barty made a dart and began stuffing them into his pockets. 'I know where he lives. I'll take yer. Then I'll bring yer back a pint, Grannam. That allus eases yer bones.'

The old woman raised her hands fatalistically then sat down on another pile of dirty straw, clasping her knees. 'Go on then. I'll watch over the lass until you send someun.'

Elly followed the boy out into the network of alleys, her face burning hot, her heart a lump of ice. She had never felt so clear-headed, so thoroughly scoured by emotion. What fool had said there was nothing so bad that it might not be worse? There could be nothing worse than this. All the feeble troubles she had totted up so recently were as a zephyr against this tornado of destruction, this terrible loss of a vital human being with her whole life before her. When Paul knew the truth he would never forgive himself, or Elly. *She* would never forgive herself. But she could force the murderer to abandon his trade.

Within a few minutes she was completely disoriented. The lanes had become a labyrinth, directionless, barely visible. Barty, towing her by the arm, seemed to proceed on a combination of touch and instinct. Shadows slithered by in the dark, some with two legs, some with four, but Elly took no notice. In a place where she'd have hesitated to come even by day, she let herself be led, feeling no fear, nor any other emotion. She was frozen. They eventually turned into a cul-de-sac, stopping before the vague outline of a tumble-down cottage, only a grade superior to the surrounding shanties.

Barty whispered: "E's in there. I can see a light be'ind the curting.'

'What's his name?'

'The Doc. That's what they call 'im. You goin' in there?'

In answer, Elly stepped forward and knocked on the door, the panel rough and splintery under her knuckles. When she glanced behind her, Barty had gone, blending with the shadows. No-one answered her knock, but when she found the door unlatched she stepped inside into a damp smelling darkness. A slit of light guided her ahead into a cramped room furnished haphazardly with a bro-ken-legged armchair, a table and bed, and a cabinet. An oil lamp flickered on the table, lighting a heap of bloody rags, with a few dirty instruments lying in a bowl of red-stained water. Bile rose in her throat, but she swallowed the bitterness. Her gaze swept the room, past the empty bed with its suspiciously stained coverlet, stopping on the figure slumped in the chair, legs outstretched, head sagging on one shoulder. A pipe with a long slender stem had fallen from the man's dangling fingers to smoulder on the mat, a rising smoke spiral filling the room with its sickly sweet odour. Opium. She stepped forward to peer into the slack face. With mouth open and eyes turned up, Doctor Harwood slept.

Elly's trembling legs gave way and she found herself on the mat at his feet. Her whole frame shook. She dug her fingers into her thighs, keeping them there until the tremors stopped. The thought uppermost in her mind was surprise that she was not surprised, that this might have been expected of a charlatan who had brought death to so many. Having left the Settlement when it became too hot for him, he would have continued to practise his spurious medicine in other towns, until finally forced to flee for sanctuary in the heart of a thieves' kitchen. Here he lived amongst his own kind who would never give him away; and here, by all appearance, he would very shortly die. The man's bones rattled with each breath; his skin had dried to parchment. He looked a hundred years old. Only thin slits of white showed beneath his eyelids, while his lips, wizened as sun-dried peel, curled back from a mouth full of blackened teeth. Dreaming in another world, he was letting his life slip away from this one.

Retribution had come to Doctor Harwood, more swiftly and more thoroughly than anyone could have imagined. The bitter wish that he might have killed himself earlier, before doing the same for Lucy, was pointless, Elly knew that. What was done was done. But in her heart she despaired. Had there been any point in her long struggle? She'd been frustrated at every turn. With so many against her, with her friends leaving, Cornwallis lurking in wait, Paul content with friendship while her own yearning for his love all but consumed her, and now Lucy destroyed when she might have been saved if Elly herself had only been more flexible. What was left? She had given her health, her energy of mind and body, and her heart, and they'd been thrown back at her.

Barty returned for her, a reluctant escort sent by his Grannam, and Elly turned her back on the cottage whose occupant dreamt away the last days of his life. Paul had resumed his search for his cousin, so Elly arranged for Lucy's body to be brought to the hospital, to her own room. There she cleaned and arrayed her decently, then spent the rest of the night in vigil by her side.

When Paul arrived, white with fatigue, his broad shoulders bowed in defeat, she told him all she knew. He seemed scarcely to heed her sorrowful accounts, so she slipped away, leaving him to mourn privately.

In the morning Jo-Beth brought her a document signed by the acting chairman of the board of directors. Elly carried it to the window and read it carefully because the letters seemed to jump about, giving her some trouble.

Jo-Beth watched her. 'What does it say? Is it bad news?'

Refolding the paper, Elly stared at her blankly. 'I don't know. I really don't know. They write of falling standards, of too many shortfalls, of patients' complaints.'

'What? When the Board's caused all the trouble themselves? What complaints? I've not heard of any.'

'It doesn't matter. The evidence will be there if they need to manufacture it themselves.'

'Evidence?'

'Tomorrow there's to be a special meeting of the Board. I'm invited to attend and show cause why they should not dismiss me as Matron.'

Jo-Beth's horror seemed to strike her dumb, but Elly only said wearily: 'Perhaps it's for the best. I'm not at all sure whether I want to go on.'

'You don't mean it!'

'I've lost my sense of purpose, Jo-Beth. You know, Paul once warned me not to underestimate the Board's power. I thought I could win them over to my views, but they're unwilling to change. They never liked a woman standing up to them; now Cornwallis has thrown his weight against me, there's no hope of my being heeded. No-one in the community seems interested in the hospital. Even JG with his stinging diatribes will soon be gone. I'm sorry to sound so defeatist; still, we must face the facts honestly.' She let the letter fall and clutched her arms about her body, trying to warm herself.

Jo-Beth made her sit down, then crouched beside the chair, saying earnestly: 'This is partly because you feel guilty over Lucy, isn't it? But you know her death wasn't your fault. You're letting your judgement become distorted. For that matter, I'm equally at fault for leaving her to that wolf. So is Paul. But whipping ourselves won't bring her back, and giving up on your life's work would be a useless sacrifice. You've always been a fighter, Elly. You will overcome this terrible melancholy, believe me. It's not in your nature to give up.'

'It's in everyone's nature if the load becomes too heavy to carry. I'm lonely, you see. I don't have the strength to keep going without someone at my side, a companion sharing the difficulties, supporting me when I waver, picking me up when I fall. It's a sad admission from a crusader, but it's the truth.'

PART THREE

Chapter Thirty-one

It rained on the day of Lucy Whatmough's funeral. A bitter wind whipped the skirts and coats of the mourners huddled around the grave under a canopy of black umbrellas. Gazing around the gallery of faces, Elly realised that Lucy's gay, light-hearted personality had touched more people than she'd realised. It made it all the harder to bear the thought that Lucy had gone, extinguished as easily as a candle flame.

The minister's words of hope of salvation were whipped away like a flock of starlings in the wind. Elly, glancing across the gaping hole at her feet and seeing Paul's care-lined face, quickly returned her gaze to the pathetically small coffin being lowered into the grave. The world wavered in front of her, the faces, the umbrellas, the dripping trees. Anger, frustration and grief combined like a great wave rolling over her, and she knew she'd finally given in. She had made her decision. She would leave Sydney for some place far out in the countryside where she could find peace, away from all the pain and angst of the past two years. Someone else could do the fighting. She'd run out of weapons and the will to wield them.

The minister finished, the wet earth thudded on the coffin. Elly waited until people began to move off, whispering her last goodbye before she returned to the others waiting at the carriages. Only the chief mourners were to go from the burial ground to Paul's rooms in Balmain, yet Elly couldn't face even such a small gathering. She wanted to keep her decision to herself a little longer. Nor did she want to face Paul just yet. He had been too shocked to notice how much she grieved for him. Having done her best to reach through the protective wall he had erected, as always, around his feelings, she had finally left him to JG, convinced by Paul's attitude that he did not need her.

Huddled in the corner of the carriage with muddied skirts clinging to her icy ankles, she longed only to be back in her own room, with a hot cup of tea and time to herself. Instead, she heard Paul's voice as he opened the carriage door, politely requesting Jo-Beth and Pearl to allow him to accompany Elly privately on the drive back.

She said quickly: 'I'm not coming, Paul. Please excuse me. I'm needed back at the hospital. There's so much to do before I leave.'

His haggard face was impassive, but he said quietly: 'We need to talk, Elly. There's been no chance since ... Ladies, do you mind? JG and Captain Petherbridge will escort you in the carriage behind.'

Jo-Beth and Pearl exchanged glances then rose, allowing Paul to help them down. Abandoning me, Elly thought drearily, turning her face to the streaming window. She felt Paul's weight on the seat as he closed the door against the weather and took off his wet hat.

'Elly,' he began.

She kept her face averted. 'What is there to talk about? You can't possibly blame me more than I blame myself. I know I'm not the only one who let Lucy down. We all did. Yet I can't forget that this could all have been avoided had we only taken more care.'

'I don't want to talk about blame, although the Lord knows I've enough on my shoulders to sink a battleship. However, I do want to talk about you. You've got to stop this, Elly. You're letting go.'

'I don't know what you mean.'

'Look at me, my dear.'

She faced him angrily. 'Don't lecture me. I don't need that from you. I don't need anything from anyone. Just let me be in peace.'

'Peace! Since when did the word have any meaning for you, Elly Ballard? Was it peace you wanted when you faced the people who turned you out into the bush to die? Was it peace that forced your way into the hospital and led you to take on the board of directors? Was it peace that changed a filthy, vermin-ridden hole into a place of safety for the sick? You can have peace when you're fast in your rocking chair; in the meantime you'll remember you're a fighter, my girl, which means no quarter.'

She flushed. 'You can't bully me, Paul. There's no fight left in me. I've got to admit defeat when I'm dismissed; and Lucy's death is the last blow. I'm too dispirited to go on.'

'Oh, no you're not.' He took her by the shoulders and gave her a little shake. The carriage lurched forward as the horses were whipped up, and she fell against him, her cheek landing on his wet lapel. He held her there, with the smell of damp wool in her nostrils, his chin edging her bonnet aside. His voice was warm near her ear. 'You're not alone, my dear. We're all in this battle with you. It may surprise you to hear that our wake for poor little Lucy will be more a meeting of her avengers.'

Tremendously comforted by her awkward position, hard up against Paul, her body twisted sideways, half stifled in his coat, Elly paid little heed.

'You're not listening.' He held her away from him. 'Look, we won't let you lose everything you've worked for, nor will we have Lucy's death go unavenged. But you must help us. We can't do it without you.'

She blinked and gave him her attention. 'I don't understand. What could we do against the power of the Board? How can you possibly reach Cornwallis to pull him down?'

'That's what we'll discuss this afternoon over sherry and biscuits. What should have been a sad, decorous farewell to my little cousin will be a council of war.' His voice hardened, his grip on Elly's shoulders tightening until she gasped. 'You remember me telling you about my father's death? You might even have guessed Cornwallis was responsible.'

'I did wonder. I'm so sorry, Paul. The scales are heavily weighted against that evil man.' His sombre expression saddened her.

'So, will you help, Elly?'

'Of course I will.' Already her crushed spirits had begun to lift with the prospect of action. Even better, Paul had not said one word of reproach to her over Lucy. 'You must think me spineless, Paul. I was hit so many times I felt flattened. It's just taken me a while to get my breath back.'

Paul let her go and watched her straighten her bonnet. 'Elly, you are about as spineless as Pepper, who killed his sixth snake last week.'

'Ah, well, I don't presume to be in Pepper's class.' She met his smile, and for a brief moment forgot the sadness lying over them all.

They were greeted by a blazing fire in Paul's rooms, with JG dispensing sherry in fine Irish crystal glasses, Paul's wedding gift to Pearl. JG gave Elly a glass, the liquid a glowing honey-gold nectar which warmed her after the first sip. She knew Jo-Beth had provided the sweet biscuits to go with the wine and had seen Ethan Petherbridge clutching a bunch of winter iris which now adorned the mantel shelf. I provided nothing, she thought, except a self-centred whine about my own misery. It's time I took a grip on myself.

Paul raised his glass to the company. 'I'd like to toast the memory of Lucy, who will never be forgotten by us.'

'A blithesome lass, a minx, yet an engaging one,' added JG.

'A woman,' Pearl corrected him, 'whose flowering was cut off too soon. May her spirit wander in pleasant paths.'

They drank the toast solemnly.

JG refilled the glasses, then addressed the room. 'We all know whom to blame for this tragedy. The curse of the crows on you, Cornwallis. May you be a load for four before the year's out!'

'I'll drink to that.' Ethan Petherbridge downed his sherry with a scowl. 'I've seen some cruel sights in my travels, but nothing has moved me as much as this sad series of events.'

Jo-Beth sent him a glance of pride and approval. Elly knew she was grateful for his easy acceptance into their close circle. They had watched Alan McAndrew's unhappy withdrawal with sympathy, and seen him off to London with relief. His obvious misery had been a reproach to them all, and Elly knew Jo-Beth had suffered for him.

Elly put down her glass and said: 'Well, what are you going to do about it? That's why we're here, isn't it, to plan how to bring down Cornwallis? Well, JG?'

His lips twisted. 'We've already begun. Paul and I have agreed the only sure method is to attack the black hound's reputation, to expose him before his peers. He'd rather kill himself than lose his position in society.'

Paul joined in. 'He's the son of a British peer, feted and admired, too clever by half in business, monied, spoilt, toadied. He's begun to believe he's invincible. So we'll prove him wrong.'

'How have you begun?' Elly asked.

'We've inserted a death notice in all the Sydney journals, a large, eye-catching black-bordered affair, which hints at some mystery attached to Lucy's demise.'

'And you believe this will worry Cornwallis?' Elly asked.

'Oh, I think so,' replied Paul. 'He meant to punish me by ruining my cousin. He didn't mean to kill her. The Honourable D'Arcy will be carrying pistols and starting at shadows, wondering whether I've come for him.' His voice was iron. 'But I've realised he's not worth hanging for. My revenge will be more painful than a quick death.'

'You've waited a long time, haven't you?' It saddened Elly to think how long.

Ethan looked interested. 'Why? What else lies between you and Cornwallis, Gascoigne?'

To Elly's surprise Paul gave him a full answer. 'He has assaulted Elly—though thankfully she was unharmed—and caused me to be beaten by thugs who might have killed me. He had my father tortured to death. Then there's Lucy. I'd say there's quite a debt between us, wouldn't you?'

'I wonder what the Master Lao-tsu would say about such a debt.' Pearl was thoughtful.

Everyone except JG seemed bewildered. He patted his wife's hand. 'My love, he would say regrets are vain, they stifle the present, and the balanced soul would not harbour revenge. But we're out to stop evil. Cornwallis has left a trail of damaged lives, of actual deaths and, worse, minds which will never heal. Like a vampire, he feeds off the fear and misery of others.'

'Surely you exaggerate, JG.'

Seeing his wife's anxious expression, he added: 'Paul knows I don't. He's heard the tales circulating in the taverns, the faint odour which persists around Cornwallis yet is never openly discussed.'

Both Pearl and Jo-Beth raised doubtful eyebrows. Elly could read their thoughts—exaggeration, gossip, the desire to be up on the latest salacious tale to circulate amongst the boys.

'They're right,' she said, and told them about the hanging in the Darlinghurst gaol. 'I know anyone who wishes may be a witness to an execution, horrible thought though it is. But deliberately to savour the victim's terror, to want to pull the knot tight in person, is simply abhorrent.'

'My God, he's a monster,' Jo-Beth exclaimed. 'Let's get on with this plan, whatever it is.'

JG continued to expound. 'We've begun a campaign to undermine confidence in him, just hints in the marketplace, conversations meant to be overheard in the clubs, and so on. We're also conducting a thorough search into his background, to dig up anything at all reprehensible which we can publish.

'Henry Parkes has agreed,' added Paul. 'He's with us in this, particularly as there's a political angle. Cornwallis hopes to be appointed to the Legislative Council at the next elections. There's another thing. Cornwallis is a powerful member of the hospital board of directors and directly responsible for the action against Elly. If we discredit him, it will go some way towards upholding Elly's credibility.'

Elly smiled wanly. 'Thank you, Paul. But it won't be sufficient to have me reinstated.'

'You'll do that yourself, Elly. You haven't examined this clearly. As a private citizen, no longer the matron, you will be able to go to the public, approach influential members, send letters to women active in charities seeking their support in your fight to improve the hospital. They have influence by virtue of their husbands' positions and wealth. Then you can mount your soapbox in the Domain to make public speeches.'

She said faintly, 'What?'

'I like it,' Jo-Beth nodded. 'Now you're no longer bound by

loyalty to your employers you can say what you like, expose what you like. I'll help you write the letters and speeches.'

Elly felt the walls closing in on her. 'I couldn't do it.'

'Of course you can. We'll all support you.'

Before Elly could comment, Pearl added that she and JG would postpone their departure. 'We couldn't think of deserting you at such a time. As well, there are all the women you have helped since you came to the hospital. They will rally around you, I'm certain.'

Elly had to blink hard and swallow before she could find the words to thank them. 'I want to drink a toast to all my friends here, my good and faithful friends who mean more to me than I can say. To you all.' She gathered them in with her gaze, enjoying their gratification and draining her glass.

The campaign gathered momentum from that day. Much to JG's satisfaction, all sorts of information detrimental to Cornwallis began arriving on his desk, or was whispered in his ear in the street or over a glass in the taverns. Paul started to compile a list of men either bribed or coerced into supporting Cornwallis politically and commercially, and another list of those who had refused and been financially punished, even ruined, as a consequence.

Uglier rumours surfaced about street-women who refused to associate with the man, whatever the price offered; then there were the men with beautiful wives, men whose faces shut against his name. Ethan pulled his weight in the merchant houses where he was establishing his business interests and, disguised as a common seaman, in the lower taverns frequented by bully boys, questioning, eavesdropping, discovering the contacts used by Cornwallis to do his dirty work. The conspirators kept on digging, querying business associates, bribing clerks and accountants concerned with Cornwallis's many interests. Their activities could not be kept secret for long, so they knew their quarry would be aware and, it was hoped, afraid.

Then the articles began to appear in the *Empire*.

Investigations into contracts let for extensions to the new Sydney Gas Works have revealed corruption at a high level, involving bribery of council officials who will be obliged to explain the suppression of tenders and the giving of false information. It is expected that persons named in connection with the bribes, including some of our more prominent men of business, will shortly be required to appear before an investigatory committee.

There was a distinct flavour of 'watch this journal for developments', plus an inference that names would be named shortly. The next week Cornwallis headed the published list.

Another paragraph, ten days later, adopted a high moral tone over prostitution, then suddenly switched viewpoint to deplore the brutality frequently suffered by 'ladies of the night' at the hands of their visitors, and the pernicious double standard which allowed their abusers to pose as upright citizens. An interview with a retired police officer revealed the existence of an establishment consisting entirely of girls under the age of twelve, catering only to the most select clientele. When pressed, the man had revealed the owners' names, and the *Empire* promised to seek confirmation while hinting darkly that one at least was the son of a British peer.

From then on Cornwallis's name was constantly presented before readers of the *Empire* in all possible contexts, some innocuous, others less so.

These items were sandwiched between reports of the carnage in the Crimea, and the gradual perception by the public that the English governing classes were the cause of the disaster. 'Do we want the same system of government here which distributes both public and military office according to the accident of birth?' thundered the *Empire*, and even the *Sydney Herald*, traditional supporter of the landed gentry, agreed. The *Melbourne Age* trumpeted a cry for independence: 'Don't you think the time has come when we should prepare to take the business entirely into our own hands?'; while JD Lang called for independence, by force of arms if necessary.

The increasingly powerful middle class in Australia had become vocal, demanding a system of government that promoted talent rather than privilege. Paul didn't hide his delight, even while diverting most of his energies away from the cause to concentrate on the Cornwallis campaign. Twice he had been set upon, and now he went nowhere unaccompanied and avoided secluded places. He had received anonymous threats in the mail and had scurril-

Hold High the Flame

ous words painted on the wall of the house where he lodged. Fortunately his landlord, recently returned from London, took as much interest in politics as the next man. Assuming this to be a politically motivated attack, he simply had the wall repainted.

JG carried out his own similar precautions, which included an invitation to Elly and Jo-Beth to move into the house he had hired for Pearl in Woollhara, with its high fence and a sturdy gardener living on the premises vetting visitors at the gate. For Elly's supportive friends had also been dismissed from the hospital and were now unemployed.

'I'll employ you,' Elly said, when the news had been indignantly passed on by Jo-Beth. 'We'll begin with the letters to charitably minded women. I've brought with me from the files a list of those who support the hospital, the Benevolent Society, the orphan school, and such. Of course, the ones with husbands on the hospital board will probably not feel disposed to listen, but there'll be others with a more open mind, I trust.'

Jo-Beth's society background fitted her to compose the letters, so she set to immediately, co-opting Pearl while Elly sent carefully designed notes to a number of former patients. She chose only those who were not too ground down by poverty and child-bearing to have the time or interest to help better their health system. It wasn't necessary for Paul to point out the power of the rising middle class, the merchants and traders prosperous enough to give their wives the freedom to espouse causes. Elly had seen for herself the influence wielded by women like Mrs Burton, the gaol governor's wife, who could sway not just her husband, but other wives in her own circle. If these women could be enlisted in her cause, she would have a strong base from which to work.

From the number of replies, Elly realised she would have to organise a meeting.

'Somewhere warm,' Pearl advised. 'It is midwinter.'

Elly began to laugh. 'I know just the place—the Royal Hotel. They're used to rowdy political events so won't cavil if we ladies get a little out of hand.'

With the appointment of a new matron at the Sydney Infirmary, JG immediately pointed out how well Elly had performed in the position and how many improvements she had introduced.

Chapter Thirty-one

His article alluded to the incompetence of certain members of the Board, claiming fallen standards since Elly's departure. A fuming counter attack in the *Sydney Herald* only added to the publicity, giving JG further chance to sing Elly's praises and ask point blank whether the Board would care to list its reasons for her dismissal.

The following week the *Empire* revealed to its readers a story of graft and corruption which sold out the edition almost before it hit the street. Elly read the item aloud to her friends at breakfast, congratulating JG on having excelled himself. He ducked his head in false modesty, replying, 'I believe it to be one of my choicest works.'

'You're stirring up danger here, JG.' Pearl rested her hands on her husband's narrow shoulders.

Elly suddenly noted the grey streaks at JG's temples, and realised that his experience at the goldfields had damaged his health, perhaps permanently. She believed Pearl knew it, yet was wise enough not to interfere in his headlong crusade. If it were not Cornwallis, it would be another.

JG smiled mischievously at his wife. 'That's the idea, to stir that snake Cornwallis on all sides. We'll have him so confused he won't know where to strike first, although I know where the first major blow against him will be dealt.'

'Where?' the three women chorused.

JG practically hugged himself. 'Since this stir up of interest, he and his banker friends have been under investigation, with particular regard to the handling of charity funds. The board of directors of the hospital has scented scandal. They've convened a special meeting to discuss its composition and the necessary probity of its members. How do you imagine Cornwallis will enjoy that, eh?'

Chapter Thirty-two

Jo-Beth had thoroughly enjoyed Elly's inaugural speech on public health. Her pleas for the more fortunate women in her audience to appreciate the plight of their sisters forced into unendurable situations in dirt-floored slum hovels, below street level, subject to every rush of rainwater bringing in filth, their malnourished children at the mercy of vermin and disease, had brought tears to many eyes, including Jo-Beth's own.

'Did you see those women, at least a hundred, all hanging on Elly's words, and not an objection from any of them?' Jo-Beth asked Ethan breathlessly. 'As a campaign opener it could hardly have been bettered.'

'It was the first shot in the campaign. But you should be wary. Having taken the opposition by surprise, you may not be so fortunate next time.'

'What opposition? We're not attacking anyone.'

'Oh you are, dearest. You're criticising the establishment, the men who have, in your own words, "failed to care for the unfortunate, the sick and the elderly in our community". Nor have you yet clashed with the rowdy element, the cabbage tree boys and street bullies who will delight in breaking up your meetings out of sheer devilry.'

'Paul and JG have organised a band of men to keep obvious troublemakers away from future events. If any do slip through, they'll be swiftly ejected, I assure you.' Seeing him still concerned, she slipped her arm through his, adding: 'Now, you're not to worry, Ethan. With you at my side there can be no danger.' She swept him over to the others, grouped around Pearl's fireplace, deep in discussion.

Pearl was saying: 'I particularly liked Elly's plea for us to use our feminine minds to create the kind of world in which we want to live, not to leave it always to the men. The more affluent women in society have power; they're a huge, virtually untapped resource.'

Paul, standing listening with his back to the fire, took no part in the discussion. He'd done his best this evening, Jo-Beth knew, coming forward without warning to speak on Elly's behalf. He had begun by gracefully apologising for having taken so long to realise that equality of opportunity should include the female sex. He then went on to praise Elly, telling of her tenacity and fortitude in her fight to improve conditions at the hospital. Elly had been furiously embarrassed, and still refused to talk to him.

Joining her on the sofa, Jo-Beth said softly: 'Don't be cross with Paul. The way he attacked that cabal of hospital governors for dismissing you was inspired. It's just the sort of support you need.'

'This evening wasn't about me. My personal difficulties shouldn't be dragged into public view—'

'Nonsense. The behaviour of the Board is everyone's business, as well as valuable ammunition in our fight. You're not usually so thin-skinned, Elly. I think you owe Paul an apology for raking him down when he only tried to help you.' She had a shrewd idea that Elly's overreaction went a lot deeper than mere pique.

Elly flushed. 'Perhaps. Let's leave the subject, shall we?'

Some weeks later, Paul convened a meeting at his place with the promise of important news. JG met Ethan and Jo-Beth at the gate and they hurried inside to be met by Paul at the head of the stairs and ushered into his fire-warmed room. Spring had come, yet nights and early mornings remained chilly, so Jo-Beth happily adopted a seat near the hearth to warm her toes. Elly sat opposite, her expression strained, while Pearl, who had come with her, greeted her husband.

Sensing an atmosphere, Jo-Beth asked, 'Has something happened?'

'Ask Paul.' Elly's hands twisted in her lap. Jo-Beth looked up expectantly at Paul.

'We've stirred up Cornwallis with a vengeance,' Paul said. 'Although a brick through my bedroom window last night is an uncommonly weak response when we consider his earlier attacks.'

JG said gleefully: 'That's probably just the entrée. There'll be more to come now Cornwallis has been dropped from the hospital board. I heard, too, that the Australian Club has asked him to resign his membership. The whispers are all over town, and people withdraw their skirts from the path of the pariah. Why the faces of gloom? We've achieved our aim. The man's socially doomed in this country. We'll hear next that he's taken passage for England. Good riddance.'

Paul shook his head. 'There's more to it, I'm afraid. The message wrapped around the brick was specific and scurrilous in its threats to Elly and me. It's too vile for me to read it aloud. You can see it later, JG.'

'Well, it's to be expected, I suppose.' JG frowned. 'What haven't you told us?'

'This.' Paul flourished a paper. 'The information came to me privately and I've written the column myself for tomorrow's *Empire*. I'll read it aloud.'

Elly went white, and Jo-Beth moved her chair up beside her as Paul began to read:

' "Residents of our great Colony will be appalled to learn of the scandal surrounding one of its foremost citizens, a man whose advantages of birth and wealth have been grossly misused in the torture and degradation of his fellow creatures. It has been revealed that the owner of a model property in Camden, the Hon. D— C—, a man renowned for his intelligent and modern attitude towards farming and husbandry, whose horse-breeding facilities are second to none, whose animals enjoy a princely existence, is no more than a callous monster in his dealings with his own kind ... " '

Elly allowed her thoughts to drift, unwilling to listen once again to the tale of cruelty and violence which had so shocked her when she had first heard it. The evidence had been supplied by Cornwallis's overseer in a long-overdue rebellion against his master's brutality, which this time had been applied to a member of the overseer's own family. It had been stupid of Cornwallis to antagonise his companion in crime; or had he finally over-stepped the line of rationality? He had to be mad to have organised such orgies of torture involving the convicts assigned to him. Their sufferings didn't bear contemplation. Aware of sudden silence, Elly looked up at the appalled faces of the two women.

Pearl asked, 'Is it true?'

When Paul nodded, Jo-Beth said in some awe: 'This is dreadful. But how do you dare expose him? He'll be murderous.'

'No doubt. But it finishes him.'

His gaze was remote. He is remembering his father, Elly thought. Well, he has his revenge. How does he like it? JG was right to liken Cornwallis to a reptile, the worst kind, as vicious as a tiger snake. They had stirred him to a wild rage and now, with his own life in ruins, anything could happen.

Elly's decision to speak publicly in the Domain had not been made lightly. She knew she would be exposing herself as no lady should, risking being dubbed a loose woman seeking personal publicity at the expense of her reputation. But she also knew it was the way to reach people of all classes and backgrounds. If she could capture the interest of the factory girls, clerks, housemaids and labourers, as well as the masters and mistresses; if she could carry her message into the humblest homes and the grandest mansions, she would have a chance of bringing about change. Paul had been right. It had to come through the process of law, pushed for by the great majority. So she must risk anything to gain their support.

On a bright July day, with the flags on Government House snapping away from the poles and just an edge of frost to the air, Elly climbed onto a specially erected platform in the Public Domain. The unusual sight of an obvious lady clutching her hat in the breeze while addressing passers-by soon drew a crowd; although before long a coarser element began to drown her out with their jeers. She persisted, knowing she was losing the battle, that people who might have listened had begun to drift away.

Paul, beside her, wanted to take her place, to drag the crowd in with his well-known face. They were always happy to listen to politics. But Elly would not let him. It was *her* cause.

Elly's voice had begun to crack under the strain of shouting above the interjections when in the distance she heard martial music. Then over the rise marched the red-coated bandsmen of the 11th Foot led by JG twirling his knob-topped cane, followed by a party of women stepping out with precision. Jo-Beth and Pearl, demure as ever, headed the procession of nurses and ex-patients spearing through the thickening crowd to stand before Elly's improvised rostrum.

The uniformed nurses, so smart and proud; the women with babies in their arms, dressed in the best they could find and all beaming at Elly, brought a lump to her throat. So many of them, all here to encourage and sustain her. The music rose to a final crescendo of blaring brass then ceased. JG stepped up and bowed to Elly, then turned to the rapidly growing audience. People descended from carriages to hasten across the grass, while others hesitated on the edge of the group, seeking a way in.

JG opened his lungs and bellowed, 'Citizens of Sydney, you are greatly privileged today to hear a speech by one of our foremost ladies, the former matron of the Sydney Infirmary, to whom so many of you owe gratitude, if not your lives. She has something to say which you will wish to hear. I know you will do her the courtesy of listening.'

A lad in a cabbage-tree hat yelled a rude comment, but others cuffed him to silence. JG bowed to Elly once more then stood back, and before her nerves overcame her, she plunged into her speech. Its content was on the same lines as the one given at the Royal Hotel, and she noted increased interest in the women in the audience. But at the end she had a special message for the men.

'You all know what terrible reports we have had of the war in the Crimea. The despatches sent to London by newspaper journalists have revealed the shocking state of the hospitals and lack of care for our soldiers, who die, not on the battlefields, but in the hospitals, and not so much of their wounds as of disease and neglect.'

An angry roar greeted these words. She waited until it had died down.

'I'd like to tell you that something is being done about it, by a woman called Florence Nightingale, who is dedicated to caring for the sick and wounded men, together with a band of nurses trained by her—all ordinary, decent women with compassionate hearts and a good deal of commonsense, just like the women I had begun to train in our own hospital here in Sydney. The old image of the nurse as illiterate, untrained, dirty and drunken is now out of date. Nurses are people to be respected and valued. These nurses here before me are a vanguard of the army of qualified women who will forge into the future with a profession to be proud of. And you, the people of this Colony, will be the ones who gain.

'Citizens of Sydney, we are at war with a far more dreadful enemy than the Russians. We are *always* at war with disease; there will always be accidents; people will still try to kill one another. Our hospitals should be places of refuge and healing, but this will only come about if you, the people of this city, take an interest in your own health. The responsibility can't be pushed off onto bureaucrats or well-meaning charities having little understanding of health needs. We must make our will known to our leaders, by using public pressure to create the health system we want. Already we've gained the approval of several highly placed officials, of journalists, of district doctors whose experience supports all I've said about our city's needs. Now you must do your part.'

From the moment Elly stepped down she was mobbed, and for days afterwards people continued to call at the Patterson house to discuss her ideas. She found she had struck a nerve, and the women in particular were in the mood to fight for change. Committees were organised to lobby members of the Legislative Council, to raise fighting funds, to petition the Colonial Secretary, Deas Thomson, due to return from London shortly, for an investigation into the activities of the hospital board, with special reference to the dismissal of Matron Ballard.

JG kept the impetus going in the *Empire*; Paul spoke about health at his rallies, Jo-Beth and Pearl helped Elly organise further meetings and answer letters and queries.

The movement began to swell, until Elly let herself hope there would be enough pressure generated for an explosion. It was not yet clear what form the explosion would take, or whether it would be sufficiently well directed to achieve the radical changes she wanted. But while she pondered this, a letter of a different kind arrived, which she'd have liked to burn and forget, but could not.

It was a plea for help, from the former Nurse Jenkins, who had apparently fallen upon hard times after her dismissal. Typically, she couldn't resist blaming Elly for her fall, even as she begged for her help. While feeling no responsibility for Jenkins turning to whoring, Elly couldn't reject a woman dying alone and a fatherless baby to be cared for.

Pearl offered to go in her stead, but Elly, already familiar with Durand's Alley, insisted the duty was hers.

'I'll be back before supper. Don't worry about me.' She packed a satchel with food and medicine before sending for a cab. 'If matters are as bad as Jenkins says, I'll most likely arrange her admission to the hospital. Can you and Jo-Beth manage alone?' She referred to the funding committee about to meet in their parlour.

Pearl rolled up her eyes, and Elly apologised with a smile, then hurried away. As before, the cabbie refused to enter the malodorous warren of Durand's Alley, so Elly set off on foot with her satchel on her back. Since it was still daylight she could see where to put her feet to avoid the worst of the refuse. When Barty shot past with a crowd of mischief-bent allies, she waved to him and asked after his Grannam. She found Jenkins's shanty lodging without much difficulty, and at her knock was admitted at once into a room so gloomy she could scarcely discern the bundle in the corner.

'Jenkins? Is that you?'

A baby whimpered. Elly felt her way forward, stumbled over some object in her path, and was seized from behind. A heavy cloth came down over her head as she struggled and cried out. Then something hit her. Blinding pain burst through her skull, then nothingness.

Chapter Thirty-three

T he darkness had an oddly thick quality, like wool brushing her face. Her head felt as if the wool had got in to wind itself around her brain, slowing it to a plod. Even her mouth tasted of flannel, with a furry coating on her tongue. I'm mildly concussed, she thought, aware of a singing in her ears and the dull ache that accompanied it. But where am I? And what hit me?

Events prior to her waking in darkness were still hazy, but she vaguely remembered young Barty's impish face, and a door opening into a dimly lit room. What happened afterwards was still a mystery. Her muscles ached, and she lay still while mentally probing the rest of her body, deciding that she rested on something hard and chilly, neither stone nor feather-down—perhaps a straw-stuffed mattress. It smelt dank, and she shifted her head, then cried out as a sword-blade of pain thrust through her skull, leaving her limp and nauseated.

Whimpering, she tried to raise her hands but was brought up short as metal jabbed her wrists. It couldn't be … But it was true. Her hands were cuffed together and attached to a length of chain. Horrified, she yanked at the chain, feeling the gyves bite deep into her skin, ignoring the hurt as she twisted and turned like a snared animal, the agony thundering in her head not enough to drown the sudden onset of terror.

She couldn't guess how long she struggled to free herself before lying back exhausted, tears sliding down her cheeks into her hair. She was trapped. There was no way the chain could be torn from the stone wall that grazed her fingers.

Time passed in periods of panic interspersed with moments of clarity when she fought to understand what had happened to her. She realised almost straightaway that Cornwallis was responsible, and hot waves of anger poured over her, only to recede, leaving her shivering with cold fear.

Perhaps she had already been missed. Pearl and Jo-Beth would be anxious if she hadn't returned by suppertime. Midnight might have come and gone, for all Elly knew. The men would mount an immediate search. But where? Cornwallis had gone into hiding after the *Empire*'s final indictment, and would use his wealth to cover his trail. She wouldn't be imprisoned in his city house or the farm at Camden. Both could be too easily searched. Yet Cornwallis might own any number of properties in any part of the Colony, not necessarily in his name. What if she had been unconscious for days and carried into the outback? No. Unlikely. People struggling for existence in the bush did not bother with stone cellars. Why did she think it was a cellar? Perhaps the smell, the faint aroma of spirits bringing back a memory of the hotel in the Settlement? That was it—a waft of spilt liquor underlying the thick, musty atmosphere. Which meant she had most likely been confined beneath an inn or a wealthy private home in a large town.

She was pleased at having arrived at a conclusion, even an unprovable one. She still had charge of her wits and had not been reduced to the status of paralysed prey. Yes, that was the way to stave off dread. Plan and plot to out-think the enemy; be ready for him when he came. That thought almost tipped the scale back into panic, but she hurriedly regained her balance. She must not meet him already demoralised by her own fears. He would be hoping for it. That was how he worked, letting his victims create their own frightening scenarios and suffer unnecessary torment. Well, she would not play the game. He would have to do his own bloodcurdling, and work hard at it to make her knees knock before him. With renewed courage, she sat up, swinging her legs over the side of the cot she lay on. But the short chain would not allow her to sit forward. She drew up her legs and curled back against the wall. When he came, he wouldn't find her prostrate and helpless ...

Suddenly a key turned in a lock and a glimmer of light appeared outlining a door opposite. Cornwallis entered, an oil lamp held high in one hand.

Elly waited until her eyes had adjusted to the light, then looked up to see him standing over her, smiling unpleasantly. She knew he was savouring her powerlessness. His smile became a sneer, an effort to degrade her as if she were an object of dubious value. Raising her chin, she glared back at him.

'Well, Miss Eleanor Ballard, who is now the victor?'

She allowed her own lip to curl. 'Do you call it victory to be forced to skulk like a rat in a hole? I'd call it ignominy.'

Her thrust had no noticeable affect. 'You sing loud, my dear, but you are still a caged bird.'

'The rat versus the bird. Do you plan to eat me for supper?' Elly was pleased with her steady voice.

'Something of the kind. I've not yet decided on your fate, but I assure you it will be as poetic and demeaning as I can contrive. That's simple justice, considering what you and your assistants have done to me.'

'We only had to point the finger. It was hardly difficult for us to smirch a life so tainted with cruelty and self-seeking.'

Cornwallis carefully set down the lamp then bent down to slap her cheeks, two hard cracks with an open palm, almost splitting her skin open. Tears jetted from her eyes. She tasted blood.

'Keep a hold on your bold tongue, mistress.' He straightened up. 'I'll leave you to summon a little humility while I break my fast. Are you hungry? I regret that I cannot invite you to sit at table with me.' He picked up the lamp.

Elly turned her burning face aside, waiting for him to leave. The light faded and she heard the door close heavily. What now, she wondered? Starvation? Or was he toying with her, intending to return with some new form of torment? Her impotence, which left her open to any kind of attack, would be a stimulant to a man of his type. If he came to her in the mood for rape would he be excited more by resistance or by feeble capitulation? What a useless exercise, in any case. She could never bring herself to submit tamely. She'd fight him whatever the cost.

Winter cold had entered the cellar, and hunger and thirst added to Elly's misery. By the time Cornwallis reappeared an hour later, Elly was racked by tremors, her jaw clamped tight, not to mislead her captor into thinking her weakened. But the man had changed tactics. In one hand he carried a wine flask, while over his arm lay a thick padded quilt which he wrapped tenderly about her. She took the proffered flask, clutching it with icy hands, and drank it all. Her head began to spin and she huddled into the comforting folds of quilt, hazily trying to fathom Cornwallis's motives.

Settling on the end of her cot, he smiled without a trace of a sneer. 'I am not the monster you think me, Eleanor.'

She eyed him warily.

'I want to talk with you. I'd like you to appreciate my motives. You are the most sympathetic of all the women I've known.'

She was incredulous. Why should she care what drove him to such depravities? But let him talk, if it was what he wanted. Talking did no harm.

In a voice growing more taut by the minute, Cornwallis began recounting his experiences as a young boy, caged in luxury deep in the British countryside while his parents travelled or enjoyed the London Season, forgetting his existence. He rambled on about loneliness and the perversions taught by servants, the beatings by a cruel tutor, the encouragement of a streak in his nature which could take pleasure in the torment of others.

'I grew to love pain, even my own,' Cornwallis said. 'Yet masochism, over indulged, ends in self-destruction, and I wanted to live life to the full, to extract the maximum enjoyment in payment for what had been withheld from me. I knew I had been deprived of something immeasurably important, although I could never name it, and the knowledge filled me with rage. I wanted to smash other people's pleasures, to ensure that they, too, were deprived. Then, in maturity I learned the exquisite joy of subtlety, of luring men and women into a pit of their own digging. I disciplined myself in order to experience greater heights of pleasure. I dealt in pain, but at a distance, watching it administered by another.' He paused, and Elly, sick at heart, struggled to hide her revulsion in case it enraged him.

Suddenly Cornwallis was on his knees beside the cot, his hands imprisoning hers, his expression wretched. 'Elly, tell me you understand, that you can still be a friend.'

'A friend! When you've made me your captive and tormented me!'

'Can you not see why I did it? You brought me down; thus you must be punished. My honour demands such payment. But you must understand and forgive me.'

'Did you ask forgiveness of all the men you had beaten to death?' She tried to withdraw but his grip tightened, forcing the iron into her wrists. She paled and ceased resisting. His expression frightened her. His customary smooth assurance had gone, replaced with a half-crazed, restless energy.

'You have to die. Don't you see?' He looked up, his head thrown back in appeal.

In the split second that he relaxed his grip on her, Elly whipped her chain up and around his neck, pulling on it with all her strength. Caught off balance, he fell against the cot, his fingers gouging furrows in his throat as he tore at the links and wrenched them away.

'Whore!' He tugged the chain sharply. The iron wristbands cut into her and she screamed, feeling the blood slippery on her skin.

Cornwallis wrested the quilt from her, bundling it under his arm as he picked up the lamp. 'You can do without comforts. Endure the cold in fear and darkness, before I end your suffering permanently.'

He's crossed into insanity, thought Elly, watching the light disappear as the door banged shut. I'm at his mercy. Oh God, what can I do to save myself?

For a while she slipped into despair, but gradually she roused. The cold was creeping in to stiffen her muscles, chill her flesh, slowly paralyse her will. She made herself lie down and exercise her legs, driving the blood around her body until she could feel her extremities once more. If she were to have any hope of escape, she must be able to move quickly, to respond to whatever tiny fraction of a chance Cornwallis might leave her. It was a forlorn hope.

Whatever death he envisaged for her would be staged as a performance for his particular enjoyment. Mad or not, he would plan meticulously to extract the most from it, as he had from the hanging in the gaol.

As time passed and Cornwallis did not come, Elly's courage began to fade, and she weakened in her determination to exclude from her mind all the things she cared about. Paul's image pushed forward, claiming her attention. Her dear Paul who might never learn what had become of her, and certainly wouldn't learn how much she loved him. Curled up against the cold stone, Elly realised there was nothing about him she did not love and dread to lose. Oh, Paul, Paul. Would she ever see him again? Sobbing, she laid her head on her drawn-up knees.

It seemed only minutes later that the door was flung back with a terrific bang and Cornwallis erupted into the cellar, the oil lamp jiggling wildly in his grasp as he flew at Elly. She cringed in the corner, her heart slamming in her chest.

'What is it? What's wrong?'

'Whore! Did you set them on? How did you do it? Tell me before I shake the life out of you.'

'Set on whom?' Elly grasped his free arm as it sought her throat, and hung on with all her strength. The lamp wavered before her face, oil slopping, the chimney smoking.

Cornwallis's face was greasy with sweat as he panted, 'The mob outside. They're threatening to fire the house. Don't you hear them?'

Still desperately holding him off, Elly became aware of a distant sound like heavy surf. A mob? How had they known where to find him?

'I swear to you, I didn't set them on. I don't even know where I am.'

'It had to be you. Bitch! I'll finish you before they come for me.'

Almost without thought, Elly brought up her knees and knocked the lamp flying. At the same time she jerked her chain forward, dragging Cornwallis across her. His face hit the stone wall along with the lamp, and flaming oil mixed with shards of glass jetted into his face. He fell back, screaming, tearing at his eyeballs, then began to stagger blindly about the cellar. Elly rolled frantically on the smouldering mattress, strewn with broken glass, and managed to extinguish the flames; but she couldn't extinguish Cornwallis's screeched imprecations. The darkness terrified her. It hid them from each other, but she knew he'd come for her.

She held the chain taut so it wouldn't chink and give away her position, trying to still her hammering heartbeat in her ears. Cornwallis was quieter now, although still spewing words of hate and vengeance in a voice thick with pain. He had only to feel his way around the walls to find her. There was no escape this time. She could sense his groping hands, the long fingers clawing, seeking to meet around her throat and snuff out her life.

The distant noise of the mob had become a roar, mingled with the sound of breaking glass and mysterious thuds. They must have broken in. But they wouldn't know where she was, beneath their feet. No-one would come to save her. Then she smelt smoke and knew that a worse death might be in store for her. They'd fired the house.

'Do you hear?' Cornwallis cried. 'They're trying to burn me out, but they'll fail. There's a warren of cellars under the house, and an exit from the far end. They haven't trapped me.'

He was terribly close. He'd spoken almost above her head. Cowering back she felt his breath on her cheek, heard the brush of his sleeve sweeping by only a fraction of an inch away. She held her breath and stayed rigid.

'Where are you? You can't hide from me. Speak, dammit!'

A mighty crash overhead shook the floorboards, making Elly flinch. Running footsteps followed, then the sound of doors flung back, a voice she knew calling her name. Fingers touched her chin and she let out a piercing shriek. 'Paul. I'm here. Quickly—'

Hands around her throat … crushing pressure … no air … light searing her eyes … pain, terrible red raw pain … Then, quite suddenly the pressure was released and air flowed into her straining lungs. She lay breathing in great gulps. Torchlight flickered on stone, and now she was aware of new sounds, animal grunts, the hiss of breath expelled by force, the thud of a body hitting the door.

Pulling herself up on her elbow she saw the two men grappling, hands clawing for eyes and throat. Cornwallis, who must still be half blinded by the oil, struggled to hold his adversary close, his arms tightening around Paul's chest in a rib-cracking hold. Elly saw the strain in both men's faces, felt the tension of muscles ready to burst through skin. Then Paul broke free, landing a terrific blow on Cornwallis's chin. The two staggered back against opposite walls, panting, gaining a few seconds' respite.

In the brief silence, Elly heard the fire raging above, the crack of exploding timbers and windows blowing out as Cornwallis's house of treasures melted into a funeral pyre. She could smell smoke, even thought she could see it sifting through the boards overhead, imagined it billowing down the cellar stairs and through the open door. How long before they suffocated, before the building fell in upon them?

Cornwallis made a sudden dart for the torch lying inside the door. 'You bastard!' he snarled, swishing it before him like a flail, holding Paul off. 'I'll best you yet.' He began edging around the wall to where Elly crouched on her cot. 'I'll set her hair alight, and you can watch her burn.'

'Not before I choke the life out of you.' Paul lunged, and the flaming torch arced down, narrowly missing his face, the heavy wooden stave connecting with his shoulder and throwing him off balance. His shout of pain coincided with Elly's horrified gasp.

Cornwallis sprang at Elly and she kicked out, hitting him in the chest, but before he could raise his arm, Paul was on him. The two men swayed, locked in a tight embrace. Cornwallis was mad with rage and lust to kill. Breaking free, he used his fists and knees, gouging, tearing at Paul's hair, even trying to sink his teeth into his flesh. Paul, just as powerfully built, fought with his mind as well as his body. She could see him accepting the blows without attempting a defence, all his concentration on cutting off his opponent's wind.

His long, strong hands ripped aside Cornwallis's collar, closed around the throat, and began to squeeze. Paul's shoulders hunched as he gathered all his energy, pouring it into the muscles of his hands, his fingers digging deep into the flesh. The torch fell from Cornwallis's grasp. His fists battered at Paul's head, then clawed for his face. But Paul now had him bent back over the end of the cot, locked in a position where he could bring all his strength to bear. Cornwallis, his face engorged, blood dripping from his nostrils, frenziedly tore at Paul's hands.

Elly could smell his terror. She covered her face. The cot shuddered as a weight lifted and she peeped between her fingers to see Cornwallis heave upwards with a mighty effort, bringing both men erect before toppling to the floor. A beam overhead creaked, floorboards sagged. Smoke and hot ash billowed into the cellar.

Elly screamed, 'Paul, the fire's breaking through!'

He staggered to his feet, swaying, the key to Elly's fetters in his torn fingers. Cornwallis lay still at his feet, his eyes turned up in his head.

'Is he dead?' Elly searched Paul's face as he undid the cuffs then hugged her to him, his face buried in her hair.

A moment later he released her, saying hoarsely: 'No, not dead yet. But we'll all die if we don't get out of here immediately. Can you walk, Elly?'

Cornwallis stirred. Paul swept Elly up in his arms and headed through the door into the adjoining cellar. Here a doorway high in the wall stood open, a gateway into a hell of flame. The steps leading up to it were alight and the floor above crackled. Even as Paul dashed through another opening opposite, burning boards fell behind him, sending sparks in all directions. They were in a narrow corridor with several openings on either side.

Elly felt Paul hesitate. Remembering Cornwallis's boast, she said urgently, 'There's a way out through the end cellar. Keep going.'

A curtain of smoke poured in to envelop them. Coughing, Elly hid her face in Paul's coat as he rushed up the corridor, with the sounds of destruction following close behind. When he stopped and set her on her feet, she saw their way was blocked by another door.

'Stand back, Elly.' Paul launched himself at the panels. The door shuddered, but stood firm. This time he smashed at the lock with his booted foot and wood splintered.

'Hurry, Paul.' Elly could hear another sound, mingled with the roar of flames, a voice that raised every hair on her body, the howling, inhuman voice of a creature treading in their footsteps, almost upon them.

Paul's boot smashed once more into the lock and the door sprang open, creating a suction and drawing smoke and burning debris upon them as they hurried into the next room. The furnishings and other comforts showed it had been Cornwallis's lair, but now it, too, was alight. In one corner, the ceiling had given away and a heavy marble-topped table had smashed its way through. Fire licked overhead and dropped onto the floor; everything that could catch alight had done so. They stood amid a forest of dancing flames.

'Where in God's name is the way out?' Paul scanned the walls feverishly. 'The house above is an inferno. It'll collapse any minute.'

'There! In the far corner. Quickly! He's right behind us.' Elly dashed through the flames, which licked at her skirts, beating at them with her bare hands, making for a narrow iron door tucked almost out of sight behind the remains of a burning book cabinet. Paul caught up the bedding and used it as protection for his hands, thrusting the cabinet aside to get at the door, slamming back the bolts, top and bottom, then flinging the door open. A blast of chill air hit them in the face just as Cornwallis plunged through the opening behind them, his eyes manic in a face so deformed with hate that Elly's heartbeat stumbled.

The three faced one another for a long moment. Then simultaneously, the ceiling gave an ominous crack and Paul kicked down the burning book cabinet straight in Cornwallis's path; then he threw Elly through the doorway and followed, catching her up as he ran.

A tortured howl rose, culminating in a shriek cut off by the thunder of tumbling brick and stone as the house collapsed behind them, burying the cellars beneath an avalanche of fiery debris. Flames shot triumphantly into the sky, dimming the stars, while the band of men surrounding the conflagration scattered in panic.

Elly burrowed into Paul's embrace and drew in great breaths of blessedly frosty, fresh night air, savouring her freedom, her rebirth into a world she thought she'd never see again. Then she said a prayer of gratitude and sent it out into the darkness.

Chapter Thirty-four

'There isn't much to explain.' Paul had been cornered by the women in the sitting room of the Woollhara house, watched by an amused JG and sympathetic Ethan.

A week had passed since Elly's rescue, and Sydney had rocked with the news of the Honourable D'Arcy Cornwallis's perfidy. The *Empire* sold out each day's edition an hour after it came on the street, its banner headlines heralding JG's exclusive reports on the secret life and eventual dramatic demise of one of the city's most esteemed citizens.

Cornwallis had perished in his own cellar beneath the ruins of his town house filled with treasures, and with him went the iniquitous records that held so many people in thrall to him. Only this close circle of friends knew the truth of that night, all agreeing it was best kept between them.

Elly had spent the past few days recovering from her ordeal, aggravated by concussion as well as prolonged exposure to the cold, and had been in no fit condition to receive the many curious and concerned callers who had knocked on Pearl's door, only to be politely turned away. Today, however, she'd been well enough to insist on a meeting with her friends to clear up all the details that had thus far been kept from her.

Paul held up his bandaged hands. 'All right, I'll explain. Just what did you want to know, Elly?'

'Firstly, how did you find me?'

Paul's gaze flickered to JG and Ethan. 'Cornwallis's town house was the first place we three searched, but it seemed deserted. The main cellar apparently had a false wall concealing others behind, so we found no trace of you there. It was … disturbing.'

She glanced at him sharply. What was wrong with Paul?

JG took up the tale. 'Young Barty from the Alley put us onto your trail. He'd seen you go into that wretched Jenkins's house, but when you didn't reappear, he sensed foul play. So he followed the cart taking you away, wrapped in a roll of carpet, to Cornwallis's back door, then scampered home to report to his Grannam. She roused the neighbourhood and, the inhabitants of Durand's Alley being what they are, they marched off to the rescue. If you ask me, any excuse for a mob demonstration and a bit of house burning would have been enough, especially where the notorious Cornwallis was concerned. I suppose they searched the place for you before deciding to fire it. If they thought at all.'

'I'd come back to check for any news while the others were out searching,' Paul interposed. 'I found Barty's Grannam had also sent word here, through the hospital. Thank God someone knew where to find me. Otherwise the mob would have unintentionally finished you off.'

'Cornwallis would have done that.' Elly shuddered, and Paul moved over to sit beside her on the sofa.

'Don't think about it, Elly. Let the memory fade. You have so much ahead of you worth thinking about.'

In a low voice Pearl said: 'I've seen a great deal of violence lately, and none of it worth a single life. The rule of the mob is insanity, whether it be vagabond ruffians bent on mayhem, or soldiers and police licensed to murder in the heat of battle. It only achieves misery and destruction.'

JG patted her shoulder and she turned her face to him. 'There will always be violence in the world, my love,' he said tenderly. 'The trouble is you've seen too much of it in your short life. God willing, we'll settle somewhere peaceful and you can be content.'

Even Pearl smiled as Elly pointed out that JG Patterson and

peace were hardly synonymous. In the midst of the general amusement Pearl said directly to Elly: 'There's talk of changes to be made
in the hospital board of management. Your supporters have raised
such a commotion, I shouldn't be surprised if you are able to continue your work, Elly, and I could go off to mine.'

Elly shook her head, but all she said was, 'You'll be sailing soon?'

'In early October.'

'I'll miss you,' Elly said simply.

Jo-Beth, hearing them, interrupted. 'But before they leave, JG
has a duty to perform. He has agreed to give me away at my wedding, while you, Matron Ballard, are requested to carry my train.
Will you?'

'I'd be honoured, Jo-Beth.' Elly swallowed the sudden lump in
her throat and widened her smile.

Paul added abruptly, 'Ethan has asked me to act as his grooms-
man.'

'And I'm to bring up the rear as a matron of honour.' Pearl
smiled.

Paul got up and strolled to the bay window with a view of an
early blooming rose garden. There he faced the room. 'I'd like to
finish this off and never have to mention Cornwallis again. So let
me say this. We've been in contact with evil and have, thankfully,
come away unscathed. We've been very fortunate. As for myself,
I've learned a difficult lesson: that a man's whole life may be twisted
by a desire for vengeance. I thought I'd be satisfied on the day
Cornwallis died, but now I only feel regret for the years wasted in
hatred.

'Let me also say how grateful I am for the friendship which has
helped me through to this point. I know now what should be valued and cherished, and what should be laid to rest in the past.
Thank you, all of you.'

Paul did not meet Elly's eyes as the friends murmured their
appreciation and Pearl hastened to provide wine to toast their
friendship.

Elly, hiding her growing unhappiness, spent some time pondering the best way to shake up the establishment and achieve some

results before Pearl sailed off to her new life and Jo-Beth stepped into another milieu. She arrived at an idea so revolutionary as to be greeted with acclaim by her supporters, who went into action immediately.

Ten days later the town was rocked by an unprecedented event—a march upon the Legislative Council by women. It was unheard of, a scandal not to be missed. People turned out of houses, taverns, restaurants and clubs to watch the women go by, some pushing their children in carts with older ones almost running to keep up. Ladies beneath shady parasols rubbed shoulders with shop girls and tarts in grubby satin and lace. Housewives in calico and cotton, maid-servants, merchants' wives dressed to impress and poor women dressed mostly in darns, all stepped out together. Their boots clattered over cobbles and pavers, through dust and dung, from the far southern end of George Street to the new Semi-circular Quay, past markets, livery stables, taverns and fashionable stores, driving shoppers back onto the footway, forcing carriages to the side.

To a cacophony of jeers and cheers, they waved and called out slogans, were barked at and ankle-nipped until the roaming dogs were driven off with the handles of placards proclaiming: *Good health for all*; *Our men will vote for our hospital*; *Where are the trained nurses?* and much more besides.

Heading the procession was a huge wool dray pulled by a team of Clydesdales, their manes beribboned and hung with bells. On this dray stood a group of men waving to the crowd, among them Paul, JG and Henry Parkes. Behind the dray strutted Barty with a cohort of his friends bearing drums and banging more or less in unison.

Elly marched with Pearl and Jo-Beth, arm in arm with their women supporters, their faces bright with anticipation and determination. From the Quay, the procession turned right up the hill to Macquarie Street, past Government House, then right again towards the building which housed the Legislative Council.

There Elly was lifted bodily onto the dray to stand beside Paul. Henry Parkes had taken his place on a raised dais at the back and prepared to address the crowd. They shuffled to silence, listening as he reminded them of their great responsibility as citizens of the new Colony about to attain constitutional self-government.

Elly was grateful to have, thanks to Paul's influence, such a popular public figure spearheading their cause. The crowd would be won over and in a mood to listen when it came to her turn. A message had been sent asking the members of the Legislative Assembly to receive publicly a petition from the marchers; and, as Elly had foreseen, curiosity, if not apprehension, had brought the members out onto the verandah of the building. Parkes now addressed them directly.

'Gentlemen, you are no doubt surprised to see ladies as the petitioners, yet you should realise what a force they represent in this new climate of freedom. The day is about to dawn when their husbands, brothers and sons will vote for their own representatives in a parliament of two Houses, and the will of the people will be paramount. They will demand your attention when they speak.'

James Macarthur, a Wentworth supporter and member of the constitutional committee, stepped forward to face him, raising his squeaky voice in outrage.

'Sir, you are premature. There has been no word as yet of a royal decree granting constitutional government to this colony. You and your comet's tail of females are out of order and causing a public nuisance. I call upon you all to disperse to your homes.'

Parkes grinned then turned to the crowd. 'Ladies, are you prepared to leave yet?'

'No!' A sea of bonnets and parasols surged forward, and Macarthur stepped hastily back amongst his fellows.

Parkes held up his hand; as the noise subsided he introduced Elly, then stepped down to the accompaniment of approving claps and shouts of 'Hurray for Matron Ballard!'

Pink and slightly flustered, Elly tried to compose herself, to project her voice as best she could. This hour was the culmination of so much effort by so many people. It had to achieve its purpose. She searched the crowd then fastened upon one eager young face, framed in brown curls topped with a nursemaid's cap. The girl smiled back at her and, encouraged by a complete stranger, Elly began:

'Good citizens of Sydney Town, we all know the only way to achieve lasting change is through proper legislation, properly administered, which is why I've joined my efforts with those of the men who will soon represent you in your own Legislative Assembly. I hope to persuade you that health is one of the greatest concerns facing this colony. Even the richest among you are not immune to disease and accident.

'We need a proper medical school to train our own doctors. We need a nursing school to train staff for our hospitals. We need a new administrative order for the Board of the Sydney Infirmary and Dispensary, not directors appointed politically or through nepotism, but men qualified to make improvements to health care for patients, men who will be held responsible for any abuses in the system and required to bring about reforms. We need new hospital buildings. The old ones are insecure and vermin-ridden and should be torn down.

'We need to appoint a commission of trusted leading citizens, men and women, to enquire into all branches of hospital administration, and to advise the Board. We need to raise funds by public subscription and to have these carefully and honestly dispersed amongst such institutions as hospitals, asylums, orphanages. Above all, we need, each one of us, to be committed to the cause of good health in the community.'

She turned to the men on the wagon behind her and swept her hand to include them, before addressing the members of the Legislative Council.

'Gentlemen, these men here with me have given their promise. If elected to government, they will strive to bring about such changes throughout the community, also setting up more clinics, clearing slums, improving drainage, forcing the polluting industries out of the city and cleaning our water supply—enormous projects, but essential. I ask you gentlemen, members of the Legislative Council, to join with them when the time comes, to support this work of saving lives. I ask you to begin now, to demonstrate your vision and greatness of mind, and not be forced to follow where others will shortly lead. Sydney will be a great city one day. We want to be proud of it and of her happy, healthy citizens. Thank you, all of you, for listening.'

There was silence when she stopped speaking, then thunderous applause. It came, not only from the marchers, but from the crowds who had gathered to listen, spreading as Elly's speech was repeated in shortened version to those beyond the reach of her voice. Caps were thrown in the air, boys whistled and clapping didn't cease until Paul handed her down from the dais and took her place. Even then he had to wait some time for silence.

'People of Sydney, there has been a great injustice perpetrated against the former matron of our hospital. As many of you know, she was dismissed without good reason, without adequate explanation by the current board of directors, and, I may add, in the absence of the chairman, the Honourable Edward Deas Thomson. I demand that an investigation be held into the circumstances of Matron Ballard's dismissal. I demand an investigation of the board of management of our hospital.' There could be no doubt of the crowd's approval.

The council conferred until finally a spokesman stepped forward, projecting his voice far over the crowd.

'Ladies and gentlemen, it is not the practice of this Council to submit to pressure in the matter of the government of this Colony.' Amidst rumblings, he quickly continued. 'However, we are happy to accept a petition on a matter pertaining to the general good, a matter which is not yet the subject of legislation. The issue of the governance of the Sydney Infirmary and Dispensary, an independent body, may well be judged worthy of enquiry by a further committee of concerned citizens, within suitable guidelines and subject to the Governor's overriding authority. We are willing to appoint such a committee—'

He got no further, as a stentorian bellow from Henry Parkes caused everyone within ten yards to leap.

'*Unsatisfactory!* No more appointments of committees stacked to suit anyone's favour, if you please. Let the committee of enquiry be nominated by the people of this town. The people know who in public office has worked honestly for them in the past, and who has merely feathered his own nest.'

The members of the Legislative Council turned a collective purple. Their representative could scarcely get his words out. 'That is an iniquitous accusation, sir, and the suggested mode of choosing your philanthropic nominees is quite unworkable. How would the people nominate?'

'Quite simply, through the *Empire*. Each copy on the street would have a nomination form printed on it, to be filled in and posted through a locked box kept on my newspaper's premises— to which you may hold the key, if you choose. On a given day the names will be counted, publicly, and the most popular ten or fifteen, or what you will, announced as our committee to appoint a new board of directors. What could be fairer?'

Elly choked back laughter. Henry Parkes's audacity had to be admired, as well as his brilliant notion for increasing his newspaper's circulation figures. She wasn't surprised to find the Legislative Council agreeing to the scheme, in the face of the crowd's overwhelming approval.

Henry Parkes hadn't finished. 'Fellow citizens, today you have seen democracy in action. Now let us have justice. Let the post of matron of our hospital be added to the nominations. Let it be open to anyone of fit standing and qualifications. Let the slur cast upon the finest woman ever to devote her energies to the care of others be done away.'

The rest of his speech was drowned in an enormous shout of 'Vote for Matron Elly!' She was swooped upon by Paul and JG and lifted high above the crowd where she could be seen. Wild cheering broke out, while Barty's friends began a frenzied drumming. If the reception accorded her own speech had been enthusiastic, this was pandemonium. Deafened, overcome with emotion, Elly could not respond with anything more than a wave and smile. No-one could have heard her speak over the racket, she thought. Anyway, what could she have said—that she was touched by the support of so many people, humbled by their trust in her, delighted to the core at the thought of another chance to mould the future of 'her' hospital? The Clydesdales snorted, tossing their ribboned manes, scattering those standing close by, while the political aspirants on the dray now unfurled a new banner of their own. Admirably succinct, it read: *'Free beer and sausages in the Domain.'*

The rush began with those nearest the dray, then spread rapidly. Men and boys tumbled off walls and out of trees, balconies emptied and soon Macquarie Street had cleared, even Barty and his friends succumbing to the lure of free food and drink.

Jo-Beth, Ethan and Pearl, who had climbed on the dray to take refuge from the mass exodus, suggested a withdrawal of their own for a celebratory lunch.

'You can't run off yet,' exclaimed Henry Parkes. 'We've softened them up, and now we go in with the speeches, tell them what we stand for, what we'll do for them when the elections are held early next year.'

Paul glanced at him sharply. 'You know something. Come on, Henry. Out with it.'

Parkes winked. 'I've had a private message from London, telegraphed overland and carried by the fastest steamboat. It'll soon be official. Westminster has passed the bill. We have a constitution, my friend.'

Paul threw up his hat, yelling like a schoolboy, and Elly flung her arms around him and kissed him, heedless of propriety. 'I'm so happy for you, Paul. We'll see you in parliament next year, I'm sure of it. What a day! What a glorious, wonderful day!'

Elly held out her arms to embrace her two dearest women friends. 'Who would have thought, a few weeks ago, that we'd have achieved so much? I can't wait to get back to the hospital. There's so much to do. Oh, I pray the people of Sydney will vote in my favour.'

The three women descended from the dray, Elly linking arms with Pearl and Jo-Beth, surrounded by new friends and supporters, knowing there was just one thing lacking in her life to make it perfectly fulfilled. And now it only needed a little courage to try for that.

Chapter Thirty-five

A few days later, Jo-Beth's wedding to Ethan was celebrated quietly, without any of the splendour and pomp she might once have wished for. Elly helped dress the bride in her simple silk gown, her glorious hair crowned with a wisp of lace and early narcissus. Jo-Beth's beauty and serenity filled Elly with pride and thanksgiving for her friend's blessed happiness.

The private ceremony took place in St James Church, just a step away from the hospital, its cool marble interior filled with flowers arranged by the bride's many friends and well-wishers. Afterwards the guests adjourned to the Earl Grey Tavern, closed to the public for the duration of the wedding luncheon, then walked down to the Quay to see the newlyweds aboard a ferry going upriver, their final destination a carefully kept secret. They bore with the good-natured chaffing, although Jo-Beth's glowing face could be seen like a beacon amongst the crowd on deck as the boat steamed out into the harbour and the guests on shore dispersed.

While it was still light, Elly slipped away from the others, around the back of Government House grounds to wander alone in the Botanical Gardens. From there she could see the main hospital building on the crest of the hill, its roof slates gilded by the sunset. Had she really spent two years of her life struggling to bring system and order to a medical dinosaur? How different she was now from the woman who had sailed into battle against the Board, full of self-confidence, proud of her ability to stand alone. The confidence had been severely shaken, although it had survived, and she had known for many months that she did not want to be solitary for the rest of her days.

With a sigh, Elly removed her large hat garlanded in blossoms and laid it on the seawall. She looked out over the harbour where swells as smooth as satin reflected the lamplights just beginning to prick out on the opposite shore. Sadness welled up in her, a product of the lonely hour and place, and of her own heartache. She knew she would have to make her final bid for happiness soon.

'You seem so sad, Elly,' a familiar voice said behind her.

She forced a smile before turning to face Paul. 'Not at all. I couldn't be, not in the face of Jo-Beth's joy.'

Paul rested his back on the wall and searched her face. 'You'll be lonely with your dearest friends gone. Even with Jo-Beth living in the town, she'll have a full life of her own.'

'Need you remind me?' Then she added painfully: 'I'm sorry. I shouldn't snap at you. I've been trying not to think so far ahead. Pearl sails tomorrow and I don't know whether I'll ever see her again. And I'll miss JG terribly.'

Paul glanced aside. 'He's my closest friend, my companion since boyhood. It was he who brought me to the attention of my benefactor, you know. The man was a surrogate father to me; he educated me and gave me a chance in life. He's dead now, but he was a very great gentleman; and JG is another. We won't find his like again so easily.'

Hearing the wistfulness in his voice, Elly moved closer, touching his arm fleetingly. 'I'd forgotten you were losing someone as well. That was selfish of me.' She studied the strong face grown so dear to her over the years since they'd met in the lonely bush.

Paul had drawn back a little, as if her touch disturbed him. 'I still have other friends—Frenchy and all the other men who work for political change.'

'It's not the same. We each need someone close to confide in, to tell our deepest thoughts, to comfort us … Paul, that night you saved me from Cornwallis, something important happened to me. When I lay chained in that cellar, believing I would soon die, I suddenly knew how much I had to live for. I told myself that if I did somehow escape I would do things differently in the future.'

Paul stepped forward, hesitated, stopped. 'Elly.' He cleared his throat. 'That night changed me, too. I realised what mattered to me, and it wasn't what I'd always believed.'

Their gazes met and held. Elly could feel her heartbeat in her ears, not racing, but measured and deep, like combers breaking on a cliff wall. Would he say it? That all that mattered was to be loved?

'Elly, darling,' he said softly, with a note of tenderness she hadn't heard for so long. 'I've been an idiot. I've known it for a long time. Only stubborn pride has held me back, and fear that you'd ceased loving me. I couldn't admit to my own stupidity. I couldn't face another rejection.'

Elly stiffened, peering into his face, now a pale blur in the dusk. 'Do you mean to say you knew you loved me after all, yet didn't say so? You've let me exist in misery for months, vainly striving to kill off my own love for you? Is that what you're saying?'

'I suppose it is. But—'

'You worm! You unfeeling toad! Ohhh! I could hit you.' She shook her fist at him, and had it grasped as he pulled her towards him.

He said, half laughing, 'Elly, you spitfire!', as his mouth descended on hers. An instant later he released her hands and gathered her to him again, burying his face against her neck. 'My own dearest girl. I've hungered for you so. Forgive me. Forgive me.'

Elly closed her eyes, her mind reeling. She pulled from his clasp, saying, 'I ... think I'd better sit down,' and, regardless of her finery, sank onto the grass. She smelt the sweetness of clover crushed beneath her, saw Paul's anxious face hovering above hers as he knelt beside her.

'Paul, are you sure this time? I don't think I could bear it if you found you were mistaken. This isn't about pride or self-esteem, it's about breaking a heart.'

'What can I do to make you believe me? If it's any consolation, I've suffered like the damned for weeks, thinking I'd lost all chance, not daring to approach you after my ridiculous high-flown words about the impossibility of our loving each other and how we should simply remain friends. God, what an idiot I've been! I knew what a dreadful mistake I'd made on the night you saved my leg. But I thought it was too late. You had made your life without me. Then when Cornwallis took you, when only *my* strength stood between you and a horrible death, I knew I would lay down my own life to save yours. I couldn't have gone on alone if you had died.'

She cupped his face, bringing it closer to study it. 'Don't! We must bury that memory. My love, I was the one who kept us apart. When we danced together at Botany Bay, then walked on the beach in the evening wind, you told me you wanted to spend your life caring for me. I remember every word you said, the way you held me. It's been like a fire in my body ever since. Yet, like a fool, I mouthed about my ambitions and the sacrifice I'd have to make if I became your wife. How little I knew then.'

Paul drew her back into his arms, his lips against her forehead, stirring her hair. She began to tremble.

'What do you know now that's so different, my darling?'

'That there's such a thing as compromise. It's been a hard lesson.' She sighed. 'Like your program for vengeance which turned out so sterile and destructive. I finally saw that I wasn't some sort of heroine put on earth to save others; I needed love and support, like most other people. But I thought I'd cut myself off from your love.'

'You could never do that. My ambitions are no longer paramount in my life. They're important still, but not as valuable as you. You're the pulse in my veins, the very breath that keeps me alive.'

Elly had no reply. She raised her mouth for his kiss, which started gently, then swiftly grew more demanding. Held fast in his embrace, she surrendered wholly, offering herself and accepting his own wordless offering, knowing the freedom she discarded would be replaced by a lifetime of loving support. Paul would always be there beside her, no matter what difficulties they might face. She need never feel solitary again.

With her head on Paul's shoulder, Elly gazed out over the harbour, the lights reflecting back from water like black glass, and saw a different world, no longer sad in the dusk, but brilliant, vibrant with promise for the future.